DEADLY C.

About the authors

Born in Switzerland, Oliver Frey a.k.a. Zack ended up in London and, after attending film school, plunged into gay art and publishing. Innumerable illustrations poured from his pen and brush for British magazines *HIM International*, *Vulcan*, *Teenage Dreams*, the *HIM Gay Library* series, and *Mister* magazine. For *HIM* he created the mold-breaking Rogue comic strip and later *The Street*, which was part of the inspiration behind cult TV series *Queer As Folk*. The Internet has spread his reputation to an enormous global fan base through many sites and blogs. Some of his comic-strip work has been published recently by Bruno Gmünder—*Bike Boy*, *Hot For Boys: the Sexy Adventures of Rogue*, and *Bike Boy Rides Again*. As Zack, Frey has taken gay erotic art and comics to new dimensions. He lives with life-long partner Roger Kean in a medieval town on the edge of Wales.

British-born author Roger Kean, who met Oliver at film school, has had careers as a movie cameraman, film editor, journalist, and magazine and book editor. As an author he has written books on historical subjects both factual and fictional, and gay fiction, including: *Felixitations*; *Thunderbolt–Torn Enemy of Rome*; *A Life Apart*; *Gregory's Story*; *What's A Boy Supposed to Do*; and for Bruno Gmünder *Boys of Vice City*, *Boys of Disco City*, *Boys of Two Cities*, *Boys of the Fast Lane*, *Boy of the West End*, *Blood* and *Lust and The Warrior's Boy*..

BOYS OF IMPERIAL ROME

DEADLY CIRCUS OF DESIRE

by ZACK

BRUNO GMÜNDER

Copyright © 2014 Bruno Gmünder GmbH
Kleiststraße 23-26, 10787 Berlin, Germany
Phone: +49 30 61 50 03-0
Fax: +49 30 61 50 03-20
info@brunogmuender.com

All text and artwork © 2014 Reckless Books-Zack/Oliver Frey & Roger Kean
www.zack-art.com

At the point of the story, all characters depicted are 18 years of age or older.

Printed in Germany
ISBN: 978-3-86787-785-5

More information about Bruno Gmünder books and authors:
www.brunogmuender.com

In memory of Colleen McCullough, Lindsey Davis, and
Steven Saylor who have given ancient Rome vivid and lusty life.

~ A POTTED HISTORY ~

When this story starts Trajan is on the throne. There have been twelve emperors of Rome, commencing with Augustus in 27 BC—some good, some super bad. Augustus made himself supreme commander of the army, the *Imperator*, or Emperor, and ruler of his domain, the *Imperium* (Empire). But the ordinary people still thought of their state as *res publica*, a term meaning "Thing of the People," the Republic, which only goes to show that the common Roman citizen wasn't all that clever. On a modest day, Augustus (and his successors) referred to himself as the *princeps*, or "First Citizen," and when he felt a bit grander—probably most days—he called himself Caesar. Julius Caesar, who nearly made it as an emperor until some concerned senators murdered him, was a real person, but those who came after stole his name and made it into a title. Those who followed Augustus used the titles "Augustus" and "Caesar" interchangeably, just to confuse historians. Of those first twelve "Caesars," few died of natural causes.

Octavianus / Augustus 27 BC to AD 14; sweet, jolly, virtuous, totally despotic; died in bed, though his wife Livia might have poisoned figs to hasten his journey to godhead.

Tiberius 14–37, stepson of Augustus; dour, sour, mean, and sexually dissipated; died in bed, though his grand-nephew Caligula may have suffocated him.

Gaius Caligula 37–41; adored for a month or two before he went mad as a hatter, slept with his sisters, fucked boys, killed whoever he liked; Cassius Chaerea, the Praetorian Guard commander, finally lost his cool with the brat and assassinated him.

Claudius 41–54; considered an idiot by his parents and grandfather Augustus, but rather good on the whole, if you discount a few dead senators who didn't do as they were told; murdered by his wife Agrippina to put her son Nero on the throne.

6

Nero 54–68, adopted son of Claudius; degenerate, deviant, and completely bonkers—pity it took people so long to figure this out; last of the Julio-Claudian dynasty, the Senate deposed him and he killed himself. At least he died "an artist," as he claimed with his last breath.

Galba 68–69; first contender in the "Year of the Four Emperors," the greedy elderly governor of Spain was mean to his second-in-command, Otho, who expected better of his boss and had the Praetorians murder him.

Otho 69; young and nice (discounting Galba's murder), but defeated in battle by General Vitellius; he took his own life.

Vitellius 69; venal, greedy, gluttonous, and obese—stupid as well; executed by forces of Vespasian.

Vespasian 69–79, first of the Flavian family; common sense countryman, fair in attitude; started the Colosseum; died in his bed (some thought Titus poisoned him).

Titus 79–81, son of Vespasian; much loved, completed the Colosseum, saw Pompeii disappear under Vesuvius; died suddenly of an illness, but some thought it was his brother Domitian who poisoned him.

Domitian 81–96, son of Vespasian; dour of disposition, he started well but turned tyrannical, terrified everyone until his wife conspired to do him in. She and her co-conspirators looked around for a nice respectable senator to be next, and found…

Nerva 96–98; elderly, solid, dependable, he removed Domitian from the record and damned his name. He looked outside the usual suspects and before dying of natural causes he went to Spain to choose as his successor…

Trajan 98–117; nice guy of the Spanish Ulpia family, generally regarded as Rome's finest emperor and one hell of a builder; bit of a fiend with the young lads, though, and downright nasty when it came to conquering territory from less deserving nations.

Many patrician and senatorial families disapproved of the new licentiousness that Trajan (and Hadrian after him) brought to Rome, that permitted men to lie together as they pleased, either taking or giving… or both, if it so pleased them. Like the Greeks of old, virtuous Romans held that a man who allowed another man to penetrate him—either end—was not a real man. Any appearance of effeminacy was considered deviant behavior, whereas an older man taking a younger man was simply acting in a dissolute manner—neither condoned nor condemned. It was commonly understood that when he grew older, the younger man would in turn take a juvenile male partner of his own.

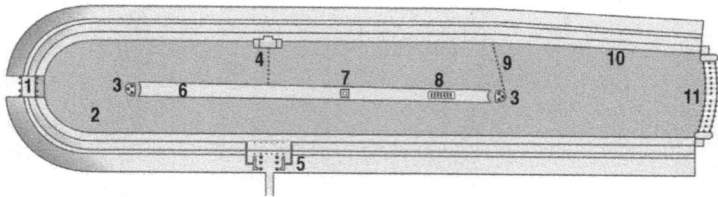

The Circus Maximus of Trajan

1 Triumphal Arch of Titus
2 Median walkway separating plebs from upper classes
3 The two *metae*, or turning posts
4 Finishing line and referee's box
5 Imperial box, or *pulvinar*
6 Long masonry rib running down the center of the track called the *spina*
7 Obelisk of Ramesses II taken from Egypt by Augustus
8 Raised rack supporting 7 bronze eggs and 7 dolphins. A dolphin is turned down and an egg raised when the lead chariot completes a circuit
9 *Alba linea* (white line), starting line
10 First third of the right-hand stand angles inward to give an equal break from the starting gates
11 The 12 *carceres*, or starting gates. The curved line of arches is not at right-angles to the track. This, combined with the angled side and angled starting line gives all 12 chariots an equal chance to arrive at the start line together

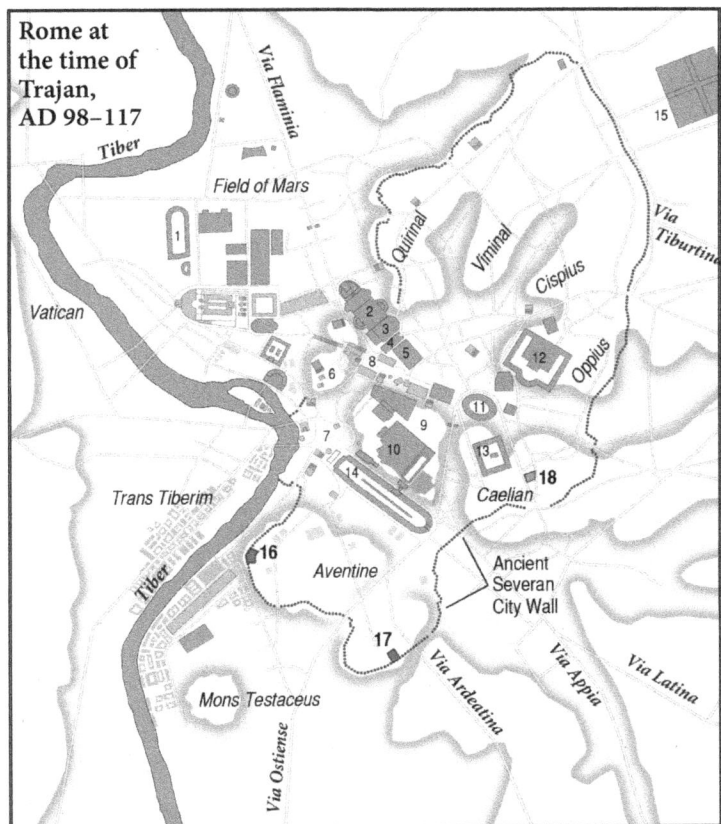

Rome at the time of Trajan, AD 98–117

Via Flaminia

Tiber

Field of Mars

Vatican

Quirinal

Viminal

Cispius

Via Tiburtina

Opplus

Trans Tiberim

Caelian

Tiber

Aventine

Ancient Severan City Wall

Mons Testaceus

Via Ardeatina

Via Appia

Via Latina

Via Ostiense

1   Circus of Domitian

2   Forum & Market of Trajan (under construction)

3   Forum of Divine Augustus

4   Forum of Nerva

5   Forum of Vespasian

6   Capitol (Temple of Jupiter)

7   Beef Market

8   Roman Forum

9   Area Palatina

10   Palatine Palace

11   Colosseum

12   Baths of Trajan (under construction)

13   Temple of Divine Claudius

14   Circus Maximus

15   Praetorian Camp

16   Tullius Emporium of Artistic Excellence, Headquarters of "We Are Celebrations and Festivities)

17   Domus Alba

18   Domus Fabii

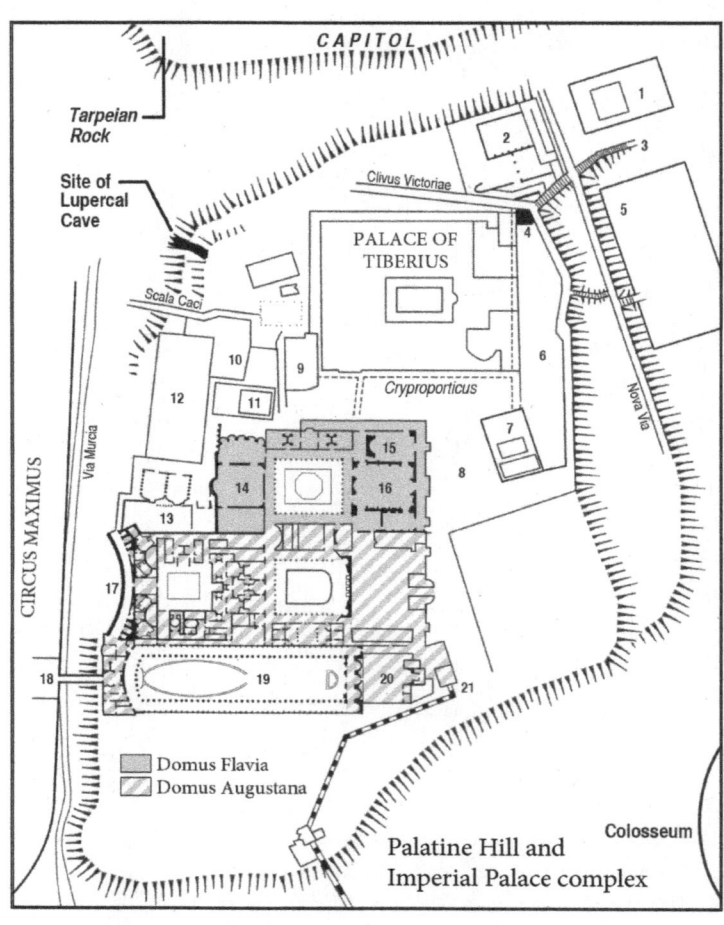

Palatine Hill and
Imperial Palace complex

1 Temple of Castor & Pollux
2 Vestibule and Great Ramp
3 Steps down to the Forum
4 Bar of the Imperial Forums
5 House of the Vestals
6 Tiberian Administration block
7 Temple
8 *Area Palatina* (Forecourt of the palace)
9 House of Livia
10 House of Augustus (amid houses of the later Republican era)
11 Temple of Apollo (built over the original *domus* of Augustus)
12 *Paedagogium* (below the hillside)
13 Libraries underneath open court and garden (site of the Hecatoncheires)
14 Banquet Hall
15 Basilica
16 Audience Chamber
17 Gallery
18 Pulvinar
19 Sunken "Hippodrome" gardens
20 Baths
21 Cistern and aqueduct crossing to the Caelian Hill

P·R·O·L·O·G·U·E

Wavering flickers of flame from surrounding oil lamps pulsed through a miasma of burnt incense and hemp that writhed about the undulant bodies in the contorted throes of sex. Splayed on assorted cushions and low couches on the circular mosaic floor of a crepuscular colonnaded chamber a dozen or so young courtiers engaged in the pleasures to be had from the clutch of five pretty slave boys in their midst.

The intimate gathering of young patricians enjoying wine and snacks amid ribald banter, accompanied by the gentle sounds of flute and lyre while being served by three fetching youths in the skimpiest of loincloths, quickly degenerated to crude erotic suggestions. Intoxication and the heady fumes of hemp had done their work—the moment the pretty flautist and the lyre boy were plucked from the floor and hauled onto the laps of the nearest revelers, the conclave turned into lascivious sex play. The three serving lads, too, were quickly tumbled among the aroused men to join the musicians.

A clutch of eager fingers, hungry to claim their lissom bodies, caressed, pinched, teased, probed, and aroused. The rhythm of grunts, breaths, moans, and slurps of sexual excitement replaced the stilled music as the courtiers feasted on the nubile flesh wriggling so enticingly between their tangled limbs. They all but smothered their prey. Rampant cocks slid between stretched lips, opened up and speared peachy bottoms, busy mouths enveloped youthful hard-ons, suckled tender balls, as multiple men at a time ravished the submissive boys. Forceful hands bent their naked limbs to their will, twisted and turned their bodies as if they were playing with dolls. In a gently heaving, slithery circular dance of lust the helpless youngsters were tugged around from clutch to clutch of men ravening for the varied fare of their writhing forms.

Lost in their sex play, the revelers were oblivious of the solitary figure lurking in the shadows of the pillars that circled their scene of debauchery, and remained unaware as its form slunk away, black as a raven in the night…

Filthy animals! Pigs at the trough… defiling helpless, subjugated youth with no say in the matter. Their slaves… but themselves enslaved by their own carnal urges. Gods, but I have turned a blind eye to the excrement that surrounds me. The Roman beasts bestride the world they call their Imperium. But now—after the ghastly news that has come today… how can I control my righteous anger any longer? This changes everything. I must hit out and pay them back the pain I've suffered… with interest. My body demands revenge… and in the kind the Romans so freely deal out. If by domination ye live, so by its heavy hand shall ye die.

They are so easy to seduce. A sway of the hips, a suggestion of a back-thrust bottom, pert under the barely adequate tunic, a sly flutter of eyelashes from under the hood and a come-hither look. There's not a young Roman aristocrat can resist. Like animals. Rutting beasts with sex bubbling in their bovine brains like milk curdling over a fire.

This one's on the hook. A good catch. So long have I restrained my craving for justice. Now, it is my time. Sex is my revenge. No! It is the instrument of my revenge. Cocky, big-cocked boys hardly men, stride the world and think they own whatever they see or touch. Like the bastard who did this to me, a cheap puppet of the Romans who now has the effrontery to come to Rome. Who was he in his unbounded Oriental arrogance to decree that I should lose everything that was precious to me? One day—I swear this to Sin, goddess of the night, of the Moon, patron of the dark soul and El-Gabal, god of the Mountain— my vengeance shall fall upon the foul monster who ended my life. But for now… now I am forced by cruel circumstance to take some minimal pleasure from exacting partial retribution whenever I can.

A dark alley. Perfect. He follows. He wants me. So pretty, so delectable, so gently beguiling am I. One last lingering look over the shoulder. And oh! The wall, He takes me against a crumbling wall, he presses me to the rough surface. Hands scrabble on my bare ass under the hem of my tunic. I can see his cock, all hard and eager, shiny with excitement. Silly teenage Roman aristocratic fucker, fucks me, all grasping hands, eager balls, and poking patrician's tool.

This rich father's boy will never inherit. I hope he's enjoying his last moments. At least I provide the goods before I extract payment. And that's right…Oof! That was a hard plunge. Yes, it's right he thinks me a common whore. Ha ha ha! If only he knew who it is he's screwing, he'd be pissing himself with fright instead of… coming.

They're always so raring to go, to jam, butt, poke, and prod, they never bother to check the blade tucked into the straps of my boots. My fine shoes, worth more than this boy's life.

He cries out in ecstasy. I feel his seed spurt, and then his blood. Darkness is my revenge.

O·N·E | I

Rome in the reign of Trajan, in the year of the consuls
Appius Gallus and Marcus Bradua (AD 108)
Palatine Hill, February 10

"I feel like a boy tonight." Flaccus leaned against a corner of the tavern and rubbed his back against its rough edge.

"You don't look like a boy." Libo loosed a harsh chuckle at his predictable wit. In a literal sense he was right, his fellow night watchman was a well-built hunk in his twenty-eighth year. His regular regimen of exercise at the baths gave him a figure that frequently drew admiring glances from women in the street.

"Very amusing." Flaccus hawked and spat a gobbet of phlegm on the cobbles. The sharp corner failed to satisfy the itch somewhere unreachable under the uniform strap over his left shoulder blade. The wall belonged to the grandly named Bar of the Imperial Forums. True that from its vantage point at the junction of *Clivus Victoriae*, the Slope of Victory, and the dizzying steps down to the Roman Forum it was just possible to see the great forums of Julius Caesar and Octavian Augustus, both gods now, but that was about all that the fleapit had to recommend it.

"Soon as the damned subaltern brings our relief, I'm off to Lucretia's," he grunted. "She's a nice range of boys, and I really need a good tight ass to fuck tonight." He rubbed his back up and down the ragged stonework more vigorously. "By the Emperor's right testicle, this is a terrible itch."

"You should go to the baths more often, I've told you. Can't imagine any lad of Lucretia's wanting to shag on a hard bed with you like that."

"Har har! I'm itching because of the rubbish material they use for these tunics. I haven't got fleas, so stuff it!"

As members of the Vigiles—the force of *vigilant* watchmen responsible for keeping peace in the city at night and acting as firemen—Flaccus and Libo were standing duty on the Palatine hill just outside the imperial palace. They were bored. Up here they were unlikely to encounter burglary, robbery, runaway slaves, or a decent spot of public fornication. Fire was the most frightening threat, but on the Palatine everything was constructed of stone. For a hundred years since the time of Augustus emperors had built and built until now the imperial palace complex occupied almost all of the huge hilltop.

"Bored shitless, I am."

"You weren't bored this time last week." Libo's throaty chuckle turned into a harsh cough. "That murder down near the Portico of Octavia. What a mess."

"Yeah. Vetranio will never get over seeing what the murdering bastard did to his son. Castrated and dumped in a dirty alley like a sack of refuse. I wonder if they'll ever find out who did for him, or why."

"The why's pretty obvious. Picked up some whore who killed and robbed him. Poor young bastard." Libo sighed, the sound of a man who's seen it all. "Ah well, it's down to the fucking Urbans to do the detective work." He gave a short, mocking bark of a laugh. "So that means we'll never know. Anyway, forget that. What about Lucretia's? Are her girls any good?"

An enormous thump shook the ground. On the other side of the Forum a dust cloud billowed up into the night sky, hellishly lit from underneath by the flames of a thousand pitch torches. The vertical face of the quarried hillside opposite slid downward, gathering speed as tons of rock fell. His question momentarily forgotten, Libo swore brutally. "There won't be anything of the Quirinal hill left by the time that fucking Greek architect's finished. Look at it…"

He waved an arm in a wide arc from left to right, from the Temple of Jupiter on the Capitol to the flanks of the distant Colosseum. "Apollodorus has made the whole of Rome a damned building site."

"Day and night, at the orders of the Emperor, mind."

"By the mound of Venus, it goes on and on. How many slaves have they got over there chopping away the hillside?"

"Thousands," Flaccus asserted confidently. He knew because on the way to report in for work he had ogled some of the handsomer near-naked specimens through the viewing ports in the boards put up to keep people out of the dangerous building site. One of them reminded him a bit of young Rufio. Now there was a lad... "The other day I looked at a notice on the hoarding keeping people out of the site," Flaccus said, avoiding saying he liked to look through the viewing gaps at the hunky slaves. "Says there's going to be a multi-story shopping arcade above the forum bit. You ever heard the like of that? All those steps to go up and down, laden with goods?" *Gods, will Rufio ever let me get inside his loincloth?*

"At least the Circus is finished in time for the races after Lupercalia." Libo broke into Flaccus's little reverie of gorgeous Rufio. "More than six hundred feet in length it is and more than sixteen tiers of seating in some parts—"

"Seats two hundred and fifty *thaasand*," Flaccus said, not to be outdone. "By Pluto and his dark legions, it's earned the name of Maximus now."

"Mind. All that stone seating is going to be a lot harder on the bum than the old wooden bleachers." Libo patted his right buttock. "Gives you piles, you know, sitting on cold stone. I reckon I'll get my Livilla to make up some cushions."

As the dust settled over the way Flaccus returned to his back rub. "What was it? Girls you asked about?"

"Huh?"

"Lucretia's girls you asked about— Ay-hup! Litter coming!"

They snapped to attention at the clattering of four bearers

16

coming up the steep incline from the direction of the river and the beef market. The senior slave, a hulking black Nubian, bellowed out, "Make way for the noble Livius Caecilius Dio!" The slaves' panting filled the narrow confines between the Palatine buildings as they passed the two night watchmen and made a sharp right-hand turn onto Upper New Road, which ran along the Palatine rampart between administrative buildings. Their hobnailed sandals played a loud tattoo on the paving stones and then faded as the litter disappeared around the far bend into the gardens and forecourt of the Domus Augustana, the House of the Augustus.

"Another knobhead for palace fun night," Flaccus muttered sourly. "Make way for the noble Assus Prickus," he whined in mockery of a nasal aristocratic voice. He relaxed back against his sharp corner again. The Bar of the Imperial Forums was the last commercial building left on the Emperors' sacred hill, tolerated because it served men of the Vigiles, their rivals the Urban Cohort ("nothing more than jumped-up policemen"), and those Praetorian Guards on palace duty who didn't mind slumming with their militarily inferior colleagues.

Libo scratched behind his ear, an itch set off by the one Flaccus couldn't satisfy. He spoke softly, after checking no customers were hanging out of the one window in the bar behind them. "I heard from this friend of mine, a Praetorian fella, that his nibs up there…" he dipped his head in the direction of the palace, "is a bit like you. Prefers boy ass to the feminine kind—"

"I never said I prefer it, just—"

"—and that relative of his, *Hadrian*," he whispered, "likes 'em even younger. So, what about Lucretia's girls. Any good?"

Flaccus straightened up and took a few paces out into the street to ease his feet. He turned to look up at the bulk of the massive palace. "Girls? I dunno. I go to Lucretia's for the boys, so I don't know about her girls. Try it out for yourself. For a piece of cunt I go up the Viminal to the Sign of the Rampant Cock, in that alley off Tavern Street."

17

"Out of interest, you ever had one of them up you?"

Flaccus spluttered indignantly. "What are you saying! Are you suggesting I might turn my ass around for a boy?"

"Now, now, there's no need to fly off the sword handle. I'm not suggesting you… you know, take it up the ass. At least, not much—"

"Fuck you, Libo. Thought we were friends. You're trying to say I'm like a woman? I tell you this, you jumped up Campanian cockerel, I'm a good Roman. I don't do it with citizens, and if I bugger a boy it's because he's a good tight fit, right? I give it. I don't ever take it. Right?"

"Fine. Sorry. I was just curious, seeing as how you like screwing boys. But you are a funny old-fashioned thing, though. Hasn't anyone ever told you that's all so last century? Maybe in the time of Divine Augustus—all that moral rectitude bit, all that marry and raise fifteen kids for Rome and the Republic—maybe that was how it was back then. But these days everything's a lot more liberal. No one cares any more if you like to take it up the ass. Me, I don't. Can't get into the pederastic thing. But that's why I felt I had to ask, cause I don't know. Anyway, sorry. Forget it."

For a pregnant beat of the heart, it looked as though Flaccus might snap back, but instead he eased his arms and took a couple more paces back, almost to the top step of the vertiginous staircase where he could see down onto the roofs of the Temple of Castor and Pollux and the round Temple of Vesta, to the edge of the Roman Forum. He was clearly not going to answer back. Instead a picture of Rufio filled his mind. Tullius Rufio, a vision of tightly packed muscles, wicked come-to-bed eyes (or come anywhere for that matter), a neatly wrapped and bulging package pushing at the front of his tunic, and a ready smile, which turned to laughter as easily as he slipped out of the very same tunic (and he often didn't wear a loincloth underneath). Not to forget the most beautiful butt in Rome. Unfortunately a pair of the shiniest, smoothest, most perfectly rounded buns off limits to Flaccus, who had tried several times to get his prick in between them.

When it came to boys, there were none to hold a candle to Rufio, and if he wouldn't put his ass online for Flaccus, at least he never minded offering a hand in consolation… well, once. His cock stiffened as he thought of tangling with Rufio's sturdy limbs, of being able to run his fingers up and down the silky smooth skin of his inner thighs, to stroke the sensitive purse of his balls, to entice his rosebud asshole to open… *No. Rufio wouldn't let him.* Flaccus sighed. Lucretia's then, for a fuck, and pray that his occasional daylighting employment as security for Rufio's mother's business might lead to an opportunity to part those delectable ass cheeks one day.

"A denarius for them."

Flaccus started. Rufio with his astonishing head of flame-colored hair dissolved into the image of nighttime building mayhem on the Quirinal. "Sorry?"

"You were miles away," Libo said with a chuckle.

"Ah… yes. I was just thinking on how things happen in life. How you mostly never get what you really want—*like Rufio's ass*. Look at you and me. Stuck up here on this damned hill, bored shitless, while up over there fucking noble Livius Cacius Whatsisname gets wined, dined, probably bedded. Isn't fair."

"Life isn't fair, Flaccus."

"You been taking lessons from the Stoics, Libo, or whatever they call themselves? Hah! Look at this," he said and pointed up at the glowing windows of the palace. "Light blazing everywhere. Our glorious Emperor must be having a hell of a party up there."

"Yeah. With his highborn boy-ass-poppets," Libo whispered with an evil grin.

Flaccus threatened with a clenched fist.

"Just saying…"

T·W·O | II

"Livius Caecilius Dio."

Hadrian drawled the way he did to avoid sounding like the provincial he was. Livy was sure of it, but he bowed low enough that he had to huff for breath, lungs squeezed against his potbelly. He straightened and smiled unctuously. The two men knew each other slightly but the hostility was mutual, as evidenced on Hadrian's part by his unnecessary use of all Livy's names as though there was no previous acquaintanceship. Livy felt like snapping back: *How good to see you, Publius Aelius Hadrianus, and when will you be adding* Traianus *to your nomenclature?* But of course he didn't. Hadrian acted like a prince even though all Rome knew Trajan had done nothing to indicate any favor toward his Spanish relative, let alone adopt him.

Livy had to be pleasant. He needed the Emperor's patronage desperately and antagonizing the primped, Greekly popinjay standing so arrogantly before him, who might, just possibly might, succeed Trajan would not be prudent. Hadrian wasn't even dressed properly for a dinner, wearing nothing more than a clingy, skimpy tunic that hid little. Only a broad purple striped hem indicated his membership of the senatorial order. Livy was a broad-striper as well, but he held that his membership of the Senate was a duty as much as a privilege of his birthright. Jumped-up country bumpkins like Hadrian just didn't understand.

Hadrian smiled with imperial condescension. "You really needn't have worn an elaborate synthesis. Caesar likes his informal dinners to be... well informal. Still. It's a very *handsome* evening synthesis."

Why did "handsome" sound like a calculated insult? Livy fumed inwardly. His lightweight and elegantly folded ankle-length garment of silk, dyed in a light but vivid ultramarine, had cost a pirate's ransom from *Domum Vestiarium Ithacae*, just about Rome's most fashionable clothier in his exclusive emporium on the Caelian Hill. "With its stitched folds it falls like a full toga, but at a fraction of the weight of those horrid woolen grotesqueries," proprietor Ithacus claimed. "When you sweep into a room, all will fall at your feet and marvel at its beauty." Well, Hadrian hadn't. Livy wished he'd asked Appius, his patron, how to dress for the evening. Too late now.

A comely young slave hovered to the side, waiting to remove Livy's street shoes and replace them with slippers. As Hadrian indicated the chamber beyond in a sweep of his arm, the boy gently wiped Livy's hands with a dampened warm linen towel that gave off an aromatic fragrance. Finally the slave handed him a dinner napkin embroidered with Trajan's monogram. Hoping he was to be his personal slave for the evening, Livy followed the pretty boy, who showed him to his place in what the invitation had described as a *small, intimate gathering of the Emperor's close friends in the modest seclusion of his private dining room. Dress style informal; please do not address the Emperor as Augustus, he prefers the title of Caesar at soirées with his* comites.

To Livy *small and intimate* meant a handful of one's *comites*, one's closest companions, in a cozy *triclinium* with a few attractive boys to serve, not thirty diners in an ornate chamber built to cyclopean scale. Those present were all male, and apart from Trajan and Livy's patron the consul Appius—the eldest guest present—none older than Hadrian, who to much fanfare had turned thirty-two in the previous month of January. Indeed, several of the guests were barely adults, which reflected the primary sexual predilection of his host for hunky young men, preferably of military bearing. It was Trajan's fondness for firm, young male flesh that Livy fully intended to prey on. He had a plan, and it was absolutely essential that it worked; critical to his brother-in-law's large family, and far more importantly vital to his own interests.

After pausing to lower his head in a respectful genuflection to his august host at the high dining table some twenty feet distant, he took his place beside the consul Appius Gallus. Livy had done Appian a few small favors in the past and now wanted a pay back from the influential man. The first part was done: he'd angled for and received an invitation to an imperial soirée. The second Appian was yet to deliver: the Emperor's ear for a man-to-man chat. Livy intended to be a plain speaker. Trajan was said to be an ordinary man who disliked overt ostentation—he was dressed only in a simple army tunic—which made the excessive surroundings seem out of place. But this was the palace Domitian built, a man who relished extravagance.

Columns of Numidian yellow juxtaposed with Phrygian purple supported a ceiling of richly painted panels set between ribs of cedar wood adorned in lapis lazuli. Egyptian granite sparkled with the myriad glints of feldspar, quartz, and mica, while the marble floor was an expanse of pink to blushing red and sea-green malachite. It was pleasantly warm from the underfloor heating system. Somewhere in the depths of the palace underworks, slaves toiled to keep the *hypocaust* furnaces burning to heat the air forced through tubes below the marble and up through the walls.

However, the beautification of the Circus Maximus was down to Trajan and, as an ardent fan of chariot racing, Livy certainly appreciated the result. Just below the walls of the palace the once primitive track girded by low wooden bleachers was now recast from one end to the other in stone and marble, its outer walls raised high enough to blot out the sun from the surrounding streets.

"Are you well?"

Livy turned at the question to Appius Gallus reclining on the couch next to him. "Er… I am, thank you. Being a consul obviously suits you."

Appian dipped his head sagely. He could afford patrician airs. Descended from the ancient Annii Regilli family, his cousin was Hadrian's brother-in-law, which gave him a degree of clout in the imperial court.

"I am grateful for the influence you brought to bear on my behalf—"

"Yes, yes. That's all right, Livy. It's what friends are for." Appian sounded impatient. "I spoke with Caesar and he has consented to hear your petition."

"It's a great honor—"

"It is, Livy. See you make the most of it. You have a small gift? Something of interest for Caesar? Trajan doesn't condone bribery, as you know, but a modest show of your appreciation...?"

"Yes, I took your advice." Livy felt the edges of the offering hidden in the folds of his synthesis dig into his ribs.

"I say, Livius." It was one of Hadrian's *comites*, a young fop he dragged around called Cassius Quietus, calling out across the serving gap between their respective tables. "As a Caecilii Alba, which faction are you for?"

Those close enough to hear the question looked up with amused interest. Livy resented not only the pun on his brother-in-law's branch of Caecilii, for Alba meant "white," the jokey implication being that he must back the White racing team, but that the callow whippersnapper didn't know he was of the Dio branch of the family. It would, however, be demeaning to point out this stupid error, so he swallowed the insult along with the olive he was chewing. "As a matter of fact," he said, spitting out the pit, "I'm for the Greens, though my brother Lucius *does* favor the Whites."

A polite ripple of laughter greeted this. The forthcoming chariot races to follow the festival of Lupercalia were intended as the official consecration of the reconstructed Circus Maximus. They were a subject of constant discussion and argument. Livy backed the Greens because he knew Trajan did, but also because he had

an arrangement with one of the idolized charioteers, a flibberty-gibbet boy from the island of Rhodes called Scorpus. He boasted of a powerful "sting in my tail"—a pun on his name, which sounded like *scorpius*, or scorpion—because he was known to enjoy vigorous bouts of copulation between races. The jockey was even-handed about whether he pleasured a senator's melting wife or her husband, and was ambidextrous enough to turn up his pert bottom for a daddy senator. Scorpus had his rules, however: he only let men of equestrian rank and above get their leg over, if they had the wherewithal to afford his price. Livy had been such, another reason for repairing his fortunes urgently.

"Green!" scoffed another young dandy. "I call that sycophancy." He dipped his head at the top of the table to indicate Trajan. "I tell you, the Blues have it all this season. I was down at the training track yesterday, and believe me, you'll be throwing good money after bad if you bet on any other than Blue."

Appian spoke up with a senator's firmness. "You, Cornelius, are a whippersnapper. You understand nothing about equine form, otherwise you would know the Reds' horses are by far and away the finest in Rome. Put four of those beauties in a chariot with a man like

Endymion of Ephesus and no team can stand in the way of the Reds."

Voices rose up around Livy, jeering bets were offered, refused, or taken, but Livy's attention had turned toward Caesar... and the handsome young man to whom he was feeding a grape. "Who is the fellow to the Emperor's right? I mean *Caesar's* right." Livy hoped his tone sounded neutral, merely curious, when in fact he had been surreptitiously regarding the boy with the attractive shock of jet-black hair since the meal began. But it wasn't lust that aroused him, more a misgiving that Caesar's interest in the young man might cut across and thwart his plan.

"My consular colleague Bradua's son. Atilius is on leave from his unit in Germany."

"A military tribune?"

"I hear he shows promise, hence his promotion to head of the table, where no doubt he will shortly be expected to show his gratitude in a suitable manner."

Disturbing news. If Trajan planned on a night of bliss in the tribune's arms, he, Livius Caecilius Dio, would have to get in soon, and before Bradua's handsome son overshadowed his little gift for the Emperor (*must remember to address him as Caesar*). If Trajan

25

didn't fall for his nephew Quintus and so justly reward the uncle, Livius faced almost certain ruin and consequent ejection from the Senate. He was gambling everything on the undeniable charms of brother-in-law Lucius's youngest boy.

Appian's neutral tone didn't fool Livy, who detected in his companion's body language distaste for the dissolute attitude of juvenile men who offered their bodies to their elders and betters in return for advancement. According to that scurrilous scribbler Suetonius, of the first five emperors Claudius alone had displayed a normal taste for women—much good that had done the poor sap, but everyone knew Suetonius only wrote what Trajan wanted to hear. By smearing the two previous dynasties, Suetonius made Trajan look good to his subjects and to history. But in truth Marcus Ulpius Traianus was more boy obsessed than any of his predecessors, excepting perhaps wicked old Tiberius. However, the changed morality of the Ulpian court suited Livius.

"Oh so modest, so moderate in his behavior," Livy muttered under his breath while chewing on a chop of goat roasted Greek style. "If his subjects could see him dripping in fit, good-looking young men..." he let the thought trail off and wondered where Empress Pompeia Plotina was. No doubt stashed safely well away in her private apartments. Still, he reflected, smiling around a succulent duck breast smothered in garum, Trajan's sexual proclivity for male charms played to his own purposes perfectly... he hoped. He felt for the umpteenth time to make sure his little gift was safely tucked away.

"The delicacies are to your taste, I see," Appian rumbled.

"Oh yes, indeed. Quite splendid. Er, when do you think I might make an approach to the Emperor— To *Caesar*, I mean?"

The consul chewed and swallowed before replying. "If it goes according to the usual way of these things, Hadrian will get up and declaim some Greek hexameters in Trajan's honor. When he resumes his couch, Caesar will pick out some likely young fancy and disappear with him. My bet—a gold aureus if you're willing to take it, Livius—is on young Atilius Bradua tonight. Your best time is to approach him between those two events. And it won't be a long gap. Now, about that bet?"

Livy sighed and agreed. He could hardly refuse his patron, especially after Appian had eased the way for him to petition Trajan. The Emperor (*Caesar, dammit!*) appeared relaxed, in good humor; pray he would listen and grant Livius what he needed and then he would gift Caesar with the lovely Quintus. Oh bless those Ulpians and their sexual urges.

The man good Nerva picked to follow him was born in Italica, a town in Spain, from where his second cousin Hadrian also came. Detractors called them jumped-up Spanish provincials with an accent to prove the point, when in truth both were of good Italian stock, families that had settled Spain in earlier generations (it was a fault of their upbringing, but neither could help their loose-voweled Iberian Latin). Interestingly for Livy, the Ulpians also enjoyed a far looser moral code than most Romans. Trajan's court had swept all that fusty old righteousness away. What men did together in private—or in like-minded company—was their business now. Even the younger Greek men of Livy's acquaintance fucked each other as busily as rabbits along the Appian Way. Same, it was salaciously rumored, as the boys of the Imperial Charioteer School and the adolescents who studied for the civil service in the Paedagogium. Both those venerable institutions, founded by the monster Caligula, were handily placed across the way from the walls of the Circus Maximus, an area notorious for its bordellos. Along the narrow Via Murcia, sandwiched like a canyon between the vast walls of the Palatine palace and the Circus, just about every other doorway sported a large erect phallus above the portal. These *Herms* might bring the city good luck, Livy remarked to himself, but they were also an unrepentantly rampant symbol for the kinds of "luck" a man might purchase within.

T·H·R·E·E | III

Imperial palace, Palatine Hill, February 10

Slaves plied the guests with unwatered wine on a regular basis and the level of conversation rose with every serving and every course of the lavish banquet. Livy noted that while he drank sparingly, Trajan made sure that Atilius Bradua's glass was always topped up. The boy's complexion was flushed. Drunk, he'd be more easily led to Trajan's bed.

Livy was suddenly aware of the conversation across the table, the young men wondering whether anyone had news of the investigation into the brutal murder of one of their companions. "No, Spurius, Gnaeus Vetranius has never been to the palace… *had* never, I should say." Livy recognized the speaker as the dandy called Cornelius.

"Will we ever know what occurred?"

Titus Spurius was another effete youth who dressed in a pre-pubescent manner and affected an innocence he did not possess.

Cornelius sniffed. "Last I heard the Urban police are no nearer a solution. I suppose we won't know… unless, of course, the murderer strikes again."

At that point, before the talk between Hadrian's pretty companions grew maudlin, Cassius Quietus piped up. "When is this Nabataean barbarian showing his greasy face?"

Appian's voice growled from beside Livy. "I suppose you are referring to Obodas? Quietus, I would recommend you do not call a friend and ally of Rome a barbarian. As to his presence here, well Caesar has invited him—"

"Don't you mean ordered?" Spurius gave the company a smug grin.

Appian swung his protuberant eyes on his interrupter. "Indeed, I don't. It's to be a state visit." He glared at the young patrician. "There will be all the courtesies and ceremonies due a friend and ally of Rome."

"With respect, Consul," Spurius came back with an oily smile, "I imagine this wily oriental prince will have his own agenda, probably to do with why Caesar hasn't confirmed him as the king of Nabataea."

"I should have thought that was obvious to one and all," Cornelius scoffed. He seemed to have recovered from the sour mood of a minute ago when reflecting on his murdered friend. "It can't have passed his attention when Caesar sent the legions into Nabataea that Rome was taking over. It's no longer a kingdom, it's the Roman province of Arabia. To all intent it has been since his father King Rabbel Soter died. Hah! Soter... isn't that Greek for Savior?

"Yes, sire. It means Savior."

The pleasant baritone voice came from a tall Greek who appeared suddenly from the gloom of a corner to stand at a respectful distance behind Hadrian's cronies. Livy took his first close look at Imperial Chamberlain Bardas attired in a full-length robe of costly white wool. Handsome, almost pretty in that inimitable Greek way, the functionary was extraordinarily young for the office, to Livy's thinking. His stance—at once proud yet obsequious—was that of a classic *kouros*, the statues of noble-born youths sculpted standing tall and upright, arms held to the sides, the left leg stepped slightly forward of the right, as though frozen while marching. As Livy knew, *Kouroi* were depicted naked, cocks proudly jutting though not usually erect. Livy reckoned Bardas would look fine naked, without his robes of office.

"Well, he didn't save his country, did he?" Spurius said. "Now his son claims the right and has the nerve to demand an audience with Caesar. Doesn't Obodas understand the meaning of a Roman sword?" Spurius shook his head in disgust.

"To date, young man, the Senate has not officially given the territory the name of Arabia and neither has Caesar, so until such time as that happens Obodas is a potentate of some importance." Appian glared at the youthful insolence visible in the expressions of Hadrian's companions. "After the initial unpleasantness when the legions went in there has been peace, and as far as I am concerned I'd like to see it remain in that way. Bardas," Appian addressed the Greek freedman, "as Caesar's chamberlain, have you had confirmation of our esteemed friend and ally's visit arrangements? The House has yet to hear dates."

"Sire, I have." Bardas produced the end of a small scroll from the arm of his robe and showed it briefly before tucking it away again. "I shall discuss it with Caesar tomorrow. My secretary Acacus will no doubt make Caesar's decision known to you in good time."

The delivery was polite, but it was clear even a senator and consul of Rome did not command a senior minister of the Emperor.

Cornelius broke the tension the chamberlain's words caused. "This Obodas is a notorious pederast, I've heard. I mean, the desert-dwelling Nabataeans might have been fine noble savages at one time, but these days they're basically Greek, and we all know what they're like."

Bardas coughed quietly.

Cornelius had the decency to blush. "Oh, present company excepted, of course."

"When you say 'pederast,' Cornelius, what exactly do you mean?" Quietus asked amid loud chuckles. "In comparison with your own... er, preferences?"

"Oh, hah hah. Bit of pot and kettle there, if you ask me. No I mean Obodas likes his boys young..." Cornelius blushed again, more deeply this time, as those around him fell silent and shuffled uncomfortably, all aware of Hadrian's similar weakness. Fortunately, the prince took it in good part. He peered around his immediate couch companions to frown teasingly at Cornelius.

"Exactly how young is young?"

The embarrassed patrician coughed awkwardly, cleared his throat and mumbled, "Oh, very young, sire. Much younger than…"

At that point he wisely decided to quit while he was ahead, indeed while he still had a head.

Hadrian gave vent to a throaty laugh. "Cornelius, you must not paint all Greeks with the same color, boy. However, I shall ensure that when the noble Obodas graces us with his presence it will be you who has the task of seeing to all the potentate's oriental pleasures and comforts. And I mean *all*."

After this gentle wrist slap, the conversation turned to other and less contentious avenues. Slaves came and went, wine was quaffed, food disappeared in a bewildering array of dishes. Barely attired dancers pirouetted daintily to sistrum, flute, and harp; fountains tinkled; guests belched and ate more. After a while, Hadrian stood with a flourish, and in a pleasing baritone delivered an encomium to Trajan's greatness in what Livy assumed was flawless Greek, which of course hardly anyone understood. Spondee followed dactyl until Hadrian concluded with a bow to Trajan. Once Hadrian had returned to his place at the tables, Trajan sat up and swung his legs over the side of his couch to make room for petitioners to sit beside him.

As if it were a signal, the atmosphere in the chamber subtly shifted to one of overt eroticism. Hands began to reach out for handy slaves, dancers, partners.

It was the moment Livy was waiting for. In spite of his corpulence, he was off the starting blocks like a Lupercal athlete. He reached the Emperor's side and executed a sweeping obeisance. Trajan glanced over his shoulder and received a faint nod from Appian. He looked at Livy and patted the couch.

"O gracious Caesar," Livy began a bit breathlessly, pleased to have remembered how to address his Emperor. "I am most grateful for a few grains of sand of your precious time—"

"Which is running," Trajan pointed out with a tight smile. "I can make time for one of the Caecilii, Livius, but it must be brief."

"Of course, Caesar."

"And to the point. Sit, please. Speak."

As quickly as he could, Livy outlined the position he found himself in: possessed of clients who earned him his wealth through the mining and supply of stone and marble to the Roman building sites; of his clients who worked two of Rome's largest brick and tile companies; of others who acted as haulers…

"And your problem, dear Livius. There must be a problem?"

Livy smiled unctuously. "I always hesitate to point the finger of accusation—"

"Why do I have the strange feeling that that is precisely what you are about to do?"

Livy looked down at his fidgeting hands, clasped in his lap, two fingers fretting at the gift beneath the fabric of his robe. "The Ahenobarbi, Caesar, and the Fabii. These families have massive vested interests and like me, as senators, may not engage in trade, and so work through the intermediaries of Equestrian men who—"

"I'm well aware of how things work around here." Trajan gave a patient sigh.

Close up, Livy could detect a far stronger Iberian provincial accent than his cousin Hadrian had. All praise to Hadrian's elocution tutor.

"The heads of these families don't really understand the construction business, Caesar, whereas I have made it my life's work—at a remove, of course," he added hastily. "If Caesar could see his way to giving me patents to act in Caesar's name, I am confident that my companies will be supreme in delivering the very finest materials for all Caesar's wondrous building programs."

"A patent, Livius, that gives you the right to mint coins, effectively." Trajan's tight lips broadened into an amused smile, but his gray eyes remained cold and calculating.

Livy spread his arms to show how utterly disinterested he was in filthy lucre. "If I were to ask for myself, I should be worth less than the slippers on Caesar's feet. No, no, it is not for me, Caesar. I ask only for those in my family who one day will inherit Caesar's generosity. Like my youngest nephew. Oh, how silly of me. I almost forgot that I have brought Caesar a small gift, a mere token of my unworthy esteem."

Livy produced from the pocket within the folds of his robe a small thin rectangle of wood and tentatively held it out for Trajan's inspection. Although he lowered his gaze respectfully, his head ached from the strain of peering up from under his eyelids at Trajan's expression as the emperor took in the painting. One imperial eye widened a fraction, the eyebrow above arched so slightly only someone close by would have noticed. A corner of his downturned mouth twitched and lifted infinitesimally.

"That, O Caesar, is my young nephew, Quintus Caecilius Alba, son of my adored brother Lucius, a senator who prefers to keep a low profile and stay retired at home reading his books to enjoining Roman society."

A nod of the head, too small to be graced with the description, more like an inner vibration rising to the surface of Trajan's cheek, and a greater furrowing of the creases curving up onto his broad brow from either side of the long Spanish nose indicated interest in what he saw.

"It is for Quintus, I ask this of Caesar... and of course," he hurried on, "to serve Caesar in his endeavors to glorify our Rome by delivering the best marble, travertine, the neatest bricks and—"

Trajan raised a hand to quiet Livy, and then he took the small painting and held it closer to his eyes. "This is a true likeness?"

Livy thought quickly and looked suitably abashed. "By the honor of Jupiter Greatest and Best, Caesar, no it is not. The boy is so much more beautiful than any painter's poor art could possibly do justice. My brother is truly blessed with a son surpassing in looks and figure and nature anything that even Zeus snatched for his own."

Trajan inhaled deeply through pinched nostrils. Then his eyes swiveled up over the picture to transfix Livy. "Since, as you say, your nephew Quintus, this veritable Ganymede, will one day inherit your wealth—a fortune that I will have generously supplied—I feel it is only fitting I should see him in the flesh. I like to know those to whom I am giving my blessing, patents, and... wealth. If I am satisfied as to the youth's... how old is the boy?"

"He is just turned eighteen, Caesar, on the twenty-fourth day of January."

Trajan looked up and turned his head, sought Hadrian's attention. He held aloft the portrait. "This young man shares your birthday, Publius."

Hadrian leaned over his table on one elbow and peered a little short-sightedly at the picture. He shook his head so that the neat heat-tongued curls of hair rustled like crisp leaves in a breeze. "Hmm. Attractive, if you can believe the painting, but already too old for my taste." And with that dismissal he returned to his chat with those clustered around him.

Trajan threw Hadrian a sharp look of reprimand, but it was ignored. "I shall keep this," he said to Livy.

"Please, Caesar. It is my gift to you."

Trajan narrowed his eyes and the dimples either side of his mouth deepened in displeasure. "I shall only deem the gift received when you bring Quintus to see me. The quicker this is accomplished, the sooner you will receive those patents you crave, Livius Caecilius Dio."

"And... I hesitate to ask, but the Ahenobarbi and the Fabii, their interests—"

"Will be reconsidered. If I am satisfied."

Trajan's eyes added the unstated "You understand?" Livy managed a straight face, but a cauldron of glee boiled inwardly. Of course he understood. Perfectly. He only hoped Quintus would when it came to pleasing the most powerful man in the entire world. Anyway, Livy had his suspicions as to the kind of company Quintus liked to keep. Shy, demure, and a raging tempest of adolescent desires. Yes, the boy would do his dear uncle's bidding. Or else.

"Caesar," Livy said, standing and bowing low as soon as he gained his feet. He shuffled back a couple of steps and bowed again.

"Coordinate the arrangements for your nephew's appearance... *appearances*, with Acacus, my chamberlain's under-secretary. He's bound to be lurking somewhere..." Trajan glanced around. "Probably in one of the darker corners. You can't miss him. He is sublimely beautiful... though not as this portrait suggests Quintus might be."

As Livy bowed a third time, Trajan swiftly turned his attention to the young man at his side. Knowing looks ran up and down the gathering when Trajan stood and held out a hand to the military tribune. Atilius took it and, in spite of the wine he'd consumed, rose gracefully from the couch. Without a further word, Trajan led the boy away across the expanse of marble to disappear through a darkened portal in the far corner.

Around Livy, the party moved rapidly into lechery, concupiscence, and lovemaking.

* * *

Obodas! The very name makes the Earth shudder. I must not let a glimmer of my feelings loose, lest they be seen. Though any who did would think I was suffering a debilitating fever and not the almost uncontrollable rage that name always releases in my breast. That slimy toad, offspring of a man whose rotting flesh even hyenas of the desert would disdain. Hah! They called Rabbel "Savior," when he was a miserable excrescence, but certainly a shining example of nobility compared to his son. Obodas! Warted skin of poison pustules. Flesh robber. Made from the corrupted seed of degraded Seleucids. How is it possible for such a dog's turd to carry the blood of Alexander the Great in his veins? All Olympus cries for vengeance against his crimes.

And he's coming here. To Rome. To grovel at his master's knee. To make pretty-pretty faces at these catamite whoresons of Hadrian's lust. None will know of the turgid filth sloshing about in the black heart of Obodas like bilge water. But I do. I know it well. And it will spill here, along with his putrescent guts, so he never again can rob innocent boys of their future.

F·O·U·R | IV

Trajan's apartments – Imperial palace, Rome, February 10

It was the floor that first caught Atilius's imagination. Spread out before him, *tesserae* in a multitude of colors glittered in the low light from sconces high on the painted walls. In stark contrasts, the mosaic's swirling lines depicted a series of gladiators, their muscled bodies shown against a pale blue ground. Lighter and darker shades of flesh colors defined the contours of their naked bodies. White stones sharply edged prominent muscles in glistens of sweat. Mosaics of gladiatorial combat were almost commonplace, but not usually with each combatant fighting the other with his huge, erect phallus held at the ready. At the corners, fighters—swords and shields discarded—entwined their bodies in various decorative sex acts.

He had little time, though, to admire or be disgusted by the writhing images beneath his feet, or those of painting-covered walls. The presence of the Emperor was the dominating factor in the surprisingly intimate bed chamber; and the more surprising fact that he was utterly alone with a force so powerful he could only tremble at the thought—the ruler of the world, leader of the new Imperium, before whose sandals barbarian warriors and foreign kings bowed. Not even a body slave lingered in the private chamber, all sent away at the commanding sweep of an arm. In awe of the man and his surroundings, Atilius remained close by the doorway through which they had entered the bedchamber.

Trajan stopped halfway toward the bed to loosen the belt that cinched in the simple, plain white army tunic around his still-lean waist. Not even the thin purple stripe of an equestrian or a senator's broad stripe edged its hem. This lack, far from demeaning its wearer, only emphasized Trajan's dislike of ostentatious clothing, and more, Atilius thought with an excited shudder, his supreme indifference to the need to impress anyone as to his status. After the belt, the tunic went, in an effortless lift over the imperial head, to land in a soft mound on top of a huge dress-chest at the foot of the massive bed.

"I dress as does the legionary, Atilius, without under-clothing, ready for action." Atilius gave a nervous half-laugh at the ironic joke. Legionaries liked to be well padded about the loins when going into battle. Naked and aroused, Trajan turned and advanced on the young tribune.

"C-Caesar…"

"In here, you may call me Marcus. And you…" Trajan ran his fingers through Atilius's hair. "So thick and firm, such a lustrous black tangle." A thumb traced a line down to Atilius's brow. "And matching eyebrows of obsidian. See how they arch into thick noble crescents, anxious to meet over the bridge of…" The thumb was exchanged for an index finger, which trailed down the ridge of his nose, finally to the tip and down onto his pursed lips. "You, my dear Atilius, I shall call Niger for the color of your hair."

Trajan pressed closer and Atilius-now-Niger fell back against the wall, his wide eyes unblinkingly regarding the deep brown of Trajan's irises, shot through with flecks of a tawnier color. He felt the pressure of Trajan's erection as it thickened and rose up to catch on his tunic. In his own lovemaking—mostly adolescent fumblings if he were honest—Niger had been the instigator, the leader, but he knew in the presence of his Emperor he would submit. When it had become obvious that this might be the outcome of the night, the thought frightened him, but now he resigned himself to its inevitability. And yet, in such close proximity, Trajan excited his natural lust. And pride. How many of his age were there who could boast, "I caught the Emperor's eye and he wanted me"?

Trajan began working the belt buckle loose. "I think, Niger, you are overdressed for the occasion."

"Yes, Caes—"

"Marcus! There." Stiffened leather clattered on the mosaic and the belt seemed to form a neat coil around a two-dimensional gladiator's rampant cock. "That's better."

Trajan worked a hand lightly to lift the hem of Niger's tunic and played with the shape of his cock in its protective covering of a small loincloth. Trajan took this unexpected defense by storm and a candle flicker later the underwear covered one of the immodest gladiators beneath their feet. The probing hand cupped Niger and the cool touch on his balls caused him to arch back. The back of his head thumped lightly against the wall when Trajan stroked up the stiffening length of his cock.

"I haven't made up my mind yet whether I prefer to lift a tunic over the head or if I enjoy this new fashion for shoulder fastenings." Trajan stepped back a little to take in the reaction of his partner. "What do you say, Niger. Do you enjoy unbuttoning your conquests?"

"I... I like the choice, Cae— Marcus."

"Indeed. Of course a button-up tunic may be lifted off as well as one without. But I think..." Trajan bent his head, momentarily nibbled Niger's neck before taking the nearest ivory toggle between his teeth. When the method proved cumbersome, he quickly gave up and unfastened the three on the left shoulder, then the three on the right. With a deft down stroke, Trajan freed the tunic so if fell down around Niger's ankles and left him bare but for two *armillae*, arm-ring decorations for bravery awarded for facing down a rabble of German barbarians. They rattled as his sudden nakedness acted like an aphrodisiac surge. His cock reared up, the foreskin peeled back, and his entire frame shook when Trajan again took hold of his aroused flesh and pressed his cool lips against Niger's. He tasted wine as the Emperor's tongue invaded his mouth and took control of his teeth. For a long moment they exchanged Chian-flavored breaths.

"Now you are mine, Niger most glorious." Trajan pressed in close with his hips enough that their cock shafts just rubbed together, a tantalizingly light touch. His tongue found the hollow just under Niger's Adam's apple and wet it. Imperial hands stroked Niger's flanks, inner thighs, across his taut stomach, the length of trapped arms, squared shoulder muscles, up and down his back until he thought he might ejaculate without any physical stimulus to his cock.

Trajan must have sensed his close orgasm for he stepped back suddenly into a gladiator's stance, his torso and trunk a patchwork of scars, his own *armillae*. "Ah, the young. So urgent. Kneel, Niger!"

He did so, in awe, submissively before the Lord of the World, who now approached again, one step, two, his out-stretched sex

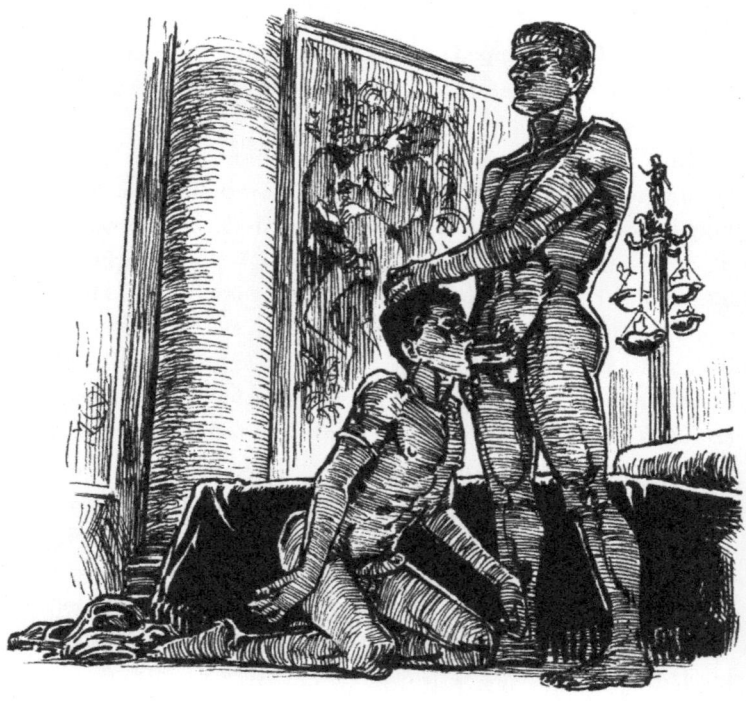

rigid, demanding. Trajan's hand reacquainted itself with Niger's hair, the better to pull his head forward until the tip of the Emperor's extended cock touched his lips. His tongue flicked out, wet his dry lips and the imperial crown. Trajan sighed, increased the pressure on the back of Niger's head. His lips parted, allowed ingress between them, the taste of excited cock filled his mouth, and then Trajan leaned in, pressing inches of heated flesh toward Niger's throat. He almost gagged at the unexpected girth of the mushroom-shaped head that forced his jaws apart and his tongue aside.

He might have expected impatience, perhaps an unavoidable violence on the part of Trajan, but in these opening minutes, the Emperor gentled him, slowly pulling back and then inserting himself again, until Niger could suck his full length with something approaching expertise. And for Niger it was like wrapping his lips around a long soldier's *botulus*, the common sausage that for its rarity on military rations was all the more eagerly devoured. Even better, the fat, rustic and spicy pork *lucanica*, beloved of soldiers stationed south in Lucania. Niger loved the taste of *lucanica*, and the taste of his *imperator*'s sausage, now plunging in and out between his tautly stretched lips, was arousing him again. When he reached down between his legs to grip himself, Trajan knocked his arm aside.

"Oh no, my fine Niger. For that pleasure, you must wait." He pulled his cock from Niger's mouth and raised him to his feet. He reached out to grip Niger firmly, turned toward the bed, and led his conquest by his stiff prick as a man might take his leashed pet dog for a walk.

Orgasm built inexorably in spite of Livy's natural disinclination to perform in public. But when he spared an eye blink to take in the cavorting figures promiscuously crammed around his sweating body, he accepted that all were too engrossed in their own pleasures to watch his own stimulation. The young slave boy who had served him throughout the evening was performing this invigoration of Livy's stubby *verpa*, his erectile tissue, used his mouth with such exquisite expertise he convinced Livy he'd been transported to Olympus. In moments his quickening climax mounted to an unbearable burn of unexpended energy.

And then he came.

Through narrowed eyes he stared down at the head bobbing up and down on his organ, squeezing the last spurts of his ejaculation from his aching balls through his pained cock. The hair color was wrong, too light, but in most other respects the brilliant little fellator reminded Livy of his nephew Quintus. Was that why he summoned the boy over when the informal dinner party took a turn for the less than formal?

On the other side of the low dining table, still littered with remnants of the feast, Livy thought he recognized Cornelius and

Spurius. He couldn't be entirely sure from their adjacent rears. He levered himself up on his elbows for a better view of the naked young patricians. Their asses humped in military precision as they fucked two more slave boys who knelt on the dining couch. One turned to the other so their faces almost touched. Livy saw it was Cornelius. He said something and then laughed in a competitive, feral way. Spurius, for it was he as Livy saw from the youth's noble profile, almost spat back his reply, and they both fucked their boys even harder. In response, as at a given signal, both slaves strained and bent their legs at the knees to kick their calves into the air around the aristocrats screwing them, and wiggled their toes at Livy.

In a far corner Livy saw some of the dancers and musicians all tumbled together with others of the party on cushions: arms, legs, bare rumps, upthrust erections entangled in an orgy of sex. Livy looked for Hadrian, but couldn't see the prince and supposed he was buried somewhere under that writhing mound of humanity. As for old Appian, Livy assumed he had taken his leave before the descent into licentiousness. The freedman Bardas had also vanished, a mute signal of disapproval?

"I say, Livius, are you finished with him?"

It was another of Hadrian's young clients. Livy struggled with the name and then it came to him. Cassius Quietus.

"It's just that thinking what Caesar must be up to with Atilius, and those two over there..." he waved vaguely across at Spurius and Cornelius, a vision of thrusting thighs, backs and slapping balls, big cocks disappearing into tight slave holes, all accompanied now by rhythmic shouts as the two men egged each other on to shoot, "... has just got me so aroused and I saw how well your boy did you. You seemed to enjoy it..."

Quietus trailed off and like an eager puppy made big appealing eyes. The thought of Caesar with Atilius soured Livy's mood. *It should be Quintus... give it time, give it time.* He flapped a limp hand at importuning Quietus, who read the gesture as permission and happily took the cock-sucking slave by the elbow. The adoring look the boy gave his abductor only made Livy feel worse. At times like this he sometimes washed up, at least compared to the virile youths fresh from the Paedagogium who made up Hadrian's camp followers. Time to adjust his synthesis for decency, wake up his lazy litter bearers, and go home. He only prayed that in the morning when Trajan finished with thrice-damned Atilius, he would remember Livy's little gift, and fantasize about Quintus and all the pleasures of the flesh the boy would bring him.

Atilius had never submitted to another man before, but as a lowly tribune of the army he might as well stand before the statue of Jupiter in the Capitol and say "no." And it was not as brutal as he'd imagined it might be. Trajan cared also for Niger's own enjoyment. As their joined bodies ground toward extreme arousal, Trajan reached under and rolled them both onto their hips so he could grasp Atilius by his hard cock and masturbate him in a steady rhythm with the fucking. The intensity of feeling in all his limbs, the lubricious rubbing of his insides, the urgency of release in balls and cock, all this merged visually with a mural painting to the side of the bed of a priapic satyr deflowering a young nymph with a howl of sexual triumph etched on his face by a masterly hand.

"My Niger," Trajan breathed in his ear in between savaging the lobe between his sharp teeth. "Oh bliss my hard-but-yielding Niger." The hot breath in his ear acted like the trigger of a tensioned ballista, and like that forceful weapon, Atilius-Niger shot his bolt through the moving grip of Trajan's hand as he felt himself injected with the imperial seed and its urgency of release fill him. Caesar's hand gentled in time with the relaxing of his own muscles and Atilius sensed that this second fucking had satisfied Trajan. For his own part, Atilius found it hard to believe that he had come twice while being fucked in the ass, and an odd feeling of accomplishment swept away any residual misgivings as to his now undoubted effeminacy.

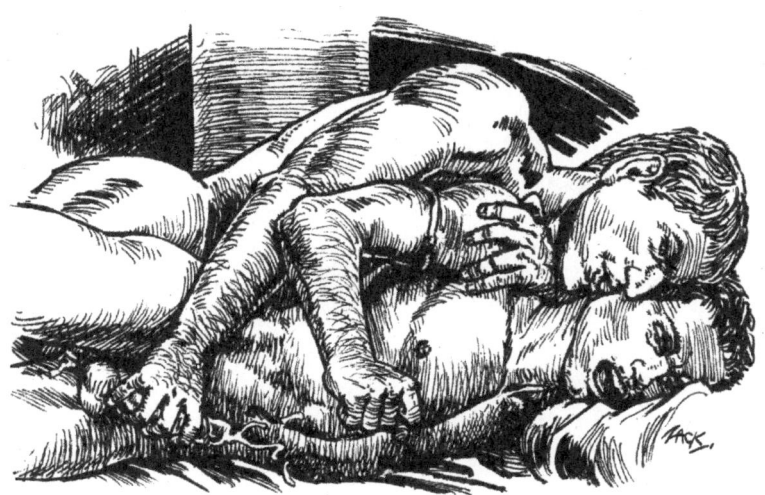

If he were painted as such by an Emperor, an immortal-in-waiting, surely the label of "deviant" that his military colleagues might hurl at him if they ever found out was an honorable one? Atilius, with all the pragmatism of a Roman youth of military bearing, decided to treat it as so.

Trajan fell back on the bed and stared up at the ornate ceiling. In his pleasantly enervated state he was definitely the mortal, in his vulnerable nakedness almost ordinary. As he had done between the first and the just finished sex, Atilius leaned over and traced some more of Caesar's scars.

"I often wonder at how the gods perceive us, my Niger. When I was born and Claudius still ruled—at least for my first year on Earth—did any god pick me out and place my toddler's feet on the path to majesty? Who should have known that an infant in a distant Spanish town was destined to rule over the Imperium of Rome?" He sighed and watched Atilius's finger moving. "Ah, that one I was given by an enraged Jewish rebel in Syria. It's faint now, but when I was twenty-two it hurt like Hades and bled a torrent. There, below, just above my hip, a sword thrust from a dishonored soldier fighting

45

for the traitorous dog Antonius Saturninus. My fault. I let my guard slip in the midst of a short but furious fight on the banks of the Rhine."

Atilius had to lean right over Trajan to run a fingertip over a criss-cross ridge of scar tissue on the side of the Emperor's abdomen.

"Those look worse than they are, all gained in Domitian's Dacian and Pannonian wars."

Atilius drew in a sharp breath at the mention of the Flavian emperor whose name was erased from the records, but Trajan seemed not to notice his reaction. Evidently, Emperors were allowed to disobey their own edicts, or in this case that of Trajan's predecessor, Nerva. But when he spoke again, it was as if in response to Atilius's unspoken question.

"It is expedient for a new regime to discredit the previous one, Atilius. In Domitian's case that was easy, since he'd become feared and hated by just about everyone."

It didn't escape his notice that Trajan called him Atilius and not Niger. The intimacy was nearing its end.

Trajan turned his head to look him in the eye. "Nerva had Domitian denigrated, but you know he never made any important changes to the way Domitian ran the Imperium. Do you know why?"

Atilius shook his head.

"Because Domitian's legislation worked. In fact, it still does." He let that sink in. "The Senate and the people call him a terrible tyrant. I think of Domitian as more of a troubled soul, but in any case, just because one is a despot it doesn't mean he can't be a clever legislator. That, young Atilius, is something to think on and remember: don't judge the entirety of a man by his worst faults."

F·I·V·E | V

The Ides of February dawned crystal bright but cold for the naked youths taking part in the annual festival of Lupercalia. Its roots went back to the very founding years of Rome and honored Lupa, the she-wolf who suckled the twins Romulus and Remus in a cave known as the Lupercal. No one any longer knew where this holy grotto was situated other than somewhere on the lower slopes of the Palatine. Certainly Tullius Rufio didn't know but he didn't have to worry because the divine Augustus long ago solved the problem by having a new grotto dug out under his *domus* on a shoulder of the Palatine (that was the small house he owned before the Senate built him a modest palace). From the grotto's mouth there was a fine view down to the rotunda temple dedicated to Hercules and the tall temple of Portunus, the god who looked after the harbor, both silhouetted against the Tiber's bright line.

Rufio, his head a blaze of red-gold in the sunshine, was dressed ready for the fun, which is to say he wore little more than a strip of bleached cloth around his loins to preserve modesty until the festivities began in earnest. His everyday tunic and belt were in the keeping his friend Crispin's mother. A third acquaintance called Octavian was with them. This stocky youth was happy to tell everyone that while he was the eighth child born to his father, "I only have two older brothers and a sister, the rest kicked the bucket at some point, probably between his third and fourth wife." Rufio thought Octavian coarse and cocky with it, but Crispin seemed comfortable with him.

The gathering onlookers were cheerily noisy, exchanging loud greetings and sharing breakfast nips of wine. For Rufio, Crispin, and Octavian there had been several offers of wineskin or flask, and Rufio was just the littlest bit tipsy. He loved the way the girls, women, and men crowding the starting point ogled his neatly muscled body. He stood out well among his fellow Luperci, as the youthful participants were traditionally called: a sea of flesh in movement, loosening up shoulder and back muscles, working out biceps, doing athletic crouches and stretches. There was much suggestive hitching and adjustment of the contents of loincloths to tantalize the girls with what would soon be freely revealed. Rufio felt young, fit, aware of his coltish good looks, and just damn glorious. He and Crispin exchanged exuberant hand slaps, eager for the events to get under way, while Octavian contented himself with ogling any girl under the age of twenty who dared smile at him.

Rufio thought back to his old school teacher who tried to hammer home the deeply religious meaning of the festival's rituals. This in spite of the way Mark Antony infamously cheapened it by throwing off his clothes and joining the two chosen Luperci, to the great joy of all women present who could judge for themselves the rumors of his colossal manhood. His profaning the rites had not stopped the sacrifices from still being made in the ancient tradition, but since Antony's disrobing the two Luperci had swelled in numbers to include any brash boy who wanted to show off his wares as he ran around the base of the Palatine hill. To those taking part, the most enjoyable aspect was whipping all the female bystanders packing the circular course with bloody strips cut from the hides of sacrificed animals.

Schoolboy Rufio asked his teacher what was the point of it all and received a stern response. "Some say we honor the she-wolf, others the god of shepherds, Lupercus." Which didn't explain to a puzzled Rufio why it was that the priests sacrificed goats and dogs. "When a girl or young woman receives a lash across the hand from a Lupercus it ensures her fertility, which is why females crave it," the teacher explained. Well, that was a few years back and Rufio wasn't confused about anything now because he didn't care. Once the boring religious rituals were done, he'd be off, howling like a wolf as Romulus was said to have done, dealing blows with his goatish whip *dextra, sinistra, et media.*

A wintry sun began to warm the fresh air as everyone waited impatiently for the priests to arrive at the altar specially erected outside the Lupercal grotto of Augustus.

Crispin shivered suddenly. "I don't like it here, this part of the hill," he said in a sudden gloom.

Octavian was staring fixedly at covered breasts and didn't hear. Rufio furrowed his brow, only barely interested. "What's wrong with it?"

"On dark nights Cacus haunts between here and the steps over there named for him. He snatches maidens and boys—"

"And devours them alive, I know."

Crispin frowned at Rufio's tone, but said nothing.

"The legend says he snacked on cattle—"

"And humans."

"What can you see down there, beyond the corner of the Circus starting gates?"

Crispin looked, as though he didn't know. A natural defensive response. "The Temple of Hercules."

Rufio snapped his fingers. "Exactly! Hercules happened to be passing by and slew Cacus. So that's that. The monster gone, and Hercules' temple proves it. Crispin, I thought you were beyond silly old tales like that."

"If I was, I wouldn't be here today, would I?"

"Good point." Rufio grinned, refusing to have his happy mood spoiled by argument. "Where are the fornicating priests? I want to get going."

Octavian made a rude gesture. "Waiting for more aristocrats to turn up?"

"If that's the case we're doomed to be here until Pluto opens up

Hades. My mother says this used to be a festival for the families of better-off citizens, you know, equestrians, patricians, senators—"

"And snotty-nosed freedmen, think their farts are perfume."

Rufio ignored Octavian. "But in recent years it's become too rough and tumble for the aristocrats, she says. Still, if the nobs are thin on the ground, at least the rest of us are all out for a good time."

He laughed out loud for the joy of it and with sheer animal energy, which must have communicated itself to Crispin because his friend joined in and they exchanged a loud hand slap. They pressed in close with their fellow Luperci on the side of the altar away from where officiants would stand, eager to see the sacrificial blood flow.

"Here they are!"

A line of priests and acolytes filed down the hillside. At their head one man stepped up to the altar. He was dressed in a full toga and wore an enormously tall conical hat made from olive wood on his head. Two scarlet bands tied under his chin held the strange object precariously in place. He was the current Flamen Dialis, a priestly position the divine Julius Caesar once held before he became dictator. After the Pontifex Maximus, he was the most senior of Rome's priests of the state religion. He began a litany of arcane incantations in a form of Latin so old it was incomprehensible to the onlookers. The Flamen seemed to get the invocations correct, otherwise he'd have had to start all over from the beginning, and that would have been more than Rufio could stand. Finally, the priest finished.

In another modern deviation from the ancient rites, where once the sacrificial victims had been two goats and two dogs, a long line of bleating goats now awaited swift dispatch. Behind the makeshift altar several braziers glowed hotly, with priests ready to cook the meat for the banquet that followed the religious aspect of the ceremony. As in tradition, there were still two dogs to be sacrificed—but only two, since no one wanted to eat dog meat for the sake of custom. So they went the way of the goats as far as the throat cutting and bloodletting, but not on to the flensers and the barbecue.

Ignoring the increasing clamor from nervous bucks and nannies, in quick succession with the efficiency an abattoir owner would appreciate, the Flamen Dialis sliced through goat throats with a fine hand, while lesser priests caught the blood in various bowls. Behind the officiants, acolytes flensed the hides from the corpses and jointed the meat before throwing it onto the griddles.

Rufio elbowed and shoved to make sure he was among the first in line, aware of Octavian and Crispin pressing hard behind. "Steady there," shouted the priest holding a blood bowl. "Step up! There you go!"

A hand reached out to sweep Rufio's tangle of curls clear, and a dripping carmined finger painted a diagonal of blood across his bared forehead. The iron tang filled his nostrils, earthy-fresh, still warm, a sticky mark of Lupercus. As he turned away to allow Crispin to be anointed with fresh goat's gore, Rufio stuck a finger under his locks. He wiped the tip in the blood and smeared his cheeks in two horizontal stripes because no one would be able to see the priestly insignia on his forehead under that cascade of coppery hair. One priest along handed him two thin strips of coarsely cut and freshly oozing goat hide. Doing as others did, he removed his scant loin covering and bound it around his left arm. Blessed and naked, Crispin, Octavian, and Rufio began the run. The route would take them right around the base of the Palatine hill, the line of the Romulus's ancient city. Almost immediately, Rufio scored a hit on the hand of a maiden nearly hysterical with excitement.

With loud whoops and bawdy suggestions, the cavalcade of youths ran north away from the river, past the Tarpeian Rock— from which sheer height convicted traitors were once hurled to their death—and on up the steep slope between the tall flanks of the Palatine and Capitol, over the crest of the hill and suddenly as steeply down into the Forum. Due to the narrowness of the passage at this point the bystanders on either side were forced into single rows. Rufio whipped no end of girls and young women, every one of whom would have loved for him to bring truth to the promise of their fertility. He could see it in their eyes as they took in his lithe figure and… well, exposure was making it a bit tumescent. He saw he wasn't the only one sporting something of an erection, and that was a far more interesting sight to Rufio than the women aspiring to have his virile seed.

He waved back at one enthusiastic matron, but that was Junilla Rufia, his good-looking mother. What mother wouldn't be proud to see her strapping son with everything on show petitioning the gods for a fertile year ahead and honoring the she-wolf who looked after Rome? He heard her shouting to all who would hear, "That's my Rufio, my lovely son. Look at the cock on him!" Junilla was always wiling to express her inner thoughts to all and sundry, but fortunately embarrassment wasn't in Rufio's vocabulary… nor hers.

Soon, on the right, the Palatine fell back, and the leading Lupercus ran down the paved slope alongside the Portico of the Twelve Gods rising up on the left, and then it was a sharp right turn in front of the Temple of Saturn and into the packed Roman Forum. Here, a sprinkling of nobility leavened the lowly citizens and proles. Rufio let loose a loud wolf's howl, jumped a few feet to the side where the crowd was thickest between the row of honorific columns celebrating past victories, and lashed out with his goat thong. The girl he'd aimed at screeched jubilantly and waved her blessed hand at her mother and proud father to show them the faint bloody imprint on her skin. The man nodded his gratitude and Rufio howled again.

And that's when he saw him. Tall and slim but under his expensive looking cream tunic obviously deliciously well formed. A helmet of tight-cropped raven-black hair glinted with purple highlights under the now well-risen sun. Serious eyes fired Cupid's arrows straight to Rufio's turbulent heart, but of course the aim was off and instead it was his groin that exploded with instant lust. For a couple of heartbeats he faltered as the marauding youths thundered on along the pavement of the Sacred Way past the Temple of the Divine Julius toward the Arch of Augustus. A combination of the wine he'd imbibed and the sheer lustiness of the festival went to Rufio's head. Taken by the lad's absurdly good patrician looks, a wicked wood-nymph thought made him sidestep and lift his whipping hand as he drew close to the cute vision.

The boy was clearly a part of his family group, for several pairs of eyes widened in surprise and then alarm as Rufio ran up, took aim, and slapped out at the young aristocrat. The thong whipped out to catch his victim right around the back of his taut upper thigh just where it began to swell to his rounded butt under the

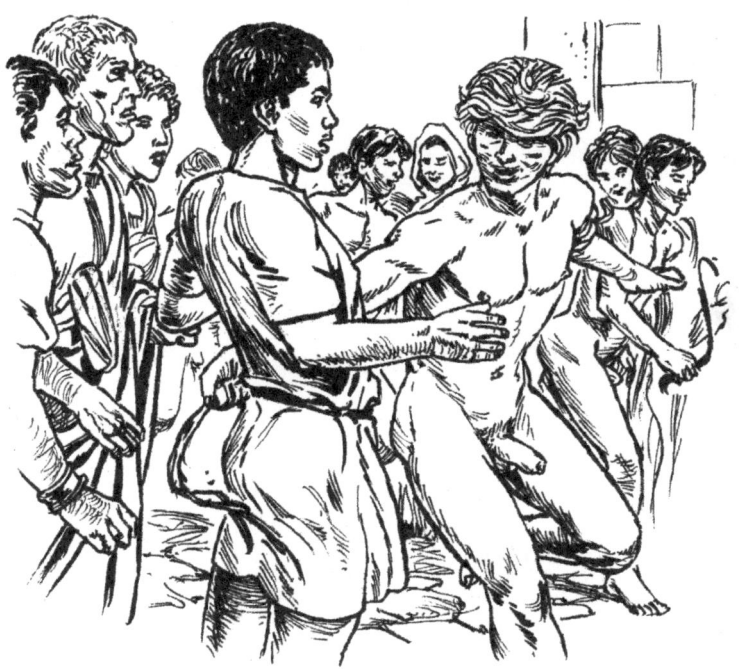

hem of his elegant tunic—a beautifully shaped buttock, Rufio noted approvingly. He just had time to register his victim's startled reaction, a gasp, dark pools of eyes thrown wide in mixed horror and shock.

From the first sighting to the moment of whipping and then passing on by with a cheekily turned head to wink, the act took less than the time it would take for ten grains of sand to fall through the waist of an hour-glass. Rufio felt deliciously wicked. He hoped the boy had gotten a good look at his prick. And then he was through the Arch of Augustus and beginning the climb past the House of the Vestals, curving to the left to run around the complex of old Nero's Porticoes toward the Colosseum.

Not much more than another hour of running and whipping and howling and then… Ah, then. Some wine, some song, and lots of fun.

Shame clothed Quintus Caecilius Alba as effectively as his tunic. Not the one he'd worn to watch the Lupercalia. That had a smear of goat's blood on the hem. "Not even steaming it over sulphur at the fuller's will entirely remove the stain," Ashur said forlornly.

Quintus barely listened to his body slave's grumbling. The stain on his flesh was far worse than the one on the expensive woolen tunic. How would he ever live it down? To be whipped like a swooning maiden by…

And there was the rub. Struck by a wild, whipping redhead with… yes, with wicked cornflower-blue eyes. Quintus shook his head in dismay. It had been so embarrassing, to be treated as a girl in front of his family, and so many strangers staring, smirking, even laughing outright at the joke. If he hadn't been struck dumb at the lout's sheer effrontery of laying hands—well, a thong of smelly goat hide—on a senator's son, Quintus would have taken hold of him and thrashed the Gallic peasant to within an inch of his barbarian life; better still, run him through with the long *spatha* cavalry sword he was learning to wield.

Big cock, though, and cocky with it.

"I'll take the garment to Metronia's, dominus, and urge her to pray to Minerva to remove the stain..."

To my honor! "Yes, yes. I'm sure Minerva will prove far more effective than Metronia at stain removal, the one a goddess, the other a bitch-dog."

Ashur slipped without another word from the suite of two rooms Quintus had for his bedroom and dressing area. He couldn't blame his slave for escaping. Ashur was getting the sharp blade of his temper for suffering such a public indignity. A keen blade he'd love to run right through that prole for the insult.

Large balls hanging below as well.

The color of his unkempt hair marked him as a Gaul, but he wouldn't be allowed to partake in the Lupercalia unless he was a freeborn citizen. Anyone of lesser status who put on the guise of the Luperci would certainly find themselves in the bowels of the Flavian Amphitheater, as his stuffy father Lucius insisted on calling the Colosseum, before they could say "*gladius*." And they'd be lucky to get a gladiator's sword to fight with.

How was it that he remembered the color of the boy's eyes when the entire stupid incident took less than a heartbeat? *Such a contrast to that brash hair. And the dimples.* Yes, Quintus could reconstruct them behind closed eyes, the way they tucked in so neatly to bracket the lips, bared in cruel humor at his joke. He could also recall in disturbing detail the callous way the runner's ass cheeks waved at him—up, down, up, down, sideways—as the bastard ran swiftly on toward the Arch of Augustus, carefree and unaware of the damage he'd done. To be hustled off home by his family, furious at the shame he'd caused. And that was so unfair because it hadn't been his fault, to be singled out for such extreme humiliation by a...

A dead boy! Dead when I'm done with him. A vision of the boy strung up on a cross, blood trickling from the nail wounds in his hands and feet... *Big cock on him, though.*

garden. The afternoon sun caught at the dark evergreen of the plane tree so it looked as if it were a flat cutout against the rubbly wall behind it. The irregular stones piled one atop another separated the Domus Alba from the steep hillside down to the Via Appia. His father Lucius claimed the wall was an authentic bit of the ancient city defenses built by King Servius Tullius in a time so long ago no one could remember it, not even the historians whose work Quintus studied. Now the city spilled far beyond that old sacred boundary. Marcus, his third brother, wit of the family, had joked that they could dig up the wall and sell the stones as artifacts to antique dealers. A wealthy home, yes, but Quintus knew that the family's wealth had ebbed badly. They were keeping up appearances without the means to do so.

The upset in the Forum made him squirm. He couldn't put it from his mind. It had even knocked right out of his mind a poem he'd been carefully formulating for days in praise of the festival. And it was even more of an insult to his honor because he was now an adult. Not a month had yet passed since the celebration of his coming to manhood in that very spot, on the auspicious day when the new consuls were installed. He'd put aside his *bulla*, the amulet every boy-child wore about his neck to protect him from evil until he donned his stiff new toga *virilis* to be ushered into the Forum by his father and shown off to other leathery senators. "My son, the man," Lucius said with touching pride. What sort of man got marked out as a woman by the lash of a Lupercus? Quintus strongly doubted the bastard who'd done it to him would be embarking on the *cursus honorum*, the path of honor marked by increasingly important civic and political offices, which every patrician male was expected to follow. The lout was evidently lowborn and therefore had no honor. It wasn't expected of his class.

He must go out to sit at dinner. It was time. Overdue, in fact. He hoped no one would bring up the sensitive subject of a madman whipping him. Or perhaps—if it were brought up—he could turn it to advantage by claiming it as an omen of good luck. Something that might help to rescue the Caecilii family fortunes.

Fuck that redheaded prick! If only I knew where to find him. I'd do anything to get my hands on him.

S·I·X | VI

Rome, Subura, February 13, AD 108

It was some time later when Rufio caught up with Crispin and Octavian in the vicinity of the Lupercal grotto, once again decently dressed and flushed with the enjoyment of the morning's running and whipping. "I single-handedly seeded at least twenty virgins," Octavian boasted.

"Here." Crispin held out Rufio's tunic and he quickly dressed. "My mother's rushed off to buy ground produce before everything in the vegetable market gets sold and the stalls shut up for the afternoon."

Smoke and the strong smell of cooking meat rose into the air. Clumps of idlers stood around the braziers still gorging on free goat meat. Others complemented their feast with flat breads and pulse porridge purchased from the super-expensive street vendors, whose ramshackle stands littered the roadway leading down off the hillside. At the bottom, where it met Via Murcia, the street between the palace and Circus Maximus, there rose the roofs of the charioteer school and adjoining Imperial Paedagogium. Crispin pointed down at its barely visible tiles. "I've always dreamed of getting inducted," he said with a longing sigh.

Octavian laughed. "Dream on, my little Crispin, that place is for the fucking nobles, not street rats like us."

"Speak of yourself, Octavian." Rufio squared his shoulders in a haughty manner and his tummy rumbled, hungry for some roasted goat. "I have a calling."

"Your mother's an entertainer," Crispin pointed out mildly.

"Hah!" Octavian barked. He tapped the side of his squat nose. "And we all know what that means."

Rufio's sniff contained all his disdain. "My mother… and myself… we're merchants in antiquities. But we do also have a business in *arranging* entertainments for the great and the good."

Having got his barb in, Octavian lost interest in Rufio's occupation and Crispin's hopeless desire to be admitted to the Paedagogium to be trained as a high-up civil servant. His mind had evidently turned to a subject that interested Rufio, or would do as soon as he had satisfied the hunger pangs above his waist.

"As this is the Lupercalia and we've been rushing about as wolves, it's just right we visit a *lupanar*," Octavian announced, using the Latin slang for a brothel, a wolf den. He said this with a leer and handful of genitals grabbed through his tunic. "How about the Urgent Bull?"

"Which one's that?" Crispin's glance of doubt at Rufio only increased his look of perpetual surprise, the result of highly curved eyebrows, a long pointy nose, and a small, pursed mouth.

Rufio raised his own eyebrows: more disdain. "What, that stinking hole in the third arch along under the Circus?"

"It's not that bad." Octavian said with a sniff of his own.

"Not if you want to choke on soot from lamp fumes and come out crawling with vermin."

Octavian sneered. "I bet you've never been in there."

"Have so! For two blinks of an eye." Rufio bared his teeth in an appropriately wolfish grin. "I'm starving. Let's get something to eat first and then cut across to the Subura. Find somewhere there."

Octavian wrinkled his nose. "Do you know the Sign of the Rampant Cock, on the corner of Tavern Street?"

Crispin lifted a hand. "That's all the way up the Viminal. We've had enough of that sort of exercise for one day."

"Lucretia's Lupanar in the Subura is a nice clean place." Rufio gave his two friends his most engagingly innocent smile.

Octavian's sneer widened into a grimace. "That place! There are at least three cocks to every cunny, but then, you'd know that Rufio, wouldn't you? It's always the same with you Gauls. Can only get off with a man up you."

Rufio's bright whoop was so full of joyous humor, people from all around looked at him with happy smiles. His voice was much lower than the brazen laughter, though. "Octavian, when you're finally forced to join the legions to avoid starving, I'll guarantee you'll learn what the centurion does with his vine rod and the meaning of his stern instruction on the parade ground to 'man up'!"

At that, even the butt of Rufio's joke had to chortle

Later, with stomachs satisfied, they made their way back around the Palatine and crossed the Roman Forum and slipped into the Nerva's Forum. This long passage was squeezed between the Forum of Augustus to the left and Vespasian's Temple of Peace on the right. There was a time, Rufio remembered his schoolteacher lecturing his class, when it was Via Argiletum, the ancient way linking the Subura to the Roman Forum, as indeed Nerva's Forum still did, though of the original street there was no longer a sign. That hadn't stopped the booksellers and shoemakers who had always lined Via Argiletum from colonizing the narrow place. Normally busy, on this festival day it was quiet. At the far end, Rufio led the way past the temple of Minerva and through the opening in the monumental wall that ran all the way behind the imperial forums to where Trajan's vast forum and markets were under construction. The tall wall served as a firebreak to protect the public and civic areas from the frequent incendiary incidents that characterized the rabbit warren of the Subura beyond it.

Out there, narrow streets filled the old gulch as it rose steadily between the projecting shoulders of the Viminal and Esquiline hills. Apartment blocks of up to six stories towered over the district's crooked streets and alleyways. On the ground level most buildings housed shops, taverns, and cookhouses. The shops offered for sale every conceivable object known to the Imperium, from hammers and nails to eastern delicacies, from curios like lucky hares' feet to the foreskins of twelve-year-old Jewish boys preserved in oil. And there was an endless parade of *lupanaria*—the brothels for which the Subura was famous.

On every street a pervading stench of overcooked vegetables, stewed meats of indistinct provenance, piss and feces from the public latrines and even more urine from the tanner's stores, made every intaken breath an olfactory adventure. At some point lost in the mists of time Lucretia's forebears had garnered one of the better sites in the district, a corner position half way up Suburan Hill, the nearest thing to a main road, where one of the wider cross streets rose up steeply to the Cispian hill.

Predictably, after such a sexually arousing festival, eager customers in party mood crammed Lucretia's. Octavian pushed in through the street door, Crispin and Rufio close on his heels. What seemed a narrow street frontage, inside spread from the initial foyer like a Minoan labyrinth. After dropping the giant Nubian slave guarding the entry a few low-value *asses* to keep his temper sweet, regulars melted away in this direction or that, along this hallway or up the narrow stone steps to the upper levels. Tambourine and sistrum blended with the general buzz of conversation. Above a small cubbyhole in the foyer wall, the various rates for the "prostitutes of the day" were advertised on a large board, including prices for the *lupanaria*'s popular "take out service." The minimum rental was an hour and the establishment's majordomo monitored matters strictly. His decision in any dispute was final. Discounts for bulk-booked hours were available on application to the management. Below, tucked snugly in the cubbyhole, Lucretia scanned all her clients with a careful eye as they crossed the lewd mosaics on the floor, which left little to the imagination as to the nature of the house.

"Hey! You lot. You may have sucked up to Daroua," she crowed, referring to the monstrous Nubian, "but there's a cover charge on tonight." She held out a hand like a grasping claw. Leaning forward from the gloom of her lair, light from the nearest lamp made her hennaed medusa's nest of hair glow the color of fresh gladiator's blood. "Oh, it's you," she said with a scowl at Rufio. "By Jupiter's priapic phallus, your hair's a worse shade than mine. Does your Ma know you're out on the fuck-trail?"

Rufio squared up to the harridan whose bark he knew to be a great deal worse than her bite, but a shade less heavy than her hand when it came to dealing with clients reluctant to part with their *denarii*. Lucretia didn't really need Daroua to deal with rowdy customers, but she liked to provide employment. Besides, as rumor had it, the huge ebony-skinned man was the only one with a dick big enough to fill her leisure hours.

"She gave me an advance on my wages specially, Lucretia." He smiled and coaxed the slightest twitch of amusement from her full, scarlet lips. He dropped a few coins into the still outstretched palm.

"You are an imp and you will die a terrible death because of it. But not yet. In you go then. The courtyard's got a special Lupercalia live show on. I recognize your horsey-faced friend. Won't interest him, if you know what I mean." She winked. He did. "I don't recognize the big thick one, though, but I'll judge he fucks women."

Rufio smiled at hearing his friends' discomfort at her coarse descriptions. "I'll see you both later," he said to Crispin and Octavian. "Or if you get happy, maybe not."

And with a small wave, he pushed through a drape and turned left, soon swallowed up in the dim-lit interior. His friends, he knew, would go the other way to where the female prostitutes plied their trade in numerous small rooms set aside for the purpose. On this side, there were the same kind of spaces, simple and equipped with a stone bed topped by a thin straw mattress, the rooms mostly open so passers-by could get a dark glimpse of the action inside. Rufio's cock twitched in anticipation, but first he wanted to see the show.

The corridor came out into a large open space, actually the block's central well. Looking up, he could see five floors of windows and balconies, crowded with the apartment dwellers who occupied the top three floors of the *lupanar*. They were getting a free show, and none peering down seemed bothered by the all-male action below.

The substantial cover charge he'd handed over evidently included the wine that scantily clad boys were pouring from jugs into clay mugs for those who wanted it—which seemed to be everyone, including the slaves, servers, and sex partners. He took a mug and tried the contents. Typical Lucretia. *If it's included in the price, don't expect a Falernian!* He screwed up his face at the sour stuff, but it was strong, unwatered, and would do. He leaned back against the wall beside a line of graffiti that read: *Felix bene futuis*—"You lucky guy, you get a good fuck." The wall on the other side of the passageway bore the even happier legend: *Hic ego pueri multas futui*—"Here I fucked many boys."

On a raised stage a dance troupe was performing something that looked decadently oriental. Exotic, olive-skinned Emesene boys circled fair-haired Teutons, warm-skinned Berber youths sinuously wound themselves around their darker cousins from the interior deserts. But Rufio was particularly taken with two black-skinned Africans from—he guessed—the far south of Egypt. Their undulating bodies glistened enticingly in the orange lamplight as they caressed each other, wiggling their jutting little buttocks at the audience and bouncing their long, slim erections at each other. Rufio's cock twitched and burgeoned at the prospect of invading those delectable bottoms.

Around the stage, in the flickering light of the sconces, regularly replaced by slave boys, customers ranging in age from youths no older than Rufio to elderly statesmen relaxed on couches with whatever boy they had chosen. He was familiar with the rhythm of the place; as popular as Lucretia's was, there were always more customers than fuck-rooms available and it was customary to lounge about out here until the majordomo approached the next man in line to let them know that the previous client had vacated a room. At that point, the customer handed to the same functionary the sex-slave fee as advertised on the board in the foyer. It was up to the customer to reward his boy on completion if he'd been satisfied. At least tonight the waiting was spiced by the sexy show the naked dancers were putting on.

As a couch came free close to the stage, Rufio quickly slipped between occupied ones and grabbed it. Fortified by the wine, he made eyes at the two black boys to be rewarded by a blindingly white smile from the slightly taller of the two. And then he relaxed and watched the dancing, happy that because Lucretia and his mother were old friends, the madam would see him right. *I'm going to get to fuck those two beauties!*

A slave topped up his mug, and then to prove his faith in the power of who you know, it was the majordomo who approached to inform him that a room was free and did he have in mind any...?

"Those two," Rufio promptly answered. *Oh yes.*

"A fine choice, if I might say so. I'll take you through and then fetch them."

The room was spacious by the standards of a *lupanar* and equipped with a sturdy wood-frame bed, not the usual stone ledge and mattress, and a moderately clean drape across the door. As the majordomo showed him in, a cleaning slave was just smoothing down a fresh bed covering.

"Hurry up, boy!" The majordomo gave Rufio an apologetic look and a shrug that said you just couldn't get the staff these days.

Rufio stood aside to the let the blushing boy pass by with the previous client's soiled bed covering rolled up in his arms. Then he handed over the correct amount of *denarii* and went to sit on the bed. The majordomo disappeared. Rufio unfastened the belt around his waist and slipped the tunic over his head. A flick of the wrist loosened his loincloth and left him naked, aroused, and ready for sex.

And that is how Menankouda and Tapi found him when they stuck their woolly-topped heads around the curtain and gave him shy grins. Rufio knew their names because they were engraved on the slave collars they wore—which was all they wore, though they were carrying two mugs of their own and a large jug of wine. He beckoned them in. More drink was poured and taken. Hot bodies were hungrily explored, cocks stroked to full arousal, balls fondled. And then Menankouda dropped to his knees and began sucking Rufio, who pressed Tapi down on the bed so he could stroke the boy's long black cock and free the pink glans from its rose-petaled sheath. He shared none of the reservations of that funny Flaccus his mother hired from time to time, so desperate to get a hand up inside Rufio's tunic, yet self-declared old-fashioned when it came

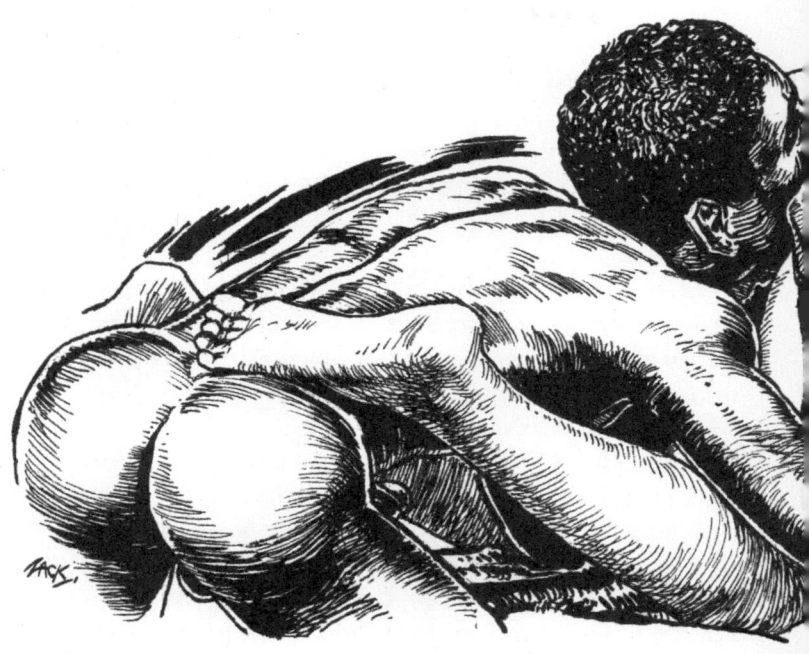

to the more interesting aspects of men having sex with other men. Rufio leaned down and took the succulent rod of flesh between his lips, sucking Tapi as Menankouda sucked him.

The excitement of the day fired his senses. All too soon he took spasming, gasping Tapi's copious load as he urgently shot his own between the second Nubian's thick lips. After relaxing, nestling languidly amid satiny limbs, and slurping more wine, Rufio made Tapi fellate his black friend, which he did with gusto. His loins flared with titillated excitement when Menankouda shuddered and climaxed, and his cum flowed down from Tapi's mouth stark white against his ebony shaft.

That got his own so excited that it was a delicious torture to spend time checking which boy had the tightest asshole. That turned out to be Tapi, the smaller of the two, and Rufio laid him on his back, folded his legs up and back over his torso into a nice tight parcel that left his twitching little bud vulnerably exposed. Rufio

anointed it with a swirl of his spittle and nudged the inflamed tip of his rigid cock against it. With a sigh of victory he punched his way in, invaded the steamy channel to the hilt, and fucked him hard. As Rufio's orgasm mounted, Menankouda—needing no command—ducked his face down into Rufio's bucking rear and used an amazingly prehensile tongue to dicker at his asshole. In spite of the hard fuck, Menankouda managed to keep his tongue engaged, evidently relishing the butt-cheek slapping his face cheeks received.

When he started to cum, deep inside little Tapi, the Nubian slave, mouth agape, eyes rolled up in abandon, jerked his own hard cock up between his thighs and stroked out a stream of cum that jetted upward to catch Rufio under the chin. Moments later Menankouda straightened up and brought himself off over Rufio's shuddering back. They slowly collapsed into an entwined sandwich of white between black, slippery with their mutual emissions, for the moment content like satiated puppies. Rufio thanked his foresight (and his mother's generosity) in paying the majordomo to let him keep the room for the whole night—he was not finished yet...

Menankouda's girlish squeaks spluttering past his lips wrapped around the root of Tapi's swallowed cock filled the room. Rufio had him sprawled on his spread knees over his friend's squirming body, and his rhythmic fucking of his juicy ass forced the lad's erection deep into Tapi's upturned mouth. Rufio lost himself in the pleasure of probing deep into the hot, clenching flesh, the sucking retreat to the gaping mouth of the boy's passage, the glimpse of pink insides

before boring back into the fleshy furnace to hit bottom and elicit another frothy squeak from the young Nubian. What pleasure! He wanted to go on forever, to bugger a boy, to feel the near-painful climax rushing through his bursting, gushing cock and lather it with hot cum…

An intricate web of cracks skittered across the low ceiling, brought to pulsing life from the light seeping around the gaps in the door drape of a flickering oil lamp in the corridor. Rufio stared at them from his Nubian cocoon as a quiet snore told him Menankouda had slipped into slumber. Tapi soon followed, but Rufio found sleep elusive. A face kept looming in his vision like an avatar. At first it was blurry in detail, but then he realized who stared back at him from the cobweb of cracks above. The dark-haired patrician lad he'd so wickedly misused with his goatskin whip. As the memory strengthened, Rufio even saw the faintest smear of blood he'd left on that creamy thigh. The handsome youth in the Forum smiled at him. Unaccountably, considering how many times he'd just come, Rufio's cock sprang into hard life again and found the nearest moist orifice to plunge into.

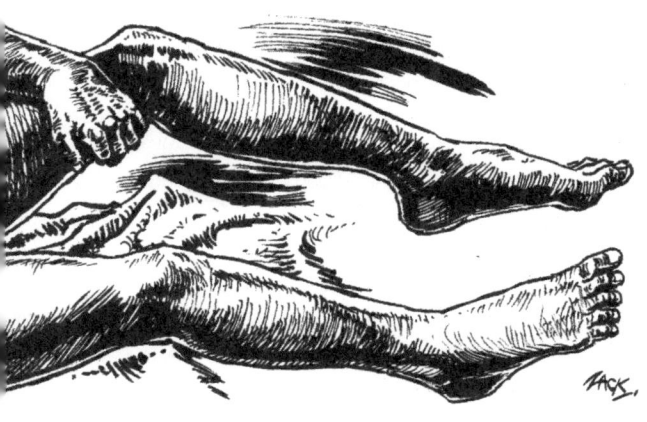

S·E·V·E·N | VII

Rome, Aventine Hill, evening, February 13

Dinner at Domus Alba was always a solemn event, held strictly an hour before sunset. Quintus recalled with fondness the easier-going meals at the family seaside villa when he was younger. But those days were gone. Then, Lucius Caecilius Alba's business concerns thrived and so they could afford to leave Rome for holiday resort of Baiae in the hot summer months. Quintus dreamed of restoring the family fortunes and getting back that beautiful villa overlooking the wide Bay of Naples where they could leave stuffy Roman values behind for a while. In Rome they had a formal *triclinium*, a dining room with three couches arranged around a single square table, and room for three persons to recline on each couch, which meant a formal dinner was only for nine persons. Also in accordance with ancient tradition, the couches were graded in importance: *summus*, *medius*, and *imus*—top, middle, bottom. Of his few friends, Quintus didn't know one whose family were still so stuffy in their dining arrangements.

The Caecilii were equally unimaginative over naming their children. Unlike Quintus, his three older brothers at least received real names. Primus as the firstborn was named after his father, but to avoid any confusion everyone called him Lucius Primus. Secundus took the name Livius Secundus after their mother's brother, Uncle Livius Caecilius Dio. The third boy, Tertius died in a childhood accident, so his name of Marcus (for their mother's father) was transferred to Quartus. But Quintus, the fifth son—he was just Number Five. Plain Quintus. The two sisters, one older, one younger, were Fabia the Younger after her mother, and Julia after an aunt from somewhere.

"You're late," Lucius snapped out as Quintus stepped into the dining room.

Eight pairs of eyes looked up. He was last. He saw that the first course of hard-boiled eggs, baked white fish, raw vegetables, and dips of variously flavored ground chickpeas in olive oil was already on the table. A trail of oily drips between the dishes and edges of the table told the tale of how late he was.

"Take your place." His father was still smarting from the insult of the morning.

Quintus nodded and quickly settled himself on the bottom couch above his sisters. "Be quick!" Fabia the Younger snapped. "I suppose you've been mooning over some poetic composition while we all starve to death waiting for you. And don't be so clumsy."

He apologized for knocking her ankle. Julia gave him a tiny smile of complicity over Fabia's fashionably piled up hairdo, probably thankful she wasn't getting the sharp end of her sister's waspish tongue. Julia was the only one who complimented him on his poetic writing. Across the low table, Quintus faced Lucius Primus and Livius Secundus, who reclined next to their father. On the middle couch his mother Fabia had placed herself so she and his father were close enough to engage in private conversation. Beside his mother were Maia, the wife Lucius Primus, and his fourth (now third) brother, Marcus. All in strict, proper, order; "Ship-shape and Misenum fashion," as Marcus was wont to say—often. Marcus, who was on leave from the huge naval base at Misenum, near Naples, had been regaling the diners with his exploits aboard a war galley. He was an optio of marines, second in command under a centurion. Quintus knew that the older brothers teased him because the Roman navy simply didn't compare to the majesty of the army; and also because they suspected (as did Quintus) that Marcus was too inexperienced to really be an officer.

He continued his story, interrupted by Quintus's arrival,

"We were no more than three hours out of harbor when the

bugler sounded an alarm and the legionaries armed themselves ready for battle. The rowers speeded up and—"

"What battle?" Skepticism hung about young Livy's head like a screen of smoke.

Quintus picked at a fishy fragment, not really hungry, still brooding on the morning's events and the sense of parental disapproval, which wafted like a bad stench from the corner where *summus* and *medius* met.

Not my fault!

"There are still pirates about, you know, Livy. I know most people think that old puffed up Pompey Magnus cleared the nests out, but don't forget his son turned to piracy and there are many he inspired. Anyway, we came about and prepared…"

It was obvious from the stiff demeanor that much as he might like to, his father was not going to raise the subject of his embarrassment, but Quintus knew he would not be able to avoid discussion of the impending marriage.

And now his eldest brother was taking a turn sniping at Marcus. Quintus didn't take it in.

"I'm sure he knows quite what he means." Her reclining position forced Maia to snap over her shoulder at Marcus to back up her husband. After a couple of years as a junior legate on the Rhine, Lucius Primus was an expert on military tactics—at least he thought so. Not that he'd know anything about war on the sea, but then neither did Marcus, Quintus suspected with a rare spark of humor for this awful day.

"Were the accommodations at Moguntiacum comfortable?" Fabia the Elder wanted to know. "I can't imagine things in Germany have improved much since we spent a year up there." She shuddered, but Quintus knew his mother had quite enjoyed the challenge.

"Oh, Mother-in-Law, your dear son found us a lovely little villa on a bank above the Rhine a little distant from the camp."

"We were very comfortable, Mama," Lucius Primus added. "As

much, anyway, as is possible in that damp, gloomy, and backward land. Thank Jupiter we had a proper working hypocaust to heat the rooms in winter."

"And in spring," Maia said, with a sniff.

"I note you aren't running the central heating here," Lucius Primus said to his father.

"It costs money. You've no idea how much the wood merchants have jacked up prices this winter. When I complain I'm told we've used up all the locally available timber and now it must be hauled from Belgium and Germany at great cost. You'll never see a poor timber merchant, that's for sure." Lucius chewed for a while and everyone remained quiet, familiar with his habit of considering what he wanted to say next. "I should like to know how my brother's prospects fare with the emperor."

Quintus noted surprise in the expressions of his older brothers across the table. Marcus next to him gave him a questioning look, but Quintus shook his head. It was the first he'd heard of Uncle Livy having prospects with the emperor. He was never sure about his uncle, who was really his mother's brother, but brothers-in-law always regarded each other as though they were of the same father—unless there was a divorce.

"What is Uncle Livy up to with Caesar?"

Lucius swallowed another morsel before answering. "As you know, Primus, we have joint interests, and Livy has been angling for an introduction to Trajan through his patron, Appius Gallus."

"The consul?" Marcus sounded excited. "A consul as a family patron would help my career no end."

"*Is* there such a thing as a *career* in the navy?"

"Oh ha ha, very amusing, Secundus—"

"There is nothing to laugh about," Lucius said with asperity. "Our finances suffered terribly with those—" He couldn't bring himself to mention the rivals by name. "Those other families using underhand tactics to secure contracts for their clients to earn them all fortunes.

Livy has been trying to change that by swaying Trajan's mind against our enemies and placing us in favor. But these are delicate negotiations that require careful handling. They take time, and I'm waiting for him to advise me how his plan is progressing."

"I hope his plan includes us." Lucius Primus held his father's hard stare.

"What are you implying?"

"Nothing… I hope, father. But you must admit that Uncle Livy tends to consider himself before others, and does he not own the lion's share of the family's interests?"

"He does, Primus," said Fabia, joining in. "But my father awarded your father a very generous portion when he married me, and I'm confident that while he is a Dio Livy will see to the benefit of all the Caecilii when he gets what we hope for from Caesar."

The discussion faltered when slaves started to bring in the main course of cooked vegetables and roasted duck, rabbit, and cold eel terrine with jellied eel compote. As the used dishes were cleared away and replaced with the new ones, Livy Secundus looked across brightly at Quintus.

"I'm sorry I missed the fun this morning."

Quintus choked on a fragment of the fish he hadn't finished.

"I hear we gained a new sister we didn't know we had."

"Livius Secundus," his father warned.

Quintus knew it would take more than one admonishment and the use of Livy's full name.

"I always knew your interest in history and the scented words of poets set you apart from the warlike rest of us, brother, but I had no idea it had so emasculated you—*ow!*"

If Livy was accusing Quintus of being girly, he couldn't joke about the manly accuracy of his young brother's aim. The chunk of jellied eel struck Livy just below his left eye, dead on target. *Wouldn't want to blind him.*

In a blur of movement, Livy was on his feet. "You little—"

"Enough! Livius be seated." Lucius's voice brooked no dissent, his normally mild manner folded under a seething anger at his sons. "We do not brawl at dinner. We do not brawl in the house of Caecilius Alba at all." He glared at both of them. "What occurred this morning was... distasteful and reflects badly on the family. However, it was not the fault of Quintus, and neither is he marked by its implication. It was a tasteless, blasphemous prank. I want to hear no more of it. Is that clear?"

Livy's scowl slowly melted. Quintus stared ahead, unwilling to give in first.

"I don't hear you."

"Yes, father," they both said.

After an uncomfortable silence broken only by the sounds of mastication, the conversation slowly picked up and moved in the direction of the girls' marriage prospects. Fabia the Younger was comely in appearance, but her short temper put suitors off once they got to know her. Her prospects of betrothal to the son of a well-to-do family were fast fading. Julia was possessed of a pleasant nature, much like his own, Quintus thought, but where everyone said how handsome he was, no one said anything encouraging about plain Julia. Lucius Primus married Maia before the Caecilii fortunes slipped, so there had been no pressure brought on him to marry for wealth, and Maia's portion was modest, while Livius Secundus discovered his wife's father had suffered a financial dislocation similar to that of the Caecilli shortly after the wedding.

Aurelia, his attractive spouse who he loved, sensibly declined invitations to dine at Domus Alba where she felt uncomfortable under the disappointed gaze of her father-in-law and the disapproval of her mother-in-law. Marcus was under a similar pressure to Quintus, but not much could be arranged until he'd finished his stint in the navy, which would not be for another year at the least.

Even as his father opened his mouth, Quintus sighed.

"I shall speak with Numerius Metellus on the next day we are in court together," Lucius said, pointedly looking at Quintus.

At a call, Lucius's secretary appeared in the doorway and bowed. "When am I next in court, Pallas?"

"The twelfth day before the Kalends of March, dominus."

Lucius swiveled around on the couch. "In four days? That long. Hmm. Thank you, Pallas." He turned back to address Quintus. "Well, it will have to do. I doubt the caseload we'll be hearing will be so heavy that I won't have the time to persuade Numerius to speed up the engagement. I've no doubt you will like Vipsania Metella, Quintus."

Quintus swallowed spit. "What—what if she doesn't… like me?"

"Her opinion is less relevant than yours, my boy. Her father's wealth most certainly is, so I don't care whether she looks like the back end of one of Marcus's biremes—"

"It's a quinquereme, Father!"

"Last time you wrote you mentioned a twenty-man Liburnian," Lucius Primus said with a mean smile. Livy Secundus chortled and held his palms a foot apart to suggest the tiny size of a Liburnian ship.

"Shut up!" Lucius roared before Marcus could make a retort. "Now, as I was saying, Quintus you are expected to make Vipsania feel comfortable when you finally meet your bride to be. Numerius tells me her appearance is far removed from the rear end of a *plaustrum*…" he paused meaningfully to glare again at Marcus and then Livy Secundus, having removed any cause for the trading of further insults by changing the unfavorable comparison to that of a waddling farm cart. "So you will make her feel loved. Indeed. Whatever you think of the maiden, you will be married to her before March is out. The moment her father and I have settled on her wedding portion. Now I want my third course."

They might have fallen on hard times, Quintus reflected bitterly, but expensive tradition remained. None of his friends' families stuck to the old principle of having slaves remove the table on which the first and second courses had been eaten to replace it with one already laden under the weight of fruit, but oh at Domus Alba never let penury stand in the way of virtue and ancient custom.

"Mmm, figs." Marcus reached and picked one out, so ripe that at the press of his fingers purple juice ran down them. He licked his lips as he prised the fruit apart to reveal its delicate inner secrets. He nudged Quintus with his foot and smirked as he held the fig to his mouth. "I'll bet your Vipsania will be as easily opened up and moist inside as this." He buried his mouth in the succulence, flickered his tongue into the soft cavity, in and out like an eager lizard, and slurped.

Marcus spoke quietly so no one else heard his lewd words, for which Quintus was thankful. The very notion of what Marcus suggested revolted him. He felt sick, and couldn't wait for the torment of dinner to end.

At last. Peace and quiet. His own room. His own space. Alone. The thought of Vipsania Metella filled him with such a deep unease the notion of vomiting welled up again. Quintus might dream of restoring the family fortunes, but he did not wish to be the sacrificial victim who made it possible. Unwilled, the vision of the flame-headed youth came back. Carefree, unfettered.

Such a big cock on him. I wonder if it gets any larger when it grows hard, or it one of those that doesn't alter in length, just gets thicker...?

Without thinking consciously, he stroked the skin of his inner thigh and registered the tickling sensation in his balls.

He became aware of a soft, intimate scratching sound. Ashur. On the wall outside the dressing room. His usual signal to request entry. Quintus smiled and called out softly. Ashur pushed aside the heavy drape that closed off the two chambers from the hall and offered some privacy. The Syrian body slave approached the bed with a look of quiet anticipation, awaiting a command, but with hunger in his eyes.

"Do you require help undressing, dominus?"

Quintus's breath came out as a sharp, amused-yet-bitter laugh. "I need comforting, Ashur. Anything to take my mind off what is planned for me."

Ashur bent over and began to unfasten Quintus's belt. "And what is that, Quintus?" he asked softly, allowed to use his master's name in the privacy of his chambers.

"I'm sure you know. You slaves know everything." He half sat up so Ashur could pull the tunic up over his head.

"Because there is gossip on the other side of the *atrium* does not mean I believe it." Ashur carefully folded the tunic and set aside on top of a wooden wardrobe chest.

Quintus fell back and allowed Ashur to unknot and remove his loincloth. The process meant the slave's hands coming into contact with his flesh in a place that made Quintus tingle and his cock twitch. He smiled. "This you know, you lying scoundrel; that I'm to be partnered with a girl I haven't seen since we were infants. It's not fair because she has seen me. At least I suppose so. That was why I had to endure sitting for that portrait father and Uncle Livy insisted on having done. I'm to be put out to stud because her dowry will be as colossal as her backside is now."

"I hear the Lady Metella is very beautiful."

"Hah! Then why did my father describe her as being like the rear end of a naval vessel?"

"He didn't." Ashur frowned.

"You were listening."

It wasn't a question. Quintus knew Ashur liked to know what was being said, and because it wasn't a question, Ashur didn't bother answering. "He *said* it didn't matter to him—or you—if that were to be the case." Ashur quickly slipped out of his own tunic, and visibly aroused, curled up beside Quintus. He began to stroke the muscles of his master's stomach, following with a fingertip one side of the pronounced abdominal V toward the groin.

"If my father has his way of it, we'll be forced to start the wooing process in no time. So how do you know she's beautiful?"

Ashur shrugged. "All virgin girls of marriageable age are described as 'beautiful', so I'm sure she must be."

"What rot! I don't want to marry."

Ashur caressed away the nonsequitur and traced his fingers along the stiffening curve of cock. Quintus breathed out raggedly, and tried to relax his body.

I hope Uncle Livy's plans with the emperor work out, then the need for banking money from a dowry won't be necessary and I needn't marry. Not now, anyway. I haven't lived yet.

He closed his eyes and let the skilled Syrian work his oriental magic with lips and pointy tongue, which played around inside Quintus's foreskin until he was completely erect and his cock head fully unsheathed. Gentle at first, Ashur soon firmed up his lips, spread wide around the rigid shaft, and sucked much harder. Quintus couldn't quite visualize the stern of a war galley, though the back end of an ugly *plaustrum* was too easy to create mentally, but gradually, as Ashur sucked, the imaginary visage of Vipsania Metella melted away as though into a blazing sunset. A fiery creature of wild hair framing eyes so blue they shamed the summer sky—naughty eyes that held a challenge in them; dimpled cheeks, cheeky in smile and smirk, also provoking a response. The thrice-damned redheaded Lupercus...

Ashur gulped furiously as the response came, and his working throat flooded with his young master's seed.

E·I·G·H·T | VIII

Rome, Subura and Aventine Hill, dawn, February 14

For a terrifying moment Rufio thought a monster of the Underworld had him in its pestilential grip, maybe Crispin's Cacus come back for a late snack. He groaned and the creature mimicked him. He opened a crusty eye.

"Gods alive, Daroua. Fucking put me down. I'll die in the corner over there."

The giant Nubian made a sound that might have been a laugh or a terminal cough. "Der cleaners come, you go."

"I can walk. Put me down. *Aarrgh!* I didn't mean drop me on the damned floor."

"You may well be my favorite baby customer, but even you have to make yourself scarce."

Rufio looked up blearily at Lucretia in the cruel daylight, and thought his eyesight must be damaged by the quantity of cheap wine and all that fucking, because the madam had looked a whole lot better by the dim light of a candle. His brain must be starting to work because he thought better than to say so. Daroua gave vent to a gusty laugh and lent a hand to haul him to his unsteady feet.

Lucretia tutted unsympathetically. "I'm not surprised at your state, the way you left poor Abba and Nasri."

"Huh?"

"Costs me money when they're laid off. Fucked 'em half to death, poor mites."

"I thought their names were… oh, what were they? Menankouda and Tapi?"

Lucretia shrugged, a maneuver that involved an enormous

amount of flesh rearrangement. "Pah! You don't expect whore-boys to use their real names do you? I've no idea what their mothers called them. Bastard probably."

The wheezing chortle was almost too much for Rufio and his gorge rose. He leaned weakly against the hallway wall and looked dubiously at the morning light that streamed in through a distant open door. It looked too bright for his present state, but it was evident that Lucretia was about to have Daroua throw him bodily onto the street. He took a brave step.

"You owed me five denarii."

"I did?" He fumbled for the small purse affixed to his belt.

"I took the liberty of taking it already."

"Ah. Then… I'll be on my way."

"Straight to your mother's, I hope. It is a working day. Me, I'm off to my bed as soon as Daroua seals the street door. Have a good day."

"Tullius Rufio you are the drunken son of a bitch sow," he muttered under his breath. *One foot in front of another, that's the way to do it.* "Why do I do this to myself? Still… it was a fucking good fucking night." He wondered briefly how Crispin and Octavian got on while idly checking whether Lucretia had left him any coins in his purse. She had. It renewed his trust in humanity. Briefly.

He pulled up at a cookhouse on the first street junction he came to. Like nearly all others, it had two counters either side of a corner pillar. He leaned on the cracked stone top. Only one other customer stood at the other counter waiting to be served. He gave Rufio a cursory glance, a look of mixed suspicion, mild curiosity, and disapproval at his disheveled appearance.

"A good morning to you," Rufio said, the edge of sarcasm aimed more at himself than the stranger.

The man gave Rufio a second appraisal, and then grunted. "Will be when Septimius gets me my food." He raised his voice on the last few words.

"Hold on to your thunderbolt, Gaius. It's coming right now."

The owner appeared from behind a buttress, a haze of blue smoke following him out. He slapped down a steaming bowl in front of the man and added a hunk of ready-torn flatbread from a basket. He looked across enquiringly at Rufio.

Rufio's stomach growled. He needed something solid in him, and not a Nubian cock. The bowl sitting on the other counter contained two sausages and a mess of steaming pulses. It looked as tasty as it smelled. "I'd like the same, but how much?"

"Two *asses*."

The man named Gaius tucked in. He dipped a piece of bread into the porridge and took a large mouthful, followed by a bite off a sausage held in his other fist. "It's good." He finished the mouthful and then, without looking around as he prepared a second helping of bread and pulses, said, "Septimius makes the best breakfast this side of the Forum."

"I'll have it. Thanks."

As the cookshop owner disappeared through an opening behind the counter into his kitchen, Rufio gave Gaius a second look over as well and realized what he hadn't in his hungover state that the man was passably attractive—if you liked the rugged river stevedore type. His look was returned with a lazy wink. Rufio was wondering what to make of it when Septimius returned with a second bowl, added bread, and placed it on the counter in front of him. He tore of a piece of bread hungrily and dipped it into the hot pulse porridge, then took a bite of sausage. Rufio had eaten at enough hot food stalls and along with a human need for food the customers had to accept the quite probable run for the nearest public latrine to void the part-digested result. "Inedible" might be the slogan for many such cookshops, so Rufio marveled that he had never come across this one before.

"It *is* good."

Septimius, who had been standing stiffly as if preparing for attack as the best means of defense relaxed and looked pleased, even smug. "You'll only get the finest local produce served here. I pride myself on the quality of my food. I use only the freshest ingredients, bought every morning in the great market above the Forum, and I make my own sausages fresh *every* day, cased in the best quality pig intestines. That's a medium-coarse porker with some onion and sage mixed in."

Gaius next door swallowed the tail end of his sausage and mopped the bowl out with the last corner of bread. He belched appreciatively.

Septimius lifted a cloth from over his arm and whipped it down smartly on a fly wandering on the corner of his counter. He flicked the small carcass away into the street dismissively. He disappeared into the kitchen again briefly to return with a bowl full of cucumbers, which he placed on the counter top beside Gaius. He took one out and started polishing it with a cloth while Rufio, filled with pulses and sausage, began to feel more human. Even the bread wasn't too coarse.

Septimius kept polishing, carefully piling the cucumbers into a decorative hill on the counter. "I get a fair bit of custom from Lucretia's Lupanar in the morning," he said apropos of nothing." Rufio looked up. Gaius screwed the corner of his mouth into a sly grin at this. "The ones who can afford to sleep it off usually look a bit worn at the edges," Septimius went on. "In need of a quick feed to restore some vigor for the day ahead." He dipped a cucumber in a bowl of water and carefully dried it on his polishing cloth.

Gaius reached out and snatched a particularly magnificent specimen of the long, green fruit. He held its gracefully curved length out across the corner at Rufio. "Ah, a beautiful *cucumis*." The way he said the word made it sound salaciously erotic. His narrowed eyes came up to engage Rufio's, full of leery knowing. "A sure cure for a night at Lucretia's, lad." He wiggled the cucumber suggestively and lovingly cupped his right hand around its girth near the pointy tip, then slowly stroked it down. "Of course, if you aren't partial to a nice bit of *cucumis* in you—and some say it gives them the burps—I'm sure I could find a length of something more to your taste to fill you with."

"Stop your teasing, Gaius, and don't play with my produce. The boy isn't like that. I can tell."

"Nice cucumbers," Rufio said. He treated both men to his more usual cheery smile, and finished his breakfast.

Gaius looked as if he wanted to add something, but Septimius cut him off.

"They're a popular dish, either quartered lengthways, or thinly sliced and served in vinegar and olive oil with a pinch of salt. Salted, pressed slices with dried anchovies...*mmm*... And I sell a lot as a balm for scorpion bites in the summer and—seeing as it was Lupercalia yesterday—to women who want to get pregnant."

Gaius snorted into his hand. Septimius saw Rufio's arched eyebrows.

"You never come across that old wives' tale? They string several around their waists." Septimius took the one Gaius had put down and waggled it suggestively in front of his apron in an obscene echo of what Gaius had just done, though evidently with different intent.

"All the nice girls like a cucumber." Gaius guffawed. "Just like the nice boys."

"Shouldn't you be at the harbor by now?" Septimius asked with pointed sarcasm.

Still chortling, Gaius slapped down a two-*ass* coin. "Yeah, I can take a hint. I'm off." He turned to peer around the corner pillar at Rufio. "And I hope I'll see you again, lad."

Not if I see you first, cucumber puller.

Rufio nodded, followed suit by pulling out two single *ass* coins from his purse and placing them on the counter top. He thanked Septimius just long enough to give priapic Gaius time to amble down the hill toward Nerva's Forum before following. For a while, their mutual paths coincided, so Rufio made sure to keep well back as they crossed the Roman Forum and climbed then descended the spur in the narrow valley between the Palatine and Capitol. It was the reverse of the direction he'd run as a Lupercus yesterday. Only yesterday? It seemed an age. And that brought to mind the handsome boy in the Forum he'd whipped. Rufio daydreamed about him, the look of shock in his lovely dark eyes.

When he reached the chaos of the beef market, his route took him along the river bank for a short block, before turning past the buildings in front of the Circus starting gates to begin the slow climb up the side of the Aventine, while the distant figure of Gaius continued on along the riverside into the maze of wharfs. He had just reached the bulk of the temple of Minerva when the distinctive voice of his mother rose above the general clamor of a Roman day.

Junilla Rufia's booming voice rang out above the noise of the walled enclosure encompassing house, slave quarters, workshops, and warehouses. "Cato, you little Samnite snake, where in Hades have you got to?"

Tullius Rufio's urchin brother of fourteen years, in trouble again. Though he had a good home, Cato liked to run with the Little Foxes, the junior gang of the Aventine Foxes. The orphaned and abandoned boys of the district named themselves after the cunning foxes that roamed wild through the wooded lower slopes and the flat area over toward the Mons Testaceus. Rufio stepped between big gateposts and smiled as he rounded the corner into the yard of his mother's business property. The sight he found so amusing was that of scruffy Cato emerging from under a wooden storage hut. The boy swaggered nonchalantly over to Junilla, the picture of complete innocence. Rufio was too far away to hear what he said, but Junilla's laughter rang out in response even as she delivered him a smart clout across an ear. Completing the affectionate punishment, she turned and saw her eldest son watching from the gate.

"Oh, the lone wolf returns from his arduous tasks. What time do you call this?"

Since Rufio had no way of knowing accurately because the horological man had not been around yet to repair the water clock, he simply shrugged apologetically as he walked over the yard to them.

"How many fat girls did you lash? None, I'll bet."

Cato was pissed because Junilla refused to let him go and watch the Lupercalia. Rufio aimed a box at his brother's other ear. "I got plenty, little squirt."

Cato ducked, easily avoiding the blow, and stuck out his tongue, a startling red between equally bloody lips as if someone had thrust a sword into his mouth and shaken it all up in there.

"You'll get the shits again, if you keep on eating bilberries," Junilla said to her youngest with an indulgent smile, which she then turned on Rufio. "And I hear you whipped a good-looking boy when you ran through the Forum yesterday."

How does she know that? But he did know. His mother's network of female spies was dotted all over the city. She didn't miss much.

A wicked humor wrinkled the corner of her eyes. "Is that where you got to last night, making him pregnant?"

Cato doubled over in juvenile merriment at his mother's jibe.

"Very funny, Ma." But Rufio returned her smile. "I suppose you already had an account from some little birdie flown over from the Subura."

Junilla winked broadly. "One of Lucretia's slaves did pass by not so long ago. Now answer my question. What time is it?"

"Late, I suppose."

"Sleeping off a hangover, no doubt. Well my priapic offspring, I can't run everything all on my own. Damianus is only a secretary, after all." She looked up at the cloudy sky. "Winter hours are short, yet there's as much to do as in summer." The affectionate arm she placed around his shoulders belied the nature of her complaint. She addressed her younger son again. "And you, get off to the school before your paedagogue comes looking for you and shouts at me."

"Aawww, Ma…"

"If your father was here he'd have you over his knee and tan your unfeeling hide. Now, get! And for the love of Venus, wash your mouth out at the fountain on…"

But Cato ran off before she could finish.

The Tullius Emporium of Artistic Excellence was sited on a sharp corner of the Aventine plateau. To the northwest the house overlooked the Tiber and the red roofs of several long warehouses crammed into the narrow area of flat bank between the hill and the river. To the southwest the ugly hump of Mons Testaceus rose above clusters of the pine trees that hid more warehouses and the hovels of port laborers. The hill was man-made, the city port's great rubbish dump, named for the *testae*, the broken up pottery, that formed it. Here, over the centuries, traders had dumped damaged amphoras, the ceramic containers Romans used to transport goods, from wine and olive oil to cereals, across the Imperium. The pile rose up behind warehouses lining the curve of the Tiber below the Aventine, and continued to grow year by year. It was a popular hang-out spot for the Little Foxes.

Rufio liked his brother's free spirit. In that they were alike, though not in appearance. It was blindingly obvious to anyone that Rufio inherited his red hair from his mother and her father's line of Celtic Gauls who had come to Rome in the wake of the Divine Julius Caesar one and a half centuries ago. Of course, Caesar was just an ordinary army commander then. At what point the tribe of flame-haired warriors descended from the far north—some said from beyond Thule itself—into the Celtic heartland of central Gaul, no one knew.

On the other hand, Cato's dark brown bird's nest was inherited from their father, Tullius. He came from a lowly equestrian background, but made a good life for his young family through a canny eye for antiquities and a glib tongue. Tullius could sell a fourth-rate stone figurine from one of the Rhodian production-line art factories as a genuine Greek marble statuette from the Homeric period to a rising star of the Senate in need of an instant injection of culture and status, or find the right buyer for a genuine sculpture by Praxiteles in Naxos marble, rescued from a shipwreck discovered at the bottom of the Ionian Sea.

As he often told young Rufio, when he met the daughter of a freed Gallic slave who, he said, matched everything written of her race by Strabo, he'd met his match. "The geographer said the Gauls are, 'Lofty in stature, of fair or ruddy complexion, terrible from the sternness of their eyes, very quarrelsome, and of great pride and insolence.' Only for Jupiter's sake don't tell her I quoted the last bit," he said with a wink. "He also said that they are terrifying warriors. 'A whole troop of foreigners would not be able to withstand a single Gaul if he called his wife to his assistance who is certainly strong like him and with blue eyes.' Just like you, my son, fiery of hair and sky in the eyes."

Sadly, Zeus in the process of raping Ganymede ripped Tullius from his spirited wife and sons when a huge statue depicting the god's sexual prowess toppled from a high pedestal and crushed him. This misfortune occurred in the Tullius Emporium of Artistic Excellence's monumental storage facility and was the consequence of sloppy installation work by slaves of the importer who sold it to him. A blow of such magnitude would have destroyed many a Roman matron, but with her ancestor's Celtic blood running in her veins Junilla was made of sterner stuff. And she enjoyed another advantage. Before his death, her freedman father made a fortune importing rare metals from Britain, and he was the financial mainstay behind the Tullian antiques business. Tullius had full use of his wife's generous dowry, but the canny Gaul had insisted on his daughter being the real holder of the purse strings and so the wealth remained in her name after her husband's unfortunate death beneath pederastic Olympian lust.

When Junilla stepped in and took over the reins of the emporium, she was already an established businesswoman in her own right. She had, however, opted for a different (and many would say barely more respectable) line of entertainment to that of her dear friend Lucretia. As the sole proprietor of *In Celebrationibus et Festivitates*, Junilla Rufia was one of Rome's foremost party planners. We Are Celebrations and Festivities brought in a handsome additional return for her efforts.

And she loved her wayward children, no matter who they chose to screw (though she hoped Cato was still too young to have begun loving anyone).

"You had a good time with Crispin and, what's his name, the thick one with the big dick?"

"Is it?" Rufio gave her an arch look. "Octavian, you mean, like the first emperor. And yes, I did, though not exactly with Crispin and the thick one with the winky prick. They prefer cunny."

"Well, they will until they collect a dose of something from a young maiden in the guise of a fifty-something street-walker, or should that be the other way around? Stick to fucking with the boys and you won't go wrong." Junilla Rufia was nothing if not a broad-minded free spirit.

An organized chaos of comings and goings went on around them as they talked. Workmen and slaves crisscrossed the courtyard on missions of their own, some hauling statuary on trolleys, in pairs humping a rolled floor covering, or staggering about with nude marble women and young men in deathlike grips (Junilla did not tolerate breakages).

"I've an important job for you this morning... or what's left of it, my little horn-headed Pan. You know the Satyr of Capri? That statue of a rampant satyr Emperor Tiberius once owned—"

"Allegedly."

She swept his skepticism aside with a wave of her hand. "It came from Capri and is inscribed on the base: *I fucked a few boys below this statue.*"

"Only a 'few,' I bet it was loads, the rampant old satyr, Is the inscription signed?"

"Tiberius Claudius Nero Caesar Augustus."

"Oh, authentic then." Rufio grinned. "What about it?"

"I sold it and promised delivery today. I'd go myself, but…" She pulled him in close and lowered her normally powerful voice. "It's all very hush-hush." A quick tap of the nose. "From the very top, if you know what I mean. There's been a request—more in the way of an order, really. Can I organize a series of events. Apparently an Oriental of some importance is due to visit Rome. From Nabataea, or somewhere. Can't say more yet, darling, but the contract is worth the mint. In fact I've already prayed to Juno Moneta in thanks." Junilla straightened up to her imposing height. "And if the goddess of making money doesn't answer it… well sod her! So I'm busy and you'll have to make the delivery. Go smarten up. Put on a decent tunic. Take Zeno, Phokas, and Alexius with you. I told them to load up… just in case you did decide to come home this morning."

Rufio pecked his mother on the cheek.

"Oh come here." She pulled him into an embrace and for a long moment they hugged. And then she thrust him away. "Off with you and bathe. Get rid of the stink of the *lupanar*."

Rufio made for the house, but looked back over his shoulder at her call.

"By the way, how many?"

"Last night?"

She made a flapping gesture to show how redundant the question was.

Rufio grinned. "Only two. Nubian boys, horny as Zeus. Fucked them stupid."

N·I·N·E | IX

Rome, Caelian Hill, mid-morning, February 14

It was a long trek from the slopes of the Aventine, past the rounded end of the Circus with its triumphal arch to good old Emperor Titus at its apex (the one he got for destroying Jerusalem; and he died young, not old), and along the valley formed by the sharply rising bulk of the Palatine hill to the left and the steep flank of the Caelian hill on the right. Far in the distance, grayed by the mist, rose the Colosseum's stacked arcades.

The little cavalcade of slaves pulling and pushing the handcart, with Rufio at their head, made its way to the point where a spur of the Claudian aqueduct soared overhead on its way to supply the palace cisterns. Here, rising up alongside the aqueduct's arches, *Clivus Scaurus* was a steep street that led up to the Olympian loftiness of the Caelian. On its refined heights the wealthy lived in quiet seclusion behind the temple gardens of Divine Claudius. Zeno, Phokas, and Alexius huffed and puffed as they hauled the cart over bumpy paving stones and heaved it over steps in the road when the angle became even sharper. Rufio even helped on the worst bits, though mainly to ensure the statue's safety. He was dressed in his second-best tunic of fine linen. The flax thread from which it was woven had been well scutched and hackled, so it felt smooth and sexy against his skin, and the pale blue dye only heightened the flame color of his voluminous locks, while matching his eye color—unfortunately it also showed up sweat patches too readily, so helping haul the cart was out of the question. Besides, his hangover precluded too much effort (although if he was honest, its effects had almost faded), and it never looked good to lend slaves a hand in public.

The weather was unseasonably warm and the humidity only added to the haulers' woes… and grumbles.

"Give it a rest, Phokas. We're almost at the top."

"Just a breather, master Rufio."

"Very well."

Rufio took the opportunity to look back at the great slab of the imperial palace rising like a glittering white wall through the green sward at its feet. It occupied all of the Palatine visible around the mass of the temple to Claudius on his right, which also hid the Colosseum from view. The Tullius Emporium of Artistic Excellence had several clients on the Caelian, the kind of aristocrats who would once have lived in elegant residences over the way on the Palatine, until the emperors kicked them off. The heaped piles of monumental masonry on the other side of the valley fascinated him. So big, so complicated, it was impossible to tell from the exterior what the inside of the Domus Augustana must look like. Was it possible the "hush-hush" order from the top was from the palace? A stab of excitement in his stomach made him think. Was it possible that he might get to see the interior?

Finally, the *Clivus Scaurus* reached the top of the incline and met the street named after Claudius at an angle. His destination, the Domus Fabii, sat at the highest point, the third house along the street before it plunged down the other side of the Caelian toward the Ludus Magnus, the gladiator school beside the Colosseum. In this exclusive enclave there were no shops occupying the frontage either side of the broad doorway, as was usually the case with homes in less salubrious precincts of the city. The large, two-storied house presented a blank face to the world. On either side of the grand entrance a slightly faded mural painting of a bucolic scene alleviated the building's unfriendly aspect, but did not do the same for the door slave who opened the heavily ornamented timbers.

"The master is out and we're not buying. So hop it!"

Rufio was well used to unwelcoming greeters. There was little point in having a friendly doorman who let anyone in. He sniffed contemptuously, squared his shoulders, and drew himself up to his full height. "My good fellow. We are expected. I am from the Tullius Emporium of Artistic Excellence." He moved slightly aside and indicated the three gasping slaves, the handcart, and the over-sized satyr rearing up on the cart's groaning bed.

The doorman glared at the visitors and then at the half-man, half-goat, his goat-tail, goat-like ears, and goat-like aroused phallus jutting triumphantly at the sky. He turned back, scratched at his backside, and shouted something unintelligible into the dark interior.

A moment later a young man of very different appearance emerged into the light and gave Rufio the kind of appraisal that spoke volumes of interest and left him feeling shaken… and almost as aroused as the marble monster behind him. Slender as a reed, the youth might have been older than he looked, but his small, compact face lent him the features of a young adolescent. His doe-like eyes slowly roamed from Rufio's face south down his torso, lower to his legs, then back up to linger briefly, but tellingly, on Rufio's middle, before returning to his face. He gave Rufio an elfin smile.

Rufio shook himself and pointed again at the statue. "I'm Tullius Rufio from the Tullius Emporium of—"

"Of course you are. I am Ambrosius."

Slave, lover, son…? Rufio couldn't tell. His attire gave nothing away and the name could be Greek or Roman, or almost anything in these cosmopolitan days.

"Thank you," Ambrosius said to the doorman. His voice carried a hint of authority, and the big fellow stood aside obediently so that Zeno, Phokas, and Alexius could maneuver the cart up the single low step and through the wide double doors.

"Virius Fabius would like it placed in the garden. Please follow me," Ambrosius took Rufio by the elbow, a light touch and gentle pull. The entry hall was wide and more tastefully decorated than Rufio expected of a collector of pornographic statuary. But then, the Fabii were purveyors of fine marble and other construction materials, so it should be expected that their home be well appointed. Plain white pilasters at regular intervals set off the maroon walls, between which shelves held row upon row of ancestor busts, innumerable generations and hundreds of years of the Fabii. The floor was of pale gray polished slate. Each perfectly square tile met at its corners with a flush-inset pale yellow diamond of stone, so the effect was both quiet and fluid.

Beyond the hall they walked into the most public space of the *domus*, the *atrium* where Virius Fabius would greet his clients, the men who really ran the construction materials businesses. At the center of the *atrium* sat the *impluvium*, a shallow square pool designed to catch rainwater falling through the *compluvium*, the matching square opening above. For the season, a thick canvas covered the opening to keep out the wintry chill. In summer, light would flood in and illuminate the magnificent room.

Underfoot, through the sole of his sandals Rufio felt warmth from the central heating system rising up through the floor. As the only natural daylight to penetrate the *atrium* at this season came from the end of another hallway leading to the garden, oil lamps placed at intervals on the walls provided a low light. Their carefully trimmed wicks spoke of a well-ordered household.

Ambrosius led Rufio around the pool, following slaves and rolling satyr. "To the left and right are the family's private chambers," he said, a hint of pride in his tone. "Ahead to the right, the family dining room and next to it the *tablinum*," he added, referring to the study of Virius Fabius. "Over on the left we have a larger dining room for banquets, and stairs to the upper level where there are more private family rooms." And then they were out in the formal garden, open to the sky but with a sheltered portico on all four sides. To the left, an opening in the wall evidently gave access to a side garden. "That's the orchard," Ambrosius explained. "Opposite are the kitchen latrine, slave quarters, and a small bathhouse."

"It's very grand." Rufio looked around in some admiration. A small circular pool sat at the center of paths laid out in a grid between copious planting. At each junction sat a plinth with a statue on it and Rufio's keen eye spotted some fine pieces, as well as one or two well-done fakes. The largest plinth, at the right-hand end, was empty and evidently intended for the alleged satyr of wicked old Emperor Tiberius. Rufio still had his doubts as to that attribution, but he would never say anything.

Ambrosius smiled from the corner of his delicate mouth. "Virius Fabius likes to own things that are… on the big side."

Virius? Does this sleek Ambrosius enjoy his virility, I wonder? Rufio glanced at his guide from under lowered eyelashes in time to catch a returning flutter. And then he looked across at the slaves in alarm. "Careful! By Poseidon's right tit, Alexius, that nearly went over."

"I'll summon aid." Ambrosius called and two household slaves ran out from the kitchen doorway opposite. He patted Rufio on the arm consolingly. "We really wouldn't want him to bump into something and lose that magnificent appendage… or an arm. Ah, you *do* laugh."

"And more!" The boy's flirting was having a predictable effect and in response Rufio became conscious that he was posing to best show off the mound pushing at the front of his tunic. And Ambrosius knew he was doing it because he dropped his gaze again to Rufio's midriff.

"And *hup!*"

The rampant Satyr of Capri wobbled once, steadied and, fearsomely inflamed, stared with lustful stone eyes down the length of Virius Fabius's garden. The five slaves stared up at it in awe, transfixed by the statue's magnificence now properly mounted.

"Oh my." Ambrosius placed a hand across the top of his chest. "He certainly is…" he sought a suitable word and settled breathlessly for, "…big."

Rufio sniffed dismissively and gave a cheeky grin. "Seen bigger."

A single raised eyebrow greeted this assertion. "Big as a *gladius*?"

Rufio took it as the challenge he knew it was intended to be. "More like a *spatha*," he boasted, comparing his length to that of a cavalry long-sword.

When Ambrosius suggested dismissing Zeno, Phokas, and Alexius, and offered Rufio the use of a litter to get him back to the Aventine in comfort later—and made it clear that a further advance would be welcomed—Rufio didn't hesitate. Still anticipating a retreat to the slaves' quarters, he was surprised to be led to the seclusion of a small but nicely furnished bedroom at the top of the stairs on the upper floor.

So, son or lover, then?

A window at chin height looked out over the orchard and the wall separating the Domus Fabii from the next house. The view did not engage Rufio's attention for more than a quick glance after slender hands snaked around his waist from behind and cupped his balls.

"Mmmm." Ambrosius breathed in his ear and then he sighed at the grasp of Rufio's hand pushing behind him to feel him back. Rufio turned in the grip so that their hands mutually gripped each other's ass cheeks, their stiffening cocks wrestled side by side, hip bones ground together, and their eyes and lips engaged. Rufio wasn't big on kissing, but Ambrosius had the most delicious mouth and when his lips parted, Rufio's tongue slipped between them as naturally as if they'd been doing it for years.

Head to tail, they sucked each other before Rufio rolled Ambrosius onto his back and fucked him. And Ambrosius turned out to be a super fuck. He wriggled like an energetic eel, sighed, groaned, and moaned with each deep thrust into him. Once, on a vacation, Rufio was given the chance to ride a horse. The beast didn't take to him one bit and did everything to chuck him off. Riding Ambrosius was a similar experience, except the boy clearly didn't want to throw him off. Rufio positioned himself with the confidence of practice and

mounted Ambrosius with an ease that suggested his ride was equally well trained. His vigorous bucking matched the urgency of Rufio's fucking, and if his dimensions were predictably less than that of a *spatha*, or indeed that of the Satyr of Capri standing proudly a few walls away, they seemed to more than satisfy Ambrosius.

Since he'd started ejaculating at the age of twelve, Rufio held that the best cure for a hangover was some hard sex, always better with a partner than by his own hand, and the unexpected pleasure of plowing Ambrosius was certainly blowing away the last cobwebs. He wanted to come, but struggled manfully to prolong their mutual enjoyment. When he made motions to turn Ambrosius over, the boy responded eagerly and in a trice went doggy so Rufio could kneel up behind him and stick his cock back in the waiting asshole.

With Rufio deep inside him, Ambrosius began to roll and twist and cry softly in encouragement. Together they moved like one being, Ambrosius in a squirming counterpoint to Rufio's digging cock. And then came the tightening of his balls close up under his shaft, and the sweet pump feeling as he began to come.

With his last after-shots still squirting, Rufio pulled out and rolled the boy over to take the deliciously wet muzzle of Ambrosian cock in his mouth. In no time Rufio brought his partner off in a mouth-filling orgasm, which he swallowed as naturally as his morning bowl of cow's milk. Junilla always insisted the milk was the reason for his sweet complexion, whereas Rufio knew it was the frequent application of a well-fucked boy's fresh seed smoothed into the skin. That is when he could resist swallowing it all.

Ambrosius let his head fall down on the mattress and rested the back of his right hand across the bridge of his nose, still gulping down short breaths. His generous mouth looked a picture of happy fulfilment. Rufio leaned over him and kissed his lips. Ambrosius responded briefly. "You must go. Virius Fabius will return soon."

"And he wouldn't want to find us like this?" Still probing.

The arm moved to reveal Ambrosius's eyes, wide and amused. "No. Not like this."

"What are you and he…?"

"I'm a cousin of sorts, if you go by the name. My grandfather was secretary to the father of Virius and when he freed him my grandfather naturally became a Fabius in name. He was allowed to marry a cousin of Virius's father. But I am now adopted."

Rufio nodded understanding. "And he wouldn't want to find his son being made love to by a commoner."

"A commoner's cock is as good as anyone's in my book. And yours… well, not quite as big as that fellow out in the garden, but…"

"But?"

"A nice one, the way it juts out from that nest of red pubic hair. Is that what we were doing?" The grin was a sly one.

Rufio shuffled upright, lowered his feet to the warm floor, and wiggled his feet into the sandals. "What, what we were doing?" He grabbed his discarded tunic and threw it carelessly over his head, until he remembered it was his second-best, and took more care in retying the belt.

"Making love?"

He shook his head in a way to let his disheveled hair fall naturally into place and grinned back. "No, that was a fuck. I have to know you better before I make love to you." He stroked the inside of Ambrosius's nearest thigh. The boy lifted his chin in question.

"Does that mean there will be a next time?"

"As soon as you can persuade your adoptive father to buy another rampant satyr from my mother at the Tullius Emporium of Artistic Excellence."

Ambrosisus screwed his brow up in a mock frown. "And what would your mother think if she knew what you were up to when out delivering?"

"Oh she'd be thrilled,"Rufio retorted airily. "Consorting with the patriciate for a change. Even if you are an adopted aristocrat."

The litter was clearly not Virius Fabius's conveyance, but it was adequate, indeed much better than Rufio, who mostly traveled by the power of his own legs, was used to. Ambrosius had kept his promise, and now Rufio lounged back and luxuriated in the comfort. Occasionally he peered through a discreet gap in the curtains and hoped the crowds in the streets would wonder which patrician was on his way somewhere.

Back to headquarters now. Just another fun-cum-filled morning for Tullius Rufio.

T·E·N | X

Aventine and imperial palace, February 16

"The honorable Livius Caecilius Dio to see you, master."

Lucius peered up from the scroll he was reading, seated at the worktable in his *tablinum*. "Thank you, Pallas. Why don't you show— Ah, there you are, Livy. You always were a little ahead of everyone else."

Livy had no time to waste on courtesies when it came to family, and he had less time for his brother-in-law's humming and hahing over important matters. He'd followed Pallas straight in, and Lucius's mild admonishment washed over his shoulder as easily as a breath of air. He looked down at the table Lucius used for a desk and noted the cheap paper squares stacked at one corner, next to his stylus and pot of *atramentum* ink.

"As usual, it's good to see you, brother. But the fact that you have poor pulp paper for writing instead of a decent vellum or some rolls of Egyptian papyrus is symbolic of the situation we find ourselves in."

Lucius raised a bushy eyebrow. "I am studying the report published by the scribes of Apollodorus. It lays out his requirements for the coming two consulship periods. It's a lot of building material to deliver, and waste to be distributed outside the city."

"I'm aware—"

"So how are matters progressing with the Emperor? Is Trajan responding... sympathetically?"

Livy flushed. He was unaccustomed to being interrupted. Lucius might rule his sons with a traditional rod of iron, but not his brother-in-law, not Livius Caecilius Dio. "That is why I am here," he enunciated clearly, and settled his heavy frame on the stool in front of the table. "The races on the morrow." He looked expectantly at Lucius.

"We shall attend, of course, but what of them?"

Livy sighed, the resignation of a man of the world dealing with a retiring relative, the sigh of a sorely tried man. "Caesar has requested the presence of Quintus. You know this, Lucius. Have you had a word with the boy?"

"I have put him in his place regarding his marriage to Vipsania Metella. The dowry she—"

"Lucius! Let's stick to the important item. We must have Quintus ready for Trajan tomorrow. The wedding will... well." *It will have to wait. Doesn't the fool realize Quintus can't marry anyone until the Emperor is finished with him, which may be months yet? Hopefully many months.*

Lucius grunted irritably. "I can't think what Trajan wants with my youngest son. He reads poetry, studies history. Wouldn't the emperor find a military minded lad like Primus or Secundus at his side for the racing more engaging? Come to think of it, isn't Hadrian a lover of history and poetry. I should have thought Quintus would be of more appeal to him."

He's too grown up for Hadrian's taste, you stupid old fool. "That is beside the point. The gift of the patents is not in Hadrian's hands. And I am sure Trajan has no interest in discussing dactylic meter with Quintus, Lucius. He enjoys the company of lively young persons. It makes *him* feel young again, and blessed in front of the vast audience that will be gathered in the Circus." *And he'll fuck the balls off the boy after (like I wish I could), and then hand me the contracts and patents and make us all rich again. And make sure those bastard Ahenobarbi and Fabii are put in their places.*

"I'll send for him."

Livy rose to his feet. "No, brother, I'll find him and speak with him. I will impress on him how important this is to us."

And keep my hands to myself. Unfortunately.

He had never liked Uncle Livius, though to be fair, he hadn't found any reason to really hate the man either. There was something Quintus couldn't put his finger on, something a bit sly in the expression, something you could see only from the corner of your eye for a fleeting moment.

In a cruel jest, Marcus had once suggested that Livy would love to get a hand up his young brother's tunic. "You can tell by the look in his eyes whenever he enters a room and sees you." Quintus had scorned the suggestion and buried his head back in the scroll he was reading. It was Claudius's history of the Etruscans, written when the Emperor was merely a lowly student with no thought of ever ascending the imperial throne. And on the score of hands going up or down there, only Ashur was allowed to do that on the rare occasions when Quintus needed a lift of his spirits.

His uncle's hand on his shoulders felt hot and heavy as he guided Quintus firmly from the hall out into the small and rather dusty formal garden that acted as a backdrop to the dining room. Along with two very fine statues depicting Venus at her toilet and Apollo admiring her, his father had sold the two slaves who were responsible for the Domus Alba's horticulture some months back.

"Now, my boy, this is a very great honor for our family."

Quintus pulled his shoulders up tightly. "But why does he want me beside him, Uncle? I'm not even interested in chariot racing much."

Livy coughed. A sign of uneasiness? Quintus was sure he wasn't being told the whole truth.

"Trajan has seen you—"

"When?"

Quintus saw impatience bloom in the hooded eyes at the insolent interruption.

"He has seen you at a distance. When I dined with him we had a little head-to-head and he mentioned you very favorably. The house of Ulpius is in the ascendant, and the Caecilii can rise with it... as long as we do whatever Trajan wishes. And he asks—commands—your presence."

"But, I don't understand. What will I have to do? Read poetry to him?"

"For the sake of Hecate, boy! Just be your charming self." He dropped his hand from Quintus's shoulder and stepped back. "Be engaging and enjoy the races." Livy's choleric simmered a moment, and then he seemed to pull his feelings in again. In a quieter voice he said, "I'm quite sure the emperor will tell you what he would wish of you."

It was no good. Quintus just didn't like what he saw in Livy's expression; guarded while trying to be enthusiastic. Nervous too. "Is my presence something to do with this business, you know, the family concerns my father was speaking of the other day?"

Livy thought a long while, lips pursed, gimlet eyes boring into Quintus as if assessing his potential. He drew a deep breath. "In a way, yes. If you are pleasant, Trajan will present us with inestimable gifts. I will be able to direct my clients to contracts for stone and other building materials of much greater value than we currently enjoy, and keep my worst rivals at bay."

"And my father? Our family? How will we benefit?"

The hand snaked back and pinioned Quintus by his other shoulder this time. Livy drew him closer. "Of course all the Caecilii benefit, my boy. You're a good son, and I know you will do as Lucius your father bids you."

This was news to Quintus. His father wanted this as well! The emperor had requested him... for what? He might prefer history and poetry to the cut and thrust of politics, or military advancement, but that didn't mean he was a gullible fool. And there were rumors, always had been since Trajan came to the throne, although as far as he'd heard, Trajan's preferences were for hunky military tribunes. So... it couldn't be that. Could it?

"I'll call for you an hour before the games start. Just make sure you spend time in the bathhouse tomorrow. And wear your finest tunic. Preferably a calf-length one for... modesty. And then," he leaned in conspiratorially, "you needn't wear a loincloth underneath."

The litter rocked gently from side to side and, now and again, front to back like the wallow of a sea-borne vessel whenever the porters had to slow for another palanquin crossing their path.

"Hardly ever been in one, and then two rides in as many days," Rufio said.

Junilla patted his wrist. "I do hope Cato doesn't drive his aunt to distraction this afternoon. Antonia doesn't have my patience with the boy."

"Mother. No one does."

"You were no better at his age."

Rufio felt there was no real answer to this, so instead he changed the subject. "When is Flaccus expected?"

Junilla gave him a sharp sideways look. "What's it to you? Has he been trying it on with you again?' She snapped her head forward with an irritable lift of the shoulders. "I don't mind about your... interests, but I do wish you would make arrangements with more suitable persons. You are freeborn, after all, and while Flaccus is nice enough, he is only a fireman."

"A Vigiles, Ma."

"Quite. I employ him in the capacity of security when I need it. Not as a diversion for my over-sexed, bored, teenage son. If you need to let loose, make sure it's with some nice slave boy who rents out, or an aristocrat, like that poor boy you lashed in the Forum."

Rufio laughed happily. "Him? Hah! Don't worry, Ma. I'm not planning on settling down yet. I always take your advice. You know that. Stop worrying about Flaccus. He makes me laugh when he gets desperate to feel me up."

"And it touches your vanity, you wicked Celt."

104

"Perhaps it does. But now my vanity is being fed by the thought of actually visiting the palace. To think, we're going to the top of the Palatine, to meet the emperor's chamberlain, and see the sights."

"Don't get too excited. It's a job."

But he could see his mother was as thrilled as he was. Would they see the great Trajan, even at a distance? Probably not. Though it was cool out, his palms were sweaty where he gripped his waxed tablets and stylus, ready to take notes.

The litter ride was relatively short from the Aventine, for just after passing under the end of the Circus the bearers turned off the Imperial Way leading to the Colosseum and entered the Palatine by a private gate guarded by a bunch of Praetorians. From there, a narrow road led up the incline by three switchbacks until it reached the main cistern. There, at the palace's back door, so to speak, the bearers lowered the conveyance. Rufio and Junilla stepped down to be met by a handsome young man, to the eye barely out of his teens and to the ear younger than that, finely featured, with a creamy smooth complexion. His dark almond-shaped eyes hinted at a Syrian origin, but his Latin accent in its boyish tenor was decidedly educated Greek.

"Sir, Lady, I am the chamberlain's secretary, Acacus. I am to take you to him."

Rufio bridled at the cursory look the minion gave him and the way he addressed his every utterance at Junilla, while always punctiliously calling him "Sir" first. He apparently dismissed Rufio as being of no consequence because of his age. Rufio took an instant dislike and thought the youth's shifty look hid his contempt of them, mere commoners to be treated as patricians. Fortunately, he disappeared the minute he brought them into the presence of Bardas, another immoderately handsome Greek, older than Acacus but still young and with an equally closed-up attitude, as if dealing with the proprietor of We Are Celebrations and Festivities was entirely beneath his dignity. He gave Rufio an appraisal that evidently left him a little confused.

"My son," Junilla clarified.

Bardas raised one arched eyebrow. "Were you not bringing your secretary to take notes?"

"My man Damianus is indisposed today. He has a sore thumb and that would make his writing difficult."

"I assure you, Chamberlain, I can write," Rufio said.

Bardas lowered his eyebrow with a snap and treated them with a cool politeness as they began the tour.

"The reason for your presence is for me to show you the staterooms we have designated for the visit of Obodas of Nabataea. There are chambers set aside for several banquets when many guests will be present, and those for more... intimate occasions." He turned grave eyes on them, with particular attention to Rufio, who suddenly felt he was being undressed. "By 'intimate,' I trust you understand?"

Junilla gave an explosive little laugh. "Oh, don't worry, Chamberlain. I know how to arrange a damn fine orgy all right."

Rufio flinched inwardly as his mother gave the functionary a familiar slap on the arm. Bardas looked like someone who has realized to his refined horror that he has stepped on a squishy dog turd in his open-toed sandal.

Rufio made his own quick step. "Sire, we are aware of the sensitivity of such events." He bowed slightly and saw that his use of "sire" mollified the scandalized chamberlain a little.

"Be so good as to follow me."

Icy-icy! Rufio tried not to grin at the chamberlain's haughty back in case he turned around. Instead he flipped open the top cover of his hinged wax tablets, extracted the stylus from a cunning set of leather loops that held it against the spine when not in use, and began scratching out his impressions and Junilla's dictated notes. He was relieved to see that she had decided not to treat Bardas like a regular drinking crony. For his part, Bardas led them through a bewildering maze of chambers—lofty and wide, long and narrow, oval, rectangular, and circular—and broad hallways that connected with more halls and staircases leading up and down several levels. They crossed two open areas with fountains, stilled for the winter, and were treated to an excess of decoration in white sculpted plaster, stone, colored marbles, gilt, and adorned in every corner with fine statuary.

"Gods alive, Rufio," Junilla whispered, "I could retire and buy the whole island of Capri with this lot."

"Ma, you're forgetting they already own Capri."

"You may instruct your staff to use this area for storage of props, costumes, instruments and whatever may be needed," Bardas said as he showed them into a gaunt and oddly shaped set of rooms somewhere in the depths. "These are the foundations of the palace of the Divine Claudius," he added in an offhand voice. "The rooms are no longer much used, so they will suit your purpose. And now, follow me again…"

Soon after they emerged from the divinely Claudian basement, Acacus returned with a foppish young patrician in tow. Bardas introduced the man simply as Cornelius.

"I represent the interests of my Lord Hadrian," the newcomer announced in a nasally haughty voice.

If it were not for his sticky-out ears, Rufio thought he would be handsome. *Actually, come to think of it, those ears would be great to hang onto if I was fucking his ass or his face.* He caught Acacus surreptitiously regarding his appraisal of Cornelius, and gave the secretary a sly wink. Acacus glowered back darkly. Rufio also took note of the way Cornelius looked at Acacus when the callow noble thought no one was looking. Rufio sensed the vibration of sexual interest Cornelius had in the cute young acolyte of Bardas. These two then accompanied them on the remainder of the reconnaissance.

"My, what is this?" Junilla waved a hand over an ornate waist-high parapet. "We could do something magnificent in the space down there."

They were walking along a covered arcade high above a long hippodrome-shaped sunken garden.

"Indeed, my Lady," Bardas said, "but not in February I'm afraid. Caesar is most keen to keep Prince Obodas warm, since he is from a country where it is rarely cold."

"I have a vested interest in keeping our visitor warm," Cornelius said cryptically.

Rufio could not read the inflection in the aristocrat's tone but saw his eyes were fixed on Acacus.

"Unless Acacus would prefer to take that responsibility from my shoulders. Obodas, I think, prefers younger—"

"Let us proceed." Bardas stalked off, leaving his secretary glowering at Cornelius's back as he followed the chamberlain.

The walkway followed above the garden's semicircular end. From there the gathering had a spectacular view way down into the Circus Maximus. At this point the sides of the Palatine were hidden behind cascades of stonework. Across the narrow way an army of workers was busy preparing the great stadium for the days of races that would celebrate the official unveiling of Trajan's comprehensive remodeling. A jockey was racing a *biga*, the two-horse chariot, around the track, presumably testing it out, Rufio thought. When he looked back down the length of the stadium toward the towering wall of arches that formed the starting gates, he could just make out a four-horse chariot, the popular *quadriga*, being prepared for similar activity.

"This way!"

Bardas's commanding voice jerked him from his scrutiny of the monument. The party continued through a series of large rooms with windows that opened onto a vast area overlooking the circus constructed on the roof of what Bardas called the libraries.

"Plural! One library isn't enough!" Rufio sniggered quietly.

"Silly boy," Junilla said, as softly. "One will be for Latin books the other for Greek, and I shouldn't be at all surprised to discover the works of Ovid luridly illustrated for the perverted taste, or perhaps depictions of Platonic pederasty. Just the kind of educative reading you would enjoy—"

"If you would follow me, my lady."

Junilla quickly apologized and winked at Rufio the moment the chamberlain's back was turned. "Make a note of that space out here. I have a marvellous idea of how we might use it."

"What should I write, Ma?"

"Water organ."

Rufio shook his head. Water organs weren't anything special, but he noted it on his tablet, as they hurried to catch up with the others.

After what felt like several double-backs on different floors, Bardas announced that they were now stood in the massive hallway that connected the Domus Augustana with the imperial box.

"Down this staircase, one more level, a passage leads over the lane below and directly into the *pulvinar*. Rufio noted it down, the fancy word for the emperor's box, "the cushion." *Must remember to call it that.*

Bardas led the way down the wide marble steps. "To one side of the hallway here, we have an intimate arena, where Caesar entertains select guests who appreciate the beauty of gladiatorial fights."

A wide entryway opened out onto a three-tier seating arrangement around three sides of the deep rectangular arena. The floor, clean stone now, but thickly sanded when in use, was some four feet below. The place could seat a maximum of thirty guests, Rufio noted, with little more than a grand central seat as the emperor's throne. Intimate indeed. The spectators would be almost nose-to-the-combat. He saw Junilla's eyes glow with creative excitement.

"I have a splendid idea for a fight in here," she said. "A spectacle never before seen. We must include it in the week's events."

"As you will, my Lady," Bardas said with his typical seriousness.

Cornelius leered at Acacus. "We could pop you down in there and pit you against, let me see... me, perhaps."

Rufio thought Acacus was going to snap back, but the dark-eyed young man contented himself with another nasty glare at his tormentor. *What's between those two?*

"I'll let you pause here a while to absorb the dimensions and possibilities." Bardas dipped his head, and stepped back toward the hallway. Rufio watched Acacus start to follow. As he reached the door Bardas turned. "Pit yourself against Acacus, my Lord Cornelius? I should advise you to be careful of what you wish for." And with that, he stepped out. Acacus smiled with thin lips, but there was no humor in the expression. The two Greeks disappeared around the corner of the exit to the hall.

Cornelius shrugged, and then engaged Junilla in details of the fights he had witnessed. "You really get a feeling for the combatants, smell the fear and sweat in this intimate little arena, partake of their peculiar skills with net, trident, shield, and sword. The two shuttered doorways on the other wall down there are where the gladiators emerge from the preparation rooms."

He chattered on. Rufio moved back to the doorway and leaned against the cool stone frame.

"I loathe the man as much as you."

"How can you?"

"I have my reasons."

Rufio recognized the deeper voice of Bardas. *What reasons?*

"I'm sure you know exactly. His very presence sickens me..."

And then they moved away and Rufio could no longer discern the words clearly.

So, the palace had the same kinds of jealousies and strains as life outside its walls.

His mother and Cornelius finished their discussion and Rufio walked ahead of them out to rejoin Bardas and Acacus, who seemed also to have concluded whatever it was they were talking about.

Neither of them seemed pleased to see Cornelius again. For his part, the patrician acted cheerily unconcerned at the sudden atmosphere.

"Sire," Junilla began, remembering her manners, "Might we just have a tiny little peek into the imperial box?"

Rufio knew the wheedling, gently flirtatious tone well. His mother usually got her way.

The chamberlain hesitated.

"Can't do any harm, Bardas, old fruit. This way." And Cornelius strode off. Weak sunlight streaming through regularly spaced side windows made his light green tunic shimmer for a moment before becoming dull in between. Ahead the hallway crossed over Via Murcia where all those prostitutes plied their trade under the arches of the stadium above. He thought he could just make out the sign advertising the Urgent Bull and smiled at the thought of Octavian wanting to visit there after the Lupercalia.

Sadly for Junilla's hopes, Cornelius came to an apologetic halt. "Ah, workmen must have blocked it off." He indicated the wooden boards barring further access. "Behind those there are separate latrines for men and women. And beyond that the pulvinar descends on several levels of seats for the court, down to the thrones on the lowest level for the games' editor and the imperial family."

Junilla hid her disappointment at not seeing into the "throne of the gods" behind a bright smile.

Cornelius slipped past to return them to where Bardas waited impatiently with Acacus. As they recrossed the bridge, he waved a hand airily. "This, you know, is where the Praetorian Prefect Cassius Chaerea slew Emperor Caligula, er... sixty-seven years ago. There was blood everywhere," he added with evident relish. "While back there," he pointed toward the pulvinar, "Caligula's crazed German bodyguard was stuck, held up by a senator planted there to chatter with them, so the conspirators got away."

"What happened to Cassius?" Rufio was eager to know.

"Oh, his Praetorians Guards got all panicky at the thought of becoming redundant without a god-ruler to cherish and went and found stammering old Clau-Clau-Claudius, rammed the crown on his bald head, lifted him on their shoulders, and made him the new Emperor. And of course he had all the conspirators rounded up and executed, Cassius among them."

"Thank the gods we live in a different era," Junilla said feelingly.

"Yes," Cornelius responded tartly, "Trajan has banished murder."

Like two stoic Greek warriors, Bardas and Acacus stared wordlessly at the brash young patrician.

The arrogant piece of bat shit thinks he's so clever, so above the functionaries who really run this place. I've seen them all, all with their bare legs waving in the air, their asses filled with one another's cocks, like rutting beasts. Chattering as do the locusts of the desert. They joke about barbarians, men who can only say "bar bar bar bar" for words because god-blessed Romans can't understand the speech of foreigners. "Bar bar bar barbarians." But they are all idiots under the braggadocio.

Oh so clever Romans, brave men who get others to do their dirty work for them. Filthy creatures of the deep like Obodas. Men of creeping tentacles, snakes that slither on their oriental bellies, hooded bats who suck the blood of innocents, lemurs who haunt the dark in search of flesh to devour. Men like stupid Cornelius. Animals like Obodas. When it is analyzed with a cool mind, there can be no argument. They are alike, bound in their deviousness. Bound by the need to dominate, using their sex to subdue, and if they are ever jealous of another's sexual prowess, remove it!

Enjoy your remaining time, all you arrogant pricks, for I will have revenge.

E·L·E·V·E·N | XI

At the Circus starting gates, race day, February 18

As he descended from the Aventine, Rufio paused to stare at the seething mob. A quarter of a million people—roughly half on the Aventine side, the others on Via Murcia—which took its name from the ancient stream long ago vanished under the Circus Maximus—were filing through more than a hundred and fifty archways into the massive underworks of Trajan's rebuilt stadium, to climb seventy-five monumental stairways to the upper tiers. He was thankful he would not have to join them to gain access to the stadium.

A cohort of Urban police blocked access to where he had to go, the large square in front of the Circus starting gates. He hoped he would be allowed through at this end and so save at least a mile's walk down to the river, through the beef market, and then back under the Palatine to reach the other side just two hundred yards from where he now stood. There were several people badgering the senior officer. Rufio waited his turn impatiently and fingered the small box in the pocket sewn inside his tunic. It wasn't heavy, but it was an irritation. His mother had given him the mission. "You'll get to see Scorpus close up!"

Oh joy! Scorpus might be everybody's idol, but he was a Green and Rufio, not surprisingly, supported the Reds. Now if he had a gift to deliver to that sexy beast Endymion of Ephesus that would be something.

In a disguise Rufio thought somewhat overdone, Lady J— had arrived surreptitiously after dark the previous evening. She slipped from a litter and bent her head in a hurried, whispered conference with Junilla. The noble lady handed over a small letter along with a considerable sum of money, and vanished again into the night. The missive, written on the small square of parchment now in Rufio's hand, bore her husband's seal and a line of writing. The terse missive bade those on duty to let the bearer through to visit Scorpus.

"Of course, Lady J—'s husband has no knowledge of what his seal will permit," Junilla told him with a pleased and rather sly little smile. In the morning she handed over the letter and the small box wrapped in a (naturally) green silk ribbon. "But make sure you don't dawdle, Rufio. It's a great honor to be asked to join Chamberlain Bardas in the imperial box."

"Even if it is half a mile away from the Emperor."

"Oh ho! One visit to the palace and you think you own the place. Be thankful for small mercies. It's not everyone like us gets to be in the p–p—"

"Pulvinar."

"So behave and be on time. Bardas seems keen to have us get a flavor of courtly life before I finalize the party plans for this Obidos."

"I think he called him Obodas of Nabataea, wherever that is."

"Well, we are to meet Acacus at the main vestibule. You know it? Behind the temple of Castor and Pollux?"

"I know it, Ma. Don't worry. I'll be there at the third hour."

Now there was only one fellow in front of Rufio arguing with the officer. Behind the cordon of Urbans stretched the gently curving façade of the starting gates, a long and tall edifice of thirteen great arches. In front of the central arch a superfluity of priests gathered, ready to march on and perform all the necessary rituals before the start of the day's events. Six arches on either side were the actual starting gates. Already, race officials were discussing with team leaders the random selection of the gates for the four factions, each fielding three chariots in every one of the twelve races planned for the day.

At last! Rufio thrust the parchment in the officer's face.

"What's this, then, Copperhead?" The policeman took the scrap from Rufio's outstretched hand and peered suspiciously at it.

"You do read?" Rufio smiled engagingly.

The policeman frowned. "A token of appreciation for Scorpus?" He showed the note to the man next to him in the cordon."

"That's Senator J—'s seal."

The officer wrinkled his nose and regarded Rufio with the same suspicion he'd leveled at the note in his hand. "I s'pose it's all right then. Straight to the Greens' building and no messing now!"

He stood aside. Rufio took back his note, thanked the officer politely, and began the hazardous crossing of the chaotic space. From the upper windows and balconies of four large buildings banners flew in the light breeze: red, green, white, and blue. Flitting this way and that, slaves ran around the square on mysterious missions as if the god of the Underworld was on their heels. Just behind where the priests had collected a large cage announced its purpose by the clamor of exotic wild animals intended to entertain everyone before the races. At every point of the compass around this menagerie, grooms struggled with highly-strung horses terrified of the grunts, growls, and roars from the caged beasts. Others handled the fragile chariots being prepared for their riders. At almost every step Rufio narrowly missed being run down by slave, groom, horse, or irate team leader.

Eventually he reached the six steps leading up to the porch of the Collegium Pistorum. Carved bas-reliefs on the wall depicted pistors, or millers, grinding grain in traditional querns to make flour to be baked into loaves of bread. As the millers' and bakers' guild was the Greens most important sponsor, the team always used the building as race headquarters. The affiliation earned the Greens the derogatory nickname supporters of the other three teams shouted at them—the "Grinders." The unbroken string of victories Scorpus had provided the Greens since he started riding as a mere child— almost a thousand laurels, and climbing—had made the insult an empty one.

Inside there was an atmosphere of anxious pre-race nerves, not helped by the line of men and women all screaming that they had appointments with this charioteer or that. Rufio simply pushed through, ignoring curses, and waved his passport from Lady J— at the harassed functionary who stood in his green-dyed tunic behind the desk that guarded any further ingress to the building. The seal did its work and the man waved Rufio through to a renewed howl of protest from the crowd. A slave was assigned him, who quickly sped along several hallways, past doors open to the rear courtyard and stables, a flurry of grooms and a cacophony of shouts and the clopping of hooves, to a doorway guarded by another slave.

On the other side the airy room more resembled a dressmaker's emporium than a place for a charioteer's preparation. The great man, he was told, was "at rest" in his private chamber beyond the next door. His guide bade him stay and went in. After a fidgety wait for Rufio, the boy reappeared and waved him through to the inner sanctum. With Endymion of Ephesus firmly on his mind, Rufio was determined not be overawed by the presence of the most adored man in Rome. And in fact his first impression was not special. Scorpus of Rhodes lay stretched out on a truckle bed, hands folded behind his head, naked except for a small towel draped modestly across his middle. Rufio—who had only ever seen the idol of the hippodrome at a great distance, hurtling through the dust of the track—thought him neatly built but not toned the way he expected of an athlete. Certainly Scorpus was nowhere near as sensuously attractive as Endymion (he preferred dark hair coloring)—not that Rufio had had the good fortune for closer observation of his racing hero either.

Scorpus looked to be about his own age, which was galling considering he was worth a thousand-thousand times more than Rufio's sporadic income. No, he concluded, it wasn't the Scorpion's sting that drove matrons, their husbands, daughters, and sons to want to fling themselves at his body, to be ravished by his sweaty beauty, to do his every bidding, it was that attribute all Romans loved best that drove them to adoration—the scent of victory and, above all, good fortune.

Scorpus's eyes revolved in their sockets. Colorless pupils took in his visitor. The expression of sulky boredom gradually softened toward interest as he silently examined Rufio standing a polite few feet from where he lay. A quick widening of the eyes—an unusual pale gray Rufio now saw—and a flicker of eyebrows asked a question.

Rufio took a pace forward and reached into his pocket. "I have a gift for you from Lady J—."

Scorpus deigned to untuck an arm and reach for the small box. Rolling onto his side, he undid the green ribbon. The small towel across his hips rolled with him and folded up softly on the mattress. Scorpus made no move to replace it, so Rufio was treated to a full frontal of the charioteer's cock and balls, nestled amid a soft bush of pale pubic hair. From the opened box Scorpus pulled out a small pendant in the shape of an erect phallus on a fine silver chain.

"I am to tell you that the talisman is to bring fortune in today's race, and that the lady is eager to renew her acquaintance with you later this evening. In the usual place."

Scorpus sat up and swung his legs over so his broad feet slapped on the smooth stone floor. "So tiresome."

"Sorry?"

"It never stops." He looked up wearily as though expecting Rufio to understand his petulant ennui.

The charioteer spoke with a distinctive Greek accent in imperfect Latin, which Rufio thought odd, since he'd lived in Rome for years. But perhaps it was an affectation. Rufio's silence provoked an explanatory outburst, all the more passionate sounding for the low tone in which it poured forth.

"The matrons who want me tumble them, every day, every day, this way, that way, whichever way. Like Scorpus is athletic beast. My victory rub them off. That's all they want. Never what I want. The men the same... no, they worse yet. Want me fuck them for *fortuna*. Look." He pointed at a pile of notes on the high windowsill. "Meet now. Meet later. Come to party. Worst, some fat old bastard senator type, think me his kept pet. 'Oh, my darling boy, pour you love into you adoring Livius.' I don't know. He is a Cacilius something. Yes Dio." His voice rose again to a falsetto whine. "'But all be mine for your Livius, I, your adoring plumptious sofa where to bury that big weapon…' like I am some kind of gladiator. Or maybe he think me one of those Minoan bulls."

Oddly, Rufio felt overcome with a desire to rub the top of Scorpus's buzz-cut head. Charioteers usually had their hair shorn close to the scalp. For one, it prevented long locks blowing into their eyes at crucial moments, for another, it was held that long hair streaming in the slipstream of racing slowed them down. He'd expected arrogance from such an adored celebrity of the races, and this quietly upset demeanor touched him.

"What's your name?"

"Tullius Rufio."

The sudden grin of delight transformed Scorpus to someone years younger, like a schoolboy. "Hah! Rufio redhead." He reached out a hand and took Rufio's arm. "Come closer."

Their eyes met, cornflowers on slate. A smile began at one corner of Rufio's mouth and gradually expanded across his face. He arched his left eyebrow questioningly at Scorpus's matching smile. Then the charioteer's eyes dropped down to take in the mounting bump in the front of Rufio's tunic. Very slowly he raised his left hand, under the hem and slid fingers up. The silky-light touch on the skin of his inside thigh made Rufio's pubes crackle with anticipation. The hand encountered the loincloth Junilla had insisted on his wearing as a guest in the imperial box. With his gaze fixed on the swelling shape under the garment, Scorpus found the small buckle at Rufio's waist, unfastened it, and the supple leather belt fell away to the floor, carrying the flaxen cloth with it.

Scorpus misinterpreted Rufio's quick look over his shoulder at the mostly closed door behind him for nervousness at being discovered. "No one enter, less I say so."

But the glance was more out of curiosity, for Rufio didn't much care who saw him having sex. If that got them excited, so be it. He lowered a hand onto the sharp bristles of fair hair and stroked them, which resulted in a faint crackle of static. The sexy action encouraged Scorpus. He leaned forward and used one hand to lift Rufio's tunic, the other to finally grasp his now fully extended cock.

"Mmmm…" A throaty murmur of pleasure escaped Scorpus's half-opened mouth as he dipped his head, pushed a long tongue from between his lips, and started circling its tip around the crown and foreskin.

Rufio thrust his hips forward into the wet labial embrace, and sighed happily. Still softly stroking Scorpus over the head, he used his free hand to tug up the hem of his tunic higher. *Don't want to get any cum on it. Won't look good in the pulvinar.* He was certain he was going to come pretty damn soon. The Greek boy knew a thing or two about sucking cock and was easily taking his full length all the way down. His own was rigid, standing up against his flat tummy. Rufio leaned in far enough to transfer his head-stroking palm down to grip the wet-tipped shaft and start rubbing up and down.

Scorpus moaned again, a sloppy-wet sound rich in saliva. His sucking built to a frenzied pace and Rufio knew Scorpus could feel the balls under his hand contracting and moving closer to the base of his cock. That beautiful unworldly heat of mounting orgasm suffused his weakening body, while the cum in his balls began to roil, ready to release in urgent ejaculation. Rufio sensed Scorpus tense up, his frame shudder, and he was coming in Rufio's grip. And so was Rufio, a jolting pump of pleasure and then he ejected the first jet of cum into the charioteer's eager mouth. They came and came, Scorpus from an evident need to be subjected rather than dominate, Rufio from sheer animal pleasure at the unexpected treat of feeding his Celtic cream into such a famous and willing mouth and throat. Almost everyone in Rome had to pay for this kind of

servicing, whereas Rufio felt he was bestowing a gift on Scorpus of Rhodes, a gift the charioteer clearly needed.

Scorpus loosed a great heartfelt sigh and reluctantly released Rufio's spent cock. He stood and went over to a low chest dominated by a large basin of water and a pile of towels. He dampened one and mopped Rufio's masturbating hand clean. It was a tender gesture.

"Let me." Rufio picked up Lady J——'s phallic talisman from where Scorpus had dropped it on the mattress and slipped the chain over the charioteer's bowed head. The silver cock fell tidily into the hairless valley between his breasts. Rufio patted it lightly. "I pray it brings you good fortune."

"You support Greens?"

Rufio bent to pick up his loincloth and fiddled about under the tunic to secure it once again over his almost subsided genitals. He gave a sexy sideways wiggle of the hips to settle it comfortably between his ass cheeks. What to answer? He was unwilling to lie when the boy had just sucked him off so expertly, in spite of the eager expression in the other's face. He patted his head and grinned. "I'm for the Reds, of course."

Scorpus laughed loudly, and slapped his naked thighs. "Poor you. Poor Rufio. Not to bet or you lose." He turned serious suddenly. "Thank you."

"I think I should thank you."

"No. Is me offers gratitude for you let me do something I want instead of other way around, like all others. I think the one who get your love when you bestow it will be a lucky one."

T·W·E·L·V·E | XII

In the Circus Maximus, race day, February 18

Quintus looked across the tracks at the referee's box above the finishing line. In the shape of a severe looking Doric temple, it stood tall above the steeply banked tiers of seats opposite the imperial box. That august construction, the "cushion of the gods," a real pulvinar for living deities, jutted massively from the steep incline of marble and towered above the seating only a few yards to the side of where Quintus stood.

The rows of seats on the reverse side of the massive stadium were already mostly hidden beneath a sea of humanity. He waited precariously balanced partway down one of the steep, narrow stairways serving the lower of the two great banks of seating. The lower rows surrounding the imperial box and stretching around to the great arch of Titus in the semi-circular end were reserved for the several thousand upper class citizens: senior equestrians; patricians; magistrates; members of the senatorial order; former consuls and provincial governors, their families and staff. The stadium's curved end was popular since it offered the best views of the spectacular crashes on the tight turn—the true highlights of every race.

The common plebs occupied the upper terraces, kept well away from their betters by a high wall above a wide median walkway. This ran all the way around the stadium from one end of the starting gates to the other, broken only by the imperial box, the referee's box, and the arch of Titus. Regularly placed openings in the dividing wall led back through vaulted passageways under the upper terrace to hallways that connected directly to the streets on either side.

The women of the Caecilii had parted company with their men

to take their places in the section reserved for ladies of the upper classes. Quintus trailed unhappily behind his father and brothers as they carefully descended the steeply stepped aisle to their reserved row of seats. He parked his bottom at the end by the aisle to wait for Uncle Livy's arrival. The stone was cold and hard and he hadn't had the rest of his family's foresight to bring a cushion to sit on. He felt sick with nerves. Nothing went down at breakfast. He'd nearly thrown up in the litter on the way to the Circus. He certainly could not concentrate on the light banter around him.

"Father, you know there isn't any point putting anything on Whites in the fourth race," Marcus fidgeting next to Quintus was saying, leaning around his older siblings. "Scorpus will wipe the sand with the others."

"I shall make my winnings on the first three, in that case," Lucius retorted.

"Not the third race," Primus said. "The Reds will win that one. The other drivers will be eating the dust of Endymion of Ephesus."

"I shall bet on Blues for the first two," Secundus piped up. "Then Red and then Green."

"That's treacherous," Marcus said, indignation written all over his face.

"Call me perfidious, if you will. I say pragmatic, my dear Marcus."

"Huh! In the navy we are expected to be loyal, obviously not like you army men. Well, whatever, but I do hope there will be a few shipwrecks today. Some blood on the sand."

Quintus frowned at the popular term, which he considered a fatuous analogy. What did a disaster at sea have to do with the crash of a chariot? But it was more than likely that Marcus would get his wish, he thought. A basic tactic for winning, other than being the fastest driver in the race, was to run the teams of opponent factions off the track, to make them crash or overturn on the *meta*, the sharp end corner of the tall stone central block, the *spina*. Sometimes, to let their best team get ahead, the two other faction drivers would gang up on a serious rival threat to ensure his destruction. Blood was virtually guaranteed because each driver tied the reins around his waist, so he couldn't let go if his chariot crashed, and if the rough track surface didn't flay and kill him, it was all too easy to end up smashed into body parts under the hooves and wheels of other chariots. Every charioteer carried a small curved blade called a *falx* so he could cut himself free, but nevertheless the furious pace of the races made it almost impossible to escape from being run down.

"Quintus!"

He twisted around to see Uncle Livy standing on the aisle a step above him.

"Come, boy. We'll be able to catch him as he comes from the palace to the pulvinar. Look smart!"

Quintus stood, aware of the looks his brothers were giving him. He knew they were wondering what it was Livius was up to and it made him more uncomfortable, if that was possible. His father did not turn his head and continued staring ahead into space. As he followed Livy, a sudden roar of excited approval broke from the massed spectators and Quintus received a brief impression of the distant but familiar figure of Hadrian, editor for the day of the games, at attention, arm held out imperiously in acceptance of the uproarious ovation. His appearance marked the beginning of the religious ceremonies, to be followed by some beast hunts. Then the bulk of the pulvinar cut off the view.

Livy mounted the few steps to the walkway, puffing with the effort. Here, enterprising vendors grilled sausages on braziers, sold hot and cold meat pies, fruit arranged on piles of costly ice brought from the mountains, nuts, and some goods Quintus could not identify. All around the extraordinary noise of thousands of voices shouting out to be heard, placing and taking bets on the advertised races, reverberated off the wall that separated the upper terraces from the walkway.

It was only a few steps along the path to where it disappeared into an archway set in the pulvinar's side. Two Praetorian Guards stood sentry there. In the city, the imperial guard normally wore togas, but for this occasion they were in full military uniform, all glittering bronze with gilt decoration over white tunics, with swords in their scabbards. One nodded politely to Livius when he presented a small wooden token. The guardsman studied it for a beat and then stood aside to let them pass. Beyond, a small antechamber gave access to steps ascending to one of the two temples built on top of the imperial box and connected through a second archway to the covered passageway that joined the palace to the pulvinar. Another pair of Praetorians guarded this second arch, but let them through on seeing Livy's token.

In spite of his nervousness, Quintus could not suppress his natural curiosity. He peered to the right down the long passage to the distant dimness of the palace interior, but there was little to see. In between, six openings pierced the walls on either side where the passage soared above Via Murcia. With their backs to the farther wall, a row of young slaves stood at an arm's stretch apart. Quintus looked to his left where he could see the edge of the top of the steps down into the pulvinar itself. The noise of massed voices echoed up through the complex of marble-clad walls and columns that cut off most of the view of the stadium. The only indication of where Hadrian still stood acknowledging the mob were the tops of several laurel wreaths above the thrones.

"We'll wait here," Livius patted Quintus on the shoulder, which did nothing to settle him. Instead he occupied his mind with the view facing him across the passageway. In front of another antechamber with archways at either end, both guarded by four more Praetorians, the mirror of what lay behind Quintus and Livius, stood a deputation of haughty older men in formal attire. They all looked rather apprehensive and he wondered what they wanted. Three of the senators in their purple-striped togas held tightly rolled scrolls. Quintus presumed they were petitions ready to present to the emperor.

All begging. Like Uncle Livy, and I must be the scroll he's proffering.

As this thought tumbled through his mind, a distant commotion at the palace end drew everyone's attention in that direction. A cluster of togate figures materialized from the shadow and began to progress sedately in the direction of the pulvinar. They glowed brightly as they passed each window and merged with the dimness in between. In a slow rolling wave, the slaves bowed low as their emperor passed at the head of his entourage, like a captain at the prow of his vessel of state. For the first time that day, Quintus thanked the gods he'd been forced to put on his own heavy toga because at least it prevented his shaking knees from being on view.

And then they were there. The emperor ceased walking to wave on the Empress Plotina and her ladies. One of the men opposite took the opportunity to step forward, scroll held out. Quintus had the impression of a hawk's nose jutting up in casual denial, a hand raised imperiously, and the glitter of interest in two beady eyes turned on him before he remembered to lower his own in deference.

The voice was a pleasant baritone, brushed with a pronunciation Quintus thought of as provincial. It was kindly and, in some way he didn't understand, amused and with a distinct undertone of excitement. "So Livius Caecilius Dio does not play loose with truth."

Into his lowered view came a long-fingered hand. The signet finger bore the great ring of state. At the sharp, secretive jab in his ribs from Livy, Quintus dropped to one knee and brushed his lips across the large opal set in the ring. The extended hand turned over, cupped his jaw, and lifted his head. He stood at the physical summons. The soft skin under his chin burned at the imperial touch as though Trajan's fingers were coated in pepper. He allowed his gaze to rise no higher than the glittering necklaces around Trajan's neck and the pendants that spilled over the top of his toga.

"In truth, you were correct, Livius. No artist could possibly reproduce such beauty with pigment and brush."

"Th–thank you, Sire. I hope that we—"

"It is a great shame that all the seats in the pulvinar are allocated—it's Hadrian's privilege today—or I should request your nephew's presence beside me now. My apologies Livius. I should have informed you beforehand that your nephew would not be able to attend me."

Quintus's mind reeled at Trajan's words. *What did he mean? "No artist could possibly reproduce such beauty with pigment and brush." The only painting was the one father paid for... and Uncle Livy, and where did it go? I haven't seen it since it was finished.*

The fingers swept with exquisite lightness from Quintus's neck to the point of his jaw, and the hand dropped away. For the briefest of flashes, Quintus raised his eyes shyly and met those of Trajan drinking him in. It was a very confusing emotion he felt, one he

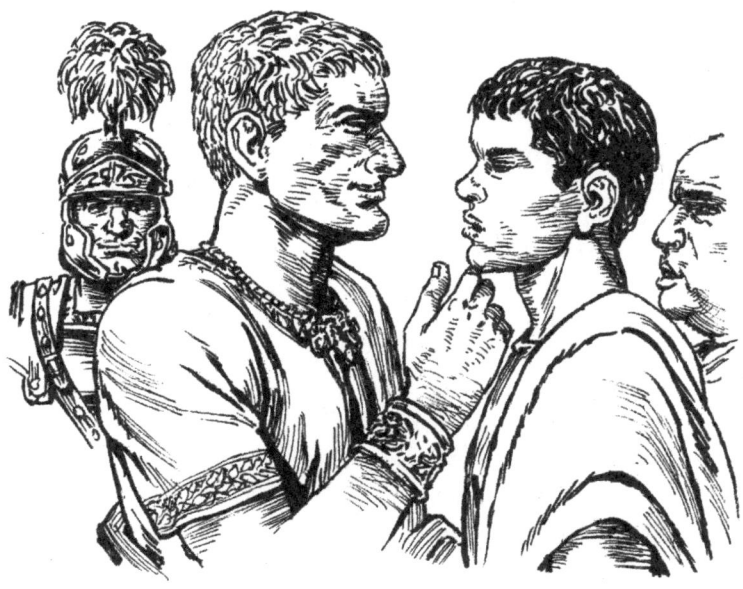

equated with the thrill Ashur gave him by touching his private parts, but also much deeper. In that heartbeat of passing time, Quintus thought he would simply dissolve into a puddle at the Emperor's feet. This close, the man who ruled the world was truly magnificent. And he smiled at Quintus, who promptly recovered his senses and dropped his gaze to the floor where he was pleased to see no evidence of his melted essence.

"I mustn't hold up my esteemed editor or arouse the ire of the priests for ignoring the rites and delaying the mob from their blood lust."

"Caesar, I am in your hands."

Livy, Quintus noted, was wringing his own anxiously. Trajan gave his uncle a hint of a smile, as slight as it was brief.

"Within two days, Livius, you may apply to Diocles in the fiscal office for the patents."

"Oh, Caesar, thank you. I assure you—"

"Not so hasty. The papers are for you to peruse, to see that they contain what you hope for. They will still require my seal to enact them."

Livius fidgeted. "Of course, Caesar. I understand."

"I'm sure you do. You could also apply to Bardas to arrange a suitable time for... Quintus, isn't it?... to pay me a visit." Trajan turned and without looking at the petitioner, who still had his scroll raised in hope, took it from him while fixing a level gaze on Livius. "I shouldn't leave it too long to talk with Bardas."

And with that parting shot the entourage churned into motion again and flowed down over the edge into the pulvinar like a herd of amphibious creatures anxious to return to their pond. The slaves all trotted in their wake, ready to do the imperial guests' bidding. Another huge surge of cheering greeted the emperor's appearance. Now the games could begin.

Suddenly, Quintus and Livius were alone, the other rejected petitioners returned to their seats, no doubt disappointed at not getting a word with Trajan as they had hoped. Only the silent Praetorians remained, as frozen as mannequins in a dressmaker's store. It took a few seconds to sink in that he'd been let off. He wouldn't be conversing at Trajan's side after all. O relief!

"It was all set up, dammit!" Livy fumed. He struggled with his disappointment before turning on Quintus as though it were his fault that the plan had not progressed as it should. "Now you won't be a disappointment, Quintus. To Caesar, I mean, but more importantly to me and your dear father."

"But Uncle, I still don't understand. What was I... am I to do?"

"Livius sighed impatiently. He leaned in close. "Don't mess around with me, boy. I know what you're like. Think I don't know what you get up to with that cute little Syrian body slave of yours? Ah..." He straightened up. "Surprised, hey? Well, I've seen you at it when you didn't know." He turned to walk back out through the antechamber, gesturing Quintus to follow. "We'd better get to our seats. When the time comes, you will do whatever it is Caesar demands of you. And enjoy it!"

Quintus stared at his uncle's broad back as he swept out. He was stunned. Not at Livy's veiled threats or the claim to have seen him with Ashur in a compromising situation, which he didn't believe for a minute. That, surely, was Uncle Livy's own dirty wishful imagination. Armed by the warning Marcus had given him, he'd fought off those octopus hands on more than one occasion since he turned twelve... or was it even earlier. No, it was what his words implied. That the emperor wanted him for... a bedfellow? And this would facilitate the release of some papers it seemed his uncle and father desperately required. *I'm to be sold, no better than a slave to despotic lust. Trajan wants me, Quintus Caecilius Alba! A plaything to a wicked... by Great Jupiter's phallus. Me!*

His loins told the real story. And a hammering heartbeat. He only hoped he wasn't reading too much into it. How awful to get all prepared and worked up only to find that Trajan wanted to listen to a reading of his latest poem. Quintus reluctantly dragged his eyes away from where Trajan had disappeared and turned his steps to follow Livius when a figure burst up from the pulvinar stairs, head down, and slammed into him.

"Hades! Can't you watch where you're going—"

Quintus stared in shock.

Rufio made it in time. Junilla was waiting for him just inside the grand entrance to the palace from the Forum, the one Domitian had had built, although the authorities preferred to call it Nerva's Porch. Try as they might to erase the tyrant's name from the official records the plebs, who never had anything to fear from him, still referred to it as Domitian's Vestibule. From its strongly guarded entryway, once past the strenuous vetting by clerks, a great ramp zigzagged inside up the face of the steep cliff of the Palatine.

Bardas wasn't waiting for them at the top. Instead, a minion intercepted them close to the summit to guide them through a maze of tunnels burrowed out at Nero's insistence and known as the cryptoporticus. These exquisitely stuccoed and painted vaults eventually brought Junilla and Rufio up not far from where they had seen the small indoor arena days earlier. And there stood Bardas, dictating to three furiously scribbling scribes. The clatter of turned wax tablet pages sounded loudly in the hall's confines.

Rufio felt almost at home when once again they were hurried across Via Murcia and into the pulvinar. Slaves flitted silently here and there still putting finishing touches to three ornate laurel wreaths arranged around the grand seats for Hadrian, the Empress Plotina, and between them Trajan. Behind the huge thrones more modest seating rose toward the back and sides of the box. Tassled, prettily embroidered purple cushions invited pampered patrician, senatorial, and consular bottoms, the men Trajan was particularly keen on impressing. Behind and around these seats was accommodation for the lesser members of the court.

Bardas showed Junilla to two wooden stools in a corner some five tiers above where Trajan would be seated. Rufio could see they would have a splendid view of the back of the imperial head.

"But think, Rufio, my sweet. The imperial box!"

He smiled, settled himself down to wait for the courtly mob to arrive, and cast his mind back pleasurably to his recent tryst with Scorpus. It amused him to think how many of the spectators were already pledging fortunes to his Green victory, not knowing that the charioteer would be carrying a small, but vital bit of Rufio around the track inside him. If Scorpus were to win—as he surely would—he would be driving something sexily Red across the winning line, just over there on the other side of the *spina*.

Thinking of sex uncomfortably reminded him that he hadn't peed in an age... and needed to.

"You should have gone before we were seated," Junilla admonished him sternly.

"There are the latrines by the entrance. You remember? That ass Cornelius said so."

She looked around anxiously, but there came a sudden flurry of activity. "Too late! Caesar is here. You'll just have to hold it in until they're all seated."

"I am holding it."

"You have no need to flaunt it."

It was as though a swarm of locusts had descended. Fluttering syntheses in a rainbow of colors, severe broad-stripe togas, lightweight dress military uniforms, all the panoply of the gorgeous imperial court flowed in and down the incline, quickly filling the available seats until the pulvinar resembled the packed stadium out beyond the imperial box's stately enclosure.

"I'm off," Rufio hissed

"Make it quick. Don't you dare try picking up one of those Praetorian Guards out there."

Rufio gave his mother his best what-me-would-I-ever looks. He shot back up the side aisle, smiling apologetically at those he passed, crossed the rear space to the steps up into the connecting passage and dashed up the stairs, head down and—

Oooff!

"You!"

"You!"

Squared off like gladiators about to cross swords, the two youths faced one other, slightly crouched, arms raised in defense or threat. Quintus glared at his assailant. The bright red hair was unmistakable. In a flash, the color of his face and neck matched that of the other's ruddy head as blood suffused his cheeks in an equal mixture of shame and wrath at seeing his flagellator again.

"Don't you ever look where you're going," Quintus said in an aggrieved tone, "or are you always too busy dashing about and striking out at people to see what's ahead of you?"

"What are you doing here?" the ruffian snapped back rudely. His blue eyes narrowed and a corner of his mouth turned up in a sneer.

"I might ask you the same…" But Quintus faltered when he realized what had escaped his notice in the moment of impact. This lout had appeared from within the imperial box! How could that be? He recovered, took a step back, drew himself up tall, and squared his shoulders. Then he thrust his left one inches in advance of the right so that he looked sideways down his nose at the youth, chin upthrust. It was the classic stance of a patrician when obliged to address a pleb. "I was standing here to be received by Caesar," he said with an icy calm that he spoiled by nervously running a hand over the neat close-cut cap of his hair, as if the encounter might have put a strand out of place.

The common pleb with his gaudy tunic also took a pace back and straightened up. Quintus was put out to see that even without trying the redhead had an inch over him. "I'm in desperate need, so I'm off to the men's pisser," he said cheerily. "That's what *I'm* doing here… or rather will be doing down there." He pointed to the steps that led down under the passage. On the wall above was engraved the more respectable description: *masculum forica*. "Do you want to join me? You look as though you're holding something in under duress."

Quintus shuddered at the very thought of baring anything in front of this crude guttersnipe, though the emotion became complicated by the vision of the Lupercalia wolf youth, proudly naked and sporting himself in the Forum as though it were the most natural way to appear. *Such a big cock on him. I wonder if it gets any larger when it grows hard?* For a fleeting shake of time he saw himself sharing the latrine downstairs to get a second glimpse of his tormentor's... *No! He shamed me before my family. And yet such sly, wicked eyes challenging me; dimpled cheeks, cheeky in smile and smirk, wanting to provoke a response.*

"I am perfectly fine, thank you." Quintus projected as much chill into his voice as he could. I don't have the faintest idea what you think you're doing in the pulvinar—"

"My mother and I, we run a company—"

Quintus sniffed haughtily. Trade was beneath his status. "I haven't the faintest interest. I am summoned to a private visit with the Emperor at his earliest convenience. So there."

Of course it was childish of him, but the vulgar youth roused his anger. Just seeing him standing there, one hand gripping a bunch of tunic at his front in evident distress, was sufficient to make Quintus crawl in his skin. There came another shudder to prove the point.. *How much bigger does it get when he's hard and...*

"Don't leave yet. Wait there. Please!"

The urgency of the plea startled Quintus into compliance as the other dashed off down the steps to the latrine, leaving him with his queasy thoughts of the pleb boy holding his prick as he peed, the way he'd so callously and cheerfully whipped him, the way Trajan's touch had made his skin tingle in the way it sometimes did when there was thunder and lightning in the skies.

A scrape of sole on stone brought him back. The unruly red hair emerged from the gloom of the latrine, followed by that sickeningly irrepressible grin, the broad shoulders, slim waist, unavoidable bulge in the tunic, sturdy legs, and...

"You did wait. Thank you."

"Don't thank me," Quintus snapped, suddenly back in control of his emotions. "You're nothing but a cheap tramp. I don't know why I bothered."

The heated words didn't have the desired effect because that damned grin only widened. "You calling me a tart?"

"More like a swindler, I'll bet."

"What's your name?"

"What!" The quietly stated request of familiarity was preposterous. In fact so astonishingly laughable that he had blurted it out in a haughty tone before realizing he'd done so.

His interrogator crossed the few steps between them and horrifyingly gripped his arm in the usual greeting. "Well, Quintus Caecilius Alba, it's always good to put a name to someone you have lashed in the Lupercalia. I'm Tullius Rufio, but for obvious reasons, everyone calls me Rufio." He patted his red hair for emphasis.

He released Quintus's arm. Quintus staggered back, shocked at the thug's sheer effrontery. He quickly recovered, as any noble Caecilii should. "I couldn't care less what any call you, even if it be Jupiter himself. If I had my *spatha* with me, I'd run you through for your insufferable insolence."

Rufio placed both hands on his hips, laid his head back and laughed uproariously. "You can wield a cavalryman's sword!"

"And a *gladius*, and if I had either, I'd soon make short work of you, you... you worm. So make sure you avoid me in future, or—"

"You're just sore because I honored you at the Lupercalia."

Quintus struggled to swallow his bile. "You call lashing me with a goat thong an honor. Who do you think I am." It wasn't a question.

"Unless you're a liar, you are Quintus Caecilius Alba, the guy with an appointment with Caesar, for whatever reason. While I'm the one who's a guest in the imperial grandstand— Oh shit! I'm in trouble with my Ma. She told me not to get waylaid by a Praetorian Guard." He glanced pointedly at the two behind him. "Not that I'd ever be so lucky."

135

Quintus winced.

"Sorry. I can't stand here talking to you all day. I have to go."

Rufio gave Quintus a happy smile and a cheery wave of the hand as he dashed back to the steps and vanished as rapidly as he'd first appeared. For a while, Quintus stared at the hole in his vision where the flaming comet had winked out. A part of him wanted to stamp his foot in frustrated annoyance while a somewhat larger part felt exasperated that he'd missed the opportunity to make a better impression on the callow, stupid, dumb idiot… yes—shit-faced cunny.

Next time we bump into each other, watch out you cheapskate guttersnipe, because I'll rip out your guts with my sword.

As he passed back out through the antechamber, uncomfortably conscious that the guardsmen's sniggers were about the altercation they had just silently witnessed, the awareness that he was already *anticipating* a third encounter with Rufio unsettled Quintus even more.

T·H·I·R·T·E·E·N | XIII

Palatine Hill and Palace, March 8

Flaccus was bored shitless, as usual. He really hated a night posting on the Palatine. The only events of any excitement that occurred up here were imperial executions or imperial assassinations, and neither fell into the domain of the poor old Vigiles. He glanced across at Libo, who wore the self-satisfied smug complacency of a man well looked after by his comfortable wife. At least he, Flaccus, had something to look forward to. The indomitable Junilla Rufia had blasted into the local Vigiles station and held a shouting match with the centurion in charge, which resulted inevitably in her victory. Flaccus was to be given a month's leave of absence in order to help Junilla with the most important sequence of festivities for some bloated Oriental potentate who was visiting the emperor. And that meant weeks of being in close company with her delectable redheaded son.

The thought of young Rufio brought a rush of blood to his loins and a rapid stiffening under his tunic. Rufio had been extra especially nice to him yesterday. They were struggling with a few gilded lamp stands Junilla wanted out for cleaning and which she didn't trust to the slaves who would be polishing them up to carry. Flaccus saw again the gorgeous heft and lithe twist of Rufio's body as they deposited the last one out in the courtyard, where a small army of dusters and polishers was at work. And then, to his delight, Rufio had leaned up against him like a large puppy and rubbed himself up and down. He'd suffered an almost incontinent orgasm at the touch, but just managed to hold back. And then Rufio strolled off toward the house to bathe and wash away the sweat of their efforts. Before disappearing into the house he looked back and gave a blissful smile of youthful innocence, and then slipped gracefully through the open doorway, leaving Flaccus with an inconvenient erection.

"That was a deep sigh," Libo said. "You feeling like a boy again?" He chuckled.

"No, but I sure am horny." Flaccus pumped his chest and arm muscles. "You'd think as a member of Rome's Finest I could get a lay whenever I wanted."

"Get married, then you can. Or get less choosy."

"You're a great help."

"Cheer up. In a few more days you'll be trotting around up there in the palace. Just you remember to tell me everything when you come back down to where us mere mortals live. I'll want all the gossip, the descriptions, the excitement—"

Flaccus grunted. "Excitement? Under this regime nothing exciting ever happens, apart from more of Rome being torn down to make way for some fucking great shopping arcade."

The deep dark of night rarely visited the Domus Augustana. The machinery of government was everywhere apparent in the intricate complex of chambers, audience halls, throne rooms, connecting corridors, grand and lesser staircases, the Praetorian Guards' way-rooms, the coming and going of slaves and paid servants, the endless repetition of bureaucratic offices for the Civil Service. Everywhere, the business of running the Imperium occupied the massive edifice. And yet, in such a vast pile there were some quiet corners, out of the way, secluded, private. Some were simply less used areas or suites of rooms whose purpose was long forgotten. Others were off limits to almost all of the Palatinate denizens, such as the Emperor's private rooms.

In both kinds of area, two young men vibrated with nervous excitement.

They were very different to one another, and the causes for their skittishness were as varied: one in pursuit of love, the other trapped by a duty imposed on him. Of the two, the young man captive in Trajan's quarters would be the more fortunate.

The sight caused his heartbeat to speed up suddenly until it was racing faster than a chariot stallion's. His unexpected proximity to what he had been seeking for weeks sparked an earthquake of uneasy seething in his stomach. Was this to be the night, finally, when it would happen? His loins fired an ache that wracked his entire body with helpless desire.

It wasn't that he pined for a lack of sex, for there were sufficient opportunities to hand, even among a few of the *comites*. And then there was the direct access from the palace to the charioteers' academy through a series of deep stairways down to the level of Via Murcia, and buggering the young trainees was an accepted recreation. Similarly, any of the hundreds of slave boys—hand-picked for their good looks—who worked in the palace confines were available. The young knights parading their prowess in the corridors of power were free to interfere with any slave they chose, so long as they didn't interfere with a boy's labors.

But in this veritable paradise of erotic luxury, one chimera had captured Cornelius's attention above any slave or exciting chariot driver. It was one among the numerous civil servants who stood out in Cornelius's affections. Sadly the handsome young bureaucrat steadfastly ignored his overtures and hid behind the robes of his office. And now here he was, mysteriously present in one of the lower-level transverse hallways used by few except some of the scribes. Cornelius knew him by his walk, the graceful sway of boyish hips, but more by a simple erotic upwelling of his desire. In the corridor's dim light it seemed as if he were beckoning. Cornelius began to follow as the shadowy figure disappeared between two stout columns. Was there the slightest hesitation just before he did, as if the siren wanted him to catch up? Or was his imagination running wild?

Cornelius reached the columns and peered around the corner. The new corridor went nowhere. Three closed doors confronted him, two either side of the dead end, one immediately in front. The dusty appearance of those on the sides suggested storage rooms long disused. Beside the third door a Herm stood on a plinth and Cornelius thought the chamber beyond must once have had a religious significance, but it was the Herm's giant penis, erect so the crown almost touched the figure's chin, which gave Cornelius a thrill. His amour must have passed through the door, and looking more closely, Cornelius could see it was slightly ajar.

Heart hammering from rampant arousal, he pushed the door inward, very softly.

The darkness is all about. It swirls as if it had a corporeal body, when really, say the philosophers, it is only an absence of light. The stoics, the sophists, epicurean philosophers know everything and nothing. They turn pain into sensation and so negate its effect; loss into a void from which man arises renewed. But it's all balls.

Who can know the pain of loss who hasn't suffered a loss beyond any redemption? Even now, as my nemesis draws ever closer, following his perception, wrapped up in his desire to take that which he feels is his Roman-born right, even now my pain is like the neverending echo in an empty basilica. I grow aroused and no longer know whether the pain begets the quickening of my loins or the stimulation that most men find natural fires the agony down there.

Another useless philosopher told me that time heals all wounds. But not this wound. Not this ghost of a feeling that screams to be freed but with nothing to release. And while it remains a ghost, it is bearable… just. But am I not like other men in all but that small respect, and do I not feel arousal? The eternal ache demands sustenance, it demands sacrifice, it demands revenge and in the violence it unleashes might I find a brief moment's solace.

Come to me now, my nemesis. Come to your Circe that you may be wrapped in the mist of your own appetite. Come to me... now.

"You truly are a vision." Trajan held up the small rectangle of thin wood and switched the focus of his gaze between what he could see on the other side and Quintus's face. "But more magnificent in the flesh." He smiled benignly and flipped the wood around.

Quintus came face to face with himself. The shock reached his toes. He'd been right, ever since those mysterious words of Trajan's in the passageway to the pulvinar. He thought he'd sat for the artist so his mother would have a permanent record of her son as a young man. But that was why Uncle Livy contributed to the artist's price. It was all a part of a plan. He knew better than to ask Trajan how he had come by the painting.

"Is it like looking in a mirror?" Trajan's smile turned a little jokey. "I think not. I'm sure Quintus Caecilius Alba is self-aware enough to know his own grave beauty is unmatched."

Quintus knew no such thing. The visage he lived with in his small polished tin mirror at home showed him a plain face, a little too long in profile, too round from the front, cheekbones too high and too sharp, like his too pointy chin, eyes too small—nice eyebrows though. His eyebrows were his best point, he thought. He would rather not have such a tightly cropped and neatly shaped head of hair. If he thought about it—and he had a lot these past few days— he'd be a lot happier if he looked more like the guttersnipe. That awful boy Rufio, *with such a big cock on him...*

"Do you know how handsome you are, Quintus?"

Trajan stepped up close. It was unnerving to be in such proximity. Quintus knew he would spontaneously burst into flame if Trajan so much as touched him again. And then he did, cupped his chin as he'd done on the day of the races. Quintus shuddered involuntarily. Trajan's smile narrowed to a more thoughtful line.

"Do you?"

"I— I don't know, Caesar."

"You mustn't be nervous. It's not easy for a man in my position to relax, but if I can do so, I'm sure you can too."

Trajan released his (too pointy) chin and his hand moved naturally to grip Quintus by the shoulder. He felt he was being pulled in, even closer. Trajan's other hand gripped his arm. It all seemed so unreal. To be here in the inner sanctum of the Emperor, in his presence, and more, becoming a part of his aura. Men like Trajan literally glowed with an inner light through the transparent surface of their skin. For Quintus, this phenomenon added to the sensation of his catching fire. To his astonishment his loins stirred at the fricative touch of skin sliding on skin, the hand gently rubbing up and down his arm. The sensation grew into a pleasurable crawling of the tiny hairs on his arms and legs, wormed its way from his chest to his groin. Trajan's gray eyes bored into him with a lustful intensity, froze him to the spot and yet made his limbs restless to return the older man's half-embrace.

As if he sensed the level of yearning swell in Quintus, Trajan pulled him into a hug that cupped their chins over the other's shoulder. The intimacy was frightening but at the same time Quintus couldn't stop his growing erection as he wrestled with the reality of this situation for which nothing could have prepared him. He knew with a certainty still tinged with innocent naivety that he would lose his virginity this night. And the gradual force Trajan exercised in moving them both toward the massive bed that had first spelled the purpose of his visit the moment he set eyes on it became a rush. In a tangle of limbs and bumped hips, they fell onto the luxurious silken covers, and this awkward opening of deeper sexual meaning actually disarmed Quintus sufficiently that he laughed. And Trajan joined in, even as he tugged at Quintus's breechclout to loosen it, and then found his stiff cock and gripped him firmly. The man's parted lips hovered above his face. Quintus couldn't take his eyes from them, full, glistening… and approaching closer. He'd never kissed any than his mother and sisters, and never then on the…

The lips met his and his breathing became uncertain. Bathing in the sea at Baiae as a child, he'd brushed against an eel, which sent a violent shock through him, but nothing like what he now felt. After an eternity Trajan lifted his head and smiled.

"I'm glad you laugh, my Quintus. I promise you we will both laugh a lot this night and it will all be in pleasure. Relax. I won't hurt you." He helped Quintus roll over onto his tummy and then everything became sensations, an awareness of Trajan's weight on his back and then the release as Caesar raised himself up over his prone form, the shock of a wet tongue on his spine, licking down, down, unbelievably into his bottom, probing, pushing. Any embarrassment at this intrusion, the clever tongue swept away in a pulse of erotic power as Trajan found his asshole and nibbled at the entrance alternately with darting the tip of his tongue inside.

It all felt so terribly wrong and so completely right that Quintus no longer knew where he was or why he was here. The ache of need in his balls made him arch his middle up off the bed to goad his older lover to tongue him even more deeply. Then there was more movement, more weight as Trajan laid himself out full on top of Quintus and he felt the imperial cock push insistently between his ass cheeks.

"Relax, my Ganymede and you won't even know when I enter your portal."

He felt the pressure increase, so weird, so wrong so—

Quintus screamed.

Palatine Hill and Palace, evening March 8th and morning after

Cornelius let his fantasy run wild. The lithe body he rode like a stallion covering a mare was mostly unrevealed, still hidden beneath the musky smelling robe of a scribe, head and face buried under its hood. Cornelius imagined the freedman boy he so desired and his mind obliged, driving him to ever more exertion in the animal fuck. They rolled haphazardly around on the old truckle bed that stood at the center of this weird room. Was this a rite? It felt like part of an inchoate ritual, an act forgotten but reforming itself from the mutual lust of their joining.

Everything he could feel wrapped in his clutching arms felt young, vital, desirous of harder fucking, but the fine linen cloaking the body he held was driving him mad. Cornelius wanted more contact.

So easy! So simple! Like a sacrificial goat to the Lupercalia altar, bleating happily under the priest's raised hand. I walk in a certain way, half glance back, and my would-be-lover follows to bury his nose in the trough. He thinks because he is inside me, that he possesses me. But it is I who possess him, his ego, his big unconquerable Romanness falls to my wiles. Giants who stride the world in their insectile segmented armor, who demand of the petty tyrants observance. Locust spawn like Obodas, who basks in Roman protection, he thinks! Obodas, fat slug and taker of children' lives.

Now my Roman stud demands more. Uncontent with plunging in and out of me, he wants the fake affection of bodily contact without clothing to interfere. You want to feel my hard blade, hard for you my bucking heroic barbarian-killer. Perhaps it is time to let you have your way.

Cornelius had no idea who had lit the small wall sconce. Presumably the one who writhing under him in evident lustiness for the arousing fuck they were both enjoying. Oh but damn the clothes, damn the bureaucrats and their false modesty. And then there came a relinquishing of the claim on the robe. The mystery figure, the young man Cornelius was convinced was the one he had for so long desired, rolled sideways. The hem of his long robe rucked up with him and suddenly Cornelius could see long legs, a pale ruddy color in the low light. Eagerly, he reached down to pull the garment right up around the other's waist.

And that's when he saw it.

Or, rather, the lack of it.

There was a cock, but no testicles. Neither filly nor colt, then. A gelding.

Cornelius paused in mid-thrust. The revelation riveted him. And then, shockingly, a bubble of mirth rose up his gullet and erupted as a barking laugh. He was hammering a eunuch! This was so far removed from his fantasy he couldn't stop laughing, and the one under him started laughing too.

A high-pitched screechy snicker.

Quintus gasped at the flowering of hurt as Trajan tried to enter him. Mouth agape, the scream he had muffled among the bed covers still sounded too loud in his ear, like the hammering thuds of his heart. He was suddenly aware of a chill on his ass, a sudden freedom from Trajan's weight on his back, and a thumping at the bedroom's double doors. Screams echoed outside.

In a trice, Trajan was off the bed and striding toward the commotion, shrugging his arms into a loose robe. In consternation—relieved that the intervention, whatever it was, had rescued him from an act of sex he wasn't at all ready to embrace, but at the same time faintly disappointed that it had interrupted Trajan—Quintus slipped from the bed and groped the floor for his discarded tunic. At first all he could feel were the proud edges of the mosaic tesserae, and then his fingers encountered the fine woolen garment Uncle Livy had insisted on him wearing for the "tryst," as he smilingly called it.

The double shock of his almost getting fucked and then the shouting and impending sense of doom robbed him of his manners and his shyness. Without realizing he'd done so, he went to stand at Trajan's shoulder, his shame at being caught in Caesar's private rooms forgotten. He recognized Hadrian's drawn face beyond the half-opened doors. Behind him several functionaries cringed, wrung their hands, and cried out in a babble of frightened voices.

"What in Hades' name is it, Publius?"

Quintus realized Hadrian, the fearless soldier, had a face drained of blood.

"Have you seen a ghost?" Trajan demanded.

"Yes. In effect. It's Cornelius."

"Wh– what of him?"

"Dead, Lord." He leaned in closer so those behind could not hear, but his low voice carried well enough to Quintus standing beside Trajan. "A slave found him, Marcus," he said, using Trajan's given name. "And he came to me at once." Hadrian shuddered visibly upset. "He's been foully murdered."

Forgotten in the emergency's imperative, Quintus followed Hadrian and Trajan, swept along in their wake by the trembling clot of slaves, servants, and flunkies as if in a flash flood. Was he Trajan's jetsam or merely flotsam caught up with palace debris in the flow?

Tension mounted as the entourage poured along corridors, across intersections, under mighty arches, down staircases wide and narrow, and so to a subterranean region of clustered rooms. Several guards held sputtering torches aloft and through the press Quintus saw a priapic Herm beside an ornate door of ancient appearance. In the flickering torchlight he made out the form of a naked man with

146

something distorting the shape of his mouth. And then he saw the dreadful mutilation. The young man had been emasculated. A raw hole of blood and torn flesh gaped where his genital should be. His balls had been stuffed in his mouth, his penis, what little was left, hung limply on the tip of the Herm's cock. And that wasn't all the horror, for Quintus in his innocence had never encountered a dildo before, and this one was only partly visible where it emerged from the murdered man's anus.

Rufio was having a good evening. The minute his chores were completed at the main warehouse where the Tullius Emporium of Artistic Excellence stored small items of antique interest—*What the fuck do people want to collect Falernian wine seals for?*—Rufio was off down the street to his favorite local tavern, not two blocks from the Emporium. The Two Balling Fighters was well known in the immediate locale as a cruising joint for the Foxes, the wild, roustabout youth of the western Aventine. There, after a few cups of a not too bad Tarraconensian wine, he intercepted the surreptitious glance of a likely lad across the other side of the crowded room and thought: *Hmmmm…*

The boy acknowledged Rufio's wink by raising a shoulder a fraction and ducking his head sideways toward it. I'm interested, the gesture said, as did the way he tucked in a corner of his mouth. And then, with a final guileless backward glance over his shoulder, he left. Rufio was but a few steps behind. The youth walked steadily along a contour of the hillside for a block and then, assuring himself he was being followed, turned aside in to a narrow alley. Rufio only paused at the entrance to the lane long enough to see his quarry disappear through a gateway. A moment later and he was within the confines of a little deserted courtyard. The boy waited for him beside a pile of baled hay, and as Rufio approached, determined smile fixed, he was drawn back out of sight of the alley, and in less time than it took to say, "Hello, what's your name?" (which neither did) they were grappling, pulling off each other's clothes, and handling the goods.

It was clear very quickly that this lithe young capture wanted it up the ass, and Rufio needed it quick and hard, so he wasted no time. He spun the boy around, spread his legs wide apart with two swift ankle kicks, hauled his arms up, palms flat up the wall to support them both, and inserted his drooling cock into the pleasantly tight hole. The boy grunted deeply, but pushed his butt back willingly against the penetration. It didn't take long. With one hand wrapped around

his slender waist, Rufio jacked his cock vigorously as he fucked him up against the wall. A strangulated *mew* blew from the boy's wide-open mouth, the only warning he gave Rufio before squirting a powerful jet of cum though Rufio's cock-stroking fingers. He heard it splatter on the rough bricks, and then, eyes screwed tight with exertion, he pumped the boy's insides with his own Celtic cream.

They parted with no more words spoken than when they started, but a companionable mutual arm grip suggested that an *encore*, as the Gauls called it, would be welcome.

Amid the panicked confusion, Quintus suddenly came to his senses sufficiently to look for Trajan, but neither the emperor nor Hadrian was to be seen. He didn't know what he would have done if Bardas hadn't swooped down on him, gathered him up, and marched him away from the blood-soaked horror that had been a young Roman nobleman. From the chamberlain's muttered words, Quintus began to understand that Trajan had not exactly forgotten him but the exigencies of the situation demanded his presence elsewhere.

His seduction, it appeared, was off.

Bardas hustled him from the Domus Augustana and through the formal garden to the open space known as the Area Palatina, where Acacus waited with a nondescript litter and its bearers. Quintus barely took in the equally cold and sneering secretary who in mock servility held the privacy curtain aside for him. As he threw himself down disconsolately on the hard bench, Bardas leaned in.

"Another visit will be arranged for you... at Caesar's pleasure. Be sure to be prepared at any time of the day or night."

Quintus felt nothing but confusion. "How... how will I know?"

Bardas screwed up his long nose in a moue of what could be disgust or the supreme suppression of a sneeze. "I'm confident your uncle, the noble Livius Caecilius Dio, will inform you."

And in that chillingly haughty manner, Quintus was ejected from the palace precincts.

His bearers padded softly through the poorly lit streets, but his heart beat to the rhythm on the paving stones of the iron-shod sandals worn by the two thugs carrying cudgels. They were hired to beat the crap out of any cutthroat or robber who dared try holding up the litter and its passenger.

Quintus's seduction, it seemed, was merely postponed.

It was perfectly clear in the Greeks' body language that they found a summons to the nether end of the Aventine as beneath their bureaucratic dignity. At least Rufio assumed Bardas did and Acacus was simply aping his master. And it wasn't so much a summons as a dispatch. Trajan, it seemed, was very keen to see the proposals for the planned week of festivities in honor of Obodas. Junilla had even ordered the household slaves to extra labors to tidy, dust, polish, and generally make the place fit for a visit by the chamberlain and his secretary. She could have spared them, Rufio thought sourly.

As she busied herself with sheaves of expensive paper with details of her ideas, Acacus and Rufio exchanged looks of mutual distrust and dislike. As he was to say later, "That oriental Greek is a slippery cove. I wouldn't trust him farther than I can throw him, which given his puny form is sadly quite a long distance. In spite of turning up his nose at the plate of delicacies the kitchen had prepared and a watered wine, Bardas did show some interest in Junilla's presentation.

"You are aware," Bardas said at one point, with a delicate cough covered by the back of his hand, "that Prince Obodas has rather particular tastes in... entertainment."

Junilla smiled calm encouragement, and inclined her head questioningly.

Rufio hid a smile, though not sufficiently, he saw, from Acacus. The look he got back said that the secretary knew Junilla was teasing Bardas.

Bardas cleared his throat again. "I mean the Prince has very, what shall I say… narrow tastes in… the personnel you will be providing as… erm, entertainers."

"Oh, you mean after the dancing's finished?" Junilla said, her face wreathed in innocence.

"Ma," Rufio warned her, still struggling manfully not to burst into open laughter.

Junilla relented. "Chamberlain, have no worries on that score. We're all people of the Imperium here. I know what a Nabataean prince is likely to enjoy. My son Rufio will be in charge of casting for each night, every banquet, every poetry reading, and every… orgy," she added with a sweet smile. "I can promise you Prince Oshobas will be very effectively catered for. Rufio will round up the most exquisite boys available, won't you, darling?"

"Obodas," they all said in unison.

Rufio nodded, and wondered what it was in the discussion that had Acacus vibrating as if he sat in an earthquake zone of his own. He looked positively ill.

"That is all very well, but you realize that security will be extremely tight and all your staff, all your helpers, will have to be carefully vetted. I have prepared tokens for you, your son, and the few you have vouchsafed for, but please pass all other members of your troupe, whether servant, slave or paid helper, through the Praetorian Prefect's office at the Praetorian camp. And as soon as possible. The officers are not, I regret, very efficient and we now have only a month before the potentate arrives in Rome. Obodas and his entourage will be residing in the Vatican palace—"

Junilla clapped her hands happily. "Oh, where Queen Cleopatra stayed when she visited Julius Caesar! How wonderful! We could organize a triumphal entry to the Forum for him like she had when she came to Rome to visit with Julius Caesar—"

"Madam!"

To Rufio's further amusement, his mother patted Bardas familiarly on his berobed knee. "I was only teasing, Chamberlain."

"Hmm, well. The man isn't as important as that! But Caesar is desirous of providing him with glittering diversions while he is here."

"Well, there will be the most splendid finale on the last night, culminating with an organ recital…"

Rufio let the remainder of her explanation roll over his head while he studied Acacus as closely as he dared, trying to work out what was wrong with the youth. Certainly someone had stuffed a prickly pear down the back of his breeches. He also wondered what that ponce Cornelius saw in him. Just looking at the secretary made Rufio shudder inwardly. Much too slender, slight, and slimy for Rufio's taste. And he thought he caught a whiff of something putrid coming from the youth's robe. Acacus, he thought, was creepy.

What a creep! Uncle Livy made his skin crawl. It hadn't always been like that. Quintus could recall a time when he actually looked forward to his uncle's visits, which made a jovial change from his father's dour and serious attitude. As a little boy, he used to squeal with delight when Livy scooped him up, tickled his ribs, and parked him firmly on his comfortable lap, there to bounce him up and down. That used to be fun, and Uncle Livy really enjoyed doing it.

These days dark suspicions as to why Livy had so enjoyed the game assailed Quintus. After his tenth birthday, Quintus began to feel uncomfortable playing along with Livy's attentions, his unease bumped along by snide comments from Marcus about how grown-ups liked to "do things" with older boys.

"Like what?"

"Fiddle about between your legs."

This puzzled Quintus deeply, because he often fiddled about between his legs and enjoyed the feeling enormously. But when Uncle Livy went to scoop him up in the old way but somehow accidentally ended up with a hand between his legs, Quintus ran away from him.

Now the gloves were off. He knew with a deepening certainty that Livius Caecilius Dio wanted to ravish him every bit as much as his uncle assured him the Emperor did. The thought of sleeping with Trajan was terrifying enough, but it lacked the revulsion he felt whenever he imagined being groped by Livy, his mother's brother for Jupiter's sake.

The velvet gloves had also hidden Uncle Livy's temper. Quintus thought he was about to have an apoplexy when he discovered the truth of the aborted tryst. Any subtlety—not, Quintus reflected with hindsight, that there had been much of that in reality—went out of the window along with those figurative gloves.

"What are you? You clumsy, inadequate fool! Have you no sense at all, no native Caecilian... *oomph*? You had Caesar in the cup of your palms, ready to pluck like a ripe plum. All you had to do was lie down and take it like a man. You wear the *toga virilis*, so take some spirit from its name!"

"You weren't there! There was a murder. I couldn't do anything about it." Quintus could see in his uncle's expression that he wasn't

believed, or he was so desperate that he didn't care. Yes, there was desperation under the surface anger. And that made Quintus pissed at Livy and at his spineless father, who obviously backed this vile plan to make him Caesar's catamite in return for some measly contracts, or something. Whatever. No one was taking into account his feelings, his desires. Of course not. As the youngest of the Albas, he knew he was little better than a daughter to be married off in an alliance with another powerful family. And that unhappy thought brought an unwanted vision of Vipsania Metella to mind. How unhappy could a young Patrician be? Was there more to weigh down on his young shoulders? A wife he must soon marry, a thought that sickened him; the most senior man in the Imperium he was supposed to please, who wanted nothing more than to ram his cock up inside Quintus's tender back passage; a family in cahoots to pander him for its own selfish gain; a stupid redheaded thug who enjoyed humiliating him.

His misery was complete. There was only one solace. Poetry. Oh, how he longed to be allowed to flee across the Ionian Sea to Greece where he could study writing in the language of the soul.

He picked up a scroll of elegiac odes he was trying to study, Ovid's epic work *Metamorphoses*. As he pondered its Hellenistic structure and the way the poet had adopted the Homeric dactylic hexameter of the *Illiad*, he kept asking himself if that single touch hurt so much, how would he ever cope with full-on anal sex?

F·I·F·T·E·E·N | XV

March 10th

Now Cytherean Venus leads out her dancers,
under the pendant moon,
and the lovely Graces have joined with the Nymphs'
treading the earth on tripping feet, while Vulcan, all on fire,
visits the tremendous Cyclopean forges.

The epic lines went out the window the moment the summons came. Quintus hoped he'd be left alone, but he kept revisiting the feel of Caesar's hard, naked flesh against his own. Virgil's *Ode to Spring* helped take his mind off the encounter with ultimate power that had ended in so dramatic a manner; almost farcical if it hadn't been so awful. But the great poet's words couldn't entirely dispel the attraction Quintus still felt.

Uncle Livy had been to the point. "Bardas wants you. Now, my boy! Now! Put down your fancy words. That written confabulation doesn't hack marble from quarries or transport volcanic ash for concrete from Sicily. On your feet, don your best—" The flow stopped abruptly. "You have already been in the bathhouse?"

Quintus felt like saying that he hadn't, but of course he had because at the back of his mind was the thought that the Emperor might—just might—want to see him again after the unfortunate interruption of their tryst as soon as he could. *Now Cytherean Venus lead out your dancer, under the light of day.*

"Who's the ugly gnome?"

Flaccus gave a start and straightened up. Rufio thought he was about to grab his lower back to ease aching muscles but thought better of it. Instead he performed a half-turn and leaned back athletically from his hips the better to accent the bulge of his package for Rufio's benefit. His eyes lit up as he smoothed down the front of his rucked up tunic and his face broke into a complex of smiles, a mixture of happiness, vulnerability, and instant lust. Rufio's question registered. Flaccus threw him a cautioning glare.

"That is Agapathus."

"Agapa-who?"

Flaccus's expression suggested Rufio ought to know better. "The organ builder."

"Ah." He remembered. Of course, the Greek engineering genius.

"We'll give them a musical finale the like of which has never been seen before," Junilla had said, once Bardas and Acacus made their farewells and took to their litters with a somewhat ungracious haste to be away from the confines of the poor side of the Aventine.

"With a water organ?" Rufio looked skeptical. "Everyone's heard one of those. There isn't a race in the Circus doesn't start without a recital and the Colosseum's is louder than the thumping of Vulcan on his anvil."

"Mark my words, Rufio my pet, this will be different to anything anyone's seen before. Agapathus is a genius," she'd said smugly.

"So what's my mother and the genius got you doing out here?" he asked Flaccus. "Oh, these scrolls are for..." he waved at the diminutive figure of Agapathus who appeared to be staring into space somewhere above the Circus Maximus. He dropped the pile of leather tubes and they clattered loudly on the paved surface.

"I thought she was sending Damianus out with the new drawings?"

Rufio shrugged and to tease did as Flaccus had just done, pulled the front of his tunic tightly back over his hips. Glancing down at himself, he saw he bulged out at the front in a way Flaccus could hardly miss. "I volunteered. Ma's got Damianus running around like a blue-assed fly. I'm not sure he'll want to be her secretary much longer if she keeps up the pressure."

Flaccus snorted. "He worships the ground she stands on."

Rufio thought he was applying the feelings of Damianus to himself, but not for Junilla. They were stood to one side of the massive formal garden that stretched across the bay formed between projecting wings of the Domus Flavia and Domus Augustana above the libraries. At their back the suite of formal reception halls towered four stories tall and before them the open panorama of the Circus and Aventine hill rising behind the far tiers of the stadium glowed palely in the early spring light. "Do you have any idea how long it took me to convince the Vestibule guards to let me in?" Rufio complained, as if it were Flaccus's fault. "And those things are heavy." He kicked one of the leather scroll tubes.

"Didn't Junilla give you one of those token things. For security?"

"I forgot it."

"So did I."

"But you're in the Vigiles. They'd let you in, no trouble."

"Ha ha. Very funny. You think a fucking Praetorian would give a fireman the time of day. The guardsmen are all jittery. They think everyone is this murderer. Haven't you heard?" he said at seeing Rufio's blank expression. "Some weirdo is going around bumping off young noblemen and now one's been done in up here it seems. So they're double-checking everyone coming in. Bit stupid, if you ask me. The culprit's bound to be of the nobility. All shit-faced inbred daft bastards.

"So how did you get in?"

"I was with Agapathus. How did you get in?"

Rufio grinned widely and patted his butt, and then burst into laughter at the expression of mingled jealousy and frustrated lust Flaccus threw at him

"Anyway, what exactly are you doing?" Rufio peered across the vast space, frowning at the complex of white chalk lines, which Flaccus had been adding to. A series of different length measuring rods lay in an untidy pile at his feet.

"It's the layout for a water organ."

Rufio ran a hand through his unruly locks and shook his head. "My Ma may be the best, but I can't see how a stupid water organ is going to impress an Oriental potentate, let alone the friends and guests of Caesar." He hadn't seen the diminutive figure of Agapathus come around behind him. The ear-splitting roar made him jump.

"Stupid! You call Agapathus of Achaea's Hecatoncheires stupid!"

The fellow's knotty-haired head barely reached Rufio's chin, but he still fell back at the unleashed fury. Spittle flew from a mouth hidden between a voluminous mustache and heavy beard.

"I'm sorry…"

"You will be when your good parent's slave force has constructed the mighty Hecatoncheires according to my plans. This is no mere cheap twelve-pipe *hydraulus*! I named it after the mythological giants who slew the Titans at the beginning of time. Towering men each with a hundred hands and fifty heads, they were. Look!" He stooped and snatched up one of the scroll tubes Rufio had thrown down, examined the legend engraved in the leather cap, grunted in satisfaction, popped the top, and withdrew a large roll of good quality papyrus. "Hold that end," he ordered Flaccus. As the paper unfurled, Rufio saw a diagram showing the elevation of a device incomprehensible in its function. Then he gasped when he understood that the ant like creature at the base represented a human being.

"How big is this thing?"

Agapathus grinned… at least, mustache and beard twitched in a manner Rufio supposed was a smirk of self-satisfied pleasure.

"It's the biggest, largest, most complex musical and performing arts machine ever conceived. This device is far more than a water organ, though it will play more tunes than there are on Olympus. There were three Hecatoncheires, and so there are three primary functions of my creation, each named after one of the giants. This section here is Aegaeon, the Sea Goat, and the pressure of water in the air dome, here," he pointed at a jumble of lines and circles in the middle of the drawing, "drives the musical parts of the instrument, as well as providing massive pressure to a series of pipes for the other two sections. Here is Gyes the Big-Limbed."

Rufio peered at what seemed to be a complicated series of interlocking and weirdly jointed crane arms.

"Gyes will cause Cupids and Narcissi to fly, to swoop over the guests' heads as if airborne on gossamer wings. Oh… and a lot of other amazing spectacles will Gyes provide. And here is Cottus the Striker and the Furious. From these variously sized tubes, Cottus will hurl all kinds of amazements from Egyptian doves to colored fireballs. Egyptian because they are small and compact, not like the great big rats on wings Rome has," the Greek felt compelled to explain.

Agapathus let go his end of the scroll. It snapped back into a roll aimed at Flaccus. Holding his end, the sudden release caught him by surprise and he had a job to keep a firm grip on it.

Rufio waved an arm around. "Won't it be cold out here, at nighttime?"

"No." Agapathus wrinked his snub nose, which just poked out above the bush of his mustache. "At Caesar's command, my fellow Greek Apollodorus the architect has loaned me a hundred of his most skilled woodworkers and even now they're up there above us, erecting stanchions for a great awning. And over there," he said, pointing at the open area above the Circus, "there will be a massive drape, so in here it will be like the inside of a deep desert dweller's tent.

"Snug as a bug in a rug," Flaccus murmured.

Rufio didn't like the gleam in the Greek's gimlet eyes, nor the way he suddenly grasped his lower arm proprietorially.

"You're a flaming beauty, aren't you? I could make you one of the centerpieces of the flying Narcissi. You'd be up there—"

"No thanks!" Rufio shook off the importuning hand. "I think I'll remain firmly on the ground as part of the organizing crew." He was amused to see the scowl Flaccus aimed at Agapathus, as if he suspected the Greek of trying to steal Rufio from under his nose.

Everyone was jumpy. There was no hiding it. From the lowliest slave even to the most senior of the palace freedmen, like Bardas, the murder had upset the quiet Ulpian efficiency of the Palatine. Quintus might not be familiar—not even remotely—with the workings of the palace, but it didn't take an expert in human emotion to detect the sense of suppressed alarm. A vicious murderer was abroad, and the serial killings that had, according the *Daily Gazette*, so exercised the Vigiles and their rivals the Urban Cohorts was now a matter for the elite Praetorian Guard. Violent death had visited the precincts of the Roman government's inner sanctum.

But perhaps, Quintus thought, he was projecting his own nervousness onto Bardas, who he did not like. There was something creepy about the chamberlain. He had noted that on the first occasion when the man had taken him to Caesar's private apartments, but now he seemed positively unnerved, while hiding it, but not well enough to fool Quintus. He couldn't understand why a man as unaffected as Caesar, first and foremost a down-to-earth military officer, should want a wily Greek—and an astonishingly young one at that (what was he? Surely no more than ten years the senior of Quintus)—and classically handsome as his leading secretary... unless...? Was Bardas another bed companion?

And here came another creep, the even prettier Acacus.

"Apologies, Bardas." Acacus sketched a light bow. "Caesar sent me to forestall you from going to the apartments. He has been detained by a matter of state and will see young..." The dark eyes flickered disdainfully over Quintus, "the young man in his *tablinum* when his business is concluded."

Bardas nodded. He turned to Quintus and said in a grave tone, "I must leave you here for a while, Quintus Caecilius Alba. Pray rest on the seating over there and I will send a serving man to you with refreshment."

"How... how long will it be, do you think?"

The ends of the firm-set lips tipped up so slightly Quintus wasn't sure he'd seen the movement. "I'm sure if I knew the answer to that I should be able to predict the future, but am I not a seer, and magic is of course punishable by death."

Had the chamberlain delivered a joke? Quintus swallowed and instinctively reached for his sacred *bulla*, forgetting that he had put away its childish charms now he was a grown man.

Bardas dipped his head, gathered his long robe and, indicating to Acacus to follow, swept off. Left alone, Quintus went to sit on a hard marble bench against the wall. He wasn't really alone, though. A constant stream of young men wearing their slave collars and freedmen wearing their importance like banners flowed along the corridor in both directions, some swerving to the side into a transverse hallway that led... somewhere. Hardly anyone spoke a word, although Quintus heard some muttered conversation between two approaching along the corridor, one of whom by the voice was a woman. The strident voice caught his attention.

"...and I want you to promise me you will be nice to the Greek—"

"Genius. I will, honest. But you must admit he's a funny little creature. I just hope you aren't misplacing your trust."

"Not according to Camillus in Alexandria. There, Agapathus put on... what?"

Quintus sprang to his feet. "What are you doing here?"

Rufio halted as suddenly, his earnest expression instantly transformed at the sight of Quintus. He gave a tight-lipped smile that could have been of pleasure or intended to taunt. Quick as a whip, he half-turned to the woman beside him and said, "Ma, this is the noble Quintus Caecilius Alba; Quintus, may I present my mother, Junilla Rufia. As I recall trying to inform you, we own a number of interests, among which is a party planning business."

Junilla fidgeted impatiently, but addressed Quintus with the deference due his patrician standing. "I'm acquainted with your father, Quintus. I'm sure I sold Lucius Alba a pair of fine statues of Venus and Apollo for the Domus Alba a few years ago. I'm sure I also know his brother Livius." She frowned in a curiously rogueish manner. "He always wants a bargain and drives a tough deal to get it. Which is why we don't ever do much business." She patted Rufio's shoulder. "You stay and chat with your friend for a bit, my pet. He's a very handsome youth." She beamed broadly and Quintus wished the travertine floor would open up and swallow him. He knew he was blushing furiously. Damn the woman!

And then they were alone, apart from the scurrying flunkies, who ran like ants and parted like a braided stream to flow around the stationary boys. Any who might have paid an iota of attention to them would have noticed a cheery-faced redhead facing a dark-haired young man with flaming cheeks and a thunderous expression.

"So, what are *you* doing here, Quintus?"

Quintus had no intention of revealing the purpose of his presence in the palace, so he was stunned and distressed when Rufio told him, with a knowing leer.

"It's the Emperor, isn't it? You're here at his request, sorry, command."

"What... how do..."

Rufio jumped on the spot and clapped his sides. Bubbles of glee made his bright blue eyes glow with wicked joy. "I knew it!"

Quintus quailed. *How does this piece of Suburan dog shit know?*

"If you'd been bothered to listen to me that day up by the imperial box, sorry, the pulvinar, your honor, I'd have told you that We Are Celebrations and Festivities, or if you prefer it with a touch of class—*In Celebrationibus et Festivitates*—often arrange small, intimate parties for…" He beckoned, and entirely against his natural inclinations, Quintus felt himself drawn into the conspiratorial whisper. "You know, the knobs who inhabit this big pile. And do you know what the biggest demand is for?"

Quintus tightened his jaw until it ached of disdain.

"Boy flesh. These Ulpians are right old Spanish Celts at heart. Oh, I know Tr… well, you know who, isn't really a Celt, but I am and I know my ancestors like to bugger boys and I'll bet you Green against Red it's rubbed off on Tr… you know who."

He took a pace back and smiled at Quintus, who felt entirely bowed under the stupid low-born, non-citizen, gutter-spawned, bastard's charisma. And then Rufio moved in close again. His eyes bored into Quintus's gaze, unblinking. Quintus found himself sinking into the cool lucid pools and all those thoughts about this wretched individual since he'd *fucking* whipped him came unbidden and libidinously, treacherously into his head.

His voice low, husky and full of constrained promise, Rufio said, "I can show you a much better time than that old man who, you know, runs things. I'd start by running my fingers through that tight helmet of black hair covering your neat round head. I'd let them fall to those… well, they are the most delicious ears I've seen in a long time. So much so I'm sure I'd want to blow very gently into their shells, one at a time, and run my tongue around the raised whorls. But I couldn't stop myself gripping your shoulders as I made love to your ear lobes, to pull you tight close to me, and drop one hand down between us to feel your erection, which—no, don't lie—would be growing with every passing moment."

To his astonishment, Rufio did indeed incline his flaming head so those vigorous curls of bright hair brushed his cheek and then he felt the hot, moist breath in his right ear. The exquisite touch made him almost curl up into a protective ball, but it also did the other thing. His cock sprang to attention and pulsed against the solidity of Rufio's thigh. The words came as warm breaths in his ear, so close,

so intimate, barely heard, but all registered with an awakening of burning desire.

"I know there are people hurrying past us, but who cares? I'm going to push you back to the bench behind you and lay you out, where I can disrobe you and take in that beautiful body I so ravished in my mind when I touched you with the Lupercal's thong. Then, I know, you thought I insulted you, but in truth you were by far the most wonderful thing on show that bright but chilly day. I've thought of your body ever since, mine to adore, to worship, to make love to. And now I'm kneeling up over you on the hard bench, but it's not as hard as your glorious cock, which I take into my mouth to work you up to a delirious state so you won't even feel me enter you and…"

Quintus came to with a start, surprised to find that he was still fully clothed and standing in the stream of busy servants, staring at a smirking Rufio. He was hard as a Praetorian spear and hurriedly cupped hands over his bulging tunic in as nonchalant a that's-how-I-always-hold-myself way as he could manage.

Rufio, regarded him with lively, amused eyes. "You did promise you'd run me through with your *spatha* next time we met, and here we are, and you know... you did." He flicked his gaze down at the protective hands covering Quintus's erection.

And then the fury overcame him. Quintus curled his upper lip into a well-practiced patrician sneer, and finally words came to him. "You low-born prick. You dirty street urchin. You worthless piece of dog turd—"

"I know, I know. For what it's worth, I am sorry, but it was nice to know that I could get you all horned up."

Quintus fell speechless again.

Rufio took advantage. He stepped up smartly before Quintus could back away and planted a light kiss on his hot cheek. "I'd like to do it for real... soon. But you've got your Emperor to satisfy first." The impish grin returned. "I only hope I got you in the mood. See you!"

He threw himself back down on the uncomfortable stone bench, furious with his failure to trump the... the... the. He'd run out of words to describe Rufio. Despicable. Yes, that would do. Rather tame, though. Contemptible. Detestable. Sexy. Vile. Sexy. Quintus sighed and gripped his errant manhood, which kept jumping at the word "sexy." But then, like a repeating onion, he saw again those amused blue eyes and saw through them an abject Quintus rendered lower than a common Suburan whore. Because that's what Uncle Livy and his pestilential father had made of him. And lowborn cunny Rufio knew it. He *knew* it just by looking at him.

I wish I could show him. Have him in the position Ashur enjoys, lips wrapped around my...

The incoherent thoughts shattered the instant the hated form of Acacus came slinking along the busy corridor. His anger at Rufio was immediately transferred with interest to the chamberlain's secretary.

"Good day to you Quintus Caecilius Alba. I see you are still here."

Quintus longed to wipe the smirk from the secretary's face. He would push Trebonius, the Alban retainer who had trained his brothers before him in swordplay, for more training sessions. For a blissful fragment of time he imagined slaying Acacus with the same swinging blow that would take Rufio's big cock off at the base. He forbade his instinct to point out that since he was seated on this uncomfortable, cold bench in the palace, he was indeed still here. Patrician sons did not bend their heads in adoration of mere freedmen, no matter their exalted position. Why couldn't he muster the same dignity in front of that stinking bastard Tullius Rufio? He stood, slowly and carefully. "As you know, Bardas asked me to wait on Caesar's convenience."

Acacus wrinkled his pert nose, which turned the smirk into a sneer.

"Oh dear. How remiss of him to forget you. In that case it falls to me to offer Caesar's deepest regrets, but he is otherwise engaged with more important matters." He sniffed dismissively and offered Quintus the final insult. "I expect you may be called on at some other time. When it suits."

And with that, and one mockingly arched eyebrow, he sailed off in a flurry of lightweight, expensive robes. Quintus stood stock still, mouth agape, breathing in the curious mix of pomade and something less pleasant, almost foul, that Acacus left behind.

S·I·X·T·E·E·N | XVI

March 10, later toward evening

The dubious look Cato gave his mother had Rufio smothering a fit of giggles.

"Is he serious?"

"Your brother is always serious, so pay attention."

Cato gave a deprecating sniff. "You want me to round up a bunch of the Little Foxes—scruffs from the streets, and then they're going to be hurled to their deaths?"

Rufio sighed. "I already told you. After a good scrub up, and suitably attired—"

"You mean stripped naked." Cato's tender years and angelic appearance might fool anyone who didn't know him better—and he used those attributes unmercifully to get his own way—but he was as precocious as Rufio when it came down to matters of the street.

"Not at first, they won't. They'll be pretty little fauns, Ganymedes and Cupids flying from the arms of this mega-organ—"

"Is it bigger than yours?"

Cato neatly ducked under the anticipated cuff and snickered. He backed off a wary pace. "How much will they get, these flying fauns?"

Junilla looked up from the lists she was preparing. "They'll get what's good for them and no more."

"Feed 'em?"

"Yes."

Cato returned his attention to Rufio. "Will there be arrows to fire? You know, into the breasts of pining lovers?" He aimed an imaginary arrow at Rufio's crotch, and loosed it. "*Twang*!"

"What do you know about love, squirt?"

Cato threw his Cupid's bow away and slid a suggestive forefinger into the cup of his other palm.

Rufio grinned at his brother's obscene gesture. "Go on, get out! I want to see forty street urchins, your fellow Little Foxes, here tomorrow. They'll each get some coins and a visit to the baths, the nice ones down by the Via Appia, courtesy of the—"

Junilla just stopped Rufio in time. "That's a secret until we're all locked down in you know where for the events. And you breathe a word of what this is about," she warned her youngest, "and you won't be using your ass to sit on for a very long time. Now, get on with it."

Rufio waited until he saw the backside of his brother disappear around the corner into the courtyard before broaching his concern. "That sorts out the organ boys, but most of Cato's gang are still too old for this oriental potentate."

Junilla looked up again. She wiped a hand across her forehead to remove some strands of coppery hair from her eyes. "There's a scoundrel down on the wharf I know. The Fisherman, only he never goes out fishing and he doesn't actually deal in fish either."

"So why do you call him the Fisherman?"

"He fishes for tiddlers to satisfy the tastes of men like Orondas. Since the Fisherman is as old as Croesus was wealthy, I think he probably supplied the emperor Tiberius with his little 'minnows,' and trained them to nibble the old reprobate's bits while he was swimming naked on his Capri hideaway. As a procurer, the Fisherman has no match, and I'm sure I can find a price to fit his imagination with the budget Bardas suggested. He won't have much trouble laying hands on sufficient tiddlers to provide Obadiah—"

"Obodas."

"Whatever. This oriental despot entertainment in his private quarters, I was going to say." She broke off. "You're looking fidgety?"

Rufio leaned back against the door frame. "It's been a long day. I was hoping to get out for a bit."

"I know that look, Rufio, my sweet. You can't keep anything from your dear mom and your look and body language says you're gagging for fuck. Oh I'm sure I can cope with everything, pet. You know, the thousands of roses we'll need for the climax of the gladiatorial combat novelty event. The stadium-length bolts of precious material needed to decorate the entertainment venues. The endless lists of staff rosters. And... oh, get on with you. If you see Damianus on your way out, ask him to come in. I need him for a task. And you—don't forget you're due at the palace tomorrow to select and vet the cutest slaves the place can offer. They're the ones to liven up the main orgy Caesar is presenting in honor of Orbalash."

"Obodas."

"Just don't turn it into a long-winded casting couch session. Where did I put that list of exotic dancers?" Junilla began hunting through a sheaf of papers. "And I mustn't forget we need a load of acrobats, midgets, musicians. There's just so much to do and so little time!"

"There's almost a month, Ma."

"Don't be reasonable. It makes me nervous when you sound like a reasoning adult."

He hardly ever kept anything from Junilla, but even so, a boy has to have some secrets from his mother, and the truth behind his fidgeting was Quintus. Rufio was surprised at how much his verbal sexcapade with Quintus Alba designed to arouse the poor boy had had the effect on himself—even more so when he thought back on it and felt sure he detected a distinct interest in return. Of course, the poor lamb had been about to be bedded by Trajan, so maybe he was all of a jigger over that impending tryst. But Rufio thought (hoped?) it was more that his own irresistible charm was getting through to the stuck-up patrician prick. If he admitted the truth, he hadn't seen much of Crispin recently because he didn't know what he could tell his friend about his mixed-up feelings for Quintus. But those feelings didn't wipe out his need for a piece of ass.

So, the fidgeting. Every nerve ending tingled with a need for relief. Junilla was right, as usual. His balls ached, his loins crawled with urgent need. Quintus had done that to him. Unfortunately, Quintus was not available to help him out, but that didn't pose much of a problem to a lad of Rufio's worldly knowledge. He was sure a visit to The Two Balling Fighters would soon elicit what he needed. And sure enough, he had barely downed half a cup of watered wine when another face he had seen hanging around the streets on a few occasions loomed out of the tallow gloom. The crooked grin revealed a broken incisor and gave the boy a feral look Rufio found attractive. Well, not really, but something animal and needy. Why waste time? *And he had Quintus's tidy, helmet-like hair...*

"I want to fuck you hard."

The boy pursed his lips and loosed a breath sideways, as though trying to blow a fly away from his narrow face. "You want to come off that bad, huh?"

"Yes. Right now, and just so we're clear, I'm not renting. I'm going to give you what you need."

The boy shrugged, nodded agreeably, and strode off. Rufio followed close behind, admiring the way his pick-up's butt swayed with each step. Just around the corner his pick-up swung in through a narrow doorway and up some steep brick steps to an upper floor. He was familiar with the building, which belonged to the tavern. The owner would claim his room hire fee at some point; he knew Rufio well enough. The tiny room—more of a cubicle—had nothing in it other than a pile of not very fresh hay, but neither was bothered by its condition.

Faster than Endymion of Ephesus cornering the *spina*, both were naked.

"Woof!"

The boy grinned at Rufio, but took a moment to reach out and grasp his bone-stiff erection. He tugged until he received a sound slap across his bottom, which he stuck out provocatively and wiggled.

"Woof!" Rufio repeated, and pushed the boy down on his hands and knees. With practiced ease, he followed suit to kneel up behind the boy, one hand pressing down on the bony pelvis, the other stroking his shaft as he dribbled a copious supply of saliva on the cock head. He wiped the tip up and down the boy's exposed crack and then simply screwed himself into the asshole with a deeply satisfied sigh that began life as a third woof but melted into a gusting exhalation.

And then, with both hands gripping the boy at the hips, he doggy-fucked in a blind fury that washed thoughts of Quintus from his head and allowed nothing but sheer animal lust to wallow in the hollows of his mind. And yet, in the middle of this furious sex, Rufio came to his senses sufficiently to reach a hand around under

the boy. He took the bobbing cock in a fierce grip and brought him off groaning into the hay as he himself shot a heavy load deep inside the saliva and cum greased ass.

If a crow flapped away from the roof of the building where Rufio and a nameless boy fucked it wouldn't have far to go in a straight line across the dip in the center of the Aventine to the Domus Alba. But the bird would have crossed from the rough side of the hill to a suburb marked out by houses of the moderately wealthy; desirable residences boasting handsome fragments of the ancient wall built by King Servius Tullius at the beginning of time as a part of their gardens.

Quintus was not thinking about Tullius the king that night, but a Tullius was certainly on his mind, all jumbled up with images of the emperor, the snide expression of Acacus, and the imagined visage of Vipsania Metella, his bride to be (nothing more from his father on that front, thank Venus for small mercies). Again and again the vision of Rufio's copper-bright head looking in the February sunshine, a subliminal glimpse of his big cock, full even in a relaxed state, bouncing from side to side as he ran right up to Quintus and his startled family. The goat thong lashed his flesh repeatedly.

His overwhelming desire was so confused with disparate feelings to the point he had dispensed with Ashur's usually calming ministrations. Instead he stroked his cock himself. And he was as hard as he could ever remember. It was Rufio in the end brought him to a flowering orgasm—*I'm kneeling up over you on the hard bench, but it's not as hard as your glorious cock, which I take into my mouth to work you up to a delirious state so you won't even feel me enter you and...*

He bit his lip to prevent a scream escaping, and then spread the coating of cum over his chest and belly, as even more poured from the muzzle of his so-hard cock.

* * *

Silken hangings sway in a seductive sea ripple, moved by a traitorous breeze that promises to ease the desert heat but then dies before it has done so. It is always too hot in Sela, which what the Romans call Petra. A dread settles in the pit of his stomach and anchors him to the marbled floor when his soul wants to fly. No, flee. Run as far away as possible. He wants to be anywhere but here. The king is dead and Obodas rules in his place, which is why he and the six other boys with him walk with terror-laden feet to meet destiny.

"It is a great honor." The Vizier repeats it like a mantra of the kind eastern mystics sing. None of them believe it, those who are feeling the first stirring of lust in their loins.

Ahead, commotion and a hot stench of heated iron and something less clean greets them. He knows this is the Grand Palace, yet it seems made only of restless drapes, insubstantial and... hands grip his arms firmly. The carved marble table, like an altar to a depraved god, is hard on his spine as they hold him down over it. The moon face of Obodas materializes from the blooming light, a sickly smile in which there is no pleasure sets all his nerves tingling in fear.

The heated blade flashes, descends in a swift, accurate arc and gelds him. In an instant of dreadful agony, he pays for being a beauteous child in thrall to the ogre's pleasure. Another favorite boy preserved forever in his youthfulness. Just as his own pleasure in sex is beginning, it is ended, to be replaced by frustration and hate, bitterness and... revenge.

The dying echoes of his waking scream could not chase away the horror of the day the palace eunuchs made him join their ranks, all for the pleasure of the greasy slob whose arrival in Rome was now impending. And—if the fates and the gods were just—whose end was as imminent.

S·E·V·E·N·T·E·E·N | XVII

A hall in the palace, March 11

"Just remember what I said about the casting couch." Junilla tried for a stern expression. "Don't make a meal of it."

Rufio's smirk wasn't intended to comfort his mother. Last night's woof-woof doggy session had done little to assuage his libido, which was attacking the underside of his tunic with every swinging step. She gave him a final tip of the head, and strode off with Bardas to inspect in more detail two of the chambers she had mapped out for an intimate dinner-cabaret party that would have "benefits," as Bardas tactfully put it, leaving Rufio with Acacus.

"If you don't mind my saying so, your eyes look very tired."

The secretary gave him a baleful glance and sniffed dismissively. *Ah, the haughty silent treatment…*

Acacus led the way along corridors, through rooms dripping in marble and gilt, the purposes of which escaped Rufio's ken. Eventually they spilled into a hall equipped with a trestle table, a wax tablet, two stools, and a host of adolescent boys wearing tunics so absurdly short they barely covered the tops of their thighs—the proposed contingent of "benefits." He gave the second stool a baleful glance—the last thing Rufio wanted was the slinky-sexy-slimy secretary looming over his shoulder, and he didn't think he'd have any trouble with the pressganged slave boys that would require the authority of a senior palace freedman. "I don't wish to hold you up from all your important duties." Rufio thought he sounded sincere, but Acacus wasn't having any of it.

"Bardas informed me that this process *is* important, Tullius."

Acacus insisted on using his formal name.

"I have to work out some sexy procedures here with these boys, and your presence might intimidate them."

"Hah! That is unlikely. They are palace slaves."

Rufio wasn't sure whether Acacus intended to imply that they were uninhibited or that they were used to strict obedience. Perhaps both. He sighed, happy at least that Acacus didn't take the spare stool. He began the auditions. First, Rufio put all the boys through their paces with some simple dance steps designed to wiggle their hips and bottoms seductively, and he speedily whittled the fifty-odd to a short list of twenty-four, discarding those too old, overweight from too much good living on palace food, cumbersome of movement, or simply too plain in their appearance. He was aware that Junilla wanted at least twenty to suit her plans, but Rufio reckoned quality should outweigh quantity.

Acacus hovered in the background, busying himself making notes on his own tablet, but Rufio sensed the secretary's reason for staying didn't have much to do with attention to administrative detail. And the frequency of notes slumped dramatically when Rufio had his short-listed slaves pair off and start to show him what they could do to arouse an audience and each other. The pace was slow at first. Rufio got up from his stool to prowl around. He slapped a bare ass here, stroked a lean flank there, and all the while exhorted them to act seductively. At the same time, close up amid the action he was mentally selecting three to take to the next level. In his perambulations he passed a partly drawn drape that partitioned off a corner of the hall. Behind it sat a long generously padded couch with a raised back and end. A small table stood just in front bearing a tray, a jug of wine, and some cups. Just as he'd ordered.

He turned back to the cavorting boys. "Enough! Thank you. Acacus has your names recorded."

A sour nod from over by the doors was all the acknowledgment he received.

"You are dismissed to your usual duties, but we at *In Celebrationibus et Festivitates* always deliver the best performances for our guests, and I know you will all want to do the same." He waved his hands to shoo the boys toward the doorway and Acacus waiting there, but the moment the secretary went through the portal, Rufio lowered his voice. "You, you, and you. Come with me."

"What do you think he wants?" he heard one boy whisper to another.

"He's wonderful! So sexy with that red hair," the other hissed back.

"Do you think his pubes are the same color?"

"I hope we're going to find out…"

Rufio swung around the drape with a beatific smile on his face.

"Attention, my fine boys. Before I'm done for the day I want trial run." Rufio stood, legs apart, hands on his hips, and studied the three slaves, naked although they had collected their tunics discarded in the latter part of the audition. Each was a fine specimen of sturdy physique for their ages, with firm muscles, flat bellies, and curvaceous butts that cried out for fondling. A palace slave could expect reasonable treatment under a benign Emperor and some of those Rufio cut out earlier had taken advantage of too rich a diet. These three had not.

Blond, brunet, and dark-haired, their faces glowed with a mixture of trepidation and excitement. In the eyes of the blond boy who had hoped to see his pubes, there was an almost puppy-like look of admiration.

"What are you called?"

"Marcus, dominus." The boy fluttered his pale lashes.

Rufio was unused to being called "master," and blew out a breath between pursed lips, which curled in a slight smile. "But you have a German name too?"

"Adalhard, dominus."

Rufio's smile broached into a grin as he snuck a glance at the thickening cock. "I think the German is more apt, Adal*hard*. And you?" He turned his gaze on the brunet.

"Marcus, dominus, from Helvetia."

"Hah, and you are also Marcus?" he said turning to the dark-haired slave.

"I am, dominus."

"That won't do. I'll get confused! I'll call you Celsus because you are taller than the others, and you from Helvetia will be Brunus for your brown hair. From which part of our Imperium do you hail, Celsus?"

"From Alexandria, dominus. I am half-Egyptian, half-Greek... I think."

Rufio paced around the table and settled back on the chaise-longue. "So, I am now one of the guests. I am, in fact, the guest you want to please the most." This was met with vigorous nods of agreement all round. "But I am a choosy fellow and I will decide which of you *I* will pleasure." In fact the decision was already made. Rufio would be delighted to have any of them, but the blond German had caught his eye in particular... *The one who wants to see if my pubes are also red.*

He barely placed his butt on the seat before the three leaped into action. Tall Celsus got to the wine jug first, but Brunus grabbed a cup and held it up to be filled. Somewhat cut out by his eager fellows, Adalhard snatched up his tunic, fell to his knees beside the chaise-longue, and started to fan Rufio with the flimsy piece of cloth. The breeze he set up was sweetly scented with traces of his having worn it. Celsus pushed him aside to deliver the wine, which Rufio took. He sipped a little.

"Now help yourselves."

"Dominus?" All three spoke at once, shocked at the idea of drinking with a master.

"Go on. Loosen up, boy. Celsus, you pour, Brunus you hold the cups, and... come here." He reached a hand to clasp the back of Adalhard's head. He caressed the short fuzz of pale hair, and pulled him forward on his knees until their lips met. Rufio slid the tip of his tongue left to right, just pushing through Adalhard's pouty lips. He pulled back and smiled. But to Celsus he acted stern. "Remove my breeches."

Adalhard swallowed and his small Adam's apple bobbed in disappointment as Celsus jumped to obey. Rufio began to stiffen as the dark-haired boy's hands busied around his cock and balls, tugging to loosen the loincloth from where the belt around Rufio's waist trapped it. He looked up to see Brunus standing beside kneeling Adalhard, his own cock now standing out in a straight line in front. Rufio beckoned him forward impatiently, making it plain what he wanted Brunus to do with his bulbous knob, and at the moment Celsus freed Rufio's genitals from the pouched loincloth, Brunus's cock punched into his mouth over Adalhard's shoulder. Still cupping Adalhard's head from the kiss, he pulled him into the action so that the German boy's mouth closed over Brunus's shaft sideways, his lips mashing against Rufio's as they sucked. Rufio worked hard on the plummy cock head and the boy's length, which forced Adelhard into the Helvetian's ball sac with every on-cock slurp Rufio made.

Meanwhile, well to the south, Alexandrian Celsus was working under the cover of the tunic on Rufio's solid erection with both his hands in a manner that suggested he was well used to performing this particular service. "They are bright red," he breathed in wonder, peering under the tunic's hem.

"Uh, uh... I shall make seed, dominus," Brunus moaned. His kneecaps, bent under the strain, beat a spastic tattoo against Adalhard's ear and Rufio's forehead, but Rufio had no intention of stopping now. With his free hand, he forced the boy's throbbing shaft up, so Adalhard dipped under to lick Brunus's balls. Rufio went down deep on the cock, gripped tightly near the base with his mouth and used his throat to massage the drooling cock head. And then the Helvetian slave shot his load and accompanied the gusher with choked cries. Rufio took the first spurt for his own, but generously allowed the rest of the copious flow to run down Brunus's cock so Adalhard could catch some of the cream on his flicking tongue and scoop it into his mouth.

"Celsus, slow down," Rufio gasped. He wasn't ready to come yet and the Alexandrian had replaced hands with his own warm mouth. It was nice, but not what Rufio wanted now.

The three slaves backed off a little: Celsus to sit on the far end of the chaise, licking his palm and the taste of Rufio's cock; Brunus to sit unsteadily on the low table, his half-hard cock slapping wetly down against his thigh; Adalhard down onto his haunches, his face lit with desire and disappointment. Rufio gazed at him, and then allowed himself a tiny smile tinged with wickedness.

"You, my Germanic Cupid, are the one I choose to pleasure me."

For a heartbeat it seemed as if Adalhard would swoon like a blushing maiden. The rush of color to his cheeks bloomed more strongly against his flaxen hair.

"Come up here." Rufio patted the seat and moved aside to position Adalhard on his back, head propped up on the arm. "Undress me," he ordered Celsus, since Brunus was in no condition to help remove his tunic. All three boys murmured appreciation as for the first time they saw the lithe body fully revealed as Rufio planted his knees to straddle Adalhard. A practiced gymnast, he placed palms on the arm of the chaise and straightened himself so his torso made a line from neck to heels. Rufio lowered his head, crowned by its shining disarray of ruddy locks and matched by a flash of bright public hair surrounding his standing manhood, so he could look back down at the German, mouth agape in anticipation, trapped beneath him. Hovering inches above the parted lips, Rufio's big cock pointed at the target and glistened from the recent attentions of Celsus.

His arms, taking the full weight of his frame, bent slowly, lowing his torso until his partly retracted foreskin met Adalhard's lips, pushed broadly at the entrance, and then Rufio lowered himself fully. Celsus and Brunus both gasped in lusty admiration as all of Rufio's inches slid inexorably into Adalhard's head. The German boy gagged. Saliva welled up around the thick cock shafting his mouth and throat, but his own erection jerked in sympathetic enjoyment at the penetration. And then for almost five minutes, Rufio went into full-swing, military-style push-ups over Adalhard, building a frantic fucking pace. When it seemed the German slave must expire of the pummeling, Rufio let up. He shook his head and the coppery halo of hair swung around so he resembled a male lion preparing to pounce.

"Turn him over," he commanded Celsus. Brunus, his legs now more certain again, got up to help and between them they hauled Adalhard up and over onto all fours. "Get his asshole nice and wet."

Celsus looked puzzled for a moment, then spat on his fingers and wiped them in Adalhard's crease.

"Not like that! Get down in there with your tongue."

When the slave still hesitated as though uncertain as to what was meant, Rufio ducked in, buried his head in between the hard, rounded buns and lashed out with his tongue. The German gave a deep chesty groan and arched his head back.

Rufio sat back. "There. See? Don't they teach you anything in this great pile? Go on. Loosen him up ready for me. And you," he turned on Brunus. "Suck me. Get me hard again." He watched in satisfaction as Celsus got down behind Adalhard and started to rim him, tentatively at first, but with increasing enthusiasm when Adalhard wiggled his perky rear against the pressure of half-Egyptian, half-Greek tongue and teeth.

"All right. Enough!"

Celsus straightened up so Rufio could climb back on the chaise and offer the head of his cock to Adalhard's well-lubricated asshole. The German strained to look back over his shoulder, his expression eager enough to give a lie to his feigned innocence.

"Please, dominus, don't hurt me."

"I won't," Rufio grunted as he pressed down on the boy's back and hunched his pelvis forward so the full length of his cock slid easily into Adalhard. "Stroke him," he said to the others. Brunus took the command literally and reached under his fellow slave to grasp his cock, while Celsus leaned around Rufio to run his hands up and down the German's back, in and out between Rufio's hands where they bore down on Adelhard.

In between harsh breaths Rufio said, "Brunus, I need more spit, here."

The Helvetian broke off masturbating Adalhard and with eyes glazed over with craving he squeezed his head in between Rufio's stomach and upper part of Adalhard's buttocks. He wheezed in pleasure as he managed to reach with the tip of his tongue the pressure point where Rufio's cock penetrated Adalhard's sphincter ring. The sensation of tight asshole and rasping tongue slithering along the length of his shaft as he pulled back and then humped in again almost sent Rufio over the top, but manfully, he held out.

"Turn him over."

Brunus and Celsus obeyed instantly, Brunus rising up from his rim-suck, Celsus from his backstroking. They grabbed Adalhard, who looked as weak as a newborn puppy, and rolled him onto his back. Instinctively, without being asked, they each took hold of an ankle and spread Adalhard's legs wide and lifted them high. Hardly breaking his stride, Rufio slammed his cock back in the offered tunnel and caught his previous rhythm. He relieved Brunus and Celsus of Adalhard's legs and immediately their hands were all over fucker and fucked.

"Oh, oh, dominus… oh…" Adalhard's mouth gaped, lips a-flutter. "Oh," he went again and came spectacularly. In a trice, Celsus ducked under his legs and started slurping up the spurting cum. For his part, Rufio did not let up on his furious fuck, working at what a navy man taking his war galley into battle would call ramming

speed. Adalhard wheezed deeply, seemed on the point of choking but somehow dragged in a breath enough to give another feeble "Oh," and began coming again, all the while gazing adoringly into Rufio's eyes. "Oh, oh, Bacchus save me, I've come twice… almost the same… time. Oh, dominus…"

Celsus made a strangely strangled gulp and a jet of cum shot from the muzzle of his cock to splatter across the mess Adalhard had made of himself. Rufio hadn't even seen him touch himself to reach a climax. Poor Brunus was clearly in a bad way as well.

"Dominus, please? May I?"

Rufio watched as a desperate Brunus leaned in over Adelhard's head and offered his ruddy-colored cock. The German rolled his head sideways to take it, and with a long and deep groan, Brunus shot his second load.

With the audition slaves returned to their various duties, Acacus returned to the hall, drawn like a bluebottle to the odor of rotting meat. As he ducked his head inside he was immediately drawn in by the sounds coming from behind the drapes in the corner. There could be no mistaking the nature of the noises—rampant sex. He knew it. He knew the redheaded barbarian would sneak off with one of the boys for his own pleasure.

Acacus stole up to the drape and peered around its edge, confident that in the hall's dimness and in the midst of debauchery he would be unseen. No, not just a single boy. Three slaves. Four naked bodies inflamed by sex, abandoned in their enthusiasm. His groin flared up in agony as the licentious scene aroused him violently. His sudden agitation almost gave him away, but the sounds the four youngsters were making, the grunting of pigs at the trough, covered his own low moan. And then the Tullius boy, his hair the color of sin, pulled free from his embrace of the slave Acacus recognized as one of the Germans—in reality sons of barbarian kings held as hostages to their fathers' good behavior. As clearly as if he were an inch away,

Acacus watched the long pale rod of hard flesh come free of the German's flaunted bottom. Tullius took it in his own stroking hand and began to fire his seed in a copious fountain of white all over the German boy's prone form.

He managed somehow to stagger back from the awful sight, awful because… it so inflamed his passion and sent darts of savage pain into his groin. It took all his waning strength to move his rebelling legs and get him across the hall and away from the horror of his own drenching distress.

Domus Alba and the palace, same day

Ashur glanced sideways through narrowed Syrian eyes. His body slave was never entirely the demure, biddable servant when they were alone, and while it sometimes annoyed Quintus, he permitted a certain degree of insubordination. Today, Quintus knew, Ashur was displeased with him because of his master's distemper.

"Are you planning on writing this morning, dominus, or has the muse remained in bed?"

"I won't have your insolence this morning. Has my best toga come back from the fuller yet? And the woolen tunic my Uncle Livius presented me with last week. The one you stained."

Ashur straightened up from the task of folding clothes and placing them in the press, interleaved with freshly dried lavender. His eyes widened in shocked indignation. "Dominus! Please, Quintus, have you forgotten how you tipped over the infusion?"

"Oh, calm down. I know it was my fault."

"It has been returned to the laundry room, but I haven't yet checked it." He paused, taking a breath. "If you will permit… you seem very out of sorts."

Quintus was indeed out of sorts. And why not? Bullied by Livy. Ignored by his family who only wanted him married off in return for a fat dowry. On tenterhooks for his next imperial summons. Confabulated by that sexy bastard Rufio. He grabbed up a scroll from his small desk and rolled it down until he found what he was looking for. "I feel like Catullus, Ashur. Angry."

"Catullus?"

"An old poet. Two of his friends had done something to piss him off, and this is what he wrote. It's called 'A Rebuke: to Aurelius and Furius.' It sums it up perfectly:

'I'll fuck you and bugger you,
Aurelius the pathic, and sodomite Furius,
who thought you knew me from my verses,
since they're erotic, not modest enough.
It suits the poet himself to be dutifully chaste,
his verses not necessarily so at all:
which, in short then, have wit and good taste
even if they're erotic, not modest enough,
and as for that can incite to lust,
I don't speak to boys, but to hairy ones
who can't move their stiff loins.
You, who read all these thousand kisses,
you think I'm less of a man?
I'll fuck you, and I'll bugger you.'''

"Wow…" Ashur actually blushed.

"Well, that's how I feel." He thrust the scroll back among his papers. "Too annoyed at life to write anything worthwhile." He went and flung himself down on his bed and made no attempt to stop Ashur from joining him. One hand stroked and soothed his overheated brow, the other aroused him. Quintus sighed as the Syrian slave's warm mouth slipped over his stiffening cock.

Towering above the parapet of the terrace-garden, the extraordinary wood and iron construct resembled a huge exotic flower. Its wide base was formed from what appeared to the untutored eye to be an entwined jumble of massive timbers. Above, its waist narrowed and from this apparently too slender center, a complex of jointed limbs were suspended, so the top resembled nothing less than a forest of crabs' legs. Ropes running through a series of pulleys connected

186

different joints of each arm to a stout central timber, which stood a further ten feet above the machine.

Junilla had thought she understood the principles of Agapathus's mega-organ, but looking up from the roof of the libraries it all seemed a chaotic mess. She shielded her eyes against the spring glare. A fan of hawsers radiating from the topmost central pillar to lines of winches ranged in an arc behind the organ made the whole structure more resemble a sea vessel than a fairground attraction. Even the small army of men crawling precariously all over it added to the impression of some crazy ship attempting to get under way.

She was uncomfortably aware of Bardas standing at her side. The chamberlain didn't have to say anything, skepticism radiated from him as strongly as the stink rising from the fish market. His unspoken disapproval made her a little sharper with Flaccus than she intended. "Go fetch Agapathus."

"Yes, Lady." Flaccus gave her a mildly reproving look, but he knew better than to say anything.

"Agapathus. Explain to Lord Bardas how this thing will look *when* it's finally completed."

The Greek needed to lay his head back on his shoulders to stare aggressively up at his tall countryman. "It is on schedule," he snapped. He waved a hand behind him. "I haven't the time to explain anything, Madam. At the moment the organ music pipes are installed but the plumbers you sent me yesterday are at work welding the water dome. It's very large, larger than anything ever attempted before. And when all the timbers are painted, the whole will make sense." Agapathus stepped back a pace, the better to see into the chamberlain's eyes. He huffed in irritation. "I see you disbelieve me. Well don't. Agapathus of Achaea always delivers. You won't recognize this area when drapes hide the back workings, cut out the backdrop of the Circus, and wrap all the way around the open side and palace walls. When it's ablaze with cunningly placed lamps and Agapathus of Achaea's Hecatoncheires is awhirl, it will be the music of the spheres, a Pythagorean perfection: Aegaeon will power the music; Gyes will give the Narcissi wings to fly above the astonished spectators' heads, and Cottus will amaze them with fiery displays—"

Bardas sniffed and spoke finally. "I really have no idea what the man is on about, Lady Junilla. But as long as you know what you are doing…"

She didn't like the way he made it a question, and was about to remonstrate when Flaccus fell to his knees. Beside her, Bardas bowed. She turned to see Trajan approaching with Hadrian and several other regally attired men. Junilla dropped to one knee in a curtsy, but in her often-difficult dealings with important men who either wanted to beat down her price for some antique or the cost of a party, she had learned to never be cowed. She knew she should cast her eyes to the ground, but habit was too strong. As the Emperor drew close she met his eyes and saw in them mild amusement at her effrontery. Well, maybe the Empress Plotina behaved as a virtuous Roman woman was supposed to, but not Junilla Rufia.

"Please, arise everyone."

Trajan's voice was quiet but authoritative, a pleasant baritone, and to Junilla's ears it burred with a faint Iberian accent, which made its tenor much less nasal than the typical Roman patrician's.

"We were interested to discover quite what amazements are being enacted out here. Hadrian because he fancies himself a fine architect, Apollodorus because he is a fine architect and ever curious. Is it not so?"

"It is, Caesar. And I wished to find out to what use my country man Agapathus has put all the workers I have loaned him for this…" Apollodorus raised his neatly bearded head to take in the Hecatoncheires water organ, "strange contraption. I declare, Caesar, you could bridge the mighty Danube with such a device!"

The courtiers all laughed politely, though Junilla noted Hadrian remained unmoved. She suspected Trajan's jibe at his architectural pretensions hadn't pleased him.

"Then I shall leave you architects to talk among yourselves," he said, indicating Hadrian as well as Agapathus and Apollodorus. "I wish investigate this wondrous machine with Lady Rufia. I shan't need anyone," he added to the courtiers. "You didn't make the full *adoratio* due the Emperor, Lady Rufia."

She glanced from the corner of here eye, suddenly shy, but saw Caesar still smiled. "I'm abject, my lord."

"I think not, Lady Rufia."

"For a start, Caesar, I'm not a lady, never have been. So I'd be far more at ease if you called me, as all do, plain Junilla." They were strolling toward the parapet of the gallery, around one side of the building site and she was aware of the shadows matching their pace at a discreet twenty-odd yards. Two Praetorians. The Emperor's bodyguard. She was equally aware that he hadn't answered, and she feared she had overstepped the mark.

He paused and turned toward her, the smile playing at the ends of his lips. "Do you actually know how this thing will work?"

"I do. At least, I know what Agapathus has told me."

Trajan took the few remaining paces to the parapet and placed his hands on the rough stone capping. He stared down into the Circus, gleaming brightly in the sunshine. "When Bardas informed me he had appointed the best party planner in Rome to organize the week's events for our esteemed guest from the Orient, I assumed it would be a man."

"You think a man would be better at the job."

Trajan sketched a step back as if shocked at Junilla's sharp tone, but she detected an interest.

"I'm sorry, Lord. I should not be so forward."

"Hah! I'm not used to it, that's true. Not in recent times at any rate. Even the senior centurion in my legion bit his tongue rather than suggest I might be wrong in something, even when I may have been. I've had the sharp edge of my mother's tongue, though that was some years ago, and Pompeia Plotina can get snappy. But

I confess I take little note of feminine distemper. You, Junilla, are different—"

"You are saying I am not a woman?"

Trajan laughed. Faces from all over the terrace looked up in curiosity.

Junilla saw the reaction, and smiled. "They seem surprised, your followers. Do you never laugh?"

"I am Caesar. I am not permitted humor. Oh, but I do... in private." He leaned in close even though no one was near enough to overhear. "The Emperor isn't supposed to have fun or even be amused. My exalted position is one of great seriousness. If it ever got out that Caesar found something funny, the Imperium would begin to crumble." He leaned back against the parapet and looked thoughtfully out over the expanse of the Circus Maximus. "Tell me, Junilla, you do not find it against your... your moral judgment to hire young men for the purposes of entertaining other men in, shall we say, compromising ways? I can't for the life of me imagine the Empress doing such a thing for the benefit of her husband."

"I assure you, Lord, I have no such scruples. As a party planner it isn't my place to pass judgment on the peccadillos of my customers. Besides, the idea of men finding other men attractive does not bother me. My eldest son is of that persuasion, and it's his life, so I let him get on with what he enjoys. In fact I've come to rely on his instincts to secure the most suitable young men for every occasion."

"Then *I* pass judgment on you, that you are a most remarkable woman. To be so open. I hope your son knows how lucky he is."

She laughed brightly. "Oh, don't worry. I tell him that every morning before he begins work for the day."

He sighed. "It's a lonely task the gods have given me. As a young man I thought the concept of making dead emperors into gods was blasphemous. Now I'm beginning to understand why after a few years wearing the purple they might think they deserved to become a god."

"I didn't figure you for a whinger. My Lord," she added for good measure. "You were brought in by that Nerva—and he was a good egg all right. But look, you defeated the Dacians, brought home untold wealth, and now you're sharing it out by giving us all these new civic buildings. If I were you, I'd rest on my laurels for that. Now I'll make sure you give your Oriental friend, whatever his name is, a fine time."

"I must tell you—and keep it to yourself—but Obodas is *not* my friend. It's politic at the moment to keep him happy. And I like your summary of my life and achievements to date. However, it lacks something in the detail. I believe I did a little more than that before 'good egg' Nerva adopted me. To be honest—it's odd but I feel I can be open with you, Junilla—to be frank, I prefer the military life to the trappings of imperial power and the never-ending palace politics. Out in the field I was free to... well, take whoever I felt like into my bed."

"And you can't here?" Junilla sounded so indignantly surprised that Trajan gave a rueful laugh, which raised startled heads over the way again.

"I can do as I please. I am after all Caesar, but I am always aware of the account that everyone keeps of my actions. With all the power at my fingertips, I'm free to do what I like and completely chained by the responsibility of the office."

It was extraordinary. Never before had he opened up so easily to a woman. They had their attractions—at least they did to most men— but even toward his wife, the Empress Plotina, he kept a guarded attitude when it came to personal discussions. If a man had to have some secrets, how much more did a Caesar need to keep the dice closed in his fist? This Junilla Rufia had all the charm of her sex, but came with a heavy charge of down-to-earthness that made it feel like he was talking to another man. And yet he would not, could not talk as he had, so openly, with another man.

A sudden flurry of hobnailed boots and general unrest alerted him. He and Junilla turned to see what was causing the commotion, to see the two Praetorian Guards holding a struggling youth with a head of startlingly golden-red hair. Trajan looked from the boy to Junilla and saw the likeness in their faces and the unmissable similarity of hair coloring.

"My son, Tullius Rufio," Junilla said.

Four more soldiers had emerged from the shadows of the palace and were advancing at a pace toward the two men who held the boy.

"Let him go! He may come forward."

Trajan watched with growing interest as... "Which name does he prefer to use?"

"Rufio, Caesar."

Trajan felt his face crack into another smile. He hadn't smiled so much in front of his companions for an age. "That is suitable, since he shares with you a head of a lustrous hue." He watched Rufio approach with a great deal more deference than his mother had showed, but yet with an air of self-assuredness so usually lacking in young men of his tender years. It didn't escape Trajan's experienced eye for a second that Rufio possessed great beauty, especially in such bright blue eyes. He sank to one knee before Trajan and brushed full lips lightly across the imperial ring on the hand Trajan extended. As he raised him up, the boy's gaze met his own, and a thrill ran through Trajan. The boy liked sex with men. From the corner of his eye he could see Junilla's expression of hopeful query. She didn't mind the notion that he might find her offspring sexually attractive? But her words were more ambiguous.

"You looked flushed, my pet. How did the audition go?"

Trajan turned to her. "Audition?"

"I charged Rufio with making a selection from among your household slaves, Sire. For the *intimate* entertainment to follow the night after the opening banquet? And it seems to me," she said in a harsher tone to her son, "that you have sampled some of the goods."

It amused Trajan that the boy showed no sense of shame. Instead he gave his mother a dazzling smile. "You always say how important it is to ensure the quality of the entertainment you are putting on." He turned to Trajan. "Especially when it is for a guest of Caesar." And the boy dipped his head in a bow, but all the while kept his gaze fixed on Trajan, a little sly smile playing at the corner of his lips.

By the beringed fingers of Jupiter, how I would like to ride this one in harness with Quintus, two fine stallions pulling my biga *chariot.*

Trajan took a deep breath. Thinking of Quintus Caecilius Alba reminded him that the lad had never answered the summons he'd issued through that fat turd Livius Dio.

"Oh, Sire…"

Bardas's secretary, Acacus sidled up anxiously, throwing out dagger looks at Rufio. Interesting. The boy was not in awe of

Acacus, as he should be of a senior member of the civil service. He was giving equally unfriendly looks back.

"Caesar, I was supposed to be looking after Master Tullius here, but I lost track of him."

"Well you have found me now, *Master* Secretary."

"Bardas has charged me with being at his side at all times, no matter—"

Trajan raised a hand. "Nonsense. There's no need for that. I shall speak to Bardas about it. Tullius Rufio has a security token, as does his mother and their immediate workforce, so there is no need for a chaperone. He may have a free run of those areas of the palace allocated to the entertainment of our honored guest Obodas, and you are free to return to your duties, Acacus. On second thoughts, remain with me for a while. I have something to ask of you."

He turned his back on the secretary and inclined his head at Junilla. "I must also return to my tasks. It has been a pleasure speaking with you and I promise we will have converse again. I shall look for you. Lady Rufia, Tullius Rufio, I bid you good day."

Their genuflections were considerably more correct than the ones given in greeting. As he crossed the expanse of the terrace, making a detour around the amazing construction at its center and the decorators who were beginning to paint the timbers a variety of colors, the secretary kept pace. "Acacus, I would like to know what happened to the boy Quintus yesterday. Did Bardas not tell you to meet him and bring him to me?"

"Yes, Sire. And I waited for him, but… he never turned up."

"He ignored the summons! Arrange another meeting tonight. And make sure the brat complies."

N·I·N·E·T·E·E·N | XIX

Domus Alba and the Palatine, evening the same day

Silence reigned. Lucius Primus had returned to his legion and Livius Secundus was absent, somewhere in the country chasing down some agrarian business, Quintus hadn't paid attention when it was decided over a meal that he should undertake whatever task it was. His leave over, Marcus had also returned to his naval duties at Misenum. Fabia, Julia, and his mother were visiting a relative—again, Quintus had no real idea who or why. He was far too wrapped up in his own problems to be bothered about the rest of his family. His father was ensconced in the *tablinum* with Pallas, and if they were true to form they would remain in there until the light failed. Even the household slaves were off relaxing somewhere well out of sight in case someone should give them something to do. Quintus didn't mind. He enjoyed the peace and quiet.

"Where in the name of Poseidon's plunging prick is he?"

Oh no! Only Uncle Livy can muddle up Greek and Roman gods. Quintus was sure his breathing wouldn't restart. A great thumping of outdoor shoes on the fine floor tiles announced Livy's arrival in the opening. Quintus wished he'd closed it, barred it, and chained it.

Hands braced on both sides, Livy's bulk filled the opening like a fleshy door. "Where in the cunny of Venus are all your slaves?"

Quintus got wearily to his feet and let the book he'd been reading roll up with a distinct *thwap* sound as it dropped to the desktop. "Uncle—"

"Don't 'Uncle' me, you pathetic little shit," Livy thundered. "What the f— Ugh! Do you know where I have been?"

There was clearly no need to ask. Quintus ground his teeth.

Livy came into the room, his seething anger seeming to fill it. "I have just come from the palace. I went there to present the imperial warrant for Caesar's authorization. But Caesar, I am informed, is in no mood to sign his warrant. This is the paper, you will recall, that will transform all our fortunes. But Diocles, who is the chief of the exchequer, made me wait for over an hour until the chamberlain's under-secretary, that slimy Acacus, came to tell me that Trajan is not yet inclined to sign his papers for me because you failed to appear when you were summoned yesterday."

"But I did!"

"Don't lie." Livy smashed a meaty fist down on the desk and made the scrolls jumbled there jostle.

"I'm not, Uncle. I even waited for an age only to be told by—well, it was Acacus who came to tell me that Caesar was busy with other tasks and could not see me."

His words did nothing to placate Livy. "This is so embarrassing for me. And potentially ruinous."

Quintus tuned the rant out. How could Acacus tell Livy that he had never turned up when the Greek had spoken to him? Light from the atrium dimmed as a figure came to the doorway. Quintus looked up to see his father's secretary wringing his hands in anxiety.

"What is it, Pallas?"

"A message, dominus. Er, for Livius."

Livy rounded on the man. "What?"

Pallas sniffed apologetically and lowered his voice. Quintus strained to hear, but the bulk of his uncle effectively cut out the whispered message. And then Livy whirled around and fixed Quintus with a wide-eyed glare.

"An imperial messenger brings a summons. A litter will be here in a short time, and this time, boy, you'd better be ready, bathed and perfumed. No worming out of it tonight. Caesar is having an intimate gathering, and you are to be the dessert."

* * *

Indistinct patches of light flickered between silhouetted bushes in the distance. A distinctly frazzled and irritable Acacus had met him in the vestibule. The Emperor's unexpected invitation to join an intimate gathering was an unsettling surprise. A kid from the bad end of the Aventine didn't get such calls every day, but he noticed his mother's calm sense of satisfaction, as if she expected such an astonishing thing. It was surely one matter to be allowed access to some parts of the palace in pursuit of fulfilling a contractual obligation, and accidentally meeting Trajan, and quite another to be invited as a guest.

Acacus appeared to be quite out of sorts. An irritable grunt of greeting was all Rufio received before the secretary strode at speed through hallways, crossed open spaces and then dived down one of the large multi-floor staircases Rufio thought he recognized from the initial reconnoiter he'd made with his mother and Bardas. Down and down they went to emerge through a grand double doorway into the sunken hippodrome garden. He followed Acacus along the nearside colonnade toward the end adjoining the palace's finest bathhouse. There, in the shelter of the towering façade, servants had planted a shrubbery of small trees and bushes in huge pots, amid which oil lamps and blazing braziers provided light and warmth against the chill of the spring evening. Guests milled about, greeting friends, or holding discussions in small groups while being served drinks and savory and sweet pastries by good-looking slaves. Several that he remembered from the audition gave Rufio a second look of recognition, and then blushed becomingly. Acacus scowled at one who had the temerity to address Rufio in a familiar manner before a word was addressed to the boy.

"I'll leave you here, Tullius. I'm sure you will find someone to talk to," he spat out.

"And thank you, Acacus, for your usual solicitousness." He watched with a sour expression as the secretary strode off in a flurry of dark robes.

"Dominus."

Rufio turned back to find Adalhard beaming at him. "Hello, you're on duty here tonight?"

"Oh no, dominus. I am not serving. Great Caesar asked for one who knows your face to watch out for you, and I volunteered. Willingly." The boy's features creased into a bright smile, but he looked away shyly. "I am to bring you to Caesar, dominus." Adalhard stepped nimbly in a weaving path between a brazier, several bushes, and a knot of courtiers, and led Rufio to a quieter spot just under the peristyle arcade fronting the baths and shielded from the rest of the gathering by miniature cypresses. The slave boy bowed low and then stepped aside to let Rufio pass.

Seated on a marble bench, caught in the flickering light of a sputtering torch fastened to a tall spike set in the turf, Trajan treated Rufio to a warm smile. As he recovered from his *proskynesis* ("You make sure you bow down properly this time, my pet," Junilla had ordered) the smile on Rufio's lips froze as he recognized the figure seated beside the Emperor.

"Come, my dear Tullius Rufio, come and sit on my other side here."

As Rufio obeyed, Quintus gave him a dark, baleful glower from a head held high. He was struck again by Quintus's refined good looks, but he wrinkled his nose in response, a gesture not missed by Trajan.

"Oh ho, do I sense you two young men know each other?"

"Not precisely, Caesar," Quintus said quickly before Rufio could open his mouth.

Rufio sniffed.

Trajan's amusement lit up his features. "That, dear Quintus, is an answer of passing strangeness." He looked at one, then the other, smiling.

"We have… er, bumped into each other a few times, Caesar," Rufio said, with a narrowed eye aimed at Quintus.

"Well, well…" Trajan leaned back and stretched arms around both their shoulders, pulling them slightly together in his grasp so they were forced to look at each other across his broad chest. "Bumped into each other. How exciting! I feel sparks building. I'm sure you know that a charioteer much prefers two stallions ready to fight each other, the better to break their spirits to his hand when it comes to the telling moment, because then his steeds can think of nothing more than the one beating the other to the finish line."

Rufio saw Quintus swallow nervously. And the symbolism wasn't lost on him either. He was sure the novice seated on the other side of Trajan was still a virgin, but then so was he when it came to taking it up his ass. He got the distinct impression that before this night ended he might be finding out what it was like to be mounted rather than being the rider.

For some further minutes Rufio and Quintus remained silent as Trajan regaled them with some of his war exploits and asked after their relatives' military careers. To Rufio's annoyance, Quintus waxed knowledgeably about his older brother's army service, to which he could only nod at appropriate moments to please Trajan (not the stuffed toga on the other side) and make monosyllabic responses. Contrary to his assertion that he was not a servant tonight, it was Adalhard who plied them with wine and nibbles, until such time as Trajan made to stand.

"Come, my bold steeds. Trot with me awhile." He slipped a hand around both their waists as if he was determined to keep them apart until such time as it pleased him to do otherwise. Rufio was in no doubt that they were all headed to bed. Trajan guided them away from the conviviality of the party and through a small doorway in the palace side of the sunken garden's long arcade.

As they walked along corridors, Trajan chided Quintus. "You never showed up the other day, as your Uncle Livius had promised me you would."

Quintus paled and spluttered his explanation. "Oh, but Caesar, I did. My uncle informed me of the time I should be here, and I was. Chamberlain Bardas brought me in, but his secretary came to say you were delayed and I should wait. But after I waited a while, the secretary came to me—"

"Which secretary? Acacus?"

"Yes, Caesar. And he told me to go away because you were too busy to see me and I should wait for a summons on another day."

"Why would Acacus say such a thing? It is true I was busy—there is never a time when I am not—but I had made time to see you, Quintus. Why would he make such a mistake?"

Rufio felt compelled to come to Quintus's defense. "I don't know why he would say such a thing, Caesar, but what Quintus says is true. I passed by with my mother and saw there where he'd been told to wait."

"It is odd behavior in Acacus."

"Bardas would know I'm telling the truth, Caesar."

"Then I must question him on the matter. But you are here now, my dear Quintus." He squeezed more tightly as they rounded a corner and passed through large double doors opened for them by two Praetorian Guards. "And so are you, my wild-haired Rufio."

It was all very well for the guttersnipe, Quintus thought, hovering between shaky nerves and bitterness, or perhaps more accurately if he were honest, envy at the street boy's obvious familiarity with sex. Rufio appeared perfectly calm as they crossed the expanse of rutting gladiators embedded in the floor mosaic toward a dauntingly huge bed. To Quintus, it looked as large as an arena and as ready for combat to commence. He hoped blood would not be spilled as they said occurred with women on first penetration. He was perfectly sure he could never manage even a semi-erection— if that was even required of his role in what was to come—let alone a full hard-on.

Trajan was clearly a very experienced seducer. Perhaps he sensed Quintus's agitation because instead of some cold disrobing, which would have only fired embarrassment and failure, he bundled them all up so they collapsed as a single bundle of entangled limbs on the bed. Caesar's easy laugh signaled that it was to be fun. In a few heartbeats—slowing, thankfully—Quintus was giggling and squirming, trying to get away from the unmerciful tickling of his ribs, his tummy, and... well, lower down. In spite of his earlier feelings, his cock stirred excitedly.

He wasn't even really aware that he was naked, so subtly had Trajan removed his toga and under garments. And then it was the turn of Rufio, and Quintus found himself staring in fascination at the boy's big cock. The one he'd seen swinging limp but heavily in the Forum that fateful day of the Lupercalia. The cock he'd seen in his fantasies ever since. He'd never before done what Ashur sometimes did for him, but now he hoped he would get to take Rufio in his mouth and suck that cock.

Trajan took off his own clothes and then rolled Quintus up against Rufio and knelt over them. His eyes roved over their bodies and his smiles lessened the satyr-like quality of his features. He fondled them both, paying attention to the nipples, tweaking, twisting, squeezing until Quintus's eyes filled. Rufio, though, seemed to enjoy the rough handling, and his cock rocked from side to side as he wagged his butt around on the bed covers. Trajan was attentive with his busy hands, one for each of them. He stroked breasts, lower ribcages, explored ridged abdomens, played moistened fingers into their navels. Then he lowered his head to take turns dipping his tongue first into Rufio's and then Quintus's belly button, while starting to lightly fondle their full-grown erections, and tickling under the balls. Quintus found himself hoping that Rufio would not think him inadequate far more than he feared the same of his Emperor. Now why was that? It had become important not to be outdone by the flameheaded twit. He was sure he could defeat Rufio in swordplay of the steel kind. Now he wanted to make sure he competed equally in the fleshy sort of sword fighting.

Gorgeous. Simply gorgeous, and the stupid twerp doesn't even know how Jupiter-be-damned handsome he is. No wonder Trajan fell for him. Gods, but I want to fuck that sweet ass. I wonder if he'll ever give in enough to let me?

Meanwhile, Rufio knew he was going to have to cope with having his own sweet ass penetrated, and his asshole clenched up nervously at the very thought. He'd seen Quintus suffering the whirly-willies, poor little virgin, but his own insides were all a-squirm as well.

Trajan cleared his throat in a commanding manner and bade them both to kneel up in front of him. Part one of foreplay was concluded. "Quintus, I want you to prepare Rufio. He is quite impressively endowed, would you say?"

Quintus pursed his lips and nodded.

"Suck it, please."

The boy's lovely dark eyes widened to show a rim of white all around the pupils. By the expression, Rufio expected embarrassed Quintus to launch into denial, to refuse in disgust, or appeal to be let off, so he was astonished when without further demur Quintus shuffled over the bed covering and dipped his head down so his smooth-shaven pointy chin struck Rufio's thighs and his warm mouth closed over the partly revealed crown of his cock. Oh bliss! Yes, he had imagined this, but never thought to enjoy it outside of a nighttime fantasy. He felt Trajan's strong arms encircle his waist and grip him tightly. He sank back in the embrace and reached out a hand to rake fingers through Quintus's close-knit cap of hair.

Long before Quintus worked up sufficient courage to take a few more inches of Rufio's pulsing shaft into his mouth, Trajan spoke. "Time to switch places," the voice breathed in his ear. "You do perform fellatio, Rufio?"

Trajan's use of the proper word aroused Rufio. It possessed such a wonderfully rounded, warm, slithery sound... fulfilling fellatio. Quintus straightened up on his knees, breathing heavily, his lips glistening with a coating of his own saliva. There was a strange look in his eyes—exultation? Rufio didn't need to be told Quintus had started to enjoy sucking him because his slightly upward curved shaft stuck up proudly and bobbed as he sat back on his lean haunches. As he did so, Rufio exchanged places, bending forward to lower his head into the lap of a boy who confused him with his stuck-up, snotty-nosed attitude, but who clearly found Rufio attractive in some kind of way. But for now, it was simple: part lips, extend tongue, lick around the foreskin to loosen it and then take the unfurling sheath between his lips.

This was nothing like Ashur. Not that the Syrian had ever failed to delight Quintus with his labial ministrations, no, this was because it was Rufio. There was a feeling of profound accomplishment in having his tormentor fellating him, and doing so with evident enthusiasm. He thought his enjoyment of it should shame him, but the reality was different. He relished the wicked freedom embracing the act gave him. There came an errant image of his brothers watching him. *Hah! If only they could see me now...* He desired to see the length of his cock disappearing into Rufio's generous mouth, but at this angle he was denied the sight by the flaming glory of the bobbing head. The feeling of all that curly hair tickling his upper thighs drove Quintus wild.

At one point he raised his eyes above Rufio's jouncing head and found Trajan staring back at him. The Emperor's features were set in an expression of lust. Quintus lowered his gaze along the up-down sway of Rufio's spine, along to the widening valley of his bottom, to the very solid imperial erection lying comfortably in that fleshy valley. He heard Trajan say, "Turn him around, Rufio. I think you know what I want you to do to him next."

The lovely sensation of Rufio's warm-wet mouth ceased as he relinquished Quintus's cock. Trajan's command meant nothing, but he aided Rufio in turning himself around and allowed himself to be guided into a position on all fours. There was a faint snuffling sound behind him. Hands planted on his ass cheeks pulled them apart, and then he felt Rufio push into his bottom with his face. It was unbelievable, the sensation as the sloppy wet tongue began probing into his asshole. Trajan did it to him that first aborted time, but nothing like this. Quintus snorted in surprise and bore back against the delicious excitement of it. He started to moan as Rufio increased both the pressure he was applying back there and the speed of tonguing.

"I think that will do, Rufio," Trajan's husky voice reached Quintus. The hands were removed. Another pair took their place, and then he felt some large object push up against that sensitive spot Rufio had so inflamed. For a moment all was confusion. He wasn't at all sure what was happening, but something eased into him. It felt wrong. It felt like the last time, the time when Caesar tried to enter him and everything fell apart with the murder of Cornelius. Only this time there was no disturbance, other than his surprised gasp of pain. He felt himself being filled, impossibly. What was happening could not go on, surely. It could not possibly all fit in.

"Woah, there, my sweet. Relax all your muscles," he heard Trajan breathe.

A hand stroked his sweaty brow. Rufio, strangely tender.

"There, there, you're taking it all. Relax, Quintus, and I will take you to the Empyrean heights."

Suddenly, the discomfort eased, and while it didn't feel even remotely normal, there was a pleasing heat beginning to rise in his gut. He wouldn't have thought it possible that what was happening to him would have an effect on his cock, which had risen again after the initial shock of being penetrated and now begged for attention. Trajan sensed and ordered Rufio to take care of it. He flopped over on his back and wiggled underneath Quintus's stomach, took hold of his cock and slipped it into his mouth. Quintus gasped and started to come, horrified at the thought of shooting his load into Rufio's mouth, but the sucker didn't seem to object. He gurgled happily away down there and politely waited for Quintus to finish before wriggling back out, a slant-eyed grin on his face.

"Come over here," Trajan barked out urgently.

Quintus groaned as the Emperor pulled out his solid member. He felt a sudden cold, a withdrawal, and realized he'd been enjoying it.

"You are a sweet lad to bugger, Quintus, but I need to sample Rufio for a bit. Kneel!"

Quintus, now released from duty, recovered by watching with interest his redheaded nemesis taking it up the ass. And to his surprise—and, be honest, to cruel amusement—he realized the street-wise guttersnipe, know-it-all, sex-crazed bastard was no more familiar with a cock stuck into his ass as was Quintus. There was a degree of malicious satisfaction to see the look of wide-eyed shock as Trajan slipped forcibly into what must have been as tight a passage as the one he'd just vacated.

"I think it only fair you return to Rufio the compliment he paid you."

Quintus started.

"Get to it, boy!"

At Caesar's command… Quintus rolled over and copied Rufio in wriggling underneath. There was less space than he'd thought under Rufio's abdominal muscle packed stomach, and his large cock, still hard as rock in spite of the vigorous hammering he was receiving from Trajan, bashed him in the eye. He struggled to get a hand under there with him to hold the damned thing steady enough to force it between his lips. Immediately his mouth filled with the taste of rampant sex. Rufio was drooling lube and far from revolting Quintus as he thought it surely must, it drove him into a frenzy of sex-driven lust.

Rufio hung on a lot longer than Quintus had done, so he sucked the throbbing shaft for some minutes before, with a huge, guttural groan, the cock between his lips jerked and began to release a flood of creamy sperm. So this was how it felt for Ashur when he did it for Quintus. Again, the shame a rational part of his mind knew he

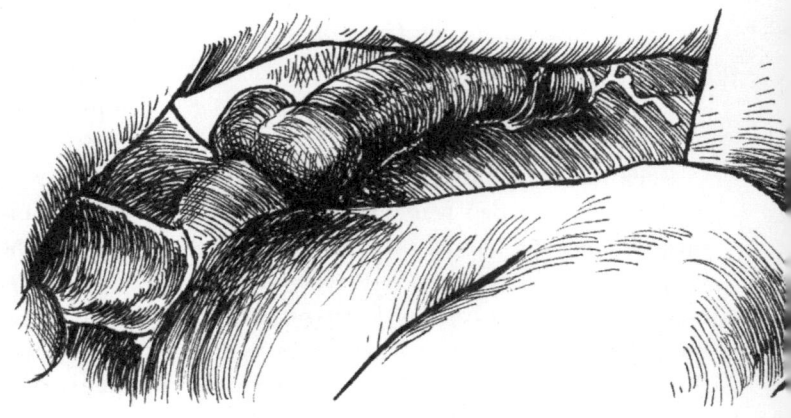

must experience was overwhelmed by the fact of the situation, or the almost religious fervor that engulfed every sinew in his young body. His mind screamed a continual mantra: I've sucked off a man; I've sucked off a man; I've sucked…

He squeaked faintly at the rough grasp of hands. And Rufio helped as Trajan threw Quintus down on the bed, arms and legs akimbo, on his back. The Emperor slipped between his splayed legs and with a practiced ease rammed his dripping cock back into Quintus.

Huh," Rufio murmured in a voice choked with lust, "That's a right royal buggering, that is."

Through glazed eyes and a haze of such extreme pleasure he had no idea from whence it emanated, he heard Trajan shout, "Take it, boy!" The first spurt felt like flood water breaching a dam. And then a torrent of imperial cum filled him.

T·W·E·N·T·Y | XX

The palace, later the same evening

Flaming anger has a name. He is the locus of all pain, the writhing agony that never lets up. To see Rufio buggering the German pig! Witnessing this act unleashed the excruciating pain of impossible orgasm. Rufio, seduced by fake innocence and hair as pure as the driven snow—even now in the dim passages it glows like a beacon in the night—the open, blue eyes, all speaking of a virtuous nature, but all profane! The creature Adalhard harbors a viper in his corrupt bosom.

When ice meets fire, fire wins. Rufio! What have you done to my poor beating heart? O heartless flame in my endless night. You torture me with your casual promiscuity and drive my impossible need for a release denied me the day the cruel blade took my manhood at the command of Obodas. Had it all been taken, it would have been better. But to leave me with the means of erection but not that of sexual climax, this was a cruelty beyond imagining. El-Gabal, made me to adore the golden-haired Celtic god-boy, and made him to torment my living soul because of Obodas and his depraved desire to keep boys forever young for his own disgusting passions. My god El-Gabal has abandoned me. He has blinded my Rufio from seeing adoration in my eyes whenever I look at him. Even on that first day by the cistern, with his mother, I adored him, but El-Gabal has forsaken me. The dirty forest gods of the Germans sent Adalhard to steal away the heart of my Rufio. Now El-Gabal demands sacrifice to restore Rufio to my heart. The German must die. By his sacrifice—and it must be a savage death, my god demands it—El-Gabal will see my plight and take pity, which is more than the mercy I will show this little German pig.

He doesn't hear me. I am right behind. The blade that has tasted blood already... I raise it. Gods alive! The brat is rubbing his bottom like some cheap whore. How dare he defile Rufio with his filthy sluttish acts?

A sly shuffling behind him in the narrow passageway was the first Adalhard knew of his impending doom. He was in something of a daze after seeing Rufio at Caesar's little impromptu party. He rubbed his bottom, happy that it still smarted from the comprehensive fucking Rufio had given him earlier. As he recalled the powerful ramrod that breached his defenses, he thought he heard rats running within the walls of this older section of the Domus Augustana. It was by sheer chance that he saw a shadow fall on the wall beside him, cast from a distant sconce. Instinct cut in and he flinched.

The screech of a blade scraping down the wall filled the confines and blended with the shriek of animal rage that was unrecognizable as a human voice. For a terrifying moment, Adalhard knew this was a demon of Nerthus come to take him to the sacrificial altar, a punishment for his dalliance with a Celt. But the indistinct whirl of dark robes settled into human form as the man hidden within the covering hood recovered from the missed attack.

The next sounds confirmed his assailant's mortality.

"Die, you befouler of decency!"

The long dagger flashed dimly in the distant light and adrenaline took over. To an onlooker, Adalhard might seem a slightly built lad, but this son of a warrior chieftain knew how to look after himself. His foe mistook his slenderness for weakness. Adalhard sidestepped the savage thrust to his chest. He ducked under the blade so it whickered over his left ear. In a flash he came up under the still swinging arm and put all his youthful force behind his right fist.

The blow landed just under his attacker's sternum and air whooshed explosively from the man's mouth. Adalhard didn't wait. He kicked out and stamped down on the undefended thigh and then followed through with a strong left to the assassin's jaw. The hood flew back and Adalhard gasped in horror.

He knew the face!

Before he could recover from the shock of recognition and prepare to continue to fight for his life, the clerical figure staggered back, struggling for breath, and spat a curse. "You will die! On the day Obodas falls to my vengeance, so will you, and all who have turned their hand against me!"

And then he turned and fled down the passageway. Adalhard didn't know whether to follow or flee. He had punched out a high up in the civil bureau. The punishment for such a transgression by a hostage-slave was death. But to where would he flee? His breathing steadied. The man attacked him without provocation. Surely he could mount a defense against that?

He ran lightly to the far corner around which his attacker had disappeared seconds before. Another long passage stretched away into the distance. It was slightly better lit, but of his attacker there was no sign.

"He can't have gone far in so short a time," Adalhard muttered aloud. He trotted on until he emerged into one of the transverse hallways, thronged with courtiers leaving the sunken garden. He looked back at the way he had come. His enemy had simply vanished into thin air. He shuddered. It must have been magic. Or perhaps a figment of an imagination overwrought by a day filled with little but Tullius Rufio and an almost crazed desire to sit on his hard sword of pleasure. There was another solution. His assailant must know of a secret passage. Popular rumor said there were many such in the thickness of the walls.

Now he knew who the man was, that surely placed him in deadly danger. He needed help.

Predawn chill air had brought down a fine mist, which softened the outlines of the Area Palatina. The fine droplets swirled around their feet as Quintus and Rufio emerged from the palace portico. At this time of night, the great ramp and lower Forum vestibule were closed, and an exit had to be made down *Clivus Victoriae*, past the Praetorians' upper-level palace guardhouse, which ironically the Guards didn't guard. That boring, lowly task was given over to men of the Vigiles.

"You're very quiet." Rufio glanced at Quintus, in his fine toga restored to his patrician status.

"Nothing to say."

The haughty tone was back. It might have made Rufio smile to himself if it didn't piss him off. No one would know from the stiff-backed stance that only a short while before this prick of a knobbish noble youth had been cavorting stark naked in his presence. More than that, waving a damned great hard-on around.

Quintus bid him a brusque adieu and climbed inside the litter awaiting him. With synchronous grunts of effort and exhaled breaths making long plumes in the cold air, the bearers set off. Rufio started to make his way home on foot, following the route the litter was taking. They both had to reach the foot of the Palatine adjacent to the beef market, and then after crossing that open space, dip into the warren at the base of the Aventine. At that juncture, Quintus's litter would carry him safely away along the northern scarp to nobland, where he would be in bed long before Rufio on shank's pony climbed the northwestern face of the big hill to the Tullius Emporium of Artistic Excellence, and his own modest truckle bed.

The litter was still in sight a long way ahead when Rufio reached Via Murcia and turned toward the river. Before the narrow way opened up into the beef market a small district of tenements and narrow lanes huddled like a dirty skirt behind the buildings that fronted the Circus Maximus starting gates. As he made his way through dark and lighted patches of the mercifully silent streets—it was too late, or too early, for the army of footpads that made Rome so dangerous to be out in alone at night—he noticed someone lurking in the semi-shadow beside a closed cookshop. His libido instantly kicked in. It was a sexy figure of a young man wearing a short cloak with a hood pulled over his head. He leaned casually against the wall, groping himself suggestively in the universal gesture of I'm gagging for it.

Rufio halted in mid-stride and stared hard at the mysterious figure. The gesture tugged at his loins, in spite of a thorough workout in the morning with the slaves (*mmm, that cute German boy, Adalhard*) and more recently with none other than the world's most powerful man, virtually sex with a god. *And Quintus, of course, spiteful little shit.* Then the young man—Rufio was sure by his stance and the body language that he was young—gave him a come-on shrug of the shoulder and started to sashay down the street ahead of him. Rufio's animal instincts took over from his sound common sense and he started to follow.

Now it is all clear. The pains in my leg, in my face, the grinding hurt of my ribs, this is epiphany! But I will have vengeance. The German cunny will die at a time of my choosing, but now is the moment Rufio will face his Great Adversary. Striking at the German pig has made everything clear. Rufio never felt a thing for me. The looks, the exchanges were not ones of demur virtue. They were of contempt! He sent Adalhard to punish me. But now? Look now, how he follows me like a dog sniffing after a bitch on heat. Except this bitch has bigger teeth, a sharper jaw, and a curse on its head placed there by Obodas that can only be averted first by Rufio's death. Why didn't I see this before? Adalhard. It was he. Sent to torment me with his pert bottom, wiggling seductively. And I see the same in Rufio.

He wants me! He wants to lift my tunic, fondle my bare ass, and then penetrate me. He's no different to the Romans. These Gauls are now as Romans, safe in their fool's paradise of supposed dominance. Well this one's had his day. He's mine, the fucking cunt, mine. Yes, just before the beef market. Isn't that appropriate? I'm leading a young

*veal to the slaughterhouse. The gap between buildings ahead will do.
Nice and dark in there, but just sufficient street light from the empty
market so he can see my beckoning gesture, wiggling fingers enticing
him. A half-turn so he can see my perfect butt. My blade is at the
ready. He is here. "Oh fine lad, come and take what your loins desire.
Come taste the wine of my ardor..."*

Now! Leap out! Strike!

The villain shrieked as he was struck by an almighty thump from
behind, from the quarter blind to Rufio's assailant. Taking full
advantage of the surprise, Quintus closed and grappled with the
wiry figure garbed in the dark cloak and hood but little else. His
first impression was that he was wrestling with a crazed prostitute,
and then they were both down on the cobbles. Quintus tried
hanging onto the wriggling body, but whoever it was managed to
get free. With a screech the sinister attacker leaped up, knife arm
outstretched and lunged over Quintus's back at Rufio, who was still
off guard through shock at the sudden onslaught.

Rufio's cry as the blade sliced through his arm galvanized Quintus.
He wished he was armed with his *spatha*, but he could hardly have
gone armed to visit Trajan; he'd never have been permitted entry
to the palace. Instead, he thrust himself up from the pavement and
wrapped both arms around the mugger's legs and tackled what
he was now sure had to be a man to the ground. Rufio looked to
be out of the fight, wounded. Quintus hoped it wasn't mortal, but
there was no time to worry about that. He tussled with the man for
possession of the knife and in doing so pulled his right arm back
a delivered and quick series of sharp jabs to his opponent's chest.
The man shrieked in agony, which seemed disproportionate to
the blow Quintus had landed. He twisted, turned, and extricated
himself from the embrace. Quintus caught a brief glimpse of the
man's face. As he scrambled to his feet the short cloak rode up
over his back and Quintus received another brief flash—bare flesh,

the mooning globes of the bastard's ass, right in his face. Then his antagonist made it to his feet and fled, dropping the knife with a clatter. Quintus heard his sandaled feet slapping rapidly away into the darkness. He felt too blown to give pursuit and he could see Rufio was in no position to do so either.

He got to his feet and took an uncertain step toward Rufio, who picked himself up and examined the wound to his arm.

"Is it—" Quintus began.

"Nothing. Really, a graze. I was fucking lucky. What in Hades was that about?"

Rufio's behavior puzzled Quintus. He took Rufio's wrist and pulled the arm closer. It really was a graze.

"I said. It's nothing. Sting like the Furies tomorrow. Oh… thanks by the way."

That's all? By the way! "What did you think you were doing? As the litter went past this corner I noticed a shifty looking character standing in the shadows. There was something wrong about it. So I told the bearers to wait, then snuck back here, just in time to see that footpad attack you. But… why did you go up to him?"

"I said thanks."

"There's no need to snap at me." And then the *denarius* dropped. A slow smile spread across Quintus's features. "You were thinking of picking him up. For sex?"

"He was encouraging me."

At that Quintus broke out into laughter. Rufio flushed.

"You've just come from having sex with the Emperor." *And me, too.* "And you are already…" Quintus trailed off, lost in wonder that anyone could be so promiscuous.

"All right. You've had your laugh. Now I'm getting home." Rufio nodded curtly and stumped off down the last bit of incline into the empty market.

"Hey! Hold up." Quintus caught him up. He raised an arm and waved. The four bearers yanked at the poles and wearily retraced their steps. "You can have a lift, if you tell them how to get to your place, and then they can take me on."

Rufio swept a sarcastic bow. "Are you sure Caesar would approve of a mere artisan's son entering one of his litters when it was reserved for a member of the great patriciate?"

"Get in. Sulking doesn't suit you." Quintus couldn't quite avoid a smirking tone, but he did prevent himself giving Rufio a patronizing pat on the bum as he climbed into the litter and shuffled over with a deep scowl to make room for Quintus. The bearers hefted the contraption and set off again. Rufio tweaked aside the curtain on his side and stared out silently.

Quintus decided to leave him to it. They were about half way up the northwestern incline when a jolt went through Quintus that had nothing to do with the lurching litter.

Rufio felt it because he turned from the exterior view. "What?"

"I've just realized. At least, I think I recognized his face. It was the briefest glimpse, but I would swear it was Acacus... or his double."

Rufio's mouth twisted into a one-corner, upper-lip curl. "Acacus? The under-secretary to Bardas?"

He got a thoughtful nod in answer. "And yet... Surely it can't have been Acacus," Quintus said. He rubbed his chin. "When this fellow scrambled up, I could see up his thighs..."

"Yuck."

"...and he didn't have any testicles."

"No balls?"

Quintus nodded again with a slight frown of admonition at his companion's coarseness.

"A gelding!"

"Eunuchs, I believe, are usually snipped. They don't have them removed. But there weren't any."

This revelation changed the tenor of the enclosed relationship. Rufio became the chatty one, with Quintus falling into silence. He suddenly felt awkward again, as if the knowledge that his attacker was castrated had reanimated Rufio and made him the one in command. When the bearers lowered their burden and by craning his neck down Quintus could see the board above closed gates bearing the legend *Tullius de artis excellentia emporium*, and underneath in smaller letters *In Celebrationibus et Festivitates*, he couldn't be rid of the pest fast enough.

Almost entirely restored to his usual insufferable bumptiousness, Rufio jumped out, only to turn, lean in and pat Quintus's arm. "It was good you came back for me, Quintus. I do truly thank you."

He shrugged his arm free of the light grip with ill grace and a noncommittal grunt.

Rufio grinned, tugged his forelock like a country peasant to his lord, and started to whistle and he went to bang on the gate.

Quintus settled back and spread out on the seat for the remainder of the trip across the top of the Aventine, deeply troubled by what had passed this night in the palace, what he'd witnessed near the beef market, and by the irritation that being in proximity with Rufio gave him the mental equivalent of a skin rash. *We had sex. With each other. Sex! I sucked his big thing...*

What did it all mean?

T·W·E·N·T·Y - O·N·E | XXI

Palatine, March 12

Rufio was excused hard graft on the strength of his bandaged arm. His protests that it was a mere graze went unheeded when Junilla saw the wound on his lower arm in the morning light. So he was comfortably slumped on a wooden bench watching his mother haranguing Flaccus as the overseer of a gang of workers in the small indoor arena they had first seen on the initial guided tour by Bardas.

"I need netting suspended above the arena and pull cords attached so the netting can be turned over to release thousands of rose petals… and that reminds me Damianus," she turned on her festivities secretary, "check on the supplier at Interamna. I want those petals delivered on the day. Not the day before. *On* the day. And chilled to keep them fresh."

"Yes, domina."

Rufio smiled to himself. Damianus went in total awe of his mistress, like most of Julia's workforce, whether slave, freed, or freeborn.

"If a single petal is wilted, you can tell him I'll have his cock and balls melted down, mixed with herbs, and returned to him as a terrine for his supper."

"Yes, domina, a terrine."

"Flaccus. Get this lot to work on the rigging."

Bolder than the rest, and perhaps emboldened as a freelance, Flaccus dared ask the obvious question. "If it's a fight to the death, what are the petals for?"

Junilla tapped the side of her nose. "That's for me to know, and you to see on the night. Oh, Damianus, I almost forgot. I need to see the fight director no later than tomorrow, otherwise—"

"Yes, domina, a terrine."

"And don't forget to send a slave around to Nathanius et Bermandius to make sure the costumes I ordered are on schedule, and that they have sufficient quantity of the plaster Corinthian columns for the orgy banquet and statues of male erotica to be spread around there and in here for the gladiatorial contest."

"Yes, domina."

"I'll leave you in charge here, Flaccus. Make sure you crack the whip."

For a second a terrible silence ensued, broken by Junilla's brash laughter. A moment later, the workforce joined in, evidently relieved that she was joking. "If you need me, I'll be in the orgy hall."

She mounted the four steps on which the wooden benches sat in a half-oval and Rufio got to his feet to follow. By the time he reached the portal, Junilla was striding down the wide passageway and then she turned in through a double-height double-doorway. Rufio set off to catch up, when a sibilant hiss stopped him. Standing in a hemicycle, half-hidden behind a statue of Trajan in full military regalia that the niche held, was Adalhard.

"Hello, my pretty German—"

"Shhh!" Adalhard removed the finger from his lips and reached out for Rufio's hand, and then pulled him behind the statue out of sight of anyone passing by in the hallway. "I need to tell you something important."

Rufio deduced the importance of whatever it was by the way the slave started feeling him up through the fabric of his work tunic. "Mmmm, I hadn't expected this."

Then Adalhard noticed the bandage. "Oh, your arm! Dominus, whatever happened to it?"

"Someone took a dislike to me and tried to chop it off. You can kiss it better if you like, though the other part of my anatomy you were handling would benefit more from your kiss. But what's so important as to drag me screaming into this hideaway, or is ravishing me the reason?"

Instantly, Adalhard's features hardened. "No, dom—"

"For Jupiter's sake, greatest and best, call me Rufio. I'm not used to all this bowing and scraping."

For a moment Adalhard forgot what he wanted to say, lost in smiles of pleasure. And then he cleared his throat quietly and became all business again. "I don't know why, dom... Rufio, but I think you are the only one who will believe me, but last night I was returning from Caesar's gathering to the slave quarters when I was attacked. I would have been killed, were it not for the assassin's footfalls alerting me, and then his shadow on the wall."

Rufio gave the boy a long hard stare. Given his own experience of the night, he was inclined to believe Adalhard wasn't exaggerating as much as slaves were wont to do. But Adalhard's next words sent a shiver of horror up his spine.

"It was Acacus."

"What!"

"Yes, but I struck out at him, and I beat the fucker up, and I kicked—"

"You're sure it was Acacus?"

Adalhard nodded his head in vigorous confirmation. "He said something about taking revenge on someone called Oba, Obo—"

"Obodas?"

"Yes! And then he ran off and I followed but he... well, he disappeared."

"You mean into another part of the palace?"

"No, I mean vanish, he did. I look, but... gone, poof!"

"Perhaps he knew of a passage or a room that wasn't obvious."

Adalhard's eyes widened. "Yes! I hear there are many secret passages. He could be anywhere and we would never know it."

Rufio screwed his brows together in concentration. What was going on here? A man attacked him last night, a man Quintus thought was Acacus, and the German slave was murderously attacked the same night, and he's sure it was Acacus. And what did the Oriental potentate have to do with it? "What was the time?"

Adalhard shrugged. How should he know? But Rufio pressed him. "The party was ended in the garden, not so late, or? Ah, I remember the water clock in the main hall was before the start of the new day."

Before midnight, then. Rufio idly batted Adalhard's wandering hand from his cock, but gave up when the boy persisted. So his attacker near the beef market struck at him much later. After all, the false dawn had tinged the eastern horizon with a pale pink glow. Were the two incidents connected? Because he'd fucked Adalhard? Acacus was loitering around in the hall they used for the auditions. Perhaps he saw them all having at each other. And that aroused his ire? But why take it out on the slave? And then there was he assertion by Quintus that whoever attacked him lacked any balls. A gelding.

"I need to discover more about Acacus's background."

"Mmmm, what?"

Rufio sighed, and leaned back against the curving wall of the hemicycle, gave way to Adalhard's mouth, and then fucked his throat hard. He grabbed the boy's head in both hands and increased the speed of pelvic thrusts until he came off.

For once, the haughty chamberlain looked flustered, though he was trying hard not to show it. But Rufio knew he had caught Bardas off guard with his demand to know more of Acacus. Bardas kept throwing little glances at the hunched backs of several scribes who scratched away on scrolls and parchment sheets scattered over tables lining the walls of the chamberlain's large *tablinum*. He tried shushing Rufio and spoke in a hushed voice, urging Rufio to keep their conversation private.

Rufio didn't much care. If what he was asking became palace corridor gossip, what of it? "I can't believe you have someone so highly placed in the civil service without knowing everything about them. I mean..." he flung his arms wide, "even my mother does security checks on anyone she hires. You can't have thieves handling antiques."

"Why the insistence, young man?" Bardas attempted to take control of the discussion again.

Rufio placed both hands flat on the tabletop and leaned forward. Bardas instinctively settled farther back in his armchair. And that was another thing. Why did Greek freedmen always get comfy armchairs, while virtuous Romans sat on stools with their backs ramrod straight? Not that Rufio thought of himself as virtuous or thoroughly Roman exactly, but really, it just looked sloppy. "I told you," he enunciated slowly, as though he were speaking to a child or a foreigner. "Acacus tried to knife me yesterday... or rather, early this morning, as I was returning home. And it seems he also tried to kill one of the slaves I auditioned."

"*Seems.*"

"Oh, he tried all right." He thought Bardas looked both alarmed and embarrassed, and realized that if it turned out that Acacus *was* a rotten egg, it would inevitably reflect very badly on his immediate superior.

"Very well. If it pleases you, I will tell you what I deem necessary for you to know. Acacus was born into a family of minor nobility, descended from the Seleucids—" He looked sternly at Rufio. "Do you know your history?"

"I know the Seleucids were a bunch of Greeks who went with Alexander the Great on his conquests."

"That *bunch* of Greeks included the great general Seleucus Nicator, and the family of Acacus was of his line. Of course, Hellenistic power in the region faded away long ago, but some aristocratic families moved south into Nabataea and came to control trade and some aspects of government. As a child Acacus found favor in the court of Rabbel II Soter, and subsequently in the household of the king's son, Obodas. Shortly after Rabbel died, two years ago, I was sent on a mission to the procurator of Judaea province to aid him in his fiscal duties during the absorption of Nabataea."

"A procurator? What does he do?"

Bardas huffed a breath of irritation. "He's appointed by the Emperor to look after a province's money matters. They often think they are the big I Am, and in Judaea's case Quintus Pompeius Falco lived up to his middle name. Now Trajan has decided he no longer wants the country to be an independent ally with its own king. That is why, to avoid unnecessary unrest, he is wooing Obodas. It was out there in Petra I first met Acacus. His Latin as well as his Greek recommended him to me as a secretary."

A wistful smile wafted across the chamberlain's features. It told Rufio something interesting. Bardas had a soft spot for his young protégé, one that went a bit deeper than educating the young man. There was something else he had to say to Bardas, but the revelation that the chamberlain was in love with his secretary made it fly from his mind. Something Adalhard said… but no. He'd remember later. For now he hoped for more information.

"And that's it?" Rufio straightened up, hands on hips.

"You expected more? Well there isn't any more."

"Acacus is a danger. Caesar needs to be told."

"Don't be ridiculous, boy!"

"I'll tell him if you won't." He turned and began to walk away.

"Tullius! My under-secretary poses no one any danger. How absurd. You should stay out of this. If anything needs dealing with, I will be the one to do it. Understand?"

"I'll see what my mother says about it." Rufio continued toward the exit from the *tablinum*, conscious of the scribes looking as if they hadn't heard a word as they renewed their eternal scribbling. And there was another sound, the scrape of Bardas getting up from behind his table in some alarm. Rufio smiled to himself. Bardas was frightened that his mother now had the ear of Trajan. He didn't care. He was heading for the large chamber being decked out ready for the big orgy, where he should find Junilla.

Out in the hallway connecting to the more public areas of the Domus Augustana, Bardas caught him up. "I don't know what you think you're trying to do, but you won't succeed—"

He shut up as Rufio turned into what was beginning to resemble a Roman bordello on an intimate but lavish scale.

"Oh, there you are." Junilla's voice came muffled from the weight of ruched fabric about her neck. "Recovered from last night?" The note of asperity faded as she gave him a sly grin. "It must have gone on for a long time?"

"Ma—"

"Never mind, pet. You will tell me all in your own good time… or I'll hear it all from our illustrious benefactor. Anyway…" and she turned on Bardas with a dark scowl. "Where in the depths of Hades is that secretary of yours, Chamberlain? I was informed on getting here that he was at my beck and call today while I get all this sorted out and I haven't set eyes on him."

"I am unsure…"

"It really isn't good enough! You must know where he is?"

"Madam, he has his duties to attend to as well as—"

"His duties are to me today. How am I to get this organized properly without a liaison officer? Huh? I can't go around ordering your staff about. I need Acacus."

"I don't think he's going to turn up, Ma."

Bardas looked as though his ineffably calm demeanor was about to crack, when the intrusion of a Praetorian Guard with an imperial summons saved him.

Rufio followed Bardas and his mother into the imperial presence. Trajan was conversing with Hadrian and Agapathus. The two tall Ulpians stood in relaxed poses, while Agapathus made up for his lack of stature by perching on a clerk's high work stool. Trajan smiled broadly.

"Lady Junilla Rufia, a pleasure to see you again. Young Rufio, please, let's dispense with the formalities." And he came straight to the point of the summons. "I have had an idea for the closing event, with that water organ—"

"Hecatoncheires, Caesar."

"Indeed, forgive me. I want to add a dash of imperial intimidation to the proceedings. After all, while we honor Obodas we must also remember that he is required to understand who is the master of his world now. Venus and Rome! I want a rousing masque of Roman power. Martial fanfares to join the organ music." He paused a second and turned to Junilla. "Have you engaged a great talent to play the instrument?"

"I have Caesar. I'm thrilled to say that only yesterday I received a positive acknowledgment to my request from none other than the brilliant Junius Sebastianus Bacchus."

Trajan dipped his head appreciatively. "Splendid. Back to my thoughts. I want to see a stylized dance featuring Mars in heroic armor as the God of War, surrounded by legionaries amid billowing smoke. But even in his divine magnificence he strides forward to bring a scroll of peace to grateful subject peoples... they will be kneeling costumed slaves. Obviously, it is vital that the man to play Mars must be a perfect Roman specimen in appearance, vigor, bearing, and righteousness, and I have exactly the man in mind."

Trajan clapped his hands smartly and in response the doors swung open to admit two Praetorian Guards, who then stood aside to show in a third figure.

"Here he is," Trajan said. "The perfect embodiment of Roman might and majesty, our young man Quintus Caecilius Alba!"

Rufio's mouth dropped open before he could catch himself. For his part, Quintus looked as flustered as Bardas had earlier. His unsettled features took on an ill-disguised look of horror as Trajan outlined what his role would be. Watching him, Rufio's initial amusement at the obvious terror Quintus felt began to ameliorate as he put himself in the other's shoes. He even felt some sympathy. When Trajan finished, Junilla stepped in and made light of Quintus's nervous protestations of his inadequacy to carry out the task, while Trajan beamed indulgently. Agapathus swung his legs in an aimless fashion, his expression unreadable under all the facial hair, and Hadrian drummed the fingers of his right hand quietly on a windowsill.

"What an honor for you, pet." Junilla impulsively put her arms around Quintus and hugged his shoulders. "I bet your father and mother will be so proud. Maybe they'll even commission a statue of you as Mars to go with those two I sold your pa, Apollo and Venus weren't they? Now, you must pop round to our place in the morning." Her look included Rufio in its embrace. "I've got the perfect costume to show you off. Then we'll schedule times for rehearsals with my choreographer and the music. My Rufio will round up a cast of suitable performers."

At mention of his name, Quintus seemed to take him in for the first time since being shown into the chamber. Caught up with her ideas for the preparation of this wonderful new scenario, Junilla swept the adults up in a gale of enthusiastic twists and turns on Trajan's idea, while Quintus advanced on Rufio like an avenging Fury. Rufio even had the grace to flinch, but it turned out he wasn't really the butt of Caecilian anger.

"You realize I'll be prancing about like an *actor*." He invested the last word with all the disdainful venom any patrician would feel for a professions so low as to be no better than that of a prostitute. "It will be a humiliation worse than the one you visited on me during the Lupercalia."

"Ah. I was rather hoping you might have forgotten that."

"Forget it! Are you mad? It's burned into my brain."

"At least you have forgiven me."

For a moment Rufio thought Quintus was about to leap on him and bear him to the floor in a wrestling match, but Trajan intervened with a hearty, comradely thumping of his shoulder.

"You will be wonderful as Mars, my dear Quintus. It's all for Rome, there's a good fellow. And now, I have much to do." The dismissal was clear. "Off you go, and prepare!"

Thanks to a curious mind, I am familiar with all the many hidden ways in this great mausoleum of Roman power. I can pop out from hiding almost anywhere, including close to the rooms Apollodorus loaned to Agapathus for his planning. There should be few around for it is the slack time when the day shift has gone and the night workers haven't yet arrived.

A real sense of cold purpose has calmed me. All emotion is banished, for I know I will unleash righteous wrath and punishment—not self-pitying revenge, not hate, not—

A final cautious check that I'm alone. Deserted corridors can always spring surprises, especially in the imperial bureau. I can always satisfy the curiosity of a slave, but a fellow scribe won't be so easy. My hood should hide me from a casual encounter, and I don't want to have to invent some reason for my being here. Best to be unobserved. There might be awkward questions to answer. Perfect! The door is ajar, so no need to force it.

Agapathus is a fool. He thinks his secret blueprints are safe, here in the depths of the palace, so he leaves them all out in the middle of his worktable without a care. What have we got here? Ah... Hecatoncheires... I'll give them fifty-headed giants before I'm through. Now, let's see... hmmm. Not much for me with the Aegaeon parts, it's just hot air. But his stupid Gyes and Cottus will probably do. Whirling and shooting things. Yesss... this will work! It will give me just what I need. Obodas will find it most amusing... until it ends his miserable life. And who knows. The Fates may let me take out a few more Romans. Not long now, by the snakes of Medusa! Soon, soon, I will be avenged, and it looks as if Agapathus's organ of death will bring me final peace.

March 13–15

If humiliation had a name it would be Quintus Caecilius Alba. It wasn't as if he was shy of taking off his clothes in front of others. After all, a visit to the public baths was a regular event. But with Rufio and—even worse—Junilla Rufia watching…

"C'mon, pet. I've seen it all before." She stood with a short military tunic dyed scarlet in one hand and a splendid breastplate in burnished bronze over boiled leather in the other, which he could see would give an instant athletic appearance to his torso.

"So've I." Rufio winked lasciviously.

"You're not helping, my Tullius Priapus. Besides, you're supposed to be shifting your pretty ass to the palace and a date with Sponsus Terpsichorus."

"Oh no, why him? There are other choreographers."

"That's it Quintus, my love, all of it off, yes. Hold that for me. Now slip into this loincloth first, then the tunic. Sponsus just happens to be the best, that's why."

"He's a pansy."

"He's in the theater, what do you expect?"

"A pansy with wandering hands. Quintus, we'll have to do some weight-lifting to get your upper arms to match that cuirass."

"I'll slap your ass, if you don't stop goading me."

"Now, now, boys. Slip your head through this. There. Rufio, pet, reach me those boots."

"But, Ma, they've got little wings on them. They're meant for Mercury, not Mars. Mars doesn't flap about the place, he stumps around with big heavy boots capable of crunching the enemy beneath his heel."

"It's all Nathanius et Bermandius had available at such short notice, but I'm getting something more appropriate for heel crushing made up. These will do for rehearsals. Quintus, sit down. You can't lace them up yourself in all that armor. Oh, you do look gorgeous."

"Simply gorgeous," Rufio echoed in an effeminate voice.

"Oh, go boil your head, you jumped-up, cretinous—"

"Off you go, Rufio, my pet. You know you have to get permission and all that from the Praetorians for Sponsus, or he won't be allowed entry."

"Yes, Ma, I'm going, I'm going. Just watch yourself with Mars there." He stuck his tongue out and waggled it suggestively. "He has a long and very sharp proboscis in his head."

The vented snort of annoyance from Quintus was his only reply to the taunt, that and a sneer as Rufio left with a cheery parting smile and wave. None of this dressing up nonsense would have been as upsetting if it had taken place at home, but here in their rambling factory of statuary he felt deeply outside his comfort zone.

When they were alone, Junilla tried soothing her charge. "Rufio really likes you, you know."

"*Hunff!* How does he act when he hates someone?"

"My Rufio doesn't hate anyone, Quintus dear."

"He shows his liking in a funny way." He sniffed.

"Let me tighten this strap, there, that's better. Now stand up for me. Do a twirl."

Quintus looked shocked. "A what?"

"You know, spin around so the tunic flies out a bit."

He took a breath in exasperation, but did as Junilla wanted and spun around twice. He felt his loincloth exposed as the force of turn flung up the lightweight tunic below the confines of his breast and back plates. "This is…"

"Just what's required. You are the embodiment of Mars."

I bet none of my brothers will think so. Oh, the humiliation.

"Now you just need to learn the routines Rufio is working out today with Sponsus…" Junilla paused at the anguished look on his face. "Oh, c'mon Quintus. It'll be all right on the night. Promise."

How would he be able to face the ridicule heaped on him by his family? And damn it all, this mess was down to his father anyway. And that bastard Uncle Livy. How unfair. There would be nothing for it. He would have to do what any noble Roman of the past did confronted by the inevitable—fall on his sword.

"No! No! Sweetie! For the sake of the Muses, you must place your feet softly in this passage of the dance." Sponsus turned to Rufio at his side. "He's worse than a Carthaginian elephant."

Rufio winced at the sarcasm he knew Sponsus Terpsichorus was trying to rein in, but the dance master's frustration with his principal was understandable. It was two days since Quintus had his first fitting, and he now wore a pair of hefty military boots in place of Mercury's winged ones. Sponsus had brought together musicians playing an assortment of different military *buccinas*, tubas, double-flutes, and reverberating tympani, while a stand-in for Junius Sebastianus Bacchus played the mighty water organ at the heart of the towering, insectoid Hecatoncheires of Agapathus (which was not yet fully working).

Evidently struggling to remember his movements, Quintus had stumbled over his own feet and brought the gyrations of spear-wielding legionaries and a small army of "subject peoples" to a grinding halt yet again. While the extras milled about in confusion and the assistants to Sponsus attempted to marshall them into order for another start, Quintus stood legs apart, one hand on his hip, the other brandishing his sword. "No one could master the steps you have worked out." He glared at the dance master.

"Such a cute young man and such a stuck-up toff."

Rufio tried not to grin at the choreographer's hissed words. "It's as well for you that all the swords are wooden exercise weapons we borrowed from the gladiator school by the Colosseum.

Sponsus curled his upper lip. "You mean *he's* lucky I don't tan his pretty backside with it. I've had enough of him. Truly, I have. Why couldn't the Emperor have hired a dancing boy from the arena—"

"Hush!" Rufio said as the entire cast bent their heads. "It looks as though you'll have the opportunity to tell him to his face," he whispered.

Trajan and entourage advanced across the expanse of terrace toward the military disarray.

"No, I can't. You must," a panicked Sponsus whispered back. "I'm a theatrical. Emperor's don't talk to players."

Rufio gritted his teeth, made his lips smile engagingly, and bowed to Trajan. "Caesar."

Trajan halted and took him in. His features remained impassive. "There seems to be a problem."

"Oh no, Caesar. Not really." He halted and glanced across at distant Quintus, and then felt guilty for doing so. "Quintus Alba is beginning to get the hang of his movements. He only needs to loosen up and…"

Trajan's eyes roved across the silenced assembly until they came to rest on Quintus.

He kept his gaze on the ornate stonework under his grotesquely booted feet. But he felt the pressure of Trajan's approaching presence and the quiet back shuffling of the extras as wooden swords were replaced in scabbards. At a gesture, those in his train came to a stop and the Emperor spoke quietly. "What is the problem?"

Quintus looked up, chewing his lower lip nervously. For the umpteenth time he cursed his uncle for placing him in this position, in the glare of imperial interest. When he answered, his voice was hoarse with suppressed emotion. "C-Caesar… acting on a stage, it's d-d-demeaning." He fell silent and tried to avoid Trajan's appraisal.

"I see. In fact I understand how you feel, that you don't relish your role in this pageant. It's wounded your pride. But…" He paused until he had Quintus's full attention. "I suspect there is a deeper reason for your reluctance."

The expression seemed kindly. Quintus swallowed some of the spit gathering in his mouth and squared his shoulders. He wondered what it could be that Caesar suspected. Trajan spoke softly and Quintus engaged him with his eyes.

"Those around me offer me assets, benefits, gifts, you name it, all the time. In almost every case it's because I am Caesar and they want something of value to themselves in return. It's how it works. So I know that the role you find yourself playing is due to your uncle's machinations, Quintus. He has sold you to me in return for valuable contracts that are in my gift, and they will restore his fortunes and those of your esteemed but too-absent father. Of course you feel demeaned by such a transaction, but that is not how I view it. Not in your case. You should realize that I value you and in fact I also rate your friend Rufio highly."

Quintus forced down the bile that threatened to rise into his gullet at the thought of being paired in friendship with Rufio.

"I would count a successful performance willingly given as a personal favor to me, not as your Emperor but as Marcus Ulpius Traianus. Believe me when I say this is a favor not tainted by any whiff of prostitution, and it is not some low-life theatrical performance. You are representing the majesty of Rome. So Quintus, I am counting on you."

The words, quietly spoken out of the hearing of anyone else, chastened him. "Th-thank you, Caesar. I h-have enjoyed t-t-the attentions you have shown me, and—"

The friendly slap on his shoulder shut him up. Trajan raised his voice to parade ground level. "Let the rehearsals resume."

"I don't know what Caesar must have said to Toff Boy, but it's certainly transformed his ability to, well, thump around with a modicum of grace at least," Sponsus Terpsichorus said with the long-suffering sigh of an artist under great stress.

Rufio wondered about that as well. Whatever exchange the two of them had had, Quintus seemed a different person. If he didn't exactly inhabit his role as God of War yet, he was at least trying.

"I don't think he'll ever be a convincing general, though. Don't these upper-class twerps have soldiering in their blood?"

"I wouldn't know," Rufio answered Sponsus with a grin. "I'm just a poor artisan."

The choreographer grunted in a way that might indicate amusement or disgust and strode toward the company waving his hands (hands he had kept off Rufio with obvious difficulty). "That's it for today, boys and girls. Tomorrow, I want the Legionaries Victorious to look more triumphant and the Suffering Female Children to look lots more happy at gaining their freedom."

Rufio trailed after him and made for Quintus, thinking how very handsome he was kitted out as warrior, even if it was all fake show stuff he wore. Images of how good he looked naked came unbidden into his mind and stirred a coil of affection, which surprised him. "Ho Quintus, that went really well. You do make a fine Mars."

He got a cool look for that. Quintus grimaced and shook his shoulders. "I want to get this stuff off my back."

Rufio went to pat him on the shoulder and grip his bare arm with his other hand, but Quintus shrugged irritably. Rufio stepped back a pace. "I'm trying to be friendly."

"Really? Why? I don't need your friendship, thank you."

Rufio backed up another pace as Quintus stormed off toward the doorway leading into the palace and the rooms set aside for the company, for their costumes and changes. He stared after the shrinking figure in his armor. As Quintus emerged from the shadow thrown by Agapathus's extraordinary construct, the sun burnished the backplate so it formed a halo of gold around him. Rufio breathed in deeply and let the air out as a heartfelt sigh. He felt the pain of frustration without entirely understanding quite why.

* * *

Evening found Rufio in the taverna just around the corner from home wondering which of the poor selection of Aventine Foxes he might pick up. The watered wine had gone to his head, partly because it wasn't much watered and partly because he'd had too much of it. He wanted that boy again, the one he did doggy style, and as if on a prayer to Cupid, the lad with the narrow face and a feral look in his eye (...*and the tidy hair of Quintus*) sauntered in. He saw Rufio and broke into a twisted little smile of recognition. A few minutes later Rufio dragged him into the small nook owned by the taverna with its carpet of rank hay and they fell into it with a great rustling, which might even have been a few rats departing in haste.

There was no ceremony this night. He speedily woof-woofed the Fox and then flipped his light, scrawny body over and took him again, legs in the air. And in the middle of the fuck, just as his second orgasm was building nicely, a sense of loss overcame him. Seeing the face below him, the parted mouth revealing the boy's crooked tooth, in the rising throes of his sexual abandon, Rufio realized there was no substitute for Quintus. As his cum began to flow, all he could see was that first sight of Quintus, reacting in astonishment when he'd lashed him with his goat thong. It was as if that mad moment in the Lupercalia had bound them together. But damned Quintus didn't understand how Rufio felt.

Woof woof! Shit!

Sleep had not come easily. Quintus was violently aroused from a dream in which a hooded specter leaped from the shadows, long knife poised to strike. As Quintus twisted desperately to avoid the blade, there came a flurry of golden light that transformed into a cluster of auburn locks caught in the weak light of a street lamp, and the shining apparition bore the black demon to the roadway. A drum kept beating an irregular pattern...

And Quintus sat up abruptly.

The thumping at the distant front door was repeated. Then he heard raised voices arguing in the entrance hall. Very awake and thoroughly alarmed, he leapt from bed and threw on the tunic he used to cover his nakedness if ever he needed to use the latrine at night. He dashed out into the corridor, ran around the *impluvium* in the atrium and into the hall. He stopped dead in his tracks.

"Lemme go, you stoopid—"

In his astonishment at the intrusion, it took Quintus a second to realize the person struggling with the door slave and shouting out his name was Rufio.

"I said lemme go you fuckin... I want to see Quintus!"

The slave, who had his arms wrapped around Rufio's waist trying to prevent him dragging them both toward the atrium, had a bloody nose. Even as he watched, stunned into inaction, Rufio's elbow connected painfully with the slave's nose again, and he yelped in pain.

"Stand back, Tredegus," Quintus ordered the slave. "Now you stay right where you are." He pointed a shaking index finger at Rufio, who swayed slightly from evidently too much drink. He took an unsteady step forward, and then another. His intense eyes pleaded with Quintus.

"We we need talk. To talk. Get things sorted."

"You have to leave." Quintus had never had to handle a situation like this and he wasn't at all sure what to do. Mostly he thought, how dare Rufio burst in like this? When Rufio took another lurching step toward him, Quintus surged into action. He pushed Rufio back toward the still open door, while bleeding Tredegus looked on in fright. For a moment Rufio staggered back, but then he raised his arms to grasp Quintus's biceps in a strong grip. His drunken intensity alarmed Quintus. Wine had never had this effect on him and it seemed weak of Rufio to have let himself get into this pathetic state. What did the silly bodkin want anyway? His breath reeked sourly of cheap wine.

Suddenly Rufio tensed up and started to fight back between agitated snatches of words. "Why... don't... why won't you listen? What I want to say?"

"Get out!"

"Haven't you noticed?"

"I'll raise the alarm if—"

"What I feel? No?"

Rufio's grip became harder as he thrust his weight up against Quintus. Panic welled up. Quintus struggled and shook him off violently. Rufio lost his balance momentarily, recovered, and lunged wildly. What happened next was purely instinctive. Quintus stepped back for room and swung his fist. It connected in a glancing blow on Rufio's cheek. His head jerked back. For a second he stood there shaking his head. Then his nostrils flared, His mouth twisted into a rictus of anger and blue fire crackled from his eyes as he lashed out.

The blow caught Quintus in the stomach and he almost doubled over from the blow, but Rufio' punch lacked the power to really hurt. Nevertheless, Quintus fell back in surprise, but recovered in time to guard against the next assault. Rufio waded in with both fists flying. In this close combat, Quintus was no slouch. What Rufio had in street smarts, Quintus made up for with gymnasium-trained boxing and wrestling holds. Poet maybe, but no pansy. And his temper was up. And he wasn't inebriated. This was his home, invaded by a drunken lout for... whatever reason.

But Rufio's blind strength forced Quintus farther back down the hall and into the open space of the atrium. The two brawled like dogs over a bitch in heat, trading blows as they passed Lucius and Pallas, open-mouthed as much as the slaves roused from their slumber, and all staring in alarm and wonder at the fight. Quintus was vaguely aware of getting splashed and realized with a shock that

Rufio's tears were the cause. Snot mingled with a trickle of blood from his nose streaked his cheeks, and Quintus saw in a mirror just before they collided with it that he was in no better state. A tall lampstand went flying when he ducked a blow and Rufio swiped it. Something banged his shoulder. It was a column he'd backed into as Rufio came arms flying again.

He took another step back, arms raised protectively against the storm of blows, and then another step... onto nothing. He had a streaked image of the world turning over and Rufio flying hard against him and then the noise of roaring water filled his ears. The cold was a shock. And then he felt the bottom of the shallow *impluvium*.

The two boys scrabbled and sloshed onto their splayed knees, hanging onto each other's arms, tunics awry, made heavy from the immersion. Pool rainwater water streamed from their eyes and they gasped for breath in unison. Quintus was barely aware through blurred vision of the faces in the low light peering down at them, his father's among them. All he knew was the presence of Rufio, his red hair darkened to almost a burned hue and plastered in coils to his broad forehead. He was aware of his eyes, now shaded to indigo, piercing him.

"I want you!"

What was he saying? Water clogged Quintus's hearing. He thought Rufio had said he loved him. *But surely not?*

The kiss came as another surprise, fervent with unspoken passion. Rufio's tongue probed at his lips, broke through as they parted involuntarily. And then both their tongues engaged in a warm wrestling match that echoed what Rufio's hands were doing, enfolding and embracing him. His grip pulled their bodies together and amazingly every part fitted together.

"I love you, Quintus. It's no good... I do."

Quintus felt overwhelmed, unsure of himself and his feelings, but somewhere deep inside he knew this was what he had wanted all along. The bluster, the disdain, the harsh words were just a denial of what he knew to be true from the moment that laughing Celtic bastard lashed him with that damn thong and waved his big cock triumphantly in his shocked face.

Rufio kissed him again on the lips, and Quintus suddenly relaxed in his embrace. Rufio caressed his face as their tongues mingled sweetly. His big, capable hands moved lower from his neck and shoulders to his heaving breast and over the curve of his shoulderblades and down his back. The both stood up. He laughed delightedly when Rufio twisted his head and tongued his chin, dipped underneath to lick his neck, forced his head slightly sideways to dip that busy wet instrument of erotic pleasure into the shell of his ears, this one, then that one. And all the while he whispered of his love, of his desire to possess Quintus, body and soul.

When he recovered some sense to peer beyond the incredible whirl of passion, Quintus realized that they were alone, calf-deep in the pool. Had he seen his father, understanding what he was witnessing, silently motion the slaves to leave? Two bore poor Tredegus between them.

"You are wet." Rufio giggled and waggled his eyebrows as he looked down. "And you are hard."

Quintus still felt too raw to reply in bantering kind. "I think I have a towel somewhere."

"In your bedroom?" Rufio sounded hopeful.

Quintus allowed himself a little smile, more a tightening of the lips with an upward curl.

"I want you, so badly. I've been a fool. It's always been there since I first set eyes on you, my Quintus." Rufio suddenly looked vulnerable, and for the first time Quintus actually thought he looked adorable. "Are you *my* Quintus?"

The smile loosened a touch. Quintus looked back into Rufio's eyes but said nothing. Instead he nodded at the edge of the pool and let Rufio take his hand and help him out. Their feet slapped on the tiled floor and left wet footprints in a trail that led directly to Quintus's bedroom, and the dry towel he'd promised.

Domus Alba, night, Ides of March (15)

"You remember that day? When I saw you waiting in a hallway of the palace? You remember the things I said?" Rufio's voice was low, husky, and full of constrained promise.

Quintus hated to doubt, but Rufio's astonishing declaration of his feelings seemed too good to be true. Was it really possible that the boy who had so tormented and taunted him really felt love for him? True love? "I remember. You said you could show me a much better time than the... how did you put it? Better than the old man who runs things." He rolled his head on the bolster so their faces were nearly touching, nose-to-nose. Rufio's was rounded at the tip, almost a button compared to Quintus's more pointy tip. "Do you remember?" As he asked, a sexual tingle shivered his whole body.

Suddenly solicitous, Rufio pushed up on one arm and looked down at him. "Are you cold?"

"No, I'm fine." *Trying to get used to lying naked with another man, naked and aroused.* "So, do you remember?"

"Of course. I said those things because I really wanted to do them. I think this was first, because..." His voice trailed off as, with the hand not supporting him half-upright, he worked his fingers into Quintus's drying hair. The stroking tips rustled and felt wonderfully cool. An erotic wave washed right through Quintus and he stirred against the rubbing of his scalp. Rufio lowered his head, closer and closer until his nose stroked Quintus on the cheek. First Rufio worked his hand down to rub at the earlobe beneath his fingers before he followed up with his tongue. "Such delicious ears..." He blew and the warm exhalation caused Quintus to twitch his shoulders in sudden thrill.

And then the tongue again, wetting the raised whorls of delicate flesh, so that the next puff came as a pleasant chill.

Rufio pulled his head back, only to descend on the other side of Quintus's face so those vigorous curls of hair brushed his cheek and then he felt the hot, moist breath in his right ear. The exquisite touch made him want to curl up into a protective ball, but it also did something else. His cock sprang to attention and pulsed against the solidity of Rufio's thigh. The blowing and licking in the other ear made him writhe very slightly, and he thrilled to the feel of their bodies pressed so close together when Rufio gripped him by the shoulder and pulled them close. He was now almost lying on top of Quintus and without the need to support his upper torso, used his freed hand to wander slowly, so exquisitely slowly down the length of Quintus between them. Words poured like syrup in his ear, "Let me handle your erection… ahh, so silky smooth, yet growing so very hard."

"Not as big as yours," Quintus murmured in a small voice.

"That's not what I thought when Caesar got you worked up." Rufio lifted his head slightly so he could look down at what he was holding. He lifted it so it stood upright like a sentinel. "It's beautiful. Like you, my Quintus."

This time the possessive gave Quintus a happy glow. He was beginning to think he liked being owned by someone as full of life, as full of beans, as full of fun and cheer as Rufio.

"You know what?"

Quintus smiled. "What?"

"When I spotted you that day of the Lupercalia I was struck by a lightning bolt like they say Jupiter hurls. I've thought of your body ever since, mine to adore, to worship, to make love to. Most of all, I want to awaken burning desire within you." As he spoke he stroked Quintus's cock, working gently at the sheathing foreskin. "And now, something I've dreamed of repeating since the night with Caesar, only all mine now…"

Quintus wondered whether Rufio could also adore what lay within him as much as he seemed to want his body. But the thought washed away like flotsam on a tide when the warm, wet ring of lips enfolded his cock. Rufio's quiet moans of enjoyment as he gently worked his head up and down added to Quintus's arousal. Rufio squeezed gently at the hard shaft and on the upstroke rolled his tongue around under the ridge of cock head, which had Quintus arching his back up off his hard mattress and gasping for breath. Ashur was never this good, this completely attentive. Nor had he ever done what Rufio did next.

"Here…" He pulled Quintus under the knees and lifted his legs. Quintus took the strain to help, wondering what would happen. Rufio shuffled up between the raised thighs and dipped his head. This time felt entirely different to when Trajan commanded Rufio to lick his asshole. On his back, legs waving in the air and one held in place in Rufio's firm press, he felt much more vulnerable, and besides, he had better view along the length of his torso, past his erection, between the thickness of his parted thighs to the mop of red-golden hair tickling his flesh even as Rufio's tongue penetrated him.

"Mmmmm…"

Rufio seemed in no hurry to finish the tongue-swirling motions up and down the groove between his buttocks and into the purse of his ass and Quintus felt reluctant to move in any way that might stop him. In the doggy position on Trajan's bed, he'd been able to lean back against the pressure of Rufio's face and pressing nose, here he could only roll a little from side to side. And then Rufio raised his head. Their eyes locked. The moment's stillness felt magical.

"Can I fuck you?"

A shudder ran through Quintus, part thrill, part fear. "You're much bigger than Trajan. It'll hurt."

"And I'm a lot more practiced as well," Rufio boasted with a sweet grin. "I'll work you a bit, give you a finger frigging to loosen you up, and then I promise it won't hurt." He spat on his fingers, leaving Quintus wondering where so much saliva came from. His mouth felt parched from open-mouth breathing and gasping. And then a finger probed its way past his opening and wiggled gently. Then two, and then three. "Ooh, that's nice. I think you're almost ready." He leaned back so Quintus had a clear view of what was about to fill him as Rufio stroked himself vigorously.

The rod of flesh almost disappeared from sight when Rufio knelt up and pressed his cock to Quintus's hole. A swelling sensation and that weird friction he'd felt when Trajan buggered him made him gasp again. Amazingly, more and more of Rufio pushed gently but insistently into him. He tried backing away up the bed, but there was nowhere to go up against the wall.

"Easy now. I'm nearly all in."

That didn't seem possible, but a moment later Rufio changed his position to lean down over Quintus so their heads were almost level. As he did, he pressed the last inch in with a grunt of satisfaction and a triumphant, all-teeth-bared grin split his features. "There, my Quintus, and now…"

Quintus felt the movement deep within him, retreating and then advancing. Rufio built the pace gradually. The grin paled to a look of concentration. He lowered his head farther, kissed the tip of Quintus's nose, and then with a mutual twist of their heads brushed their lips together. Quintus responded instantly. The pace increased and suddenly the most exquisite explosion of joy rocked his torso and limbs. He loosed a surprised squeak. Rufio saw it in his eyes, now so close he had to cross-squint to see both of Quintus's pupils. He burbled wetly, lip to lip, "I hit it, didn't I?"

"Mnnhhn… Aaaahh"

"There's something there that flowers with pleasure when my cock rubs against it. I know it because when I've hit it, the one I've been fucking has squealed just like you did."

"Aah… I didn't squeal. Oh, Rufio. Kiss me."

Rufio obliged, and also reached down between them to grasp Quintus by his cock and they rocked as one until Quintus blew a gale of ecstasy into Rufio's mouth and felt his release as a great outpouring of semen filled the rubbing fist. Rufio gasped loudly in turn and suddenly strained his head back. Through a haze of orgasmic lust, Quintus marveled at the sight and feel of Rufio's butt hammering up and down at frenzied speed. He called to mind as a child seeing two rabbits copulating, the male jacked up behind the female, his little furry ass a blur of movement. Quintus hadn't understood it really, yet some atavistic memory informed his childish brain that the rabbits loved every second of their conjunction. And then came a brief stillness before Rufio began to come. His glorious shining head dropped onto Quintus's shoulder as he pumped his seed, and with his after shots he sought Quintus's lips again, this time for a slow, languorous, and very sloppy kiss.

* * *

Quintus wasn't sure quite when he drifted to sleep. A bit dozily, he wondered what time of night it was. He was aware of a form bundled against him, warm and sleeping. Rufio! And suddenly he was fully awake. And stiff again. His cock ached for action and his balls buzzed. He prodded the sleeper, who sat up abruptly.

"What?"

"I want more."

Rufio knuckled his eyes, shook his head, and Quintus saw his grin by the way the small night candle in the far corner of the bedroom glinted on his teeth.

"Phew! Give you one and you get all sex-crazed."

"Can I fuck you this time?" For Quintus there was more to the request than curiosity and desire to try it out. That he certainly wanted to do. No, if Rufio refused him because he did the fucking—unless the Emperor commanded otherwise—it would mean he didn't feel about Quintus the way he now claimed to. And there was an underlying worry—a very patrician concern—that if he didn't take the role of fucker and always spread his legs for Rufio to fuck him, it would make Quintus into an effeminate. No noble-born Roman could allow himself the role of effeminacy. Turn and turn about... well, Quintus supposed that made things equal. He knew that Trajan was almost certainly the first man to have taken Rufio that way, how would he react now to Quintus's request?

"You're no mean slouch when it comes to the dimension department."

"I won't hurt you."

Rufio's huffed breath voiced his dubiousness at that assertion. "How do you know that? You're not practiced. You have to do it lots to get good at fucking."

"Are you frightened?"

"No!" He laughed as he grabbed Quintus about the neck and planted a smacker on his lips. "Go for it, Mars, my god."

Nerves sprang up. He wanted to. His straining cock wanted to, but suddenly he wasn't sure he would be any good. It came as a pleasnt surprise when Rufio took hold of his shaft and rubbed it fondly, kissed him again, and lay down with his back to Quintus. He pulled Quintus down while still holding onto his cock, which he guided to his ass. He wiggled a bit until Quintus felt the tip pierce Rufio's anus. And then it all happened as if Quintus had been fucking boys for years. They lay like a set of spoons in a series of perfectly fitting shapes, convex to concave, valley to mound, and moved together until Quintus was deeply embedded in his lover. For he was now sure Rufio was his lover, to let him do this. He strained hard to give Rufio the exquisite pain-joy of finding that sweet spot, and almost cried in happiness when the boy in his arms yelped joyously and twisted his head around as far as he could. If Quintus reciprocated, they could just press lips together and that's how he blossomed in orgasm, moaning lip-to-lip, sharing life, giving and taking breaths, as he filled Rufio.

When his last spurts were done, he wriggled free urgently so they could face each other as he stroked Rufio to completion, their mouths glued together in unspoken, ardent passion. And then Quintus buried his face in the crook of Rufio's strong neck so he wouldn't see the tears of joy. But nuzzling there, he knew Rufio must feel the wetness and know it for what it was.

This, surely, was the beginning of everything.

T·W·E·N·T·Y - F·O·U·R | XXIV

From the upper story of the Tullius Emporium of Artistic Excellence, Rufio could just make out the northern slope of the Janiculan hill across the Tiber. Smoke rising from numerous hearths of Trans Tiberim, the slums on the river's opposite bank, obscured some detail, but the tiled roofs of the Vatican palace were just visible.

At his side, Junilla sighed. "Such a shame. A grand opportunity thrown away."

He glanced at her, the amused question plain on his features.

"It's said that when Queen Cleopatra visited Julius Caesar, her courtiers all crossed from the Vatican to form up on the Field of Mars, and from there she was towed into the Forum on top of a hundred-foot-high sled with its own massive front ramp. The sled was pulled by a thousand Nubians... oh well, I'm sure Bardas is right. But it would have been a glorious spectacle, Slobodas arriving atop a replica of a Petran temple, hauled by a thousand Nabataean warriors."

"You have enough to look after without adding that. At least our favorite despot is now arrived."

"And soon begins the fun. How's your friend Quintus doing with his godlike role?"

"I think he has it at last. Yesterday's rehearsal with all the bits of that thing working went well enough. There's just Cato's kids need a bit more work... What?"

Junilla was staring at him. "I called Quintus your friend and you didn't bitch."

Rufio shrugged his shoulders.

"Have you kissed and made up?"

Rufio actually blushed. For some reason he did not want his mother to know his feelings for Quintus, which was strange considering he never usually minded her prying, and even volunteered what he'd gotten up to with this lad or that. He asked a question to cover the embarrassment. "Did you manage to get those modifications done to his boots I asked for?"

She pointedly glanced down at his rather ornate lace-ups. "Like you're wearing?"

"Mmm."

"I don't know why you want them. Surely the Praetorians won't let you in carrying knives."

"We won't be carrying them and anyway they are only decorative."

She gave Rufio a strange look and shook her head.

The days became frantic. Final preparations for all the events occupied much of Rufio and Junilla's time, and both had Flaccus, Damianus, and Agapathus run off their feet, along with an army of seconded freedmen and slaves. The Emperor and retinue shuffled between the palace, the Senate House, and the newly completed buildings in Trajan's giant forum, which otherwise remained a building site. Here in full majesty Prince Obodas, who would be king, and his court sat in meetings with the Romans.

We Are Celebrations and Festivities had nothing to do with the official welcoming banquet, for which Junilla expressed relief. That was left to the two consuls and their staffs, the aediles and their staffs, and the innumerable procurers of food, drink, and delicacies for the Palatinate bureaucracy. Instead, she concentrated on completing arrangements for her first set event, the banquet-orgy that followed the night after the official do. But before that she felt the need to check with the Fisherman that there had been no problems with his "catches" for Obodas's Vatican palace bedchamber.

"One or two of the little cunts didn't want to co-operate, according to the Nabataean vizier fellow," he informed her. "So I substituted them for two who were a tad more desperate for the money."

Junilla's face darkened in concern. "Did it cause a problem?"

"Nah. I hauled them out and replaced them quick enough. But there may be more trouble."

"Why?"

"Seems your eastern potentate has some very peculiar oriental habits. Not sure he doesn't even eat portions of the boys." He chuckled and hawked up a gob of phlegm and spat it far out into the sluggish brown flow of the river.

Junilla recovered swiftly. The Fisherman was renowned for his dry wit. "Does he prefer them rare, medium, or well done? Just ensure there is a constant flow over the river to the Vatican of fresh boys for him and..." she smiled wryly, "if he's devouring them, make sure they're very yummy."

"Tasty tiddlers, my lady, yes." He bowed with obsequious grace.

The Great Vestibule hummed with more Praetorians than Junilla had ever seen before, but her face was now familiar to the regular guards and minutes later she emerged into the forecourt and slipped quietly into the wing of the Domus Augustana where the "intimate" hall selected for the feast was nearing the completion of its elaborate decorations. At every corner, slaves toiled up and down ladders to string garlands of fresh laurels, sweet smelling roses, ivy, and massed bunches of herbs. Lower down, more slaves wound long trains of ivy around the freestanding columns and erotic statuary hired from Nathanius et Bermandius, while others under the supervision of Bardas laid dining knives and asparagus forks out on the dining tables.

"These need dusting," the chamberlain complained, waving a hand over the reclining couches ready for the diners. He threw his hands up. "It's all that activity. It's blowing up dust everywhere."

Junilla gave him an apologetic look. His irritation was aimed at the exotic dancers and acrobats who were fine-tuning their performances with gusto. By palace standards the chamber was small, though it would easily seat a hundred reclining diners in comfort, and their gymnastics were perilously close to the couches and tables.

On the other side Rufio stood amid a cluster of his picked boys, who were dressed in tunics dyed a dark maroon and edged with gold at hem, neck, and mid-arm sleeves. These were so short the rear hemline almost sat on the upper curve of their buttocks. The color of their skin and hair reflected every corner of the Imperium, and each was a fine specimen of his race. Among them the three Marcuses shone: Adalhard, Celsus, and Brunus. The boy servers listened attentively to Rufio's final instructions. "You must be graceful at all times while attending to the guests you are allocated, but remember what we rehearsed and be seductive in the way you deliver food and drink or remove plates. And no matter what happens, smile, be pleasant, and remember you are doing it for Caesar, for Venus, and for Rome."

This little pep talk provoked some quiet sniggers from among the boys. Rufio smiled at them. They knew what they would soon be up against—a veritable forest of wandering hands reaching out to grope whatever came to hand. He left them joking among themselves and exchanging bets on which of them would get off with some wealthy man and hopefully receive a fat tip.

Rufio found Quintus in one of the several adjacent robing rooms set aside for the staff. He smiled uncertainly at Rufio as if he were still unsure of what reception he'd receive.

"I'm relieved that your mother managed to provide a proper room with a door. I had the horrors that I'd be changing clothes and washing in one of the cubicles the dancers and serving boys have to use."

"I wouldn't have minded that," Rufio said in an airy teasing tone. "But Ma wouldn't hear of an aristocrat baring all his patrician bits in front of plebs, performing folk, and slaves."

"So I get you instead."

For a moment the two grappled like schoolboys, which Rufio enjoyed since he was dressed and Quintus wore only a skimpy loincloth. Laughing, Quintus broke away. "Hey, I still have to wash." He indicated two large bronze bowls. "The water's warm. A slave brought it in not long ago." He watched as Rufio pulled off his dusty work tunic.

Rufio glanced up while dancing around trying to unfasten a sandal. "I thought you were washing?"

Quintus arched an eyebrow mockingly and waved at Rufio's midriff. "And the loincloth. There's clean everything over there. Your mother brought the clothes in."

Rufio rocked his shoulders ironically but loosed the vestment, pointing as he did so at the one Quintus still wore. Quintus obliged, and they both started splashing scented water over their lithe bodies, Rufio's squared and muscular, Quintus's leaner but no less strong.

"Is one of your boots equipped?" Rufio said in a lowered voice.

Quintus nodded and began drying himself on the linen cloths provided. "I thought it a crazy idea at first, but you're right."

"I know I am. The Praetorians on all the watches are used to us now, so with the tokens…" he instinctively touched the small plaque worn on a chain around his neck imprinted with Trajan's imperial seal, a twin to the one Quintus similarly wore, "they won't check our footgear. The complete disappearance of that monster Acacus… I don't know. It seems too good to be true that he's really vanished."

"That's it, I'm glad to a have a dagger secreted on me, just in case."

Rufio patted Quintus's arm. "Me too. After all, I'm the one he seems to want dead, and all I ever did was act politely." He caught Quintus's expression of doubt. "I was! Anyway, you don't go around killing people because they acted a bit cool toward you. And he went after Adalhard."

"Who you had sex with, you told me."

"So?"

Quintus shrugged and started to dress in a fresh loincloth and a tunic so snowy-white it made Rufio's flashy, blue-dyed one look a bit dowdy, although it was clean.

His friend's sudden silence nagged at Rufio. Was Quintus pissed at him over mentioning having sex with others? He felt a bit guilty, an unaccustomed sentiment. "You went quiet. What is it?" That earned him a diffident glance. *Try a different tack.* "Are you worried about tonight?"

"Unsure. I mean, being asked as companions to Trajan for this dinner? Does that mean what I think it means?"

Rufio knew it did, because the request for his company had come through his Ma, who typically fizzed like a' glass of pure virgin Falernian about her darling son becoming an imperial catamite. Well, it made him laugh, even if it didn't appeal as much to Quintus. In the intervening days of closer relationship, Quintus had finally coughed up what really hurt—that his family, well his wretched uncle really, had effectively used his body as a bribe.

Rufio moved closer and placed an arm around Quintus's neatly attired but as yet unbelted waist and gazed into his troubled eyes. "But I will be there with you, Quintus. And Trajan hasn't been horrid to either of us."

"I know, but all my reading tells me that to dally with princes is to court disaster. There is always someone who resents it and waits until the day you are no longer a favorite before they stab you in the back."

Rufio smiled grimly. "And some can't even wait for that. Just as well, then, that we're armed."

Quintus gave snort of humor. "Like my brother Livy Secundus says, 'always be prepared, like a good scout.'"

The atmosphere reeked of a strange aromatic oily scent. A faint miasma of coiling smoke from many candles seemed to be the source. Multi-lamp standards scattered between the tables and couches threw sufficient light that the entertainers would be visible, but also ensured a degree of coziness. By the time Rufio and Quintus emerged from their dressing room the party was already getting under way. Brightly attired men reclined on many of the couches and Rufio's boys flitted between the candles and lamps to serve them. They swooped and flew with grace to settle momentarily like wine-red butterflies on the colorful blossoms of syntheses, filling cups as they went. Amid the tables, some late arrivals were shown to their places and the room was abuzz with muted chatter and background music from a trio of lute, sistrum, and tympanum players.

The two picked their way around the edge of the room to wait near the massive double-doors, through which the imperial party would enter.

"Oh no," Quintus began. He pointed into the smoky chiaroscuro of the room. "That's my Uncle Livy, reclining over there with… I don't recognize the other two. Why's he have to be here?"

A loud fanfare alerted the gathering to the imperial party's approach and all immediately stood. The tall double doors grated in their floor runners as two Praetorians flung them wide open with symmetrical precision. Horns sounded again to herald the illustrious host's arrival with his guest, their respective retinues, and an honor guard of Praetorians. On the slightly raised dais, the imperial couches were arranged in traditional form. Trajan's sat at the center of a cluster, with Obodas on his own couch to the right and Hadrian to his left. Functionaries of Bardas swiftly settled others of the party in their places.

"I see Hadrian's got a new piece of ass," Rufio said quietly. "Mmm-hmm, very nice."

"Shut up." Quintus dug him in the ribs just as Trajan made the slightest gesture to indicate they should join him. With all eyes in the room on them, blood rushed to his cheeks as they walked at a sedate pace between the packed couches to the dais. He had trouble keeping a respectful face when Rufio at his side whispered loudly from the corner of his mouth.

"It's not fair. Hadrian gets one fuck while Trajan gets two."

Still blushing, Quintus took his place on the couch on one side of Trajan while Rufio reclined on the other. From the instant Trajan's slight imperial wave precipitated the proceedings, the evening turned into a whirl of impressions. To his side the corpulent figure of Obodas came to resemble a sow suckling a litter of piglets on the couch he shared with no one else beside several of his specially selected boys. To his faint disgust, he saw the suckling notion was not just in his imagination. In gaps between the curtain of boys rolling on and around the potentate, he caught glimpses of what they were doing. He saw one lad glued to a nipple, his lips working like a desperate baby's. Among the tables lower down, Rufio's boys were graduating from serving to more intimate ministrations with the guests. The perfumed air seemed to be making everything waver, so that the near-naked acrobats and exotic dancers shivered insubstantially as they jumped, twisted, and gyrated to the heady music.

Quintus didn't remember eating a thing, though he felt sure he must have done. He was aware of Trajan's presence beside him, and the occasional exchange of talk with him and around him with Rufio. He did remember the moment when one of the exotic dancers sinuously wiggled up close and the visceral shock when the boy revealed the snake he held. Behind him, dancers and acrobats had shed all pretense at clothing and writhed naked and rampantly erect. The dancers paired off and began to taunt with simulated sex acts, which goaded some of the guests to pull Rufio's boys down on the couches. Sex filled the smoky air, the feel of it, the smell of it, the vibrations of it.

At a signal from Trajan, Hadrian rose from his couch with his companion of the evening. He went over to Obodas, swatted aside one or two catamites, and whispered in the potentate's ear. Rising like Neptune from a sea of boys, Obodas bowed to Trajan. His jowls quivered so the grease from whatever he'd been eating glistened in

rivulets. Then he turned and ponderously followed Hadrian, whose fingers were planted between his young favorite's thighs and the crease of his bottom.

Seeing his curiosity, Trajan said, "I feel it's best that Prince Obodas continues his… pleasures in the privacy of a room set aside for him." Trajan's nose wrinkled slightly as if at a sour odor. He turned his watchful attention back to the fray below, nodded once, and then signaled Quintus and Rufio to stand up. Without much fuss, and Quintus thought hardly noticed by the seething orgy around them, he and Rufio followed Trajan and ducked out through a small doorway almost next to the one the boys used earlier to reach their changing room. Just before a slave closed the door on the orgiastic scene behind them, Quintus was proved wrong that their exit had gone unremarked because, like schoolboys relieved at the teacher's absence, the revelers let themselves go with gusto.

* * *

*It is hard for me to believe, really believe, that this is he. By the obsidian
stone of El-Gabal, the vile slug is even more obscenely fat than I
remember, wallowing among his naked puppy-dogs like an overblown
worm of the Underworld. He doesn't know that his nemesis watches,
even as he struggles to insert the rotten tool of his pleasure into this
orifice and that one, that he is observed through the small eye of a relief
sculpture on the wall opposite the great bed provided for his temporary
lusting. The chamber I recommended to Bardas and the imperial
keeper of the bedchambers. "How suitable," they said. "How clever of
you to think of it, handy from the banqueting hall, easy to return him
to his retinue after he has sated his needs and so back to the Vatican."*

*How he ruts with his minions, with his little catamites. How lucky
they are that the monster won't be with them long enough to do with
them is he did with me. Rob them of their futures as he stole mine. No,
Obodas knows he will leave too soon to line up more young boys here
for the knife. What he doesn't know is that he's leaving even sooner!
Soon! Soon, revenge will be mine, justice will be served, and on the
despot's funeral pyre will go the sacrifices of all who would raise a
hand against Acacus or humiliate me… the German brat, Redhead
Tullius Rufio, and his Roman-pig lover Quintus Caecilius Alba…*

Trajan sprawled out comfortably on the edge of the great bed and
his presence fueled the atmosphere with need. It hit Rufio in the gut
and spread around his hips and loins. So did Trajan's low-pitched
voice, almost a growl. "Do it slowly."

For the first time Rufio wished Quintus was dressed like one of
his Celtic forebears so that there would be more layers of garments
to remove. Being made to strip Quintus with an audience—only
one, true, but ruler of the world!—was turning up the heat in his
cock and balls still trapped within his loincloth something terrible.
And Quintus, obeying firm instruction from Caesar, stood there
supine as Rufio loosened the belt around his waist and then took
his time to undo the fastenings that stretched from the neckline to

just below Quintus's rising and falling breast. Each of the three ivory toggles he freed from the embroidered holes with great ceremony, leaning toward Quintus between each one to brush lips.

At each touch, Trajan gave a low murmur, like a lion rousing itself at the sight of a herd of antelope.

Always with his eyes fixed on Quintus's, Rufio lifted the hem of the fine tunic to reveal the limber torso beneath, the trunk concealed beneath a linen loincloth, but the state of sexual excitement clearly outlined in its folds. Quintus bent his neck so Rufio could lift the tunic over his head and pull it with exquisite slowness from his outstretched arms.

"From behind."

Rufio gave Quintus a lazy smile and he sidled around, hands on Quintus's hips to turn him the small degree to face the reclining Emperor. He pressed up hard behind so his pectoral muscles mated with the indents below Quintus's posterior scapulas, the frisson of naked flesh on flesh adding strength to his stiff cock as it slipped neatly into the crack of Quintus's butt. He knew what Trajan wanted and set about nibbling at Quintus—his ears, the sides of his neck—while he played his hands sensuously up and down to caress trapezius, deltoids, pectorals, and lower to finger-tickle abdominal obliques, rectus abdominals, now heaving with the restrained excitement running through Quintus. Finally, Rufio let one hand wander down the fine hairs running from Quintus's belly button, narrowing to a trail leading to the waist of his loincloth. The hand dipped underneath to grasp the firm erection and bulk it against the fabric. With his other hand, Rufio freed the simple fastening and let the loincloth fall away. He ran fingers over the pulsing tip of cock and Quintus let go his first sound since they started the striptease. He groaned, deep in his now heaving chest and squeezed his eyes shut. A pearl glistened and stretched out into a fine spider's-web strand between Rufio's fingers and the point of Quintus's almost unsheathed cock.

Abruptly, Trajan swung off the bed and advanced on the boys. Quintus opened his eyes wide as Trajan pressed against him. The Emperor's hands encircled him to reach Rufio and pull loose his loincloth. "Turn around."

Quintus obeyed as if in a dream. Rufio moved his hips a little to accommodate their two shafts pressed together grindingly as Trajan fingered Quintus's behind. He took a small bottle from a tripod table and the scent of mimosa, plumeria, sassafras, and bergamot filled the air as Trajan poured some into his hands to grease his own powerful weapon and fingers inserted into Quintus. Rufio felt it all through Quintus from his every spasm, felt the probing fingers working at his friend's asshole, gasped in sympathy with him at Trajan's entry. Quintus threw his head back and let out a long shuddering breath as Trajan penetrated him fully to the extent of his eight or more inches of solid cock. His hands encircled Quintus to grasp Rufio firmly under the shoulders, trapping Quintus into a sandwich between them. As one, the trio lock-rocked in gradually accelerating motions. Trajan nuzzled the face of Quintus and then of Rufio, who leaned over Quintus's shoulder; his strong hands stroked down to cup Rufio's ass cheeks and his fingers slid inside in arousing play. Three lungs worked and panted in unison and Trajan's hard fuck turned Quintus into a battering ram attacking Rufio's front as he exchanged kisses with Quintus and a lip mashing with Trajan.

Every ounce of his flesh vibrated to the rhythm of Trajan humping his asshole, but Quintus was so lost in the pumping sensation that he wasn't aware of the moment of orgasm. He felt the sense of loss, though, when Trajan eased himself out and he responded to the pressure of hands on his shoulders pushing him to his knees so that Rufio's dripping cock head mushed against his mouth and slipped so naturally between his lips as he opened wide to take it.

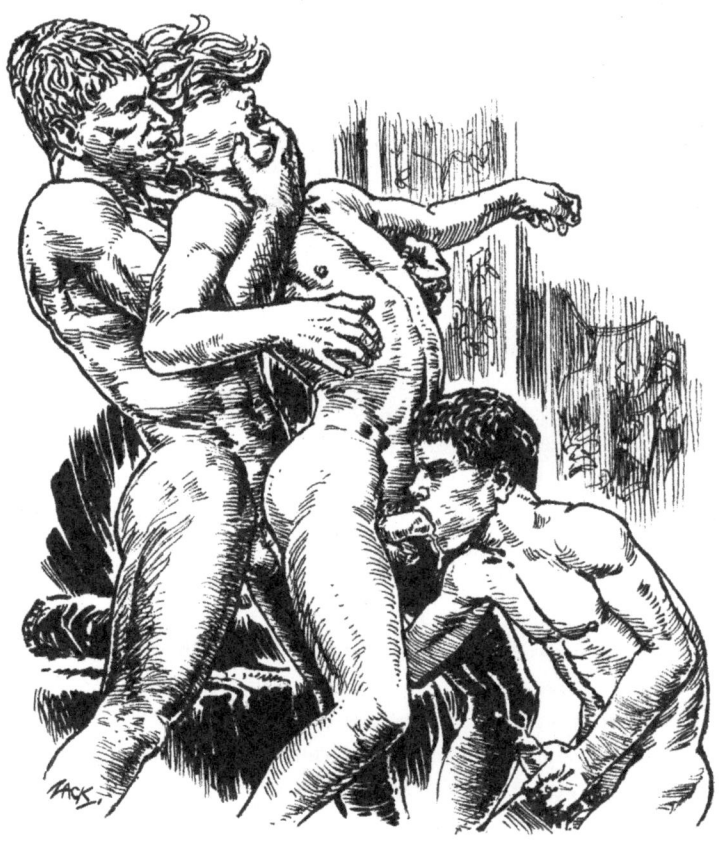

From his lowered vantage point, kneeling on a rampant
gladiator in turn screwing a brother fighter in mosaic form,
Quintus saw Trajan's powerful calves and feet planted firmly
through the steep triangular gap between Rufio's legs. He had
a ringside view of Trajan's kneecaps bending into the back of
Rufio's and a silhouette rod of dark flesh piercing up into the
crack of Rufio's ass, inches away from his stretched mouth.
Quintus grabbed hold of Rufio's thighs and teased and sucked
him, sliding down the length of the shaft in opposition to Rufio
getting humped into him.

His own arousal was agonizing, his balls begged for release, but drove him closer into the hot action so close to his busy mouth. He slid the fingers of one hand up into Rufio's fork until they encountered the clenched balls, and then on up beyond until he felt Trajan's lubricated cock. He formed a ring with his fist and relished the strength of the fuck sliding through his palm and fingers into Rufio, and Rufio being thrust forward ever harder and faster into his throat.

He felt Rufio's sudden tensing in the corded thews of his thighs that presaged his orgasm. Quintus hung onto the dubious security of Trajan's big cock pumping in and out past his gripping fingers so he could let go of Rufio's thigh and take his own cock in hand to jerk himself to a simultaneous climax. His breathing came stertorous through his flared nostrils and whistled in sucky noises in the depths of his espohagus. And then it went gloppy as Rufio began with a deep, prolonged moan to cum violently. He pumped out so much thick cream that Quintus could only gulp it down without thought, without stopping, without a further breath.

Trajan's shout of triumph announced his second climax as he shot into Rufio's gut, while Quintus sobbed around the friction-hot cock in his mouth and shot his own cum high into the air until it coated the inside of Rufio's thighs in thick white runnels, which ran down to puddle on the mosaic floor. And his knees ached. In fact, it felt as though he had just completed the run of the Greek hero of Marathon.

T·W·E·N·T·Y - F·I·V·E | XXV

Aventine and Palatine, April 10

"Obodas pronounced himself suitably impressed and pleased with a day at the races," Flaccus reported to Junilla and Rufio.

"Did they have some good fights before the races? You know how bloodthirsty barbarians are."

Rufio winked at Flaccus to taunt him. He knew the Vigiles was uncomfortable whenever Rufio flaunted his immediate ancestry, that as Gaulish Celts he and his mother were only a generation away from having just "descended from the trees." And he never missed an opportunity to point out that with animal fights and gladiatorial combats it was the Romans who were so bloodthirsty.

Flaccus shuffled uneasily. "It was Hadrian presiding and he usually puts on a good show. There were six pairs, last two to the death." He turned slightly and then paled when he spotted the young aristocrat who looked out of place seated at the homely table in the house above the warehouses of the Emporium. He wrung the woolen cap in his hands nervously. "Dominus, I didn't see you there. You know, the light is so bright out today and you in the shade there."

"Thank you, Flaccus." Junilla patted him on the arm and turned him back toward the door. "Thank you for doing that duty. I must confess, I find every minute forced to be close to that vile slug Obodas makes me want to throw up. Go find Damianus. He has some *sesterces* payment for you to date."

Flaccus dipped his head and departed with a last look over his shoulder at smiling Rufio and then at Quintus.

"Don't mind Flaccus," Junilla said to Quintus. "He tries hard, but the sight of a handsome young man turns his head to posca." She gave Rufio a quick hug about the waist and looked at him fondly. "He adores Rufio, for instance. But my wicked son just likes to flirt with the poor man and lead him on, don't you my priapic pet? It's cruel of you."

With each sip of the posca Junilla had served him, Quintus thought he knew how Flaccus must feel. His brothers always went on about drinking the vile concoction of boiled vinegar, water, and herbs—and too much coriander seed in this one—to express solidarity with the peasant soldiers in their legions. Good for them. To that point he had been spared the taste and now he knew what it was like Quintus preferred a cup of Falernian or a sweeter Chian over posca any day. He was trying to be friendly, neighborly even, by spending some time in company with the Tullius household, but the posca wasn't his only discomfort in these unfamiliar surroundings. Rufio's young brother Cato—responsible for overseeing the younger Aventine Foxes as they were called for some reason, who were to appear in the grand finale along with his portrayal of Mars, seemed to have taken a shine to him. And in a household for which loose morals were a part of the furniture, neither the boy's mother nor Rufio had done much to prevent the little brat from climbing into his lap twice already. And now here he was again. Quintus was too polite and embarrassed to complain. Cato was hardly a child after all —though he was putting on an infantile act very convincingly—and having him wiggling his bottom when tucked in there was placing Quintus in the kind of state that it would be unwise to stand up.

Finally, Rufio came to his rescue. "Cato, stop poking Quintus with your *bulla* and leave him alone."

"Aaww, Rufio, I like him." He gazed up into Quintus's face with a look of innocent yearning. "And you like me, don't you, Quintus. Say you do."

"Well…"

"Cato, you little fucker, get off him. He's not yours, besides," he added more for Quintus's benefit, "he's chasing a girl across the street, even though she's too old for him."

"Not!"

"Not chasing, or not too old?"

"He only likes doing it with men," Cato said in a sulky voice, ducking his head at Rufio while making sure as he clambered off that he groped the incipient hard-on Quintus couldn't avoid.

"That's enough squabbling, boys," Junilla said cheerfully. "Tomorrow's an important day, not for you but me. Hadrian is presiding again."

"What, the private fight, in that little arena?"

Quintus looked up with some interest at Rufio's evident excitement.

"Can we go and watch, Ma?" Cato bounced up and down on the balls of his feet, mockingly imitating his older brother's enthusiasm.

"Absolutely not. Rufio and, if you would like to Quintus, you can go along with me."

"That's not fair." Cato scowled and stuck his tongue out at Rufio, who clouted him behind the ear.

"Shutup, squirt. Besides, you're getting all the fun the day after, playing a Narcissus."

Cato brightened. "I'm not a Sissy, I'm a Cupid. That is kind of fun, whirling about round and round and up and down on that crazy machine."

They stood quietly in the shadows at the back of the compact little arena within the depths of the palace, Junilla, Rufio, and Quintus. A flourish of two buccinas announced the arrival of Hadrian with a small group of most select guests—all well-set good-looking young men—and Obodas, who trailed two of the Fisherman's boys in the miasma of his oriental perfume. Hadrian wasn't alone, since he had his arm around his own pretty catamite. Rufio was sure he recognized him as one of the lads from the charioteer academy who he'd screwed a few weeks back. Junilla managed to slap his rising arm down before he could wave to the boy as the elite took their cushioned seats on the two rows that followed the shallow curve of the oval arena.

Quintus shuddered with nervous tension, excitement and alarm. Never before had he been so close to the combat, for the arena itself was barely four feet below the balustrade protecting the spectators and the confines of the room made it intimate in a way the process of killing never was. Oil lamps mounted on the wall at regular intervals below the balustrade and around the far wall threw light onto the sanded floor, while four high-up, narrow windows cut through the thickness of the walls admitted shafts of bright afternoon light to splash in angular shapes on the interior walls of the upper level.

As the strident echoes of the buccinas faded, another music took over, provided by players hidden from sight in a gallery above and behind the spectators. It was a strangely soft sound for an event such as this. Music at a fight was common enough, but usually played at raucous levels to match the action by tuba, brass horn *lituus*, and water organ, and that usually drowned out by the noise of an overheated audience anxious to see blood spilled. Here, inside, there was no baying for gore, just the shuffling of a small group and quiet conversation only just expressing a sense of excitement at the fight to come, a few coughs and throat clearings… and the eerily soothing music, which swelled a little to introduce…

Three pairs of gladiators, representing the main disciplines of the sport. Rufio, who had no hand in this arrangement, whispered in Junilla's ear.

"You've done yourself and Hadrian proud, Ma. Where did you find these young hunky beauties?"

"Keep your voice down! In fact Damianus did the initial trawl, but we found them all at the Ludus Magnus behind the Colosseum, apart from two who are from Capua. I had Macro, the *lanista* from the *ludus* choreograph everything. Ssshh, they're beginning."

At a wave from Hadrian, the six young men approached him in a line, offered their various weapons and gave the traditional response to his raised arm. "We who are about to die, salute you!" A ripple of applause came from the spectators and the gladiators paired off, paused, and then lunged at each other according to their disciplines. Immediately, the becalmed atmosphere altered as all spectators roared their approval in general, and then specifically for each well executed thrust and parry. It didn't hurt any fighter's popularity that they were spectacularly good looking and strong specimens, whose every oiled muscle edge gleamed in the light of the lamps.

Gasps of fear mingled with appreciation met every cut that went home and drew blood. And yet there was a dance-like quality to the fights and the way in which the pairs circulated in the confined space so that each fought for a while in the front, under Obodas and Hadrian's blazing eyes. As the combatants swayed to and fro a distinct erotic flavor seemed to emanate from the moves and it became apparent that some of the gladiators were becoming sexually aroused by the contest.

A scare came when a lunging retiarius inadvertently jabbed his trident viciously upward past his adversary and nearly into Obodas's looming face. The Nabataean prince fell back in his seat, terror written in every feature of his wobbling face. Rufio and Quintus exchanged alarmed looks, but Junilla appeared unflustered by the brief event, so they both relaxed a little.

The sword flew from the hand of a Samnite, the retiarius had his net trapped, the murmillo was forced back to his knees at the point of another gladius. Suddenly, three men were pinned to the sand, and three stood triumphant over their vanquished opponents to the loud cheers from the gathering above them. As each victor raised his weapon hand to request the coup de grace from Hadrian, an amazing thing happened. As if at a signal, those lying on the floor sprang to life and either disarmed their opponent or flipped them off their feet to tumble in the sand. Rolling, grappling, grunting, the three couples wrestled frantically, hands reaching everywhere. As the battle raged, the excited spectators strained forward in their seats for a better look at the astonishing sight of six hunks arousing each other. Greaves and arm-guards were cast aside, studded belts and chest straps unwound like snapping snakes, lethal swords and pointed weapons were ignored to disappear under the growing pile of discarded protective gear and loincloths. Oiled bodies fought in slippery clinches in which the earlier drawn blood slowly dissipated.

"It was convincing, though," Rufio said admiringly, no longer required to be quiet above the general din of the fighters and the roar of the audience.

The sexual action in the arena added its heat to that rising up from the oil lamps. And then a great gasp went up to echo from walls and ceiling. Concealed slaves tipped the nets lost overhead in the dark and a thousand rose petals fluttered from above onto the writhing bodies. Amid brilliant splashes of floral color the gladiators worked themselves into three different positions and started fucking, with each pair interacting with the others in convoluted patterns of sucking extended cocks not busy screwing.

Rufio sidled past his mother, who was engrossed in the spectacle, and ran his hands excitedly over Quintus.

"Not here, not in public!"

"Sshh, no one can see us back here. Anyway, look at them. Who's watching?"

And Quintus saw that Rufio was right. Hadrian was entangled with the boy he had brought and Obodas had virtually vanished under the Fisherman's two tiddlers, while several others in the seats were beginning to feel each other up. Quintus relented and let Rufio jack him up.

But all too soon it seemed, the gladiators began climaxing, first one, then another, and spumes of jizz flew into the light. Only then did Rufio realize that the earlier quiet music had been replaced by

louder, more violent strains, and now a fanfare of tubas concluded the astonishing event. Bardas, beaming with good cheer, ushered the audience out to lead them to where a small feast was laid out for their continued enjoyment. A rustle of the drapes behind where they stood caused Rufio to let Quintus go. A dark figure pushed through a gap in the curtains.

"Sire!" Junilla turned in surprise.

"I wanted to congratulate you," Trajan said warmly. "I wasn't sure it would work, but you did splendidly."

"Thank you Caesar."

"It bodes well for tomorrow night's culmination of this state visit, your Greek genius Agapathus and his Hecatoncheires, and…" he placed a hand on Quintus's shoulder, "My all-conquering God of War, Mars."

Quintus smiled faintly—a little sickly Rufio thought—in the dim light. On his other side, hand out of sight of Trajan, Rufio pinched Quintus on the bottom.

* * *

267

It had been a long and tiring day. Bardas sighed and rolled both fists in the hollows of his lower back to ease the ache. Tomorrow was almost certainly going to prove even longer and more tiring. He dismissed his slinky young body slave with a tender fondle of his pert little ass under the barely concealing tunic. The boy reminded him of Acacus when he'd first seen him at Petra. The boy gave his master a lingering parting look before silently closing the door behind him. Bardas felt as ready for slumber as he could remember, and his bed, already prepared beckoned. He took a step toward it.

And there was Acacus, as if thinking of him had produced him by magic from thin air. But this Acacus was altered from Bardas's imagining. He was hollow-eyed, the pouches beneath darkly smudged, and he seemed hunched up. Shocked at both his physical appearance and the suddenness of it, Bardas instinctively stepped toward him. He opened wide his arms in concerned affection, intending to hold the young man, but Acacus's outstretched palm peremptorily motioned him to stop.

"My dear boy, what it this? How have things come to this? Where have you been? Is it true that you—"

"You're no different!" The words came out as a hoarse cry. Acacus shook his head in misery. "No, no different to all the others."

"What—?"

"Showed me love, but it wasn't, was it? No, you say you rescued me from Obodas, but what you really did was to lure me into depravity. Brought me here, surrounded me with bestial Romans. The people who gave Obodas power over life and death—or worse than death... a life of denial." Acacus lifted his hooded eyes and Bardas saw the lids were red. "You betrayed me."

"Acacus, this is not true. I still lo—"

Acacus's stifled shriek cut off his words as if with an axe. "Do not utter the word! Nothing... nothing you have done since first we met has been sincere. You used me for your pleasure and nothing else, just another in your succession of body-slave catamites."

Bardas wrung his hands in horrified despair. "But Acacus, you have to—"

"No! You don't understand. How can you, in your own comfort? You can have no idea of the pain that consumes my heart, the inner agony eating away at my vitals, the torments of unfulfilled bodily yearning, denied me forever by the command of Obodas."

Bardas took a step back from the spittle flying from Acacus's twisted lips.

"You, so high and mighty, you are no better than Obodas, just another despot in disguise, and you would also leave me with nothing. There is nothing left of worth to me to remain alive. But I won't go to the Underworld alone. Oh no. Many must pay and nothing can stop me!"

With these last spat-out words, Bardas grew more alarmed and wary, but even so he was unprepared for the sudden assault. Acacus launched himself across the gap between them. The terrifying knife in his fist he gripped so hard that the blood was driven from his knuckles. The blade slashed down and would have pierced Bardas to his heart had he not reacted belatedly. He twisted lithely aside at the very last moment and so his own crazed momentum took Acacus past him in a stagger. Bardas ran to the side dresser where the knife he used for cutting his meat was lying on the top amid the remains of the supper his body slave had laid out earlier.

By the time he had the dagger in his hand, Acacus had recovered and came in again, foaming at the mouth in an animal rictus of blind hate. In the brief clash that followed both antagonists took flesh wounds as they grappled in close combat for supremacy. Breathing heavily, Acacus took the advantage when Bardas tripped on the edge of a rug and fell to one knee. Acacus dived on top and bore them both to the stone slabs, but Bardas managed to get the raised knee under his assailant's body and heaved with all his might. Acacus was thrust bodily away and slid on the floor. The back of his head came into violent contact with the wooden trunk legs of the side table.

Bardas rolled over to get back to his feet, but a dazed Acacus shook his head, sprang up, and instead of renewing his attack, turned tail and ran. Howling threats and curses, he yanked aside the edge of a tapestry and simply vanished. Bardas fell back against the wall in panic. Acacus was gone and Bardas sensed he would not return now. He gasped for breath and held a hand to his side where the intruder's blade had sliced into his flesh. Not deeply, he hoped, but sore. Not as painful, though, as the nature and meaning of the attack. Fear and guilt in equal measure racked him. Duty to his master Caesar to report that his own under-secretary was unhinged, armed, and dangerous battled with the craven need to cover up the incident. Acacus was his protégé, his recommendation, and his appointment. This could only reflect badly on him in a world where failure was rarely tolerated with any sympathy and usually with fatal consequences for he who failed.

Self-serving cowardice won out. As he rummaged through a drawer in the side dresser for some linen to wrap around his waist to staunch the blood, which had slowed in its flow, he muttered under his breath. "As they say at the mimes, the show must go on. Everything will be fine and work out for the best in the end."

The walls remained mockingly silent.

T·W·E·N·T·Y - S·I·X | XXVI

Palatine, April 12

Passersby on the street rising along the northern flank of the Aventine stopped to gape at the extraordinary sight visible above the bulwark of the Circus Maximus. It looked as if the gods had draped a vast black tent over a part of the imperial palace and secured it in a spider web of ropes. For a moment some unseen hand made a fractional gap between the awnings forming the mysterious pavilion and a blaze of light emerged, only to wink out again as the opening closed up.

Within the enclosure torches, numerous lamps, and blazing braziers banished the April night's chill. A buzz of anticipation filled the humid, warm interior and merged melodiously with soft music. Maestro Junius Sebastianus Bacchus sat enthroned in his cockpit at the keyboard of the mighty water organ. More heavy drapes at his back served to mute the sounds of exertion from thirty slaves and hide them from the audience. They were the Aegaeon section of Agapathus's mighty Hecatoncheires, the "sea goats" who pumped in a constant rhythm to keep up the air pressure for the organ pipes. The enormous instrument emitted a soulful, low-register overture for the excited audience, which was arranged on a half-circle of tiered seating. In a reversal of the usual convention, the invited lesser dignitaries occupied the lowest tier. Peering through a chink in the swathes of silken curtains hanging from the gloom above the brightly lit stage, Quintus spotted Livy looking pompous and proud to be seated there. The sight made his stomach churn, but at least he could see no others of his family, which was a relief. Many of the audience nursed drinks and nibbled at delicacies served up by a bevy of attractive servants.

Looking at the next tier, Quintus saw the rotund bulk of Obodas seated in the center. A cloud of catamites surrounded him and beside them the oiled Orientals of his delegation. Immediately behind the potentate, Trajan held court with the Empress Pompeia Plotina and their close retinue, which included Hadrian and his *comites*. Behind the majesty of the imperial court, on a platform extending back to sets of hastily erected steps, a small army of flunkies under the supervision of Bardas looked after every need. And at the very rear of this construction, a line of splendidly uniformed Praetorian Guards completed the panoply.

The low buzz of conversation faded at the swelling sounds of Bacchus's playing. There came a sudden gasp of surprise, followed by a ripple of collective *oohs* and *ahs* as from the gloomy heights twenty Cupids and Narcissi floated down, every one as pretty a picture as could be imagined. Like a cluster of butterflies, the beautiful young boys seemed to float aloft, borne on a swell of enchanting organ music. The visions gyrated in alternating swoops of down and up, up and down, at their lowest barely an arm's stretch above the upturned faces of the enthralled audience as they circled round and around to fly repeatedly overhead.

Flickering spots of concentrated colored light picked each boy out from the darkness above him. It appeared to be magic, but from his spy vantage point Quintus could see that lamps on the ground, their light concentrated in convex mirrors and reflected through colored glass lenses, created the cunning effect. He, who also knew that it took two score of slaves to achieve the boys' flight, was still enchanted by the theatrical illusion. Straining his head, he could see young Cato, like his companion fliers naked but for a flimsy piece of gauze lightly wrapped about his boyish loins, trickling flower petals from a golden basket onto the gazing people beneath his diving body. Elfin organ music rose and fell in time with the pattern of the flying creatures to add to the beguiling spell.

At the controls of the organ Bacchus elicited an emotive crescendo, one which called on the tall, thick bass pipes, so that the floor vibrated with their power. As the Cupids and Narcissi retreated to a higher level, a rank of army musicians and drummers took station in the space behind the organ cockpit and faced the audience. They raised their instruments and joined Bacchus to rend the air in a rousingly martial melody.

In concert with the altered atmosphere, a colored oily smoke issued from the base of the Hecatoncheires. Slowly, it wafted out to cover the stage in a fat wave. From the dark back drapes emerged a small army of brutish barbarian warriors. They were driven into the roiling mist by gorgeously armored legionaries of the Roman army. For minutes, to the rattle of drums, the squeal of tubas, and the thundering organ, the protagonists fought a battle choreographed to perfection by Sponsus Terpsichorus. It was a ballet of thrust and yield with shield, javelin, and sword, and developed into a moving paean to determination, courage and bravery. In ones, twos, and threes, the defeated barbarians fell dead at the hands of the hunky legionaries in their showy armor. With each barbarian death, cheers rose from the audience, increasing in level to reach a roar of enthusiastic approval with the final dispatch of the warrior chief.

The scene behind the drapes that acted as a backdrop to the stage and organ cockpit resembled a pageant-tableau of a different kind from in front; as if Vulcan's forges had merged with the underworld of Hades. Here, among the forest of timber structures securing the towering Hecatoncheires, under the hellish light of a furnace, toiled the hundred and more slaves who worked the winches and pulleys that operated the jointed flying arms and steam-powered hydraulics for the as yet unused special effects tubes. Close to the massive central support column and behind the organ cockpit sat the furnace required to create steam within the huge domed cylinder that provided power for the organ. Another sixty men sweated here as they labored at different but interconnected tasks. One crew worked a bucket-chain of water to fill the dome, a second tended the furnace, and a third worked the mighty bellows that kept the steam in the water dome under constant pressure.

Junilla and a blithely confident Agapathus supervised this ordered chaos from a point as far away as possible from the appalling heat. Agapathus was concerned with the workings of his amazing construct, Junilla more with the timings of all the performers. At the moment, she was ushering the fallen barbarians and triumphant legionaries back to the costume area, which was housed outside under an awning erected at the very edge of the library roof.

Flaccus and Rufio acted as runners, taking messages and commands to and fro. For a brief moment Rufio managed a quick word with Quintus. He recognized the militarily attired butt as that of Mars, waiting in the wings and sneaking peeks through a gap in the drapes. Quintus whipped his head back at Rufio's touch. He smiled grimly at his friend's expression.

"You have a bed feeling?"

Rufio nodded. "It's Acacus. Where do you think he is? It's like no one is very bothered about him vanishing."

"He's probably miles away—"

"I don't think so. It was something Adalhard told me, something I'd forgotten. But it's to do with that thing out there. Obodas of Nabataea. Adalhard said Acacus would take revenge for something he did to him years ago. And out there the fat slug's a sitting target."

Quintus looked dubious. "Come on! Acacus can't do anything here, with all the guards about."

"Them? Huh, they're just color and pomp. I don't know, Quintus, but I'm happy that Sponsus insisted the actor-legionaries fight with real swords. There's a pile over the back there and they may come in handy. You might want to swap your wooden practice weapon with a real one." He smiled tightly. "And you are rather hot with *spatha* or *gladius*, a birdie tells me." He gave Quintus a fond pat on his metal-banded arm and flitted off into the back-stage maelstrom.

With all the coming and going, he wasn't sure why a flitting movement among the timbers, a dash of legs climbing, caught his eye, but Rufio was instantly distracted by a comment from Junilla.

"Is he ready? Is he all right?"

"Quintus will be fine, Ma. Stop worrying. Look, he's getting ready at the head of his victorious army. Where's he off to?" He meant Agapathus. The little Greek was mounting a narrow ladder of pegs set into the central support column.

"It's a better position, the first platform, to direct the next lot of operations," Junilla said in a distracted tone as she spotted something else that needed her attention.

Bacchus turned up the audible heat and the army musicians added to the clamor of a triumphal marching tune. It was time for Quintus to make his entrance. Stifling another fleeting moment of foreboding, Rufio rushed over, planted a kiss on his beloved's cheek, and patted his butt for luck and courage. Quintus grimaced, took a deep breath, and strode forward through an opening in the drapes made for him by two legionaries. More soldiers marched out behind to array themselves along the width of the stage. Quintus-Mars stepped gracefully onto a podium so he was as tall as the statue of Nike, the personification of Victory, which had been wheeled out a minute before.

Rufio quelled what was threatening to be a sob of emotion at the sight of his lover silhouetted against the bright stage lights, and he turned from the sight abruptly as the music blared to acknowledge Mars brandishing his triumphant baton. *Like a very hard prick*, Rufio had joked at the final rehearsal. He bent his head back to brush a tear from the corner of his eye... and started in alarm.

Flaccus patrolled out back of the great tent, controlling the ebb and flow of extras for the great pageant. In between scenes, he took a break for a piss. The urgent need came on him suddenly. The temporary latrine was too far away, so he slipped behind the changing tent to relieve himself over the parapet. There were only the roofs of the charioteer's academy below. No one would notice. Shaking off with a relieved sigh, he turned and stumbled over a wooden tub. Immediately, his trained nose recognized the smell of tar-pitch, or naphtha as some called it. The tub was empty, but for a few smears of the highly flammable substance.

"What in Hades' name is this doing up here?" he muttered to himself. He thought he ought to mention it to Junilla, but then another scene change demanded his attention and for a while he forgot about the mystery..

Acacus wheezed a little from the effort of trying to protect his bruises as he climbed the peg steps, past stanchions, under struts, over ropes. He passed the first platform with its oblivious operators of the crab-like arms that flew the bewinged boy Cupids and Narcissi. Agapathus was too preoccupied to take notice of a lone figure climbing on past.

More applause greeted Mars embracing winged Nike as Rome's victorious troops saluted the handsome god, waved their civic crowns in his honor, and swayed in adoration of his presence.

Rufio ran to the base of the great central pillar. He dodged under the arms of the end bellows slave to reach it, and squinted up. He thought he saw a black flag waving as it rose, but the movement seemed oddly jerky and his earlier forboding came back in force. He ran back to where a Praetorian stood over the cache of swords, but the man was so absorbed in the little he could see through the Hecatoncheires of the pageant outside that he never noticed Rufio snatch the nearest to hand. Seconds later Rufio was climbing in pursuit of what might yet prove to be a false alarm.

Beneath him, Junilla, unaware of her son's absence, waved forward a mass of extras. They streamed forth onto the stage, a swarm of cute foreigners. Following the graceful benediction of mortals, Mars stepped forward in majesty to welcome them, and they performed a dance of fear at his august presence. And then the martial music faltered to leave only the glory of Bacchus's organ playing, to which the subject nationals prostrated themselves in grateful wonder as Mars unfurled a scroll denoting peace. O great joy!

To ever-louder gasps of admiration from the spectators, upward pointing pipes ejected blasts of sparkly fire skyward in celebration of Roman munificence. Junius Sebastianus Bacchus matched the aerial display with a veritable firework display of musical score and two wider-mouthed tubes, which were aimed low over the audience's heads, discharged flocks of startled little pigeons—the doves of peace. The birds soared skyward in a clatter of beating wings, avoiding collision with their larger human counterparts still suspended decoratively in the void, taking with them the message of *Pax Romana*—the Roman Peace.

High up in the rigging of the Hecatoncheires Rufio's worst fears were confirmed. He saw a dark-robed figure crawling along one of the jointed arms from which a Cupid was suspended. To his horror, he realized the figure's odd movement was due to the two javelins clutched in a hand that he also needed to help him hold onto the wooden beam. The weapons were not practice toys but the real javelins used by the first legionaries who took to the stage.

Close to its central pillar bindings, the arm was a substantial trunk. Rufio eyed it carefully and then jumped. With the sword gripped in his right hand, he fell forward awkwardly onto all fours. He steadied himself, and then made the mistake of looking down. His head spun wildly at the brief glimpse of the stage far below. He almost lost his grip. A fall from this height would be certain death. He drew a sharp breath, gritted his teeth, and snatched his attention back to Acacus, who had now crawled to the last part of the jointed arm.

Driven by his madness, Acacus seemed able to move with the javelins, but Rufio knew he couldn't make progress safely while brandishing a sword. He needed both hands to remain safely on the bucking arm, so he stuck the blade through his belt and set off, gripping the hewn wood for dear life with knees and hands. Progress became easier as he grew used to being so high, but then the arm gave a great lurch and dipped violently. He threw his arms tightly around the girth of his support when it moved sideways and then also downward at an alarming angle.

Ahead and below his precarious hold Rufio saw the Cupid—oblivious to the drama being enacted above him—spread his "wings" and begin strewing more petals from his golden basket with each sickening low swoop over the audience. The boy seemed entirely happy, but he was safely secured in his flying harness. And then Rufio realized he was seeing Cato suspended there. The thought of what Acacus might do to hurt his young brother spurred Rufio to new effort.

Two more cannons barked with released compressed air. Floral garlands shot into the air to descend between the Narcissi and Cupids on the jubilant crowd. The crab-like arms sent the bewinged boys weaving to and fro and up and down, low overhead. The boys' gleeful joy and their jolly high-pitched voices added to the general acclamation.

Unaware of Tullius Rufio's pursuit of him, Acacus knew his moment was imminent, that his tampering was about to turn joy to terror. Swaying with the motion of the arm, he waited. Next the balls of fire…

Far below, Mars raised his arms in supplication to his fellow gods and right on cue more cannons fired. They shot cascades of glittering little globes high up in carefully calculated arcs to land among the seating and so that their delicate shells would shatter on floor, seat, or head, harmlessly releasing showers of gold and silver tinsel to delight the audience.

A few reacted as Agapathus had planned; the rest according to the interference of Acacus. Wherever they impacted, the naphtha compound he'd used to replace the tinsel ignited on impact to shower fire in all directions. Joy turned to screams of agony and horror. Acacus sputtered with glee when alarm and panic spread as rapidly as the gobbets of fire splattering the terrified guests.

Quintus saw Livy leap from his seat on the front row. Neighbors beat frantically at his burning toga, trying to extinguish the flames.

On the first platform Agapathus gasped in horror. "This wasn't planned!" he wailed, though none could hear him.

Rufio, horrified at the mayhem below, could delay no longer. He lurched across the final joint of the arm, holding on for dear life with his thighs clamped around the timber. A violent change of direction caused the hood of the man in front to fly back and confirm that he was indeed closing in on Acacus, who was clearly out of his mind. He reached the rapidly descending, wildly swinging arm's extent.

And then everything happened very fast.

Acacus reared up astraddle the slender arm as it came swinging back along the line of panicking guests below. Rufio saw the madman raise his arm, spear poised, and with a yell that sounded above the water organ's warbling, hurled it at Obodas. It was as if the potentate sensed his nemesis at hand, for at the last moment he seemed to see Acacus high above and his scream came almost at the same moment as Acacus's high-pitched shriek. Rufus watched the javelin's trajectory in impotent horror. The blade grazed one of the tiddlers to pierce Obodas in his fleshy side.

In a flash, Acacus had the second javelin readied, but they had swung out of line. The slaves working the machine were clearly as yet unaware of the unfolding disaster. Rufio realized the crazed secretary was waiting for its return path. There was nothing for it. He scrabbled onto all fours and in fear of losing his balance with every step he half-ran, half-crawled to reach Acacus. The arm swung on and up, paused, and then began its return swoop.

Rufio strained every muscle. Acacus hefted the weapon. Rufio grasped his shoulder as he readied his aim. Cato's yells of fright reached up from just below as Rufio and Acacus grappled and fought.

Quintus was thankful he had heeded Rufio's gloomy advice and now rushed with real *spatha* in hand in one hand and *gladius* in the other through the milling crowd of pretty but now terrified children playing the subject nationals. He dashed through flames, past wounded men, screaming guests—

Acacus punched madly at Rufio. Under the assault his grip on the slender arm failed. He tilted, slipped sideways. He grabbed wildly at whatever he could and found the freedman's robe of office, rent and tattered as it was. He had a blurry impression of Cato's face going up very fast, a flash of flimsy wings, a golden basket banged his cheek, and then the hard ground knocked the breath from his lungs. A split second later Acacus crashed beside him. The man's head landed hard on Rufio's pained chest.

Fortunately, the arm had been at its lowest point, but even so, the impact winded Rufio, so it took what seemed like an age to regain the ability to gasp in air.

Because Rufio had broken his fall, Acacus was first to recover. Somehow the madman had retained his spear and employed it like a staff to regain his feet. With a feral snarl, he kicked out at Rufio, reached down and snatched the sword from his belt.

Gasping for air, Rufio struggled to stand. He saw Acacus leap the now almost deserted front row of seats. Behind was Obodas, like a beached whale, mouth agape in terror.

Quintus blasted through the last line of flames. His vision hazed with heat and smoke, he barely made out downed Rufio, flying Acacus, Obodas cringing back from certain death, but there was Trajan and Plotina right behind the potentate. He heard a hoarse voice shout, "Must protect them," and recognized it as his own.

Rufio jumped onto one of the seats, which wobbled and threatened to throw him, but he regained balance and dashed at

Acacus, who slashed down at Obodas with the leaf-blade of the javelin. Blood from the first spear had dyed his splendid gown of blue-green-and-gold a bright crimson. Now more splashed up from a rent in the region of the potentate's genitals.

"Die, Butcher! Be cast into Hades, Castrator!" Acacus shrieked worse than a Fury as he stabbed down again with all his wiry strength. Obodas screamed like a horse at its gelding and his clutching hands snagged and gripped the spear's shaft where it protruded from his crotch. Acacus abandoned the useless weapon. Some sixth sense warned him. He swung out wildly with the sword at Rufio, who threw himself under the blade's path across the seats in a flying tackle.

They both went down heavily between the seats. In a brief struggle, Acacus writhed free and jumped the next row to gain the advantage of height.

Rufio faced the swaying sword point.

"It's your turn, Tullius! Lying turd! Filthy prick!"

Acacus thrust the blade in a lunge aimed right at Rufio's heart, but he ducked under the blow, and then remembered the knife secreted in his right boot. In a flash it was in his hand. But a short dagger blade against the long reach of a *spatha* gave little comfort.

Immediately behind Acacus, Rufio saw Plotina desperately trying to drag Trajan out of danger and Praetorians hustling Hadrian and most of the other elite guests to safety down the steps at the back. Trajan, it seemed, had the idea of defending himself.

Fighting in a furious daze of sweat and clashing blades, Rufio forced Acacus back. The secretary might be driven by blood lust, but he was not trained in sword fighting, nor did he possess Rufio's street smarts. They got closer and closer to Trajan…

Quintus struggled through flailing bodies to reach Trajan's side.

He might be short of stature, but the blood of Peloponnesian heroes flowed in the veins of Agapathus, and the quick wit of Greek engineers fired his mind. On recovering from the first mishap with the exploding fireworks, from his vantage on the first platform of the Hecatoncheires he grasped the magnitude of the calamity.

Grasping a speaking trumpet, he bellowed out directions to the slaves working the flying arms. "Swinging arm five! Bring it across and down—!"

On the ground, in a panic for both her sons, Junilla yelled at the top of her loudest parade-ground voice, "Listen to the man—fucking get a move on!" Across the chaotic, fiery expanse between stage and seating, she could see that one of the fireworks had set alight the bottom edge of the main backing drape at the side near the palace walls. Flames licked up the fabric. She also saw Acacus strike out at her son with the pommel of a sword. Rufio went down under the blow. Junilla began to run toward the battle, desperate to save Rufio, but Acacus instead of following up, turned murderously on Trajan.

The presence of the Empress, who refused to leave his side, hampered the Emperor. As Acacus raised his weapon for a killing blow, a figure interposed his body between the wicked point and Trajan.

"Bardas! Noo!"

But it was too late. The sword pierced Bardas in the stomach and cut him down. Shrieking his anguish and rage, Acacus lashed out at Trajan, to be foiled yet again. In a streak of glorious armor, Mars materialized. Quintus parried the blow, and returned a thrust, even as he threw the *gladius* to Trajan, who caught it with the deft skill of a trained soldier.

In the cockpit, Junius Sebastianus Bacchus kept the organ music blaring.

On the platform, Agapathus shouted orders to his crews.

As high, on swinging arm five, dangling like a morsel to be roasted in the fire, Cato saw that he was again being propelled inexorably down and across toward the fight. "Oh no, oh—!"

And then he saw his brother lying as if dead on the ground and Quintus battling alongside the Emperor with some crazy. And then... "Oh no, no, no—!" The bastard madman knocked Quintus aside and screeched with triumphant rage, his *spatha* outreaching Trajan's *gladius*. The sword plunged toward the Emperor.

"Die, Roman pig!" Spittle flew from the corners of Acacus's contorted mouth. He saw the point of the blade slide past Trajan's guard. Nothing could stop it striking the Emperor in a killing blow. And then... *What—?*

His feet left the ground at the same time a great tug on the collar of his garment near strangled him. His fingers spasmed in shock and the sword fell away. Acacus's last sight of Trajan was the man thrusting up with his *gladius*. The blow pierced his belly. Pain lashed his body, but he was flying! Bewildered at the suddenness of his elevation, the child's voice shouting above his head only added to the disabling confusion.

"Yay! Got you, bastard. Now I'm a Little *Flying* Fox... heyyy."

The strain on Cato's arms as he hung on grimly to the madman's robe was almost too much. He thought his arms would be pulled from their shoulder sockets. A voice from behind, amplified in some weird way, commanded, "Left and up, at speed."

"You all right, lad?" Rufio sat up with the help of Flaccus, who had been dashing around performing his duty as a Vigiles, dampening human fires where he could. Rufio rubbed at his bleeding brow, and stared open-mouthed at the sight of his baby brother whirling across the darkness. The force and speed of the arm's movement swung his body out on its rope like a child's toy. Even more astonishing, Cato was hanging onto the tattered form of Acacus, his spindly legs sticking out from the fluttering black robe. "More speed," he heard Agapathus yell," and the arm flew ever faster in its arc toward the backdrop, the awning now a roaring conflagration. And then a fiery hole blew out in the drape.

At that very moment the arm reached the apex of its trajectory. Cato relinquished his grip and the massive force built up catapulted Acacus onward in defiance of gravity. He uttered an inhuman wail and hurtled through the hole, where a burning shred of the blazing curtain fluttering in the updraft wrapped itself about him. To majestic music from the organ, the flaming, screaming bundle arced like a graceful comet beyond the stage to plunge and vanish out of sight somewhere over the Circus Maximus.

Enraptured Junius Sebastianus Bacchus pounded away on his water organ...

T·W·E·N·T·Y - S·E·V·E·N | XXVII

Palatine, April 12 to 20

Other organs loosed fire, accompanied by heartfelt groans of lusty release. Three simultaneous orgasms brought final relief and the combined cum cemented more than bodies clasped to each other. A bond was made.

Lesser men might have found the strains, tensions, and terrors of the evening too much to contemplate an erotic encore, but Marcus Ulpius Nerva Traianus was Conqueror of Dacia, Ruler of the World, and—according to Lady Junilla Rufia—an all-around Good Egg. Like Quintus and Rufio, the near-death experience fired up a ravenous appetite for sex. Now they cuddled, with Trajan in middle, arms on the boys' shoulders.

"I shan't forget this night. You have both proved to be true friends to me." He sighed quietly. "I would give much, though, to know what drove Acacus to such extremes."

"And Obodas?" Rufio murmured as he fondled one of Trajan's nipples and one belonging to Quintus.

"I heard from the surgeon that he will survive to return to Nabataea… no, no longer Nabataea… to Arabia. But his manhood is gone, so he won't enjoy his pleasures to the full anymore, a relief no doubt to many youngsters. And for me, I must return to normal life, to duty. In a few days I am off on a tour through Italy to see how some new welfare schemes are working out, and to see the stones laid for an arch in my name at Beneventum. For you two… I know how you feel about each other. Take my advice and make the most of your mutual affection. You are suited to each other. And Quintus, do not worry about your family's future."

He left it mysteriously at that.

* * *

Summer advertised itself in the warmth of a spring afternoon. Rufio lay on Quintus's bed, each in the other's arms, gently stroking bare flesh, exchanging soft kisses, and relishing their reflections in the other's eyes. Quintus could never get enough of running his fingers through all that liquid gold adorning his lover's head. Rufio, too, loved to stroke Quintus's thick, short-cut thatch.

"It's funny how things work out," Quintus said after a while. "With all his scheming, my Uncle Livy almost dropped dead in apoplexy when Trajan awarded my father the signed imperial warrants, the contracts for all that building work, which means the Family Alba is now secure."

Rufio wasn't interested in bricks and mortar. "And what about your impending marriage to Vipsania Metalla?"

He wriggled deliciously at the gentle laughing huff in his ear.

"My father no longer has need of her dowry and I have a feeling—a suspicion only—that Trajan has let it be known he hasn't finished with me yet... or you, come to that. So it's postponed for the moment."

"Hopefully for good?"

Rufio looked vulnerable, which rare occurrence Quintus relished. He smiled. "Yes." And kissed Rufio's pouting lips.

When they disengaged, Rufio said, "And Ma hasn't done so badly for us, either." He quoted: "'Lady Junilla Rufia, by patent of Augustus Caesar Traianus, is appointed master of imperial ceremonies and statuary.' Should make a fortune. Course, it won't change a thing for Cato. He's now cock of the Foxes, if you see what I mean. He'll run wild until some girl nails him… or maybe another boy. Who knows? He's dropped his crush on you, and I have a feeling he's transferred it to Flaccus. Said something the other day to the tune of, 'Do firefighters have big muscles? Is Flaccus built like that?' Cheeky sod thinks I'd know."

They were about to slide deliciously into a second bout of lovemaking, when there came a clamor outside and a call for Quintus. He hurriedly dressed and went out.

Standing beside the Domus Alba doorman was Junilla's secretary, his face anxious with urgency.

"What is it, Damianus? What's Rufio done now?" Quintus said.

"No, no dominus. It is you, sire. Sorry to interrupt, but it's Mistress Junilla. She asks if she can consult you urgently on a historical matter. What facts do you know, or can you find out in your books, about a famous statue?"

From behind, in his bedchamber, Quintus heard Rufio's stifled chuckle.

"She needs to know if there was more than one specimen of this work. You see she just sold one last month."

"Well, man, what statue?"

"The Satyr of Capri."

Rufio and Quintus will be back in
Boys of Imperial Rome: The Satyr of Capri.

Zack: THE WARRIOR'S BOY

208 pages, soft cover
5¼ x 7½" / 13 x 19 cm
978-3-86787-605-6
US$ 16.99 / £ 10.99 / € 14,95

Tough, no-nonsense Eric Random, an English mercenary
soer on his way to Venice in 1527, encounters rough-and-
tumble sex at every inn along thway. The randy roughneck
never misses an opportunity for an erotic adventure:
stable lads, tavern servers, and page boys all fall to his
remorseless assault, only to be tossed aside as Eric moves
on. And then something unexpected happens …
This graphic portrait of degenerate, brawling, and
licentious Renaissance Italy unfolds as a history that's
never been taught in the classroom.